Sugar Rautbord, a savvy woman-about-town, is frequently featured in the pages of American magazines. She also serves on the board of the United States Fine Arts Committee, the Chicago City Ballet, and the New York City Ballet.

Liz Nickles, a Senior Vice President of a major advertising agency, was named advertising Woman of the Year. She is the author of *The Coming Matriarchy* and has written numerous articles for *Glamour*, the *Saturday Review*, and *Advertising Age*.

SUGAR RAUTBORD and
ELIZABETH NICKLES

# Girls in High Places

This edition published 1993 by
Diamond Books
77-85 Fulham Palace Road
Hammersmith, London, W6 8JB

Special Overseas Edition 1987



Printed and bound in Great Britain by
BPCC Hazells Ltd
Member of BPCC Ltd

To M., to B., to J., to I., and to E.

From birth to age eighteen, a girl needs good parents. From eighteen to thirty-five, she needs good looks. From thirty-five to fifty-five, she needs a good personality, and from fifty-five on, she needs cash.

– Sophie Tucker

# Contents

# Prologue

*Dulles Airport, March 1982*

Catherine snapped on a brass seat belt embossed with the Intercon logo. How insane it was, she thought, that she had just shaken hands with the man who only hours before had caressed her bare shoulders, kissed her back, and entwined his fingers in her hair. During the night when intimacies, scruples, and secrets were hidden in darkness, they had been so close. She had felt nothing could separate them, yet now there were five men and two copilots between them.

Why was it that greed and lust had been compatible for centuries, but the corporate etiquette of the eighties dictated that passion could not mingle with business?

She had been careful. There was so much at stake. Their one night together was enough, she knew, to eradicate her hard-earned place in the company hierarchy. No one must ever know about last night.

She couldn't help touching her shoulder. Even after her shower she felt overheated, as if she were running a fever. Her body remembered it all; he was indelibly imprinted on her senses. Catherine couldn't erase his image from her mind but she knew she must appear purely professional on the surface. She pulled out her mirrored sunglasses and unfolded *The Wall Street Journal*. Behind the reflective lenses, she had the luxury of staring at him until a steward crossed her line of vision. She tried to concentrate on the newspaper but found herself gazing at him again. She was willing him not to look at her as she had willed him to her bed last night. But, she wondered, what was *he* feeling?

She sat straight up in her seat and forced herself to stop day-dreaming. Having worked so hard to get a seat on this plane, she could not allow anyone to think she hadn't rightfully earned it. At twenty-seven Catherine McBride had never let emotions get in the way of her carefully mapped-out career, and she wasn't about to let something foolish happen now.

At this level only an idiot would risk so much. If her sole aspiration was to be a corporate groupie, she could justify what she had made happen last night. *She* had unlocked the door between the connecting suites, an act hardly praiseworthy for a woman whose goal was to be a president or CEO.

Catherine drew in a deep breath, flicked on the overhead light, and adjusted its angle. No one should have to read *The Wall Street Journal* before six o'clock in the morning, she thought, yawning. She skimmed the headlines automatically.

The D-Mark was down. Interest rates were up. The usual. Then she smiled, pulling off her glasses. There, on the far left of the front page, was the crest and profile of Baron Eric Grunewald, the man who had changed her life so many years ago. The baron was back on the acquisition trail. She made a mental note to send him a progress report on her own career.

Suddenly there was a flurry of activity on the tarmac. Peering out the window, Catherine saw her own reflection. Sometimes it was hard for her to believe that hers was the face of a top executive. The bridge of her delicate, turned-up nose was sprinkled with freckles, and her hair, still damp from a shower, hung loosely around her shoulders. She had dabbed some lipstick on in the limousine en route to the airport, but her full, heart-shaped lips revealed a slight gap between her front teeth that gave her face a childlike quality. At least her eyelashes looked thick and dark framing her slate-blue eyes. She'd had them dyed on her last trip to Dallas. No woman who put in eighteen-hour days could afford to waste twenty minutes in front of a makeup mirror each morning.

On the runway at the private terminal, the second Gulfstream III jet shimmered in the morning light as the slowly rising sun caught the silver wings. The Intercon double-globe logo in red and blue was imprinted on the tail. The G-IIIs would travel from Washington, DC, to Intercon's island in the Caribbean.

A brown Mercedes station wagon pulled up beside the Intercon limousines and Secretary of the Interior Henry Hudson climbed out.

As if by instinct, Catherine's comatose seatmate rallied and bolted from the plane. Typical, she thought, as she watched Dr Ray Acconti hurtle down the stairs to gladhand the secretary. 'Good morning, sir,' his voice was unctuous. 'You're looking fit this morning. You're on plane number one – with Graham and myself.' Acconti could probably grease out compliments in his sleep, Catherine thought.

Suddenly the tarmac was a sea of men in dark suits, until, with a high sign to the steward, Ray Acconti led the group up the metal stairs.

Michael Picol ducked his head and emerged from the cockpit, flashing a grin at her. 'Just making sure they've got all their buttons and switches in order,' he said, slowly easing his dark, six-foot-plus frame into the cabin.

Graham Donaldson leaned over from his padded leather chair at the table unit that held the telephone and picked up the receiver to make a call. As CEO and chairman of the board of Intercontinental Minerals, he was able to command everyone's attention without saying a word. He glanced in Catherine's direction but said nothing. There was no need to talk; everyone's role, every nuance of the trip, had been outlined in advance. She knew her part.

Only last night had been unrehearsed. What had happened in her suite after dinner at the White House had not been on anyone's agenda. Who would have thought that Catherine Anne McBride, the conservative, almost prim Harvard MBA who had experienced only one serious romance in all of her twenty-seven years, would have recklessly unlocked the door connecting their suites.

It had been a gamble. Corporate politics, balance sheets, and marketing plans were familiar territory, a game Catherine could play and win. But playing with emotions was one area where she didn't know the rules or how to succeed.

She looked over at him then just as quickly back at the *Journal*. This was not the time to remember how she had curled up in the cool sheets, waiting for him, impulse and instinct overpowering reason, listening for the click of the door unlatching from the other side.

The door did open, though Catherine kept her eyes closed until she was absolutely sure. When she opened them, he was standing beside her bed, looking down at her, his face lit from behind by the street lights. She couldn't read his expression. Judgmental? Inquiring? Desirous? It didn't matter to her.

She willed him closer and pulled the sheets down to her thighs. Her breasts were round and firm and her waist gracefully tapered as she arched her back upward toward him.

Catherine heard the studs from his formal shirt drop on the bedside table, the zipper of his tuxedo trousers opening.

He folded the sheet back down to her ankles, and she shuddered as he bent over her, lifting her, pushing his fingers into her spine, his mouth sweeping over her body. She felt the roughness of his cheek against her smooth skin as his chin nestled between her breasts. He explored her body with his hands. She may have willed him there, but he was now in control.

Slipping an arm beneath her head, he stroked her hair as if she were a child being tucked in for the night. She felt his lips moving as he kissed her, whispering her name again and again, stopping each time he said it, coaxing her.

He seemed to care more about satisfying her than himself. Finding her rhythm, he paced himself, as if there were all the time in the world for his own pleasure, later.

Her body was warm and tense, responding to his searching kisses. When he gathered her up in his arms and turned her around in the bed, she shivered with anticipation. His hands caressed her thighs until she reached out for him. He moved up to kneel near her face, and before she could think about what was happening, she brought both hands up, tentatively at first, then, feeling precocious, found herself instead encircling him, enjoying the sweetness of champagne mingled with his own salty taste. Surprised by his insistence, she came together with him again and again until she spiraled into feeling she couldn't control, and had no desire to.

* * *

The cabin door slammed shut and Catherine was jolted to reality. She knew the situation was impossible. All the clichés of sex in the office came back to her. She didn't need a business degree to know that she had just jeopardized everything she had worked for, and she wasn't sure why she had done it. Would he even want to see her again? Catherine thought their night together had felt so right, so unlike anything she had ever experienced. But she had no idea what *he* had felt.

In the morning, she had awakened alone. He was gone and the door to his room was closed. She immediately wondered if she had failed to please him. He had sensed her inexperience? Maybe for the first time in her life Catherine McBride, the compulsive over-achiever, had flunked something. Maybe she should have stuck to someone her own speed. Just as she was telling herself that she should never have lost control, that she'd left herself too vulnerable, that there were a hundred other explanations for his departure – all of which fit her mother's lecture that men would always leave her – she heard someone calling her name.

'You look pretty good for somebody who gave a presentation at the White House last night.' Billy Wright settled into Acconti's empty seat.

'I survived,' she smiled.

'Well, does the Washington lifestyle agree with you?'

'I could get used to it if I didn't have to brief the President in my ballgown every night.'

Billy stretched his arms behind his head. 'That's one way to dress for success,' he laughed, pushing back a shock of blond hair which habitually fell over his eyes. Billy didn't have the look of a chief technical engineer; he had the long, graceful fingers and sensitive but weathered face of a poetic cowboy. He closed his eyes, oblivious to the maneuvering around Henry Hudson. He didn't have to care about jockeying for a good seat. His technical brilliance was established, and although he was only in his early thirties, he didn't need to prove himself. His track record said it all.

Catherine unfolded the beige linen napkin and took a croissant and a mug of coffee from the steward. As many times as she'd flown on the chairman's plane, she was always amazed at how a basically cold, metal machine could be transformed into an executive suite. The smells of leather, cigars, and freshly brewed coffee reminded her of an exclusive men's club. The walls were pale, perforated gray doeskin, with a dado and rim of glossy burled wood. Under the wood-trimmed windows stood small silver vases that Eve Donaldson, Graham's wife, had told Catherine were salvaged from the *Twentieth Century Limited*. They held tiny cymbidium orchids from the Donaldson greenhouse. Eve's touch was everywhere, even underfoot, where the charcoal carpet was woven with a pattern of the Intercon double globe. A framed picture of the President of the United States hung on the walls along with a map marking Intercon oil-drilling sites.

As the plane took off, Catherine relaxed, pushed the oversized seat into a reclining position and allowed herself to feel a sense of accomplishment. Last night's impromptu presentation had been very good but now she would have to convince some of the toughest business minds in the country of the significance of Graham Donaldson's dream: a combined undersea park and food development center, a resort complex and a research center on an island cluster in the Caribbean. The working name she had given it was A Place in the Sun.

Catherine was excited by the challenge of selling the concept to the board, which so far had been unenthusiastic. She and Graham had agreed that an all-out effort at the proposed site, propped with scale models and stocked with gourmet food and drink, was the way to sell the idea. It was Catherine's responsibility to see that *The Lady Eve*, the company's 125-foot Feadship, the Dutch Rolls-Royce of yachts on which the group would be staying, was ready and waiting offshore.

Catherine saw Graham Donaldson lean across the table to Dr Io, Japan's leading authority on undersea conservation. Adjacent to him sat Gregory Mersault, director of the Mariculture Institute, a nonprofit arm of the Smithsonian. On the tan couch, Michael Picol huddled with Secretary Hudson, while Ray Acconti, Intercon's resident environmentalist, angled for one of the two spaces Picol was aggressively filling. Catherine suppressed a smirk at Picol's deliberate immobility as Acconti approached first from the left, then the right, waving a Bloody Mary. Seemingly oblivious in his pin-striped Brioni suit, Picol leaned casually forward, his elbows on his knees, as he punctuated a point. His voice was a whisper, but Catherine knew that what he was saying was of interest to Hudson, who was leaning forward to catch every well-chosen word. When Michael Picol spoke, people were drawn as much by his intensity as by his good looks and imposing height. His speech was a finely honed skill which he only used when he knew his words would have an effect. His mesmerizing effect on juries as Intercon's corporate legal counsel was legendary. He could make even the most vituperative indictment sound like a subtle seduction. When his heavy, dark brows knitted together, masking all expression, no one could ever tell whether he felt pain, pleasure, or anything at all. His mysterious background was rumored to include kills as a fighter pilot in the Israeli Six-Day War, though nobody at Intercon could verify his involvement. Picol never answered personal questions.

As executive vice-president in charge of North and South American oil exploration and acquisitions, Picol, at forty-five, was Graham Donaldson's general troubleshooter and chief ally on the board of directors. Graham had groomed Picol for his role and now relied heavily on his protégé.

Picol's deeply hooded, pewter-colored eyes looked through Ray Acconti as if he were invisible. Acconti, defeated, slipped into the seat opposite Catherine. Although Acconti was undeniably valuable because of his PhD in ecological sciences, his conversation tended to be academic monologs. Catherine wasn't worried. Acconti never sat in one place for more than three minutes. He would be out of his seat, schmoozing around and making points as soon as he found another accessible target.

The plane gently climbed toward its cruising altitude. Catherine greeted the board members and corporate officers around her, shook hands with Secretary Hudson, and then settled down again to flip through her set of typed index cards, rehearsing the Place in the Sun presentation in her head one last time. They stopped briefly in Miami while their plane and cargo backup picked up an oceanographer and his equipment from the University of Miami, but Catherine never left the plane.

An hour after takeoff, the stewards served lunch: chicken salad on Bibb lettuce and thin slices of cold, rare roast beef sprinkled with capers, open-face on dark bread. Food was the last thing Catherine could think about. She turned away from her tray and leaned against the window, staring down at the turquoise Caribbean sea frothing lacily around tiny green islands. The water was so shallow in places that the ocean floor was visible from thousands of feet in the air.

Suddenly her head hit the side of the cabin with a whiplash crack as an explosion shuddered the air. Her ears popped repeatedly and she opened her mouth to clear them but couldn't. The pressurization was gone. Her stomach rose sickeningly toward her throat as the plane hung momentarily suspended in midair, then jolted and streaked downward. The stewards scrambled in the aisles amid upturned platters and carts. Black, acrid-smelling smoke poured into the cabin as oxygen masks dropped and swung helplessly from the ceiling; there was an unreal, deadening silence. Catherine gripped her seat cushion. The smoke was so thick she could barely see across the aisle. She felt her head and shoulders jerk back, pinned behind her as the plane veered even more steeply toward the sea. She struggled to collect her thoughts. What was happening? She searched for the one person she cared about through the smoke.

Her stomach clenched. The plane vibrated, then leveled off, then spun as the pilots made a desperate attempt to stabilize its altitude. There was a split second recovery, and the cabin was filled with voices barking instructions. Ray Acconti pushed his way past her, pulling a life raft from a compartment overhead, and struggled to inflate it as he shoved a protesting steward aside. 'Out of my way! A bomb! It's a bomb!' he shouted, wildly punching and flailing as, with a loud hiss, the bright orange rubber raft ballooned into the aisle.

The plane sustained another heart-stopping drop, and out of the window Catherine dizzily saw the sky spin terrifyingly and the turquoise water became the horizon, and she knew. They were going down.

# PART ONE
# Getting Ready

# 1

*New York, July 1981*

Twenty-six-year-old Catherine McBride looked at the clock on the rosewood-paneled wall and checked it against her watch. Twenty minutes after ten. She had been waiting for over half an hour. Why did the interviewee have to be fifteen minutes early, while the interviewer was invariably fifteen minutes late? Sitting on the edge of the comfortable black chair, she had already made polite conversation with the receptionist, who was riveted to the task of punching the touch-tone phone without breaking her fingernails. Catherine flipped through copies of *Oil & Gas* and the *Financial Times* that were neatly stacked on the granite-and-chrome coffee table. She knew it was important to project the right attitude while waiting to be interviewed, but she had run out of props and was getting bored.

Luckily, Catherine had long ago mastered the gift of masking her emotions. Her face registered only earnestness as she quietly folded her hands and hoped her suit was impressive enough. The charcoal gabardine pinstripe was an interview classic which camouflaged a woman in business rather than allowing for any trace of femininity. Sometimes she wore it with a Brooks Brothers tie, but today she had on her yellow silk blouse, buttoned to the throat. Her hair was pulled neatly off her face and knotted at the nape of her neck in a style Catherine used to offset the youthfulness of her face, still lightly sprinkled with annoying freckles. If Catherine wasn't actually considered pretty, she knew that with her high cheekbones, shiny hair and healthy, glowing skin, she was attractive. A practiced eye would see her as 'a girl with potential', though that kind of potential held no interest for her.

'Miss McBride? Mr Donaldson will see you now.' Donaldson's secretary had the look of an aloof auctioneer. Unwilling to approve or condemn, she simply accepted the goods at face value.

Graham Donaldson's office was not remarkable, but then Manhattan was not his company's home base, Catherine reminded herself. Intercon Minerals, Catherine knew, was headquartered in Chicago. In fact, there wasn't a lot about Intercon that she didn't know. She had spent the better part of five weeks researching the company after work, rereading all the relevant articles, statistics, and interviews she could find. She'd also read every profile of Graham Donaldson during his years at Intercon. She knew, for instance, that he was the man responsible for turning the sleeping mineral company, Benton and Stuart, into the mega-oil, mineral, and chemical empire of Intercon Minerals, International. It had not escaped her that Donaldson had married Eve Benton, the daughter of the cofounder of Benton and Stuart. And even though he had a reputation for being very fair, she knew that no one built a multibillion dollar corporation that ranked six on the *Fortune* 500 by simply being a nice guy or a good son-in-law. Reading between the lines, Catherine realized that Graham Donaldson had left several bodies six feet under, not the least of whom was Franklin Stuart, son of one of the original partners and heir apparent to the company.

When executive recruiters had called Catherine at Swift eight weeks ago, she had been less than enthusiastic about a position as executive assistant. The title could mean anything from a glorified secretary to a high-ranking decision-maker. Yet she knew that a fast rise would be impossible at Swift Guaranty; that she would never be able to overcome the inflexibility of its hierarchy. There was no place for hip-shooting, gut feelings, or twenty-six-year-old women at the top.

But a man like Graham Donaldson, she realized, could open doors for people. He also had a mentor potential. Donaldson had already sponsored three brilliant but unorthodox protégés, two of whom had gone on to command their own oil empires, and one who remained his right-hand man at Intercon.

And so Catherine spotted an opportunity. She would make the very ambiguity of the title executive assistant work for her by defining the position in her own terms. She had to.

Recognizing opportunity and taking initiative had been her speciality since age fourteen. In the past few weeks Catherine had developed a concept she knew Graham Donaldson could not ignore. She remembered a speech he had given at the Harvard Business School on undersea conservation. His excitement and dedication to this unprofitable subject had been a surprise to all the young capitalist vultures in the audience who had hoped to cull some hot tips from one of the world's great self-made industrialists. Keeping Graham Donaldson's pet project in mind, Catherine had put together a detailed proposal on the profit potential of combining undersea conservation with commercial enterprise. She had sent it directly to Graham Donaldson's attention two weeks ago.

She had another, private reason to go all-out for this job. The high cost of living in Manhattan and the ever-increasing nursing bills for a mother totally unable to care for the simplest needs left Catherine stretching her salary to its limits.

Although Catherine had accepted the necessity of her mother's hospitalization years ago, she still ached whenever she thought of Elaine McBride spending her days in an institution, lost in her own little world.

Catherine McBride was thirteen years old when her father unceremoniously left her and his wife, never bothering to return home to Pittsburgh from a dry-cleaning convention in California. It seemed at the time that Ed McBride had been traveling more and more on business, though Catherine hadn't paid close attention. He never failed to bring her bubble bath or a stuffed lion or some other gift when he got home, and so Catherine never doubted that he would return. She wasn't a clingy child; she had confidence that came from being loved.

Her mother, Catherine knew even then, was not so secure. She was older than her husband, but beautiful, with shimmery, wavy blonde hair and perfectly lined red lips. Catherine thought she looked like a movie star. But Elaine McBride was somehow always nervous about her appearance. She wouldn't leave the house, even to shop for groceries, unless she felt she looked perfect. And since she rarely felt she looked perfect, even after hours of preparation, Elaine spent day after day in her bedroom, sorting her wardrobe, playing solitaire, and increasingly forgetting to defrost the roast for dinner. She was prone to depression and would hibernate like a frightened animal, spending days in bed. Life was like a heavy suitcase for Elaine McBride – some days it was just too much for her to carry.

The one bright spot in Elaine McBride's daily routine was when Catherine sat on the foot of her bed and talked about her friends and school projects. She loved to share in her daughter's accomplishments. And on good days, no one could be more delightful to be around than Elaine McBride. She had the most wonderful laugh, and smelled so good sacheted and powdered in her print lawn dresses as she floated out the door on the arm of her husband. These were the days Catherine chose to remember.

She felt closer to her father, who alway let her know she was his special girl. They had their own secrets, and their relationship excluded even her mother. Since Elaine McBride was so frequently out of sorts or exhausted, Catherine took her place doing the marketing, helping at the dry cleaners, and sitting across the table at dinner while her mother ate upstairs from a tray Catherine had prepared.

Her father's desertion was a total betrayal, which left Catherine more than heartbroken. How could he leave her? What had she done wrong? What were they going to do without him? Even if Effie, the manager of the shop, and Catherine worked behind the counter at McBride Vanity Cleaners, it would be impossible to make ends meet. Ed McBride had left nothing but a mortgage, and when Elaine fell behind in the payments, Catherine had found herself suddenly uprooted from the comfortable house with the yellow window boxes on Maple Hill Drive and rudely torn from her little clique, the Maple Hill Marvels. Home was now a tiny furnished apartment, and her canopy bed was traded in for a foldaway cot behind a collapsible door in the kitchenette.

Every day Catherine had checked the mailbox, only to find her mother had already picked up the letters, and there was nothing for her. When the phone rang, it was always for her mother – her father never called. For Elaine McBride's sake, Catherine had tried to act cheerful. But inside, she felt empty, sick, and helpless.

After eight months of no news, Catherine intercepted the postman one day at lunch time and received a letter from California. Her father had written at last, but it was of no comfort. He scolded her for not writing him – but how could she, when she hadn't known where to write? He wanted her to come live with him and his new wife, an Avis Rent-a-Car agent he had met in Los Angeles. But Cathy could not bring herself to desert her mother. Elaine McBride was convinced that Ed would come back after his fling. And for a while, Catherine had believed her. How could her father, who had never missed a father-daughter day at school or a chance to hug and kiss her, who taught her to play baseball and ride a two-wheeler, not come back? But when a Christmas card arrived from California, with a Polaroid baby's picture inside, Catherine faced the truth. Ed McBride had a new daughter for his new family. Catherine's empty feeling turned to anger, and she had put the picture at the bottom of her sweater drawer and closed it, along with that part of her life, forever. She had been replaced. Her father was gone. She decided he no longer existed. She didn't need him in her life.

But Elaine McBride refused to face facts. Her depression took on a fiercer quality, and she seemed to pursue the past rather than let it go. She began to wander out at night, searching for Ed McBride in the lounges and restaurants where they had once gone. During some nights, Catherine, hearing voices, would peek from behind the sliding door to find her mother making tea for some strange, confused man whom she always called Ed.

Plump little Catherine would put on her pink robe, rabbit slippers, and most polite look and pad softly into the kitchen. At first, she wondered what to say to these men. But she soon found that all she had to do was stand innocently by the table and 'Ed' would find some excuse to leave. Elaine would then burst into tears and, as Catherine tried to comfort her mother by rubbing her temples and kissing her head, Elaine would deliver her bitter lecture: 'Cathy. Men will always leave you. A woman should never lean on a man.' Elaine wasn't the kind of woman who could stand on her own, but she knew Catherine could. She would hug her daughter and tell her to be strong, not rely on any man for anything. And Catherine would listen.

Catherine had felt totally helpless, and she swore to herself that she'd never be victimized, waiting, almost pleading to be hurt. She felt no pity, only resentment at her father for leaving, at her mother for being unable to survive on her own, and at herself for being helpless. Eventually everything disappeared. Their house, her friends; even her mother retreated into her own little world. Catherine quickly realized that she only had herself and that she'd have to make her own way in the world unless she wanted to spend her life at the dry cleaner's sitting with Effie, watching other people's gowns and fancy dresses go by on the conveyor and wondering who wore what to which party.

She had wept for her mother's increasing withdrawal. What had been only eccentric and pathetic behavior after her father's departure had escalated into a stupefying depression and, finally, a total breakdown. Catherine had sat by, feeling helpless, as her mother spent weeks talking to no one, responding to nothing, staring blankly into space. She bore no resemblance to the sweet, well-groomed woman who had baked brownies, set the table with candles, helped her with her homework, and smelled of perfume. Then she had refused to eat, even when

Catherine tried to feed her, and lost so much weight she was in danger of starving. Effie, who for as long as Catherine could remember had stepped in at any crisis, called the necessary doctors and made arrangements. She took Catherine under her wing and into her own home in the black neighborhood, an hour's bus ride from Saint Ignatius School and the cleaners. And while her mother was tube-fed in the hospital, Catherine was forced to admit that Elaine McBride needed professional care.

The doctors at the state mental hospital had diagnosed the condition as catatonic schizophrenia. That was the beginning of a long, bleak period of false hope that there would be a cure.

But her mother never did get better. She retreated forever from the real world to some sort of private, pretend place. Catherine and Effie, with the help of a part-time nurse, were able to manage between hospital visits. Eventually, Catherine had realized that the best thing she could do for both of them was to help herself. She convinced Sister Margaret, her school principal, to let her leave school at two o'clock every day to work at the dry-cleaning business with Effie. She did her homework between customers, and she and Effie managed to stay out of the red.

She sat down one night and wrote her mother a long letter, even though she knew Elaine McBride would never read it.

Dear Mother,

I would rather that you and I be together, but you have been so sick since Daddy left. And even though I've tried so hard, I know what I'm doing is not enough. You need to be someplace where they can help you. I'm still here. I'll always be here. We'll be together, wherever I am. I'll do my best to make you proud of me, so that when you're ready to come home, I will be able to take care of both of us. I will try to grow up fast, so you can hurry home.

Love,
Catherine

Effie had walked into the room while Catherine wrote at the kitchen table. Only moments before, she had served milk and cookies to her little Cathy, yet now she looked into a face that was no longer a child's.

Catherine then spent hours with Sister Margaret researching every scholarship that would enable her to attend a boarding school. They decided that she should apply to the Grunewald Junior Scholarship program for outstanding teenagers. Only two high school and ten college students from a worldwide competition were awarded the scholarship, and only one woman had ever been chosen. It was the richest scholarship available to a teenager, but it was also the most intensive. Every Grunewald Scholar spent the summer as an intern in a Grunewald company, attending seminars and observing the baron's businesses first-hand. Sister Margaret knew the scholaship would be a godsend for Catherine. It would provide the young girl, who was for all practical purposes an orphan, with a place to live and an impressive education. If the authorities had found out that Catherine was living off catch-as-catch-can kindnesses from people like herself and Effie, they would have swiftly assigned her to a set of foster parents or a court-sponsored institution. Sister Margaret knew that Catherine was too special to be lost in the shuffle of a legal maelstrom.

Catherine was ecstatic when she won the scholarship. She entered Phillips Academy and Sister Margaret helped her lease the dry-cleaning business at a small profit, which was applied toward her mother's nursing and medical care. The school years spent on Grunewald Scholarships were exciting times for Catherine, but her mother was never far from her thoughts. She hated the smell of the state hospital and felt her mother was treated more like an animal than somebody who had once been a loving woman. Each visit left Catherine unnerved and depressed, but she forced herself to work at her studies.

Ten years later, when Catherine was twenty-four and working for Swift, she was finally able to move her mother into a first-class nursing home which was, she had made sure, still close enough for Effie to visit. Catherine had first visited Wickes Manor with visions of the gruesome state mental hospital torturing her imagination. But, amazingly, the place had turned out to be as clean, pleasant, and friendly as the brochure had promised. The medical staff was actually attentive. Perhaps they could help her mother, even if it did cost most of her salary.

Catherine still tried to see her mother as often as she could. The fact that Elaine McBride could no longer dress herself, or that she spent her days staring blankly at the television, was heartbreaking. But Catherine was sure that her mother still heard Cathy when she spoke to her, and swore she saw recognition in her eyes when she brushed her hair and rubbed her shoulders. Catherine viewed her mother as a relic of an age in which women were merely appendages to men, and that helped her better understand Elaine McBride's condition. She wanted to comfort her mother and give her as much pleasure as possible.

Ten percent raises were useless. She needed to get ahead faster, make more money sooner. A company that did not go by the book, that was still under the control of one individual to whom she could report, could be just what her career needed.

When Graham Donaldson shook her hand, Catherine

immediately recognized the look in his eyes. She had seen it before. It said, 'She's too young.' Well, she had ways to address that.

As soon as the pleasantries were over and they sat down at the granite table, Catherine took charge. 'I noticed in *Ferrous Metals* that you've opened a new office in Hong Kong. I handled the financing for our Hong Kong branches at Swift. Perhaps you saw that on my résumé.'

He hadn't. 'I never look at résumeś,' Donaldson shrugged. 'They're only pieces of paper.'

There was no spark in his pale blue eyes, just bland appraisal with the nonchalance of a person who is used to having his own way. Graham Donaldson's appeal came from his elegance and intelligence rather than any physical feature. His silvery hair waved naturally over his ears, giving him a boyish look. His lower lip had an unexpected pout, which broke into a grin as he took Catherine's paper on the undersea development project off the desk top and dropped it on the table.

'This is what interests me,' he said. 'Your résumé is very nice, but there are a lot of nice résumés, and there are a lot of people with good recommendations.'

Although Graham Donaldson's eyes revealed no surprise, he had not expected, and had even been slightly annoyed, that this woman looked more like his daughter than his assistant. He wondered how someone so green, so fresh out of the ivory citadel of banking and not the hard-core corporate jungle, could survive at Intercon. He knew his own daughter, independent as she was, would be eaten alive before the first coffee break.

'There are a lot of good ideas in this paper,' Donaldson said. 'As my administrative assistant, you'd be expected to be an initiator. Pull together strategies and budgets and meet objectives.' The island project came to mind. He could use someone to stir up some dust there. But it would have to be the right someone. 'The trick is, it doesn't stop there. You have to take good ideas and implement them in order to make them happen.'

He rose from his chair as if to end the barely begun interview.

Catherine quickly countered. 'You're absolutely right, Mr Donaldson. Making things happen is important. For instance, my Bonus Business points program for Bavarian Airways . . .'

'Bavarian?' The rejuvenation of BAW was a success story familiar to anyone who watched the stock market.

She pulled a report from her briefcase. 'Here's my original proposal,' she said, pointing to her name on the cover. 'It's a three-point plan, objectives through strategies, and here's the report from the implementation team on which I worked.'

Donaldson leafed through the pages, focusing on the bottom-line figures at the end, and half-smiled. 'How did you get involved with old Baron Grunewald?'

'I was on a Junior Grunewald Scholarship from the eighth grade on, and I got a full Grunewald Scholarship when I was seventeen. BAW was one of my internship projects.'

'Didn't you have to work for Grunewald?'

'Only while I was in school. Every summer I worked at a different Grunewald company. During my senior year in high school, I interned in the baron's private offices in Germany.'

'The baron and I went shooting one day outside London with Henry Caldwell when old Eric damn near killed the gamekeeper. The bullet hit the guy right in the rump, pardon me.' Donaldson was laughing now. 'The old guy had just had cataract surgery and didn't want to admit he couldn't see.'

Catherine smiled. Now she had the interview where she wanted it. They had something in common. The baron had rescued her once again, and Catherine could tell Donaldson enjoyed telling his story.

'Caldwell advised the gamekeeper to sue for some of the Grunewald millions, but the poor sap was so honored to be shot by a Grunewald bullet that he was thrilled to accept a BMW and a lifetime supply of gas from Grunewald Petroleum. Quite a fellow, the baron.'

'Yes,' agreed Catherine. 'He certainly made a lot of things possible for me.'

'Such as?'

'Phillips Academy. Harvard, and Harvard Business School, just for starters. My family could never have afforded that kind of education.'

Catherine glanced aside. There was no need to tell Graham Donaldson about her mother's breakdown and institutionalization. She was looking for a position of prominence, not a sympathy slot. He wouldn't be interested in hearing how she had cried and lain awake nights desperately wondering how she was going to manage on her own, with just Effie to turn to, or her joy when Sister Margaret had announced that she had been selected as a Grunewald Scholar. Nor could he understand her relief when she had been sent to Phillips, far away from pitying glances and the steam-filled rooms of the dry-cleaning shop.

Donaldson glanced at her résumé. 'Very impressive. But what about your hand-on experience, dealing with real people, not just problems on paper?'

Catherine launched into her litany. 'As you can see from my résumé, I've handled some in-depth projects at

Swift. The refinancing of US Motors after they declared Chapter 11. I worked on the payback program . . .'

She noticed that Donaldson's attention was again waning, and so she played a hunch. 'Of course, I've always been most proud of my work at McBride Vanity Cleaners.'

Donaldson blinked.

'I ran the plant and the shop myself for a year when I was fourteen years old. I turned it around when it was almost bankrupt. And we made a nice profit, I might add.'

Graham tapped his pipe on the table. 'And how, exactly, did a fourteen-year-old girl turn around a dry-cleaning business?'

'I went to the campus at Carnegie Mellon and signed up some of the kids to represent us in the dormitories, for a commission. We sort of got a monopoly on the business.' She laughed. 'I wasn't old enough to drive, but one of the college kids had a van, so we could offer pick-up and delivery service. From there on, we made a nice profit.'

This was different, Donaldson decided. She had pulled herself up, as he had. True, she was young, but he'd been her age when he started. And she had guts.

The secretary slipped silently through a side door and handed Donaldson a piece of paper. He stood up quickly. 'You're going to like Chicago, Miss McBride. Charlie McBain will give you the details. You'll be a good addition to our team.'

Catherine stood, hoping Charlie McBain would tell her more about the position than Graham had.

He turned to Catherine at the door and grinned. 'If you see our friend the baron, give him my regards.'

'Yes, sir, I will,' Catherine said, the words turning into

a sigh as she left his office. She closed her eyes and sank back into a chair as she waited for McBain. Well, she thought, Intercon Minerals was her opportunity. She'd give it her all. There'd be no room in her life for soft edges or lack of control. She couldn't let herself be a victim; she was a winner. She fingered her bracelet with the gold falcon charm, the Grunewald crest. Power, prestige and success – that was what counted, that was what lasted.

And those were the trademarks of Graham Donaldson.

# 2

*Autumn 1981*

'Freesia,' Eve decided. 'It should be freesia,' so simple and fresh with its lovely white lineny fragrance. Her mind drifted as she played one of the twin grand pianos in her music room, accompanying a Heifetz recording of Beethoven that had been specially made for her without the piano parts. Yes, freesia would be a nice change from those stiffly overstuffed arrangements that were weighing down so many tables these days. Eve wanted to add just the right touch to an all-white symphony of orchids, and, perhaps, rubrum.

Eve Donaldson stood and closed the heavy, polished top of the Steinway. It was so good to make a decision. She left the music room with its fruitwood paneling and intricate plasterwork and walked down the curved stone stairway softly padded with topaz floral carpet, a polished brass rail at the juncture of each step. There was so much to do before the guests arrived. Still, she moved slowly, in a natural glide. Rushing was so unattractive in a woman, Eve thought.

Eve's smooth, poreless skin, unlined and untroubled, reflected the lifestyle of a woman whose greatest concern was the choosing of a decoration for her dinner table. At forty-eight and without the benefit of cosmetic surgery, Eve Donaldson looked like a woman in her late thirties, and her cool composure gave her an aura of grace that made her a refreshing oasis in a world obsessed with motion and hyperactivity. Her husband's world was filled with point-by-point agenda, dozens of telexes, endless conference calls, international negotiations, and interior department consultations. But Eve was her husband's island of calm in this corporate whirlpool.

She wore her long, silver-blonde hair knotted simply at the back. Her seventeen carat emerald-cut diamond solitaire and her trademark necklace were the only jewelry she ever wore. Graham had had a priceless Fabergé egg, created for the Tsarina Marie Feodrovna, converted into a necklace. The egg, encrusted with vines and flowers of sapphires and emeralds which could be parted to reveal a diamond-and-gold bird in a filigree cage, hung by a braided gold chain and nestled luxuriously in the folds of Eve's cashmere turtleneck sweater – her 'work' clothes. She would not change into her Adolfo cream silk suit until just before the arrival of tonight's guest of honor, Pollyanne Savage, the First Lady of the United States.

She passed the drawing room, its floral-carved, paneled door shut, wood ready to be lit in the fireplace, and the dining room, where china and crystal sounded like wind chimes as two maids in their black organdie uniforms rustled softly about the three round tables.

Opening the massive front door, Eve stepped out into the October morning air and skirted past the garden of her gray stone French Normandy home. The epitome of elegance in Lake Forest, Illinois. Her beige suede doeskin boots crunched the dry leaves underfoot as she passed the indoor tennis courts. She surveyed the grounds, pausing for a moment to glance at the fallen leaves skimming the surface of the large reflecting pool, guarded by two stone lionesses. Then she crossed to the elaborate series of greenhouses at the edge of the fifteen-acre grounds. The first was used as an aviary, and she smiled as she remembered that it was here, years ago when the house had belonged to her parents, that Graham Donaldson had proposed to her. He had stood at the foot of the statue of Diana, goddess of the hunt, and they had laughed, wondering who had caught whom.

They were introduced to each other at her own engagement party. She and Franklin Stuart, son of her father's business partner, were going to marry and live in a new house adjoining both family estates. Ignoring the heirloom oval sapphire surrounded by diamonds on the third finger of her left hand, Graham Donaldson, a smart but as yet undistinguished engineer at Benton and Stuart Minerals, her father's privately held company, had taken Eve into the aviary and, very directly, asked, 'Just how engaged are you? Is this one of those prearranged family things, or are you in love with this guy?'

That was the beginning of Graham Donaldson's persistent courtship. He would show up regularly and uninvited for family dinners on the pretense of discussing business with her father. One night, after a ball, Franklin had no sooner left the aloof blonde beauty at her door when Graham appeared from the shadows, coaxed her into his convertible, and drove her all the way back to Chicago to a great hot dog stand, where they sat on stools, surrounded by derelicts, till 2.00 A.M., her ivory satin ballgown trailing on the greasy floor. Eve had found Graham exciting. He was different from Franklin Stuart, who could quote to her from W H Auden, but who had never had an original thought. As her father's respect grew for this brilliant young engineer, so did Eve's feelings, until she, Franklin, and Graham became a threesome. Sometimes, Graham would bring a date, but usually he would just arrive, grinning, 'Sorry, I was working too late to get anybody to come with me.' Whenever possible, Graham would manage to drive the car, relegating Franklin to the back seat where he could only watch the sparks ignite between Graham and his usually cool fiancée.

Once, during a garden party at the Benton estate, Graham persuaded Eve to join an impromptu game of touch football. While Franklin Stuart looked on, stunned, Donaldson, former quarterback at Notre Dame, tackled Eve and sent her, white lawn dress, organdie hat, and all, flying to the ground laughing in his arms.

Finally, Graham had arrived at the house one day when her parents were out of town, on no pretense at all. He had walked Eve around the grounds and, in the aviary, held her so close she could hardly breathe, and kissed her.

'Don't marry that piece of furniture. Marry me. I've never said these words to anybody in my life – I love you and I want you.'

He kissed her again, and this time she felt what she had never felt with Franklin – magic.

With that he had picked her up, held her in his arms, and carried her right into the fountain, shoes and all. 'I know you're supposed to throw coins into a fountain to get your wish. But if you don't say yes right this minute, I'm going to throw *you* in.'

And she threw back her head and laughed, thinking that she'd better accept his proposal before he ruined any more of her dresses.

As Mrs Graham Donaldson, she had watched her husband steer Benton and Stuart from a solid but insignificant family-owned mining concern into Intercon, a powerful international conglomerate in the *Fortune* 500, with a seemingly unbreakable lock on certain critical domestic oil leases. Most of these had been discreetly acquired at Graham's insistence as he somehow charmed, wheedled, and overcame an unyielding board of relatives and in-laws with what was now considered textbook foresight. That had been the beginning.

Eve had fussed over Graham, kept house for him, entertained for him, introduced him to society, raised their daughter, Drucilla, to be his most adored confection. For thirty years, she devoted her life to him with an eagerness untinged by boredom or regret.

Her goal had always been to be the perfect wife. If she tucked a fresh sprig from her greenhouse into the lapel of one of the Huntsman Savile Row suits she had helped him choose or introduced him to operas and symphonies, she did it out of love, not concern for doing the right things. Like so many women of her generation, her efforts were simply ways of showing she cared. She had even introduced him to her old Farmington roommate, Polly-anne, and her husband, Rex Savage, who were now the First Lady and President of the United States.

Eve's primary reponsibility in life, as she saw it, was to provide her husband with diversion from a job that, without tastefully punctuated pauses of music, tranquility, and enlightened dinner conversation, would be all-encompassing. Eve had seen her father devote himself to unyielding seventy-hour work weeks, the stress of which, she was convinced, had caused his death from an embolism at fifty-five, exactly her husband's age. It was because she hoped to ease the weight of Graham's commitments as president and chief executive officer of Intercon Minerals, rather than any self-centered desire to propel herself forward socially, that the Donaldsons achieved their world-class social stature.

And so, Eve planned her parties like military maneuvers, engineering strike-force combinations of interesting personalities, culled from many fields. Food sautéed, puréed, glacéed, garnished, and served as if it were a work of art; Pratesi tables that shimmered with Lalique and vermeil; and, for a homey touch, fresh herbs, vegetables, and flowers from the greenhouse.

The right flowers were important today, Eve reminded herself as she passed the aviary and then the flask house, with its endless rows of cedar racks holding thousands of cotton- and cork-stoppered flasks and bottles, each nurturing a seedling, and beyond that a winter garden for vegetables. Eve tapped on the glass as she passed to alert the head gardener, Louis, who waved and nodded from inside. She planned to use tonight's dinner to muster ground-swell support for Graham's new project, the undersea research center in the Caribbean. Graham was anxious for every detail to be as perfect as possible, and Eve would not let him down. They were partners; her job was to ease situations and smooth surfaces.

Eve's legendary orchids were nurtured in this greenhouse. On one of her white cattleyas a record three hundred and twenty-five flowers had bloomed at once, and Donaldson blooms always won prizes at the Mid-America Orchid Show and from the American Orchid Society. The gas bill to heat the phalaenopsis house alone was six thousand dollars a year, but Eve never questioned the expenditure. Flowers made a house a home, she felt. And that was that.

The musty smell of humid air and fertilizer settled around her as she strode into the main greenhouse. Classical music drifted from somewhere overhead, mingling with the constant hiss and click of the pipes.

'Oh, Louis,' she smiled, her gold-flecked green eyes wide and sincere, 'thank you *so* much for the beautiful anemones you sent in for my dressing table. It made my morning when Cherie brought them up.'

Louis scuffed happily at the cement floor. 'Thank you, Miss Eve,' he grinned. 'By the way, this came for you.' With a tinge of disdain, he indicated a large purple cattleya wrapped in gold foil, a giant fuchsia bow hanging askew from its stem. Eve opened the card. It was a thank you note from one of Graham's friends whom she had introduced to the president of a major conglomerate. As a result, the man now had access to financing which would enable him to open a Southwest branch. If this introduction had been considered a business transaction, the finder's fee would have been in the hundreds of thousands of dollars, Eve knew. She had, after all, spent her life on the edges of the business world, quietly absorbing conversations and details at thousands of dinner tables. Wasn't it interesting, Eve thought, that in this so-called liberated age, some men still thought flowers would express appreciation to a woman for easing him into a million-dollar deal. But it didn't really matter. Eve had made the introduction because Graham had suggested it. She didn't want finder's fees or even thanks. What was important to her was Graham's best interest. Years ago she had made his welfare her territory.

'I think we'll start with just a few cymbidium, Louis,' Eve began as he handed her a sterile scissors. 'And we'll put these in the drawing room, don't you agree?'

Louis admired Eve's beautiful hands with their perfect, crystalline-peach nails. In his thirty-five years with the family, he had never seen Eve Benton, now Donaldson, with a broken fingernail or a blister, in spite of the fact that she worked in the gardens at least once a week. Of course, she didn't just dig into the dirt. She had a ritual he'd watched her learn from her own mother: first, the rich hand cream, then the pair of latex gloves, and, finally, the canvas gardening gloves. Not the kind of trouble an ordinary woman might go to but, then, Louis reasoned, the Donaldsons were not ordinary people.

He gestured to a set of six life-sized silver swans, green gardener's clay and sponges nestled in their hollow centers. 'Are these the containers we'll be using?'

Eve nodded. 'Now what would one put in a swan?' She clipped a branch of apple-green dendrobium for the drawing room. 'Let's have everything loose and fresh. Not too formal.'

They moved through the greenhouse, clipping and piling orchids into her basket until it was full of lacy sprays pastelled in shades of white, pink, and green. She knew she didn't have to worry about the arrangements. Louis always understood exactly what she wanted.

She would supervise the final touches herself, although her dear friend and almost foster son, Hughie Stuart, had promised to stop by this morning to offer moral support. Hughie had a perfect eye for detail, the kind of talent that had years ago caught the eye of one of the world's leading fashion photographers, Marshall Valeski, who worked out of Chicago. It was actually Hughie Stuart who had created some of the magnificent, perfectly proportioned setting for advertisements featuring Lenox china, Baccarat crystal, and other products pursued by those in search of exquisite taste. Some people sniped that Hughie didn't have much to do in such a position – Valeski's established trademark was simplicity. The photographer had made his name not with complicated setups, but with his black-and-white portraits of ballet dancers, movie stars and politicians, each person, male or female, wearing the same black turtleneck sweater.

Eve loved Hughie and his fifteen-year-old sister, Bambi, as if they were her own children. She had watched their talents and capabilities develop since birth and had been their guardian and mother figure since their parents' deaths over ten years ago. Eve had tried unsuccessfully to put that tragedy out of her mind, but she never forgot her responsibility toward the two children of her former fiancé, Franklin Stuart. Eve had suffered several miscarriages after Drucilla's birth and it seemed more than natural for the Stuart children to complete the family Eve had always wanted.

Hughie, she knew, was sensitive, artistic, and talented. The skill of consistently evoking the look of simplicity and taste was a rare gift, and even Valeski's work was enhanced by Hughie's assistance.

The phone in the greenhouse rang softly. 'Miss Eve, Mr Stuart is here,' Louis announced. Eve handed him the basket and smiled as she pulled off her gloves. Hughie would know just what, if anything, was missing.

Hughie Stuart surveyed the Donaldson dining room, his palette for the day. His short, plump hands were stuffed into his two back pockets as he stood under the languid-eyed supervision of the John Singer Sargent portrait of Eve's grandmother, Caroline Belmont Benton. A shaft of streaming sunlight on her auburn pompadour, décolletage daringly exposed despite the robin's egg pearls roped about her throat, a tiny, flat-faced Pekinese tucked under one arm and a white parasol beneath the other, Caroline Benton appeared by the tender tilt of her mouth to approve of the preparations for a formal dinner at her granddaughter's home.

Hughie watched the maids setting the individual swan-shaped silver salt and pepper shakers at each place, with a larger, crystal swan cradling sugar cubes between its gold-shot wings at every other chair. Napkins appliquéd with Madeira embroidery coordinated with the matching floor-skimming cloth. The round sterling service plates were set on the table, and Cherie was overseeing the placement of gold-rimmed Stueben crystal, three at each setting. Silver seashell ashtrays and tiny lacquer tubs containing cigarettes lined up in gleaming formation on trays brought in from the butler's pantry.

He noted with satisfaction the extraordinary Chinese screens of wood and semi-precious stones flanking the windows. They had been his suggestion, and he congratulated himself, as they were spectacularly well set off by the white marble floor and Eve's bleached mahogany Chippendale chairs.

Backing off into the doorway, Hughie framed the room with his hands. Height, he decided. The tables need height. And the room was washing out with all that white. A touch of color would add some relief.

He reached into the large cardboard box by the doorway and pulled out several objects wrapped in tissue paper. He unwrapped nine tiny, perfectly formed topiary deer, carved and trimmed from miniature hothouse boxwoods, and placed three on each table. Hughie had brought home these props from today's shoot as a surprise for his young sister, Bambi, because they were so appropriate to her nickname, but it was obvious that Eve's tables would not work without them. Bambi could pick them up tomorrow.

Eve Donaldson entered the room, which was suddenly perfumed with Ma Griffe. 'Hughie, how clever of you!'

She whirled around the tables, clapping her hands like a child who had just peeked under the Christmas tree.

'That's *wonderful*!' she pronounced, stopping to kiss Hughie on both cheeks. 'I'm delighted.'

Hughie grinned boyishly, his bright blue eyes sparkling and dancing as they always did when he, the ultimate giver of compliments, received one. 'I thought the famous Donaldson tables could use a touch of color, so I'm letting you borrow these. But they're really a surprise for Bambi.'

'Of course,' Eve said. 'Cherie will run them over in the morning. Are you sure you won't stay? It's going to be such a lovely party.'

Hughie shook his head. 'No, no. I promised Bambi I'd get home early one day this week to help her with her homework.'

How typical of Hughie, thought Eve. He was always so considerate of his younger sister. He had practically raised Bambi himself, insisting on keeping the tiny family together after the accident. He lived with Bambi protectively in the coach house on the old Stuart grounds adjoining the Donaldsons' property.

When the Stuart mansion had been sold off to cover the staggering debts of Franklin Stuart's estate, Eve had made sure the coach house remained intact, so Hughie and Bambi could remain there independently. The fact that Franklin had left his children nothing but millions of dollars in debt was gracefully camouflaged by Eve, who made sure the Stuart children kept at least part of the family estate and all of the good name. This Eve viewed as all-important.

At first she had made sure a housekeeper and nurse lived with them. She would have immediately adopted them and moved them in with her if Graham hadn't so fiercely objected. Drucilla had been born and even though Eve had miscarried many times, Graham was confident they'd have more children of their own. So she mothered Hughie and Bambi from next door.

When Hughie reached his late teens, however, he had insisted on running the house himself, and, more often than not, it had been Hughie, not Eve, who chose the decor and gave the orders to the housekeeper regarding Bambi's diet, exercise, or studies. Bambi had been raised by both Eve and Hughie, and Hughie had grown into a combination of foster son and best friend to Eve.

Eve gestured to show Cherie where she should place the flower-filled silver swans. 'The First Lady is coming, you know,' she tempted.

'And what is that old rascal of a roommate of yours up to now?' You could almost see Hughie's ears cock forward. The First Lady was alway news. And nobody loved gossip more than Hughie. The North Shore ladies all said that one lunch with Hughie was ammunition for a month of dinners.

Eve sighed. 'As usual, the White House Preservation Committee is on her neck. Pollyanne's repainting the Red Room this pale shade of pink, which she says is much more modern, and they're having a fit.'

'Pastels are more flattering to her skin tones,' lilted Hughie.

'Well, Pollyanne loves pastels. And she says that the deep rose of the Red Room is much too Victorian.'

'Well, it's not,' he sniped. 'It's very *Empire*. The whole room is Empire. It's that wonderful, deep color and should be left alone.'

'And Pollyanne has decided to soften things up a bit.' Eve had a habit of ignoring anything she chose not to hear. Hughie called it selective listening.

Hughie pursed his lips. 'Oh, don't tell me,' he jibed. 'Pink is her trademark. She'd like to be the Queen in *Alice in Wonderland*, painting everything *her* color. She'll leave her mark on the White House, I'm sure. Didn't she replant the entire Rose Garden pink already?'

Hughie took Eve's hand, swinging it gaily. 'Now, *you*

should have been First Lady, Eve. You're the one who knows how to do things.'

She playfully tapped Hughie's shoulder with the seating chart. 'Oh, Hughie! You're too flattering. But Pollyanne's a very serious woman, she really is. And she never asked to be First Lady. She only wanted a husband and a home, like the rest of us.'

Hughie rolled his eyes in mock disbelief as Eve picked up a stack of place cards, lettered meticulously in her own calligraphic handwriting. 'Now let's see – place cards. Come and help, you're so clever.'

She glanced at the first name on her leather seating chart from Smithson's in London, and her chiseled nose wrinkled ever so slightly. 'Governor Bob. Mmm, such a Democrat. Whom do you think we should put him with?'

Hughie scanned the guest list. 'Allison Blair. Of course! She could talk to a doorknob. She'll be just perfect.' He tucked his hands into his pockets, envisioning the aged Chicago matron regaling the governor with tales of the rudeness of the men who fixed the potholes in front of her East Lake Shore Drive co-op.

Eve slipped two place cards between the wings of two small silver swans. 'Now let's see. I'll put Dru at that table. Did I tell you Drucilla is moving into the downtown penthouse? It'll be good for her to be on her own a little bit.'

'What fun.' Hughie's voice was flat. It was about time, he thought to himself. Drucilla and her friends reminded him of an overgrown gaggle of geese, with their incessant gossiping and flurrying from party to party, extending the years of the debutante ball far beyond their tenure. At twenty-three, Dru epitomized the term postdeb. Hurtling through life, she swore that if she died dancing, she'd be buried in Scaasi. At least she was finally moving out of her parents' home, where her bedroom was an organdie-and-gingham shrine to her prolonged girlhood, Hughie thought. She'd racked up two or three engagements already, though after the second fiancé, Hughie stopped giving her engagement parties, having stumbled upon the bride-to-be in flagrante delicto with the caterer. Considering the way she and her friends had been brought up, it was amazing they weren't wearing matching tiaras on a regular basis.

Hughie believed Eve had been a much better mother to Bambi, and that Graham had been responsible for his dithering daughter. Bambi hadn't had luxuries, but Eve had made sure she had love and a sense of values. Well, Hughie thought, if Dru and her best friend Lolly Bishop moved into the Lake Shore Drive condo, Tiffany's, Cartier's, and Saks Fifth Avenue's monthly bills – which still went straight to Graham Donaldson's secretary – would double.

'What about Lolly Bishop?' Hughie changed the subject. 'Isn't she still dating Billy Wright?'

'Mmm-hmm.'

'I dropped into her gallery the other day, and she really indulges her taste,' reported Hughie. 'She had an exhibit by some California artist who makes these architectural pieces out of Plexiglas and human hair.'

'Oh, come! Really, Hughie!'

'Well, it's the truth, and God knows where it came from. There's little neon lights and balloons and hair from his own body. I tell you! It was something we thought we could use at the studio, until I got a good look at it.'

'Let's concentrate on the tables. Is this all the young people? Let's move on then.' Eve guided Hughie to her next table.

He pushed a topiary deer a fraction of an inch closer to a freesia-filled swan. 'Who else is coming?'

'Oh, Rita Butell from the Shedd Aquarium and her husband. And Dr Corbett . . .'

'Psychiatrist to the rich and demented. Put him with Governor Bob, alias Tomato Face.' He peered over Eve's shoulder at her list, pointed to a name with a flourish, and made a small 'tsk!'

'Buffy Mortensen! Isn't she the one who's putting in all those pink roses at the White House?'

'Now stop.'

'Don't tell me. She took the Jacqueline Kennedy Rose and the Mamie Eisenhower Rose and made a hybrid – the Pollyanne Savage Rose. What a name for a flower – the Savage Rose. I like it, you expect it to be all thorns.'

Eve was practically breathless with laughter, but she had to defend Pollyanne. 'Now, come on,' she gasped. 'She's been my best friend for years and years.'

Hughie shrugged and shifted his attention to the menu. Hand-written cards at each table listed cold Icelandic salmon and caviar, celery-heart salad, roast duck with cherry sauce, wild rice, zucchini squash, hot pear pie, and homemade pecan fudge. 'Very nice,' he nodded.

'Yes,' agreed Eve. 'Simple but fun. Oh, I forgot to tell you.' She arranged the cards at the company table. 'Pollyanne's flying out with me to The Golden Door for "R and R" – and it's such a to-do because we're taking Air Force One.'

Hughie's eyebrows winged toward his receding hairline. 'I can just see the headlines: FIRST LADY FLIES AIR FORCE ONE TO FAT FARM.'

'Oh, no, it's not like that!' Eve was quick to defend Pollyanne. 'We've made this trip together every year for the past twenty years and why should it be any different now that she's First Lady? She's still allowed a private life. She's given up enough for her country – why should she give up her figure?'

Hughie chortled as Eve continued. 'Rex is going out to the Western White House and he's giving a speech in Dallas, so he's going to drop us off on the way. There'll be no publicity at all.'

She rearranged a few stalks of cymbidium. 'The problem is all the security checks. I have to have my luggage ready two days early so the Secret Service can take care of it.'

Hughie rolled his eyes. 'Speaking of security, you've got enough out-of-uniform military men outside to stall off an invasion. The First Lady's personal protection, I presume.'

'The times we live in,' murmured Eve.

'Tell me about it. You should have seen Valeski's studio this morning,' he said. 'We had two armed guards there while we were shooting the Dromoldo Diamond.'

The word *diamond* sparked Eve's attention instantly. 'How divine. Is it beautiful?'

Hughie huffed. 'No, it looks like a rock on the beach. It's sixty-two carats unfaceted, you know, and insured for four million dollars. We couldn't get any dazzle from it at all. I had to sit there applying Windex with a Q-tip while these guards watched with their guns hanging out! What did they think we were going to do? There isn't a place on earth we could sell the bloody thing. But according to the insurance contract, they had to stand within four feet of the diamond at all times, so they were constantly underfoot, tromping on the seamless, edging into every shot.' Hughie shuddered at the memory.

'Goodness,' sympathized Eve.

'Finally Valeski, genius that he is, made the best of it.

He put a guard in the shot, so we'll have this pock-marked, Alcatraz-type face, and the gun and this incredible diamond up front. It should be a fabulous shot.'

Suddenly Cherie, the housemaid, burst into the dining room. 'The Secret Service is at the door.'

Eve followed her into the hall, where a group of hawk-eyed dark-suited men cut off her greetings as they moved in like a Marine landing force.

'We'd just like to check the grounds, Mrs Donaldson,' said the leader. 'Some sort of crackpot threat.' Static and garbled voices crackled over his radiophone.

The Secret Service men moved between Eve and Hughie like a flying wedge, pushing Hughie back toward the door in a flurry of official activity.

Head bent, the collar of his herringbone jacket turned up, Hughie Stuart scurried along the narrow path that separated the Donaldson estate from The Cottage. He ferreted his way through the stone-walled gate that divided the fifteen-acre Donaldson estate from what was formerly the grounds of the Stuart property, now the setting of a half-dozen million-dollar suburban residences. Only The Cottage remained standing from the original Stuart estate. After the deaths of Hughie's parents, the main house, stables, and guest house had been sold to meet unexpected debts and taxes. Eve Donaldson had managed to salvage the coach house where Hughie and Bambi stayed. Twelve-year-old Hughie had insisted on remaining with his infant sister himself, and Eve, recognizing his shock and outraged grief after the hunting accident that had killed both his mother and father, had respected his need for pride and privacy. She had come up with the coach house solution.

Eventually Hughie had redesigned the house, supervising its renovation. Working with pieces salvaged from the main house before its demolition, he had transformed the dilapidated structure into a home for himself and Bambi. The Cottage was now a place of such charm that city friends vied for weekend invitations.

The Cottage sat sequestered behind half a dozen aged pines whose needles formed a carpet that crunched underfoot as Hughie gasped, slightly breathless, definitely not used to trotting along at such a pace, but he couldn't wait to get away from the hysteria that always accompanied one of Pollyanne's visits.

Just as Hughie stepped into the small lawn and passed the huge green boxwoods sculpted into topiary deer guarding the white frame house, he heard the pounding of hooves.

'Hello, Hughie!' called Bambi as she galloped through the pines on a chestnut horse from Eve's stable. The young girl's long auburn hair mingled with the flying mane as she leaned close to the animal's neck, her blue-jeaned legs showing perfect form even though she rode bareback. When the horse trotted to a stop on the lawn beside Hughie, Bambi lightly jumped to the ground.

'Those Secret Service men over at Aunt Eve's threw me off the grounds,' she said, her huge mahogany eyes widening under thick untamed brows. 'The First Lady comes all the time. What's the big deal today? Are we declaring war or something?' She patted the horse with one hand and leaned over to give her brother a quick kiss. At fifteen, Bambi was already a head taller than he. She had inherited their father's height.

Hughie was constantly startled by his sister's ever-increasing beauty. She was a child who had never had a child's face. Her flawless peach-tinted skin, straight, patrician nose and graceful, fawnlike neck gave her a look at once sensual and innocent. Hughie, who spent his days with some of the most beautiful fashion models in the business, never ceased to marvel at the fact that Bambi somehow achieved greater beauty without ever looking into a mirror.

'On the news today, they said the American Embassy in Venezuela was bombed and somebody was kidnapped,' Bambi said. 'Is everything all right? Is that why they wouldn't let us back into the stable?'

'You know the First Lady,' Hughie brushed a leaf from Bambi's hair. 'She probably stepped up security because she had a fight with her pedicurist.'

Bambi's face relaxed into a wide grin, and Hughie smiled, too.

'Why don't you go tie up Thunder? Then we can have tea by the fire and go over your homework like I promised. I made scones this morning.'

'Oh, great! I'll be in as soon as we've cooled down.'

Hughie walked through the living room into the enclosed porch, where he lit a fire and threw in a handful of dried pine cones. Then he perched on the white rattan chaise covered with an Amish quilt and petulantly poked at the fire. Every time he came from the main house to the cottage he felt the old resentment towards Graham Donaldson. He held Eve's husband responsible for his own family's personal misfortunes. It had been a long time since Graham had to deal with anything that wasn't smoothed over first by aides, assistants, underlings, and maids. He certainly hadn't had to face real trouble since he married Eve Benton, or since he'd appropriated the Benton and Stuart Mineral Comapny at the expense of Hughie's father. True, Hughie grudgingly admitted, the company was a superpower now, but Graham Donaldson had never learned that money was *not* everything in life.

People like Graham Donaldson never understood the genteel sensibilities. The greedy bastard had rolled over two sensitive, caring souls – Hughie's parents – just to put more zeros behind his net worth. Hughie began to feel the anger that only Graham Donaldson could inspire.

Donaldson hadn't waited for Hughie to turn twenty-one so he could handle his own affairs. He had sold the Stuart estate right out from under Hughie and Bambi, the two Stuart orphans, to settle the bottom line. If Graham Donaldson could run a multi-million dollar company, he could certainly have figured out some way to have kept the Stuart estate intact after their parents had died. A quick shudder went through Hughie's body as he thought about the accident that had killed his parents.

Graham Donaldson didn't deserve Eve. And *she* certainly didn't deserve what she got from him – a lifetime of putting the company before her, Drucilla, or even human feelings.

He supposed he could live without what was rightfully his. But each time Hughie drove past the ninety-story Intercon building on his way to work he couldn't help thinking of what might have been. What *should* have been.

'Where's the strawberry jam?' hollered Bambi from the kitchen. She bounced into the room, and Hughie brightened immediately. At least some people had their hearts in the right place.

# 3

*January 1982*

As Catherine rode up the elevator to her new office, she felt totally at home. Her lifelong restless feeling of not quite fitting in was almost gone. She belonged to this building, in this position. During her six months at Intercon, she'd had to learn fast and be ready for anything at any hour. She didn't have time for a personal life, but working with Graham Donaldson was enough.

'Now I know what power feels like,' she mused. It was the height of this building. It was the freedom to make connections, decisions, to contact editors, get an article arranged, plan shoots, make projections, authorize spending. It was talking to the chairman one-on-one. It was creating something that would affect thousands of people. It was her own small empire.

Work had never felt so good. She had found herself needing less sleep, and she'd lost weight. She felt buoyant, turned-on. Standing alone in the elevator, she felt more attractive, as if power made her prettier.

If she felt like this at her limited level, she could only imagine what it might be like for Graham Donaldson. Catherine envisioned controlling billions of dollars, meeting heads of state, talking to the President on a first-name basis.

For the first time, she understood what power meant. It was having Graham Donaldson on your side and a big, new corner office. Of course it meant sixty-hour work weeks, too. But she could handle that.

She stepped from the elevator and walked down the beige carpeted hallway.

'Careful,' admonished Catherine as she directed the movers. 'The paint's still wet.' Three large men were struggling with the hunter-green, five piece sectional couch that would fill one corner of the room directly across from the round chrome and glass pedestal table which had replaced her desk.

'That's wonderful. Thank you.' Catherine folded her arms and surveyed the transformation. She had never liked sitting at her desk across from a group. People always contributed their best ideas when they felt they were equals, not being judged. A rough thought dropped in casual conversation could be the germ of a great idea, something that she could turn into a useful concept for A Place in the Sun.

Catherine had immediately seen the possibilities of turning what had been called the Trophy Room into usable office space. The room's layout was perfect. During her first six months at Intercon, she had observed that the room's sole function was as a display area for Graham's fishing trophies. The walls were colorfully hung with treasures only a taxidermist could love: Graham's fourteen-foot blue marlin, three spectacular sailfish with sword-tip bills, various record-breaking bonefish, and a giant sea tortoise. Once a month Ray Acconti met in the Trophy Room with his environmental group, but otherwise the space was wasted, Catherine thought.

When she had pointed this out to Graham, she had also mentioned that it was rather undiplomatic to meet with environmentalists in a room decorated with the bodies of dead animals. She chuckled to herself as she remembered how Ray Acconti had reacted, dropping his ingratiating façade, waving his arms and arguing that serious ichthyologists, those dedicated to the scientific study of fish, were used to working with marine specimens. Graham, however, had seen her point, and within two weeks the office manager had drawn up plans to redefine the room and outer hallway to house Catherine's growing new department.

Catherine had made an effort to become friends with Ray Acconti, at first in honest eagerness, and then, not so much because she liked him, which she found impossible, but because she realized she might need him. She knew office alliances were important, and Acconti was an office type that Catherine had encountered before. He was the kind that rarely came up with constructive ideas of his own, but who had somehow managed to edge into a position where he could cast negativism, implicit in even an arched eyebrow, that would effectively kill a fledgling idea or project.

Ray Acconti had spent fifteen years plugging his way out of academia and up the corporate ladder and had finally secured a position that allowed him some power and authority, and he clearly wasn't about to let that foothold become threatened by a know-it-all female MBA. Acconti had always viewed women as a sort of necessary support service, although he would never admit it. Instead, he loudly claimed his support of the women's movement.

'I wish my wife had a career,' he had told Catherine as he stopped in to survey her office during her first week at Intercon. Since his own office was bigger, he could afford to be generous. 'I wish Susan earned enough money so I could retire!' Acconti laughed smugly at his little joke, and Catherine smiled weakly.

Her suspicions had been confirmed during their first lunch. Graham Donaldson had asked Acconti to brief Catherine on the environmental implications of the island development. A three-volume report had been delivered by Acconti's secretary as background material. After absorbing the report, which was really a series of impossibly complex and disconnected mini-reports from Acconti's staff, Catherine had suggested that she and Ray sit down and discuss the project on a more informal basis.

Ray Acconti had turned out to be a man well acquainted with the rituals of the power lunch. He had chosen the restaurant, the International Club of the Drake Hotel, and he had picked the time. Still, he kept Catherine waiting in the Intercon lobby, sweltering with her coat on, for almost twenty minutes before ambling out with a look of serious apology.

'Sorry. Last-minute phone calls from Washington . . .'

Catherine had shrugged this off. 'Oh, no problem.' No problem for *him*.

At the restaurant, Acconti couldn't have been more charming. He had delighted Catherine with his stories of the Intercon-sponsored underwater habitat in the Caribbean, where the scientific team had made mascots out of a school of local porpoises. He told her about his wife, Susan, her hobby of weaving, and their new house in suburban Glen Ellyn, where Susan kept her loom in the study. She'd even heard about Ray Jr, and his progress on the Little League team. Catherine had almost convinced herself that Ray Acconti could be interesting and even human to work with when she noticed his possessiveness.

The salt and pepper shakers, the sugar bowl, the matches, even some of Catherine's silverware that she wasn't using, had somehow shifted to Acconti's side of the table! It was incredible, Catherine remembered later. While talking about Ray Jr's batting average, Acconti had shifted all the tableware to his side of the table in the kind of territorial display of power Catherine was accustomed to witnessing in the office. Acconti was after her space, and he probably wasn't even aware of the depths of his hostility toward her.

A month later, after Catherine had finally absorbed the three-volume environmental document, she shared an idea with Ray. What if the environmental research center were to be used for publicity purposes to attract outside funding? Perhaps Intercon could develop a proposal to link up with, say, *National Geographic*, who would photograph each step of the project and run a feature on it, or maybe even film a documentary for television? Acconti had seemed unimpressed.

She was shocked when Acconti brought up the *National Geographic* tie-in idea to Graham Donaldson at the weekly senior staff meeting. The bastard even had a chart, and a typed memo about it, presented in a folder of *National Geographic* yellow. Graham had been impressed, and Catherine had, stupidly she realized later, waited for credit. When it didn't come, she spoke up.

'I'm glad you agreed with my thoughts on this, Ray,' she said, as calmly as if she were not seething inside. 'I've already done some preliminary work contacting *National Geographic*, and they're interested.'

'Great,' shot back Acconti. 'That's the kind of follow-up I like to see.'

Follow-up? It had been *her* idea, damn it! After the meeting, Catherine stalked Acconti into his office and sat smack on the corner of his desk. Two could play his game.

'Ray, I was really disappointed that you didn't give me

any feedback on this before, so we could have presented the concept together. After all, it was my idea.'

Acconti shuffled some papers and moved the picture of Susan and Ray Jr away from Catherine's hip, as if they were too precious to be sullied by the proximity of her rear end. 'Well, your initial concept was, umm, very *conceptual*,' he said. 'It needed a little work. My group had to expand on it, pull it together, really.'

'Ray, come on. The concept was completely together. I have a report on it in my drawer!'

Acconti lit a cigar and averted his eyes. 'Around here, Catherine,' he said, 'we are a team. And we are team players. People who can't play on the team have problems. You're still new here – but you'll get used to it.'

She could see that the issue was hopeless. She had left Acconti's office cursing not so much him as herself, since she should have known better than to present an idea to someone who was threatened by her. Next time she'd buttress her concept with written documents, presented in the proper fashion. She forwarded a copy of her *National Geographic* file to Graham Donaldson – and seethed. Since that day Catherine had not given Ray Acconti any opportunity to deceive her.

Catherine walked out of her office into the hall, where carpenters were hammering partitions into place for her team. Melissa would sit in the first cubicle, and beside her, Ron. Shelly and B.J. would have the offices flanking hers. Catherine had ordered white Formica for all her people because it seemed less institutional than gunmetal-gray cabinets. Since most of her waking hours were spent in the office, Catherine felt the space might as well be as livable as possible.

Over the hammering and drilling, someone called her name. 'Catherine, I've been trying to reach you.' Carla,

Graham's executive secretary, sidestepped two men from the phone company who were carrying reels of cable and equipment. 'Mr Donaldson wants to see you right away.'

Graham and Ray Acconti were in the executive conference room. The huge topographical map that Catherine's group had designed was spread out on the conference table. One area of the islands was circled in red.

'Oh, good. Come on in, Catherine.' Graham Donaldson waved her forward. 'We need a woman's touch.'

She laughed and pointedly tapped his arm. 'There, a woman's touch.'

Then she noticed Michael Picol standing by the window. This meeting must be more important than she had thought.

'Hello, Michael,' she said.

He didn't turn around. 'It's that damned widow,' he said, his back still turned.

'Look here, Catherine,' Ray Acconti said, pointing at the map with his Cross pen. 'These blue circles indicate our successful acquisition targets. The red circles indicate our opportunity areas.'

What bullshit, Catherine thought. But she said, 'In other words, property owners who won't sell.' She pulled up a chair. 'I know the big area is US government property. That leaves . . .'

'The widow,' interrupted Picol.

Catherine glanced at Graham Donaldson. She sensed that she was going to be included in a strategic decision for the first time. Until now, her role had been promotional. She was in charge of coordinating a plan to sell the concept of A Place in the Sun to the reluctant board of directors.

She had known from the beginning that the project was high-risk. But ever since her first interview, she had worked to bring Graham Donaldson's dream to life. Turning a group of scrub islands in the middle of nowhere into a science-study center and world-class resort was not easy, but it had potential. It would be the world's first complex that combined scientific research on marine life, sea farming to provide food for underdeveloped nations, and solar water purification. And Catherine's addition to the whole idea had been nothing short of inspired. A luxury resort would finance the whole complex and make it economically and commercially acceptable to the board of hard-nosed money men. Only Ray Acconti had opposed Catherine's resort idea. He insisted that a resort would cheapen the environmental ethics of a plan that he saw as a concept with Nobel Peace Prize potential. But, as Catherine maintained, the stockholders might have a problem with a Nobel Peace Prize that drained hundreds of millions of dollars into the ocean.

'Must be some sentimental shit,' Michael Picol interjected, rubbing his forehead. 'Why else would she be holding out? We've offered her a fucking fortune.'

'This second area belongs to Agnes Palmer, the widow of Colonel Jack Palmer,' explained Graham, pointing at the map. 'Mrs Palmer refuses to sell. We sent in Michael Picol to negotiate, but even his charm didn't work.'

'I should talk to her,' said Acconti.

Graham shook his head and looked directly at Catherine. 'No, I think we need a less intimidating approach. Michael and I think it would be a good idea if Catherine came with us to Dallas.'

He pushed a button, summoning Carla. 'Carla will try to set up a meeting with you and Mrs Palmer,' he told Catherine. 'And also one with Terry Skittle, the architect you've wanted to interview for the resort.'

'When is the first meeting?' asked Catherine, scribbling notes.

'Day after tomorrow. But you'll have a chance to talk to Mrs Palmer informally at the Oil and Gas Testimonial Dinner tomorrow night.' Graham stood up. 'Michael will brief you. I'll see you on the plane. We leave at six. Let's see – it's two-thirty now. You'll be able to handle that, won't you?'

'No problem,' she nodded. Good grief. That left her less than four hours to be briefed, get home, pack, and make it to the airport. She started to plan the few items she would need to take.

'Oh,' added Graham on his way out. 'Bring something fancy. The dinner's black tie and those Texas girls go all out.' He smiled. 'I've got complete confidence in you.'

Catherine felt her stomach tighten as she mentally considered her wardrobe. Black tie! But there was no time for panic, as Michael Picol launched immediately into the briefing session.

Two and a half hours later, Catherine rushed out of the conference room. Good Lord! She'd never make it. The briefing had been endless. Proposals, pay-out plans, and the explanation of the memorial to Colonel Jack Palmer, plus the proposed private home for Mrs Palmer herself was information Catherine had to digest immediately.

Carla waved her down in the hall. 'You'd better get straight to the airport, Catherine.'

'But . . .' Catherine started to protest.

Carla handed her an envelope. 'It's all taken care of. You'll be staying at the Mansion Hotel at Turtle Creek with the Donaldsons. The hotel will provide the basics for overnight – shampoo, toothbrush, hair dryer, even a robe and slippers. Then, first thing tomorrow, Silver Key

Services at Neiman-Marcus is expecting you. They'll take care of a few clothes for you.'

Catherine had no idea what Silver Key Services was, or what a few clothes meant. She hadn't bought herself anything new in over a year – but she didn't have time to speculate. 'Thank you, Carla, you're wonderful.' She wanted to hug the woman. It wasn't often that a secretary would go out of her way for you – especially if she wasn't *your* secretary. Catherine grabbed her briefcase and raced to the elevators.

# 4

'This is a classic example of dishwater blonde,' remarked Monsieur Lupe, head colorist at the Neiman-Marcus beauty salon, as he wrapped silver foil around a strand of Catherine's hair, squinting as if he were doing major reconstructive surgery.

Catherine frowned dubiously into the mirror. But Monsieur Lupe insisted. 'This will bring highlight into the hair. I call this sunshining.' He snapped his fingers at an assistant, who handed him two squares of foil.

'In your case, we're going to use warm reds. For Drucilla, we like to do blonde sunshining. I did her at the hotel first thing this morning. But you're not the blonde type. More foil, Manuel.'

Catherine preferred not to ask what type Monsieur Lupe thought she was.

'I want to hear all about the terrorist kidnapping of Guillermo Hawks. Drucilla says they're assassins. I used to do his wife's hair when they lived in Dallas. Do you think he's dead?'

'We don't know exactly who is responsible.' Guillermo Hawks was Intercon's man in South America and currently being held for ransom. Three people had died when a plastic bomb had exploded after Hawks had been snatched from his car. The details were supposed to be confidential. Only top management at Intercon knew that the Bandera Roja, a Venezuelan revolutionary group, had claimed responsibility for the kidnapping and the bombing of the office and the embassy. That air-brain

Drucilla wasn't supposed to be discussing highly explosive issues with her hairdresser! Michael Picol had called a meeting in the executive conference room just hours after the incident to explain the delicate political balance in Venezuela and the surrounding South American countries. Intercon's Caribbean refineries were totally dependent on the good will and stability of these governments. The Bandera Roja, radical left-wing revolutionaries, had demanded that Venezuela break off all commerce with Intercon unless all profits were channelled back into Venezuela to feed and educate the hungry and indigent. Graham Donaldson's position was unyielding – Intercon would never give in to terrorist demands. But security around the Intercon offices had been heavied up, with guards at every exit and panic buttons installed in all company cars. Two new airplanes had been outfitted, and they were as anonymous as possible. Twenty-four-hour security was increased at two private hangars at Midway, the smaller of Chicago's airports, where all access could be carefully monitored.

Still, since the blowing up of Intercon's Venezuelan offices and Hawks's kidnapping, Catherine had never felt comfortable on the company plane.

All the way down to Dallas on the G-III, she'd had a blinding headache from the tension of trying so hard not to be nervous. Eve Donaldson and Drucilla had gossiped and giggled and napped most of the way, and Graham had been immersed in heavy-duty conferences with Michael Picol. But she had tried her best to tune out and ignore everything and everyone.

During the last few months, Catherine had worked fourteen-hour days, six and seven days a week. She rarely took time for herself and she knew she had to double her efforts on the projections and plans for A Place in the

Sun. The Venezuelan incident had dampened any glimmer of enthusiasm that the board might have had, and the project was, she knew, on shaky ground. But right now all that seemed very far away.

Mmm, wonderful, she thought, as Monsieur Lupe massaged her upper back and shoulders. She couldn't remember the last time she'd been pampered.

'Circulation, my dear,' said Monsieur Lupe.

'Really,' he continued, flicking his own long, black 'sunshined' ponytail. 'Drucilla was hysterical about the terrorist attacks. People ought to keep stupid causes to themselves. Dru is worried sick about her father. Do *you* think someone would try to kidnap him? I'm glad I'm just a hairdresser – what would a terrorist want with me?'

'Plenty.' He learned more information from chatty women than the CIA could access from their computer bank.

Monsieur Lupe picked up one of her hands with thinly veiled disdain. 'Do you still bite your nails? Carmelita, get over here.' He rattled through the tray of polishes. 'I think we'll use Number 22. Nothing too bright on nails that short.'

Catherine wondered what she'd gotten herself into. Since nine-thirty, when she'd arrived at the store and found her way to the Silver Key Services Department, she'd found herself in a whirlwind of hyperactivity over which she had no control.

A woman called Sunny had flashed her a perfect, toothy smile and welcomed her with a crisply typed agenda on beige stationery imprinted at the top with the Neiman-Marcus Silver Key logo.

*AGENDA*

10.00 A.M. Meet with Sunny McDonald, consultant,

Silver Key Club

| | |
|---|---|
| 10.15 A.M. | Hair consultation, treatment, and cut, Monsieur Lupe |
| | Manicure, Carmelita |
| 12.30 P.M. | Luncheon |
| 1.00 P.M. | Makeup consultation, Terri |
| 2.00 P.M. | Wardrobe consultation, Sunny |

Handwritten at the bottom was, 'Thank you very much for visiting Neiman-Marcus. Hope you have a wonderful day . . . Sunny.'

Sunny had given her a quick once-over and enthusiastically told her she had the perfect outfit in mind, and she knew Catherine was going to love her day. Then Catherine found herself propelled to the beauty salon and into the hands of Monsieur Lupe.

The first stop was the computer. Thanks to modern technology, Catherine was able to see her own image on the screen as it metamorphosized into a blonde, a brunette, a redhead, short, long, and curly-haired.

When Monsieur Lupe had finally finished, her whole face seemed to light up from the glow of shiny, strawberry-blonde hair. All the straggly ends were gone. Suddenly her eyes looked larger and she no longer seemed like an adolescent masquerading as a grown-up. She couldn't help but smile as she checked her reflection over her shoulder while two cosmetologists hurried her along to the makeup center.

'I never wear much makeup,' she protested. 'Just mascara and powder.' What had Carla gotten her into? She had had no idea that picking up a few clothes would translate into a total makeover. But then, no one was stopping her from walking out.

'This has nothing to do with makeup,' announced Terri, the taller of two cosmetologists. 'We're talking about a total look. Now, tell me about your lifestyle.'

'In one word – busy,' said Catherine. 'I don't have time to waste. I'm a business executive . . .'

The smaller redhead nodded enthusiastically. 'Wonderful! Some of our best customers are very successful corporate women. They know that looking good never stopped anyone from getting to the top.'

'You never see Elizabeth Dole without her look pulled together,' Terri chimed in.

'Well,' Catherine demurred. 'Tonight *is* important. It's a black-tie testimonial . . .'

The next thing she knew, the women had taken over. With a damp sponge, they applied light foundation that smoothed out her complexion and covered her freckles. 'But not all of them. We want you to look natural.'

Catherine's eyelashes were dyed. 'To save time in the morning. You can throw out your mascara now.' And her eyebrows shaped.

By the time the peach blusher was dusted on, Catherine could see a difference. But when the lip liner was applied with a pencil, and honey-toned, sheer lipstick stroked on with a brush, even Catherine knew the results were amazing. She had never noticed she had cheekbones before!

'This is for travel and this is for home,' said Terri, handing her two kits. 'Everything is here. So there's no excuse.' They all laughed.

'You look wonderful,' Terri decreed, surveying her subject. 'But it's two o'clock. Sunny just called. They're waiting for you in the fitting room on three.'

'Perfect!' exclaimed Sunny as Catherine walked into a fitting room almost as large as her apartment. 'Oh, Miss McBride, you look fabulous! Absolutely radiant!'

Catherine settled into one of the two flowered couches

and stared at the racks of preselected clothes. She shivered suddenly, reminded of the McBride Vanity Cleaners and the years spent watching other people's fancy dresses go by on the conveyor.

Finally, she was going to have a dress like that. She'd never had any occasion to own a full-length ballgown, much less the money to buy one. Yet suddenly, here were three racks to choose from. Wouldn't Effie get a kick out of helping her pick out one of these!

'You're going to the big oil and gas dinner honoring the chairman of Intercon,' announced Sunny. Clearly, Carla had briefed her.

Catherine rustled through the racks. She frowned. 'These are too fussy, I think.' She'd never get her money's worth out of dresses like these – even if she could write part of it off as a business expense.

Sunny pulled out a long black lace gown, caught at the waist with a big black satin bow and tiered with *point d'esprit* on the stiff laced skirt. 'It's going to be a very formal party. Everybody's dressing to the nines and pulling out the jewels.'

'Jewels.' Catherine looked at the charm bracelet with the Grunewald crest, which was her only jewelry.

Sunny stepped in front of her, holding the black creation just beneath Catherine's chin.

'Let's slip this on and see how we look.'

Catherine let Sunny drop the rustling lace over her head. Her face fell as she looked into the mirror. She looked as if she were wearing someone else's dress. The neck gaped, the shoulders drooped and the waist sagged to her hips.

'Good Lord!' Sunny exclaimed. 'I thought you said you wore a size ten! Isn't that the size you gave Carla Masterson?' She shook her head. 'No, you're a six.' Sunny pulled four inches out of the dress by gathering it in at the waist and shoulders.

Catherine examined her reflection curiously. She'd alway been a size ten! She had been pulling her belts in a few notches lately, and her skirts had seemed loose. She had worked so hard that lunches generally consisted of coffee and a salad at her desk, and she'd been too tired most nights to fix dinner. The pounds must have dropped off. But a size six?

'Why, your figure is yummy,' Sunny exclaimed. 'You don't need the funeral black.' She flung the dress over a chair.

'Red, purple, white, lilac . . .' Sunny flipped through the hangers. 'What color do *you* like, Catherine?'

Catherine sighed. She'd never be comfortable in any of these dresses. They reminded her of bridesmaid's outfits. 'Don't you have something simpler?' she asked.

'Texas men love bows and frills,' Sunny suggested.

Well, it wasn't a Texas man she was trying to please, Catherine thought. It was a Texas woman, the reluctant Widow Palmer, whom she had to impress. After all, this was a business dinner she was going to – not a coming-out party.

'My favorite color is blue,' she said. 'But do you have something tailored? Something that will pack well?' At least she'd be able to take the dress on business trips.

Sunny put her hands on her hips. 'Hmm. Blue. You do have the most remarkable blue-gray eyes. And, you know, there is a long shot. Very tailored.'

Catherine raised her eyebrows.

'. . . and drastically reduced. *And* it's a Valentino!' Sunny whirled around and darted out the door.

Two minutes later, she returned carrying the most elegant dress Catherine had ever seen.

'Here it is! A sample size six,' said Sunny. 'Valentino cuts small. Not everyone can wear a Valentino, you know.'

The long-waisted, slim bodice of shirred navy blue silk jersey had a very high, straight neck, almost a turtleneck. The long sleeves tapered from the broad, padded shoulders, greatly emphasizing her small waist, Catherine noticed as Sunny slipped the gown over her head. The severity of the tailored top made the flounce of the full taffeta skirt, which began just below the hipline, all the more surprising.

'That's wonderful,' gasped Catherine. She looked – pretty! She whirled before the three-way mirror and gasped again!

'Where's the back?' The dress was scooped out in a long rectangle baring most of her shoulder blades and her spine down to her waist.

Catherine stared at the mirror. 'I can't wear this.' But she couldn't hold back a smile. She felt feminine and elegant when the skirt rustled as she turned.

'Oh, Catherine,' Sunny exclaimed, noticing her expression. 'You couldn't have anything simpler. It doesn't have a frill or a button. My dear, what they're wearing at this ball! I've sold dresses cut twice as low in the front as yours is in the back. This is the eighties! And, after all, it's not a religious event.'

Catherine turned in front of the mirror again, looking over her shoulder at her back and her newly discovered wasp waist.

'Wait!' commanded Sunny, darting out of the room. She returned in an instant and handed Catherine a pair of three-inch long faux pavé diamond earrings, centered by a large blue stone. Catherine clipped them on as Sunny smiled. 'There we go!' she chortled. 'If you say fake in

French it's not nearly so bad.' She stepped back and examined her handiwork. 'You look beautiful. The business part is up to you.'

Catherine's image in the mirror was truly that of a lovely, self-confident young woman, capable of doing anything. And she had a gorgeous back.

She handed Sunny her American Express card, and the two women's eyes met. 'I like your Texas style, Sunny.'

# 5

Why couldn't he be on time, she thought.

Michael Picol was supposed to have met her in the lobby of the Mansion at Turtle Creek thirty minutes ago. Catherine prided herself on never being late. Graham and Eve Donaldson had already left with Drucilla and her handsome date.

Catherine checked her watch impatiently. Then she scanned the lobby, which seemed more like someone's gracious, private living room than a hotel. The combination of well-polished Old English furniture, a crackling fire, and antique tapestries accentuated by huge terra-cotta planters overflowing with bright flowers was relaxing. She peered down a long, arch-windowed promenade. Perhaps Michael was waiting there.

She started in the direction of the hallway, cinching the belt on her trenchcoat. She looked down. Her new dress was two feet longer than her coat. Maybe she should have bought an evening wrap. But the reduced Valentino had already cost almost a month's salary – not to mention the Calvin Klein cocktail dress and two St John suits she had bought from the persuasive Sunny. Enough was enough. The trenchcoat would have to do. Damn it, where *was* he?

'Miss McBride?' the blue-uniformed concierge whispered discreetly.

'Yes? I am.'

'There's a phone call for you at the desk.'

It was Michael Picol, calling from the hotel. 'Guess where I am?'

'In an accident,' she answered. 'There's no other excuse for being this late. Graham will be furious.'

'So we'll miss cocktails. I'm still in the workout room over here. I had a real high-pressure day.'

And where did that leave her?

'Why don't you hop a cab over to the Hyatt?'

Hop? She had no idea where she was, even.

'How do I get there?'

'You can't miss the Reunion Tower. Every driver knows it. See you in the lobby.' He hung up.

This was great, just great. She could imagine herself making a conspicuous entrance after all the honorees had been seated. She rushed through the glass-and-chrome doors, past half a dozen liveried men standing attentively by the hotel's pumpkin-colored façade, and got into a taxi.

The enormous Reunion Tower, a modern Dallas landmark, glittered on the horizon, rising above the entire cityscape as Catherine peered out the window of the cab. Walking into the lobby of the Hyatt Hotel, she had the same feeling of overscaled grandness. Everything seemed so large, so imposing. Women in furs and dazzling jewels swept by on the arms of tuxedoed men, and laughter filled the towers as hundreds of people pressed toward the banquet room.

Catherine looked around, but there was still no sign of Picol. Of course, it was easy to lose anyone in this crowd. But the tables were filling up now and she knew she should move quickly to secure a seat beside Mrs Palmer. She checked her trenchcoat and sighed, looking at her new Valentino. It was sort of like being all dressed up with no place to go. Well, *she* knew she looked good. She smoothed the taffeta sides of her skirt and straightened the charm of the baron's crest, which now hung on a costume gold necklace that Sunny had magically produced. She was ready, Michael Picol or no Michael Picol.

'McBride! Right? Is that you, McBride?' A strong arm caught her elbow. The slight blond man looked familiar. She was sure she'd seen him in the halls at Intercon.

'Hi, Catherine,' he said, shaking her hand. 'Billy Wright, Oil Engineering.' He looked at her approvingly and smiled. 'You look terrific!'

There was something especially warm in Billy Wright's smile, and Catherine liked him instantly.

'These are my people, he said with a chuckle, gesturing to the Texas crowd. 'I'm from Oklahoma.'

He had a way of putting Catherine at ease. She knew that once out of the office, some people made an entirely different impression. She noticed for the first time how handsome Billy Wright was, especially in his tuxedo. Then she noticed his feet. Mud-splattered cowboy boots!

'Are you taking offense at my boots, ma'am?' he drawled.

'No, I think they're wonderful!'

'Of course, they wouldn't go with your dress – and I must say, that's some dress. You ought to wear it around the office some time.'

'And you ought to wear your boots.' As they joked easily Catherine realized that the evening might actually turn out to be fun.

He offered Catherine his arm. 'May I have the pleasure of escorting you in? We company people ought to stick together. In fact I think they have a table for us by the kitchen.'

Unfortunately, only Billy Wright was assigned to the company table by the kitchen. Catherine's seating card assigned her to a table up front by the dais, where Mrs Palmer was seated on her left and Michael Picol's empty place on her right.

Catherine gave a chagrined shrug and waved good-bye to Billy. She did wish they could sit together, because he was young and seemed to have a marvelous sense of humour. She would have to get to know him better.

Since her arrival at Intercon, she had made no new friends. Instead, she spent all her spare time sequestered with Graham Donaldson or his special projects, often from seven in the morning until ten at night. Working so closely with Graham had alienated her from most of the other company people her age, who were in much lower-level positions and had their own cliques. She instinctively knew they were guarded around her, knowing that anything they said could be repeated directly to the chairman of the company. Even her seat at this choice table would be more fodder for resentment. She'd just have to find time to make some friends and some evening plans. After saying polite hellos and introducing herself to Mrs Palmer, Catherine waved at Billy Wright and he smiled at her from across the room. Yes, he was a good place to start.

Ever since her father's desertion, Catherine had lived in the company of older people, learning to please them, be they customers at the dry-cleaning store, teachers who awarded scholarships, or mentors on the job. Where other girls had idolized sexy pop singers and athletes, Catherine had dreamed of older, and, she was convinced, smarter men. She didn't need a psychiatrist to tell her she was searching for a father figure. But the fact remained that for the most part, she found older men – men like Graham Donaldson – more appealing.

As a young girl, Catherine had felt out of synch with her peers. At Harvard, the parties, clubs, and social activities all seemed to hold no relevance to her own race to finish first. The people in her classes were preoccupied with getting ready for the working world, while she had been part of it since she was fourteen. They didn't have her responsibilities, and Catherine had little in common with them.

She had no time for casual fun and romance. Her first few dates with the men in the graduate school had left her feeling as if she'd spent the evening babysitting. By the end of her first semester in Cambridge, she was almost never asked to join groups going out for pizza or to a concert. So she went to the library alone.

Until she met Brian Thundercloud, another misfit and yet a hero.

Part Cheyenne and part Navajo, he had come to Harvard Law School after fourteen years in the army. He had never been interested in fighting and war, but the military was his only route off the Navajo reservation in New Mexico. He had eventually gotten a desk job in internal affairs in Washington and earned his BA in political science and American history at Georgetown University. After seven years in Washington and three army promotions, Major Thundercloud had resigned his commission to accept a scholarship at Harvard Law School.

Catherine had first noticed him sitting across the table at the law library one January night. He stood out among the students, with his jet-black hair, dark skin, molded features, and hawklike nose. At thirty-two, Brian Thundercloud had more presence than most of the professors, and could hold an audience just as well. Consumed by great passion and a burning desire to change the grim realities of the Indian world, he had developed a reputation on campus as a man with a mission. Facing him,

Catherine was acutely aware of his almost-arrogant sensuality for three hours.

When the library closed, he had invited her for a cup of coffee, which stretched into a five-hour revelation of this enigmatic man and his dreams. At dawn, when he walked her home, it had seemed only natural that he followed her up the three flights of stairs and into her small room, where he held her face in his hands a long time before he slowly alternated between kissing her lips, her arms, and then her eyelashes. Finally he took Catherine McBride's virginity.

Catherine had been in love with a man who knew how to make love to a woman – not a college boy fumbling beneath the sheets. His fingers had felt like raindrops slipping down her back, his hair silky, as she, the girl who had barely dated, who had never trusted men, found herself entwined on the bed, reaching for his lips as they traced small circles of kisses on her breast. Then, languidly, he had flickered his tongue across her belly and she had felt no surprise, only a sense of how right it was, when he buried his head between her legs. She had arched her back and moaned as he touched her in places she had not known existed. She had been glad she waited for someone like Brian Thundercloud.

Their entire relationship had seemed ideal. He had taken her to visit the reservation in Window Rock, New Mexico, where he had grown up, and there had told her his dream of returning to represent his people in their legal battles. It had all seemed so idealistic. But two years passed quickly and Catherine found herself having to choose between his goals and hers.

When Catherine had more requests for job interviews than anyone in her class, she was forced to admit that there were no *Fortune* 500 companies near the Navajo reservation. The fact was, she had loans to pay back, a mother whom she desperately wanted to remove from a state institution, and very little interest in any Indian cause other than Brian Thundercloud.

She had tried to convince him to take his brilliant legal skills to the private sector. He could be so much more influential to his people from a power position, she had argued. But Brian's idealism could not be swayed.

Nor could she turn her back on everything she had worked for since age fourteen. She could never stop what she had started – even for the only man she had ever loved.

When she finally accepted the job at Swift Guaranty Bank, she knew it meant the end of their relationship, because Catherine McBride was always and completely a realist. Still, deep inside, a small spark of her had hoped he would come to her. Not a week passed during her first months at Swift that she didn't hope Brian would call, or visit, or move at New York, none of which ever happened.

Then one day, sitting at her desk, Catherine realized she was acting exactly as her mother had, waiting for a man who was gone to determine her fate. She immediately pulled Brian Thundercloud's picture from her wallet and filed it and him away, just as, years before, she had filed away the Christmas card from her father and the relationship it represented.

Yet her father and Brian Thundercloud had set the tone for what Catherine instinctively looked for in a man. As a woman who could not remember being young, the maturity of the two men in her life had left its mark. The Billy Wrights of the world might be interesting boys, but the Graham Donaldsons were the men who counted.

She turned her gaze to the dais. Catherine couldn't

imagine having hundreds of people honoring her, and once again she was awed by Graham Donaldson's achievements. Eve Donaldson, she noticed, sat alongside her husband in a simple cream satin sheath cut on the bias – custom-cut by Jackie Rogers, according to the all-knowing Monsieur Lupe. Her thick gray-blonde hair was gathered in an elegant French braid at the back of her swanlike neck, and she gazed adoringly at her husband. Graham Donaldson was a man Catherine could love. It figured he'd be so securely married.

Catherine sipped some wine and was about to start a conversation with Mrs Palmer when the lights dimmed. Agnes Palmer nodded politely, maintaining her ramrod straight posture, and the green eyes that matched her vintage Mainbocher gown squinted at Catherine in acknowledgement. Around her neck she wore a fist-sized cabochon emerald suspended from large diamond-studded links. Matching emeralds clips adorned ears that Catherine suspected didn't miss much. She noticed Mrs Palmer's glance flicker approvingly over her own new dress, and she knew simplicity had been the right choice. The widow was clearly not a woman who would be impressed by fluff. She'd have to stop using Michael Picol's epithet for the obviously discerning lady on her left. Where *was* Picol? Still working out at his hotel gym?

With a cymbal clash, Boy Scout Troup 337 of Dallas, Texas, marched into the grand ballroom of the Hyatt followed by the marching band of a local military academy, decked out in dress blues and gold braid. A very theatrical kleig light followed the Stars and Stripes, which led the way for country and western singer Willy Nelson's heartrending but somewhat spasmodic rendition of the national anthem. Everyone stood at attention, and Catherine noticed that Graham and all the other men, and even Mrs Palmer, covered their hearts with their hands. The large audience collectively sat after the benediction and, in the semi-darkness, Catherine groped for her chair while the honorees at the long table on the stage were introduced. The senior senator from Texas rose to introduce the governor, who then introduced Graham Donaldson, whom he heralded for his foresight, great nose for new drilling sites, and, specifically, for his success. Just as Graham stood to acknowledge thunderous applause, Michael Picol slipped into the empty seat beside Catherine, his sleeked-back hair still wet from the shower.

'Good timing, huh?' he whispered in the darkness, and she caught traces of a most unusual cologne or aftershave. It was a strange combination of something soft but masculine.

As the lights came up and waiters swarmed out with trays of trout mousse amandine, Michael Picol leaned forward on his elbows across Catherine, and addressed Agnes Palmer. 'This must be the best table in the house, Mrs Palmer,' he said warmly. 'If I'd known we'd be dining together I would have caught an earlier plane.'

Earlier plane! Catherine tried not to choke on her roll. Mrs Palmer simply nodded and pierced the molded fish with her fork.

Michael Picol seemed to notice Catherine for the first time. His hooded eyes narrowed at her, then he focused again on Mrs Palmer. 'I hope you'll save a dance for me when the speeches are done.' He smiled and winked in her direction.

'I don't dance, you know. The Colonel never liked it, either.'

Strike two.

Catherine wondered how she would ever make headway with Mrs Palmer, if someone as experienced and charming as Michael Picol got nowhere. Tomorrow's meeting threatened to be a disaster.

Suddenly one waiter crashed into another and sent a bottle of Mouton-Cadet, uncorked, into the lap of Mrs Palmer's Mainbocher gown.

'Hell,' the older woman drawled almost inaudibly. Even to Texas rich, mint Mainbocher was priceless.

Everyone at the table looked on in frozen horror as red wine splattered all over the irreplaceable dress. But Catherine knew exactly what to do. She leaped from her seat and commandeered a bottle of seltzer water from one of the ballroom's four bars and a white towel from the arm of a waiter.

'May I, Mrs Palmer?' Without waiting for a response, Catherine shook the seltzer bottle and spritzed the widow's gown.

'Don't worry, Mrs Palmer,' she said as she patted the incredulous woman's lap with the white towel. 'It's a beautiful dress, and I know just how to save it.'

The deep red stain slowly vanished, but a much larger wet spot remained. Looking to her left, Catherine noticed that Michael Picol seemed terrified. He rolled his eyes at her in disbelief, and she could almost hear him say, 'Shit! There goes the island.' The rest of the table glared at Catherine, aghast that the dowager of Dallas had been spritzed.

Catherine leaned over and whispered to Mrs Palmer. 'If you could come with me to the ladies' room, I think we can take care of this just in time. With red wine, you have to act very fast.'

Mrs Palmer drawled, 'This *is* a Mainbocher.'

'Mrs Palmer, I spent ten years in the dry-cleaning business.'

The older woman rose with the utmost dignity from her

seat and trailed after Catherine to the ladies' room.

There, Agnes Palmer was helped out of her gown and seated at the gold velvet vanity seat, dressed only in her slip and emeralds.

'Do you really know what you're doing, young woman?' she demanded, as Catherine waved the precious gown in front of the hand blower.

'Seltzer dissipates the stain, and I think we got it just in time. But you don't want to spend the rest of the evening in a wet dress. Such a beautiful color!'

'The Colonel loved emerald green.'

'He must have been a wonderful man. How did you meet?'

The old woman's eyes glowed as she told the story of which no woman ever tires. The dashing young World War I colonel had come out West to raise cattle and been seduced by the sixteen-year-old prairie girl with flashing green eyes.

'My father was totally opposed,' smiled Agnes Palmer. 'He thought the Colonel would never amount to anything.' She fingered her enormous emerald. 'But I could tell, I knew, if he cared for his land half as much as he cared for me, it was going to work out just fine. And it did for fifty-two years.'

'What a lovely thing that is,' Catherine sighed. 'To be with one man for fifty-two years. You're a very lucky woman.'

'But don't you have a young man, dear?'

'I'm afraid not. I don't have time yet. And I really don't know very many men. I've spent most of my life working. At Intercon, at Swift Bank, at Harvard, and before that, I spent ten years in the dry-cleaning business.'

Suddenly they had so much to talk about.

Twenty minutes later, Catherine McBride and Agnes

Palmer, resplendent in her now-spotless Mainbocher, emerged arm in arm from the ladies' room. All eyes focused on the social queen of Dallas and the unknown young beauty in the backless dress.

Every man at their table rose, and Catherine sprang to pull out Mrs Palmer's chair. 'Thank you, Cathy,' she said, patting Catherine's hand. 'But the next time, let one of *them* do it.' She indicated the men with arched eyebrows.

When the desserts had been served and the orchestra had begun to play South American music, the serious table-hopping began. A crowd converged around the table as all the dignitaries paid their respects to the head of the billion-dollar Palmer Foundation, which funded most of the Texas charities and arts centers. Just as the governor approached, Mrs Palmer turned again to Catherine.

'Don't forget – luncheon at Palmer Point tomorrow. I'll send my car for you at eleven.'

'Thank you, Mrs Palmer.'

'Call me Miss Aggie. All my friends do. And anybody who spends half an hour with me in my slip had better be my friend!'

Michael Picol stood and bid the widow good night.

'Are you standing to see me out, or to ask this young woman to dance?'

'Both, I suppose.'

The band struck up a rhumba as Picol guided Catherine toward the dance floor. As couples began moving to the complicated rhythm Catherine realized that she had no idea how to handle this dance. This was going to be embarrassing.

'I'm not too sure about this,' she warned him.

'Relax. You'll be great if you can move half as good as you look tonight.'

She felt his strong hand firmly positioned on her bare back, guiding her into the intricate steps. His face bent down toward hers, and she felt his breath close to her ear.

'Just what went on in that ladies' room, anyway?'

She decided to let him wonder. 'Anything that happens in the ladies' room is just between us girls.'

The ballroom lights glittered like sequins in the high ceiling as she felt herself propelled into a spin, then caught with a snap. He pulled her even closer.

'Every man here is looking at you, you know.'

She laughed, breathless. 'They're trying to see if I fall on my face.'

'I doubt it.' He was staring at her now, and she found herself staring back. His eyes were like magnets. Somehow she forgot that she'd been angry with him, that he'd left her stranded, that he was a man she had to work with. Instinctively, she arched her back to draw away from him, but his hand covered her entire waist, and she felt his thumb slide inside the fabric of her dress, pressing on her spine.

When the music stopped, Michael Picol did not loosen his grip. His gaze was languid and she was suddenly aware of his thighs against hers.

'I used to be a pretty good dancer,' he murmured.

Catherine could not answer. Her face felt hot, and she somehow had trouble catching her breath.

'Look who's here, Daddy!' pierced a giddy voice. It was Drucilla Donaldson, Graham's daughter, who flounced in an antebellum ballgown of ribbons and satin by Scaasi. 'Michael Picol. Let's switch,' she announced, and with a whirl of mauve satin, she twirled her new partner away, both arms encircling his neck.

Graham Donaldson found himself standing beside

Catherine McBride. 'How was dinner with Mrs Palmer? Did you get a meeting set up?'

'Better. We're spending the afternoon together at Palmer Point.'

'The Palmer estate? Nobody gets invited there.' Graham was impressed. Ray Acconti had been wrong. It *was* a smart move to include Catherine on this trip.

'I thought Mrs Palmer was a very nice lady,' she said. 'We got along fine.'

Graham took a sip from his brandy glass and took a close look at her. Yes, she was very bright. The human side was important in closing a deal. Maybe that had been Michael Picol's problem with Agnes Palmer. He seemed to view her as a military objective, and the woman sensed it.

Catherine accepted a glass of wine from the waiter and toasted him with her wine glass. 'I'm really impressed that all these people turned out to honor you tonight. It's a great salute for one man, though working together these past months, I happen to know you deserve it.'

Graham straightened. He always recognized transparent flattery. Tonight, people he barely knew had hugged and bussed him. But Catherine McBride meant what she said. She was with him when the rubber met the road; she saw him in action and could therefore appreciate him. And, he noticed for the first time, she had great tits, too. He checked out her dress and realized she couldn't be wearing anything under it with that backless top. Hell, he couldn't ask her to dance. Where would he put his hand!

He took her elbow and led her off the floor. 'Shall we sit this one out?' They walked into the ten-story atrium, tiered with marble and ivy.

'Tomorrow I do my real business,' Graham said. 'The Bruces have invited Eve and me and Ahmad Fashdaggi for a roundup and a barbecue.' B. B. Bruce had worn his silver-and-turquoise belt buckle with his tuxedo tonight and worn out his wife, a silver-haired, heavily lined woman with his rodeo antics on the dance floor. As soon as the music began, B. B. Bruce had started to stomp as if he were in a cattle stampede.

Catherine knew that the Bruces had just sold half of their oil leases to Intercon for three hundred million dollars, and Fashdaggi held some of the most oil-rich land in the Middle East.

'I can't wait to see Fashdaggi on a roundup,' Graham chuckled. 'He probably thinks you use polo ponies.'

'You know how to handle Fashdaggi.'

Graham finished off his brandy. 'Meet me tomorrow after your appointment. I want to know how things went.'

'Sure. Don't worry about it.'

'There you are!' boomed Drucilla across the lobby. She clattered across the atrium to her father.

'You know Catherine McBride from Intercon,' he said. And to Catherine, 'You know Drucilla.'

'Of course, Daddy. We flew down together.' Drucilla looked over the top of Catherine's head and scanned the crowd for eligible dancing partners.

Catherine guessed that Drucilla was about twenty-two years old and had an affinity for latching onto the closest man in sight. Drucilla reminded her of the girls she'd known at Harvard who had come in from Foxcroft or Madeira and had dropped out in their second year for debuts or marriages. Except Drucilla Donaldson had been more decisive. She apparently had dropped out immediately after boarding school.

'We're going to Billy-Bob's for some country music,' Drucilla said. 'What are you up to?'

Catherine checked her watch, which was tucked under

the shirred sleeve of the Valentino. The perpetual postdeb crowd was the last group she cared to join tonight. 'It's almost midnight, and I have an early appointment.' She looked around for Michael Picol, who had promised to share a cab.

'Well, I'd better run,' Drucilla said hurriedly. 'Picol and Tandy are waiting outside in the Rolls.'

So much for Michael Picol, thought Catherine. It was too late to get a ride with someone else. Even Billy Wright had disappeared into the crowd. She'd never find him now.

At the stroke of midnight, Catherine McBride found herself and her new gown on a frayed taxi seat with unruly springs, heading back to the pumpkin-colored Mansion Hotel at Turtle Creek, and she smiled wryly to herself, thinking, *So much for Cinderella*.

# 6

The bedside phone rang with a startling shrillness that awakened Catherine from an exhausted sleep. After the long flight, the weeks of fourteen-hour days, and spending all night catering to Aggie Palmer, Catherine had fallen into the blue-and-white gingham-canopied bed still wearing her makeup.

She felt confused and disorientated by the insistent phone. Where was she? At first, in the darkness, she couldn't remember. Had she overslept? Then, suddenly she was completely awake. My God, it must be the hospital! Something had happened to her mother. She groped for the phone, trying to focus in the blacked-out room.

'Yes!' she almost shouted into the phone, expecting to hear Dr Gresham's voice. Ever since last May, Elaine McBride had been almost totally catatonic; only Catherine's voice seemed to break through the heavy curtain of her illness. Because Dr Gresham had warned Catherine that a crisis could occur at any moment, she always left her phone number with her secretary at the office and the switchboard at Wickes Manor.

'I'm here,' said Catherine, her heart pounding.

'It's Picol. What room are you in?'

Picol! Catherine focused on the illuminated digital bedside clock.

'It's four-sixteen!'

'Room four-sixteen?'

'No! It's four-sixteen in the morning. What are you doing? What's the matter?'

'This is important. I have to come up.'

'I'm in room eight-o-six and it's four-sixteen in the morning and I'm sleeping.'

'I'll be right there.'

'I'm not dressed.'

'Good. I'll be right up.'

She heard the phone click before she could stop him. She pulled herself out of bed, turned on the light, and shuffled into the bathroom. She barely had time to slip a robe over her T-shirt and run her fingers through her hair when she heard heavy knocking on the door.

What was the emergency? At least nothing had happened to her mother. Maybe something had happened to Graham Donaldson. Nothing good ever happened in the middle of the night.

Catherine unbolted the door and looked up to see Michael Picol still in his tuxedo, his bow tie stuffed into his breast pocket and his dress shirt unbuttoned, the satin lapel of his coat pulled over something she couldn't quite make out.

She rubbed her eyes with both fists. 'What are you doing here? Are you crazy?'

Michael Picol leaned against the door frame and grinned. 'Hey, you look cute when you wake up. Do you mind if we come in?

Catherine blinked hard, but she didn't see anyone else in the hall. Good God, who else was on the way up – the entire board of directors?

'Well, can we come in or not?!'

She stood aside. 'Right. Why not? Why don't you *all* come in?' She pursed her lips.

Catherine collapsed onto the edge of the bed and hung

onto one of the four bedposts. 'I'm very sleepy, Picol. This better be good.'

He leaned against the dresser. 'We just got back from Billy-Bob's. It was fun. You should have come.'

'So?' She was in no mood for small talk.

'I'm on my way to the airport. I'm going straight to Love Field. They're sending my luggage. I'm taking the plane down to Caracas. Two of our refineries down there were bombed.'

'That's horrible.'

'The Bandera Roja again. Things are getting hot. The government may have to step in.'

'What can I do?' Catherine was instantly awake.

'You can meet with Welles.'

Who was Welles?

'You know, Arnie Welles. The top independent oil geologist in the country. He used to work for Colonel Palmer. I figure he might have something in that Palmer land purchase that you could use.'

'Was this Graham's idea?' Catherine asked, reaching for a pencil and paper.

'I was going to tell him, but it's no big deal. This guy worked for Palmer for sixteen years, and he really knew what made him tick. You could use some insight about the Palmers when you talk to the widow.'

'Like what?'

'Keep it personal. I was supposed to meet with him myself but I can't now. We need to know what it takes to make Agnes Palmer sell. And we know it isn't money.'

'Where does Welles fit in?' Catherine knew Intercon had a huge staff of its own geologists. It didn't make sense.

Picol shrugged. 'A company has big ears. We need to

keep this quiet until the board is behind Graham on the project.'

Suddenly, a blur of black fur hurtled from inside Michael Picol's jacket to the heavy quilted gingham bedspread.

Catherine gasped.

A tiny, long-haired black kitten with bright yellow eyes tumbled over to Catherine and licked her hand with its rough little tongue. When she jumped up, her robe opened.

'I hate cats! What are you doing with a kitten jumping out of your pocket?'

His smile widened. 'I won it at Billy-Bob's. He's a pedigreed Persian. I can't take him to Venezuela.'

'What am I going to do with him?'

Picol picked up the kitten, which was scratching at the tie on Catherine's robe, and thrust it to her breast, which was now showing quite obviously through her skimpy, sleeveless T-shirt. 'He can keep you warm at night.' Picol's eyes traveled slowly down her body, not missing her white bikini panties.

Catherine pushed the kitten away and double-knotted the sash on the robe.

Picol sauntered to the phone. 'I'm calling room service.'

'Why not?' She shrugged expansively, walked into the bathroom, and splashed cold water on her face. Who the hell did he think he was? Well, the geologist business was probably more important than it seemed, and although Picol's method might be a little unorthodox, she realized she was now part of the inner sanctum. She would be privy to the off-the-record dealings, not just what was reported on the books. The cat was another matter.

'Do you want something too, Catherine?' called Picol through the door.

'Yes. To go back to sleep.' She opened the door and the little kitten bounced over to sniff her heels.

'It's nocturnal,' said Picol. 'Like you and me.'

'Speak for yourself,' interrupted Catherine.

'He likes you. Let's call him Midnight.'

Just then, there was a knock at the door.

'I suppose this is the geologist,' said Catherine.

'No, it's room service. Get with it. Open the door.'

She opened the door and a slightly disheveled waiter delivered a wicker tray loaded with silver plates and one flower in a bud vase.

'It was too early for the morning papers,' the waiter apologized. 'But I think I've got the whole order: two orders of smoked Scotch salmon, two orders of cream, one cheeseburger rare, and a V-8 juice on the double.' He looked as if he had run all the way.

Catherine stared over the tray at Picol as she scribbled her initials. What was it about this man that made people do his bidding so readily?

'You can put in for it,' said Picol as he carried the tray to a table by the windows. 'Come on Midnight, let's eat.' He plunked the kitten on the table. Then he cut the paper-thin smoked salmon into tiny bite-sized pieces and poured the cream into the saucer.

'Want some cheeseburger?' he asked Catherine. 'You haven't had breakfast yet.'

Catherine stifled a yawn, but sat in the chair he pulled out for her.

'I'm leaving you this folder with all the information on Welles: where to go, when, even the questions to ask. It'll be easy. He's expecting you at eight. That gives you plenty of time before your meeting with the architect and lunch at Palmer Point.'

Midnight gobbled up a few scraps of the twenty-seven-dollar-a-serving salmon, avoiding the capers and lemon, and lapped a few licks of cream, then jumped into Catherine's lap, where he promptly fell asleep, purring. She stroked the space between his two ears and then laid him gently down on the canopied bed. At least one of them would get some sleep.

Michael Picol put down his half-eaten cheeseburger and stretched. 'I'm really beat. I could use a few minutes sleep myself.'

Catherine carefully avoided the hint. One strange animal in her bed was enough. She looked aside at Picol. The front of his pleated dress shirt was now completely open, exposing his broad chest. His hair was somehow perfectly in place.

His pewter-colored eyes blinked slowly, showing faint, drawn shadows of fatigue and he leaned over so close to Catherine that she could smell the heavy, oddly sweet musky scent of his cologne. For a minute, he was quiet, a flicker of warmth crossing his usually impassive face. He was a very handsome man with his high cheekbones, broad forehead, and smooth, tan skin. They stared at each other in the half-light.

'I'm sorry I wrecked your night.' His face seemed so eager for her approval. 'I hope I wasn't too much of an imposition.'

'Oh, no,' she found herself saying. 'I'd be getting up soon anyway.'

Catherine felt her anger melt away, as it somehow always did with Michael Picol. He was the kind of man who evoked apologies from others for anything he did. She wondered why he'd never married. He seemed to have everything – mysteriously handsome looks, an exciting life, intelligence, and a genuinely soft side masked by an unyielding exterior. 'Is it all right if I leave the cat with you? I'll be home in a week.' His voice was gentle.

Only a really caring man would worry about a cat at a time like this, Catherine thought. She glanced over at Midnight.

'We'll get along.'

Catherine felt Michael Picol's breath on her cheeks from across the small table. The room was now very quiet. He handed her the apricot-colored rose from the tray.

'Wanna take a nap?' His smile was an invitation.

Catherine caught her breath.

But Picol stood up all of a sudden, slapping both hands on his thighs.

'Well, gotta get to the airport and deal with this mess. I'll catch some sleep on the plane if I'm lucky.'

He walked to the door. 'You and Midnight can handle Welles and Palmer.'

Catherine said, 'See you later. I hope everything works out down there. Are you sure it's safe to go?' A worried look crossed her face as she recalled the recent terrorism.

'I'm hard to kill,' he laughed.

He turned to go when suddenly he spun around and pulled her toward him in one gesture. Tired and totally off guard, Catherine didn't resist. When he kissed her, he placed his mouth so heavily and swiftly on hers that he took her breath away. Her heart beat faster when he deftly untied the double knot of her terrycloth robe and reached inside to grasp her firmly around the waist, pulling her closer, his fingers gently massaging the soft flesh at her bikini line. He moved his hand to her buttocks and slipped it inside her panties. Catherine felt his hardness as he pressed her body against his. Her senses reeled and, almost unwillingly, her mouth began to respond to his. He ran his tongue across her teeth and she leaned into him, all better judgement obliterated. Her small hands, clenched in fists, relaxed and she reached for him just as he drew a deep breath and released her.

He twisted a few strands of her hair between his fingers.

'Take good care of this woman, Midnight,' he called over her shoulder. Then he whispered to her. 'I gotta go. See you later.' And he disappeared into the shadows of the hall.

Catherine tugged off the robe and threw it across the room.

Damn! What was wrong with her? Had she gone crazy, or was she just losing it? She had always promised herself that she would never get involved with someone she worked with. It could only lead to her downfall. Michael Picol had a reputation as a ladies' man with a hit list the size of the New York telephone directory. She wasn't about to become another entry. She had shut men out of her life for a reason, and her goals could not be jeopardized.

Catherine ran her fingers across her lips and smelled the still-pungent scent of Michael Picol.

Well, she could always explain her behavior as a response to fatigue. She'd make sure it wouldn't happen again.

Catherine picked up the kitten and stroked it. A nagging thought told her she was blocking out an entire part of her life. Emotional comforts that other women took for granted – like holding hands on Saturdays with a lover and buying croissants together on Sunday mornings – were unknown to Catherine.

For a fleeting moment taking a nap with Michael Picol had sounded very nice. But the impulse was quickly squelched; she'd be sure it didn't happen twice.

Standing in only her T-shirt and panties Catherine

shivered. Outside, the sky was a pearlescent early-morning orange and birds were beginning to stir.

Six A.M. The night nurse at Wickes Manor would just be going off duty. She dialed the familiar number to find out how her mother had passed the night. The tiny cat curled in the crook of her arm and purred.

'Hello, Midnight.'

# 7

'Mentors? Isn't that what they call them now?' Mrs Agnes Palmer asked rhetorically. 'In my day, they called them husbands. Colonel Jack was my mentor, you might say.' The old lady's emerald eyes twinkled. 'He taught me a lot about balance sheets, oil fields, and reading somebody straight out to learn whether you can trust 'em in fifteen minutes.' She pierced Catherine with a level gaze and announced, 'I think we understand each other.'

During the luncheon of scrambled eggs stuffed with native Texas truffles served on a vol-au-vent puff pastry and homemade pecan muffins with pots of gooseberry jam, Catherine had found herself talking to her hostess as she would to a friend. They discussed everything from last night's dinner to Mrs Palmer's blackberry jam recipe. Mrs Palmer's crepey neck was ringed with strong lines from her days in the Texas sun, giving her an aura of strength. The simple farm girl who had married Colonel Palmer had missed little in her life, and Catherine recognized in Agnes Palmer a kindred spirit.

They moved to the tea table set with a Royal Doulton cream-ware tea service in the parlor. Catherine had never seen such an ornately decorated room. Even the windows had two sets of draperies, one tapestry and one lace. It seemed to Catherine that flowers and creeping plants meandered over every surface, from the hand-hooked rug to the heavy plasterwork cornices.

Mrs Palmer readied herself as if settling in for an afternoon at the symphony and gestured for Catherine to begin. Catherine felt suddenly very self-conscious, as if she were violating a friendship. This was a woman with whom she longed to share secrets, not make business pitches to.

Unzipping the heavy black presentation case, Catherine pulled out her maps, blueprints, and floor plans. She was determined that this meeting would go well, since the breakfast meeting with Arnie Welles had been a disappointment. Catherine had followed Picol's agenda of questions to the letter but had only met with patronizing smiles and nonanswers. He had called her Hon twice, an insult Catherine would normally not tolerate. He had chain-smoked his way through a conversation which, for his part, consisted of mainly monosyllables. 'Yep' and 'nope' had been his most definitive responses. Catherine believed that she had blown an important opportunity. It had been obvious that Arnie Welles, with his leathery, weathered face, was not prepared to deal with anyone less than Graham Donaldson or Picol. Or at least she hoped that was so. Otherwise, she'd have to face up to the fact that she couldn't deliver the goods. She'd left Welles her card, but the meeting had ended on such a final note, she was sure she wouldn't hear from him.

Catherine patiently discussed with Mrs Palmer the plans she and Terry Skittle, the architect, had agreed upon, painting an irresistible picture of the island complex. One side of the main island was the ideal resort location, where people could swim, sail, and snorkel in protected waters. The natural white sand beach could be enlarged, and there was enough flat land for a polo field, golf course, and tennis courts. Terry Skittle had also sketched a hundred-slip marina and yacht club. On the other side of the low mountain a research facility would face the ocean and the complex would be linked by a network of roads. The second island in the grouping hinged on the transfer of certain government leases. It would house the fish farming and solar water purification facilities. Graham Donaldson's connections with the secretary of the interior were the key to acquiring that property. The third island, which was long and pear-shaped, was Mrs Palmer's. It was the only island long enough for a jetway, but Catherine did not discuss this with Mrs Palmer.

She did offer a magnificent twenty-room villa that would be part of the Intercon package to tempt Mrs Palmer. A dozen high-security, luxury villas on the main island were included in Skittle's plans, in addition to a lavish condominium and resort hotel complex. Catherine had approved the architecture of native stone, natural wood, and pale yellow tile. Mrs Palmer couldn't possibly resist this, thought Catherine as she finished her presentation and rolled up the blueprints and maps.

For three quarters of an hour, Mrs Palmer had listened politely. Then the old English grandfather clock in the hall chimed, and she slowly rose from her peach-embroidered rococo chair.

'It's time for my afternoon buggy ride,' she drawled, checking her hair in a gilt mirror. 'You'll come along, won't you? I'm hoping you will. I hate to ride alone.'

Catherine couldn't imagine what she meant. Buggy ride? She was in the middle of a presentation. Then she noticed the look on Mrs Palmer's face, the manner which left no room for questions.

'Well,' she started to say, feeling a little desperate.

Mrs Palmer interrupted her. 'You've been a good girl. You've met with old Welles, and Terry Skittle, *and* you've made your presentation to the Widow Palmer.'

Catherine was visibly taken back. What didn't this

woman know? She probably even knew about Midnight. She felt herself blushing.

'Oh come on, Cathy,' beamed Agnes Palmer, throwing her shawl over her shoulders. 'You can't be as rich as I am and be dopey!' Catherine laughed in spite of herself, and found herself being hustled along by the dowager, a force she wasn't quite sure how to manage.

'Mrs Palmer, if I knew you better, I could learn a lot from you,' said Catherine, and she meant it. 'You're a pretty special lady, and I'm very honored that you've spent all this time with me.' Business was obviously over, Catherine surmised. Even Graham Donaldson had underestimated Agnes Palmer.

Mrs Palmer led the way as they passed through the elegant central hallway hung with heavy brass chandeliers. She grabbed a handful of chestnuts from a Chinese porcelain bowl and stuffed them into her skirt pocket. Catherine followed her out the garden door to the waiting open carriage, the likes of which she had not seen since watching *Gone With the Wind.*

'Now let's get to the good stuff,' chortled Mrs Palmer as she climbed without assistance into the driver's seat. 'Why aren't you married yet?' She pulled on her gloves while Catherine unsteadily braced herself for the ride. Then Agnes Palmer gathered the reins of the two-horse team and, with a slight flick of her wrist, the pair of hackney bays took off at an even trot, then circled the gravel drive, past the beautifully manicured lawns and down the allée of oaks and pecan trees.

'I thought about it once,' Catherine started to confide. 'But I would have had to give up everything I've worked for, and it's just too important to me. Things have changed, Mrs Palmer,' Catherine added. 'There's more to it than just being married or not. There's just a lot of things I need to do for myself.'

Agnes Palmer snorted. 'Hogwash. You can have all the independence in the world and still be in love with a man. What kind of man was your father?'

Catherine cringed. This was the question she always hated most to answer. She decided to make light of it, and laughed nervously. 'Undependable.'

Mrs Palmer arched an eyebrow.

'He left my mother for a twenty-year-old rent-a-car lady when I was a little girl,' Catherine continued.

'There were plenty of honeysuckle blondes around my Colonel. Didn't your mother fight for him?'

'No, my mother wasn't the fighting kind,' said Catherine. And then she was quiet, realizing for the first time that perhaps the separation might have been caused as much by her mother's withdrawal as by her father's infidelity.

Mrs Palmer pulled back slightly on the reins as they drove down a low hill dusted with bluebells. 'Hell,' she said. 'You can't be complacent and keep a man interested. They'd all be polygamists if possible.'

Catherine had to laugh. Mrs Palmer was only old on the surface. Catherine felt she could talk as easily to Aggie Palmer as to any peer.

The Texas dowager continued, but now her expression changed. 'Right after our son Thomas's tenth birthday, my beloved Jack took up with this film star.' She said the words *film star* as if she were smelling castor oil. 'I'm sure you've seen her pictures. Anyway, she set her sights for my husband.' Catherine could see a glimmer of pain still present in Mrs Palmer's eyes.

'Suddenly, the Colonel became a film producer. It was

the only thing he ever lost money on in his life. *She*, of course, made quite a fortune.'

Catherine was incredulous at Agnes Palmer's honesty. This woman didn't pull any punches, but she could empathize immediately. 'You mean he left you?'

'Let's just say he was away a lot on business. We had a life together and I wasn't about to let some A-C-T-R-E-S-S destroy it. I put up the fight of my life. Lost thirty pounds, washed every bit of gray out of my hair, and let Mainbocher and Charlie James dress me from breakfast to bed. Bought every maribou feather in Texas.'

Now her eyes were twinkling. 'Then I did the important stuff. I took an accounting course and went over the books. And when I showed Colonel Jack the outrageous amount of funds going out, and nothing coming in from films he was busy producing for this has-been movie star, we decided the movie business was not for him.'

Both women dissolved into laughter.

'You're amazing,' said Catherine. 'My mother could never have done that.'

'Maybe not,' replied Mrs Palmer. 'But you would. You're a survivor, like me.'

It was easy for Mrs Palmer to talk, thought Catherine. She'd never had to face life alone in a fourth-floor walk-up. 'Well, Mrs Palmer . . .'

'Miss Aggie.'

'Miss Aggie. You've had a lot of advantages.' Catherine wondered how her life would have been if her mother had been as strong as Aggie Palmer. She wondered what her son was like. Did he have his mother's strong character? She looked at the woman sitting beside her and felt real affection for her.

'Advantages don't mean a thing when you lose your son.'

'I'm sorry,' Catherine whispered. She touched the old woman's shoulder. 'I didn't know.'

'All this was supposed to be for him. The business, the land, Palmer Point, even all the antiques the Colonel and I collected over the years. All for him. But he was killed in the Pacific.' Her voice went flat. Her eyes took on a faraway look.

'As a boy he had been artistic and creative. So we brought whole rooms over from European estates to make Palmer Point a showplace for him. The nursery had been built for Crown Prince Rudolph of Austria, don't you know. Young Thomas was our prince, and nothing was too good for him. The floorboards, the fireplace, the moldings – everything was imported piece by piece. It was the only Austrian Rococo nursery in all Texas. 'Course, don't you know once we had one, the neighbors had to have one too.'

Catherine chuckled, remembering that the nearest neighbor was fifteen miles away.

Mrs Palmer continued. 'The Maple Room. That's my favorite. The harp belonged to my mother, but all the Greek Revival furniture came from a Philadelphia estate. Even the paintings were collected for Thomas. He loved the Old West. Some of those buffalo paintings by Bierstadt have become kinda valuable. And the Colonel loved George Washington so we bought two Gilbert Stuart portraits of the first President and a whole slew of his silver. I had to outbid the White House for all those things.' Mrs Palmer shook her head. 'It was all supposed to go to my son. But I don't have anybody now. I suppose it'll all go to the Palmer Foundation. That's my child now.'

'You're leaving Palmer Point to your Foundation? What are your plans?'

'They'll use it as headquarters.'

Catherine felt stung by the thought. She pictured unappreciative office workers burning Mrs Palmer's burled desks with cigarettes and ringing her tabletops with coffee cups. She knew what went on in offices, an administrative environment would never mix with a museum-quality atmosphere. She remembered the old Mahoney estate in Pittsburgh, which was now an art school. It had practically crumbled behind its iron gates, the parquet floors were spattered with old chewing gum, and the Mahoney family portraits yellowed by smoke.

That's it! Catherine thought. 'No, Mrs Palmer. A foundation is just people playing with dollars and cents. It's not caring about things.'

Agnes Palmer looked startled. Nobody gave her advice unless she asked for it. But Catherine persisted.

'You can't have a bunch of unappreciative people running around ruining your furniture! You've created a memorial for your husband and son. It deserves to be . . .' She searched for the right word. 'Celebrated. Palmer Point should be a museum in its own right.'

'But Palmer Point was built as a home,' protested Mrs Palmer.

'That's right,' agreed Catherine. Her mind was really working now. When she got excited about an idea she couldn't hold back! 'If you donated Palmer Point to, say, the Dallas Art Museum, you could provide funds for its maintenance directly from the Foundation. You could specify that a curator must run it exactly like a home so visitors could see what life is like at Palmer Point.'

Mrs Palmer leaned closer. She was obviously considering Catherine's idea, but something was not quite right.

'Actually, a museum is too pretentious. It's not you. Palmer Point should be part of the National Trust for

Historic Preservation which preserves homes exactly as they are. Imagine it!'

'Yes,' enthused Miss Aggie. 'Palmer Point is a piece of American heritage, after all. Four presidents slept here in Sam Houston's mahogany poster bed. Lyndon Johnson practically ran his first senate campaign from the Victorian Parlor. The Colonel and I put together some of the best pieces of Early American furniture and paintings anywhere. Why, there isn't a museum around fit to house our collection of Americana.'

Catherine's face flushed with pleasure. The carriage was pulling under the umbrella of trees lining the front drive again.

'Why don't you draw up the proposal and send it on to my board?' said Mrs Palmer as she reined the horses in.

'And, by the way, I'm still not going to sell my island.'

Catherine nodded. 'I knew that after my presentation. I hope you didn't think I spent the afternoon here just for that.'

Miss Aggie shook her head. 'No, I know that, dear.' She turned to face Catherine. 'I've decided to give your company a fifty-year lease on my island – in return for Intercon voting stock. And I'll take that pretty house you're planning, too. As the Colonel said, you gotta live a little.'

Catherine had succeeded after all. 'Mrs Palmer, you won't regret this.' She tried to appear calm. Her future at Intercon was suddenly assured, she thought. She'd finally justified Graham's trust in her. And Michael Picol had given her more than Midnight today.

'Of course, I want you to handle all this personally,' said Mrs Palmer as she tossed the reins to a groom. 'Don't send old Casanova out here again. I'm too old for that.'

The two women sashayed on to the wicker-filled veranda. 'Now wasn't that a lovely buggy ride?' drawled Agnes Palmer, as if the abandoned child from Pittsburgh and the emerald-eyed millionairess had spent the afternoon eating bonbons, rather than closing a six-figure deal.

# 8

Eve Donaldson checked the canvas of her latest needlepoint project. Like dozens of other pillows she had designed over the years, it was an orchid. Like her music, she found needlepoint something in which she could lose herself. She loved the look and feel of the colored yarns heaped in her bedside basket and the slightly nubby texture of the bare canvas.

Right now, Eve didn't want to think about anything, especially yesterday's appointment with Dr Corbett. Since Dallas, she had felt totally exhausted and hadn't been able to regain her normal energy. She'd asked Dr Corbett for a vitamin B-12 shot, but he had insisted on examining her. When he told her he suspected a tumor in her uterus, she'd been too stunned to speak. He had assured her that it probably wasn't cancerous, but he immediately called a specialist. Eve had promised to follow up right away and make an appointment, but the phone number was still in the zipper compartment of her purse. She couldn't bring herself to dial it. It somehow seemed better not to know anything than to face the truth.

Menopause. Cancer. Surgery. The hideous words were brutal intrusions into the glazed surface of her life.

What if she did have cancer? Eve felt her chest tighten as she let a handful of seafoam-green yarn fall into her needlework basket. It couldn't be cancer. People in her family died of heart attacks, not of anything as lingering and ugly as cancer. She'd sooner take a discreet overdose than have Graham and Drucilla watch her waste away.

She knew Graham wouldn't be able to function without her. But she'd have to tell him. They'd always been honest with each other. Drucilla didn't have to know anything just yet, and, if the worst was to be – well, she knew Graham would take care of her.

But what about Bambi and Hughie? She'd carefully raised them to feel part of her family. She'd convinced Graham to leave Hughie the coach house, so he and his sister would always have a home even though Graham needed to muster every cent to pay off debts of the Stuart estate. And she'd kept Bambi's trust totally intact – even out of Graham's reach – so Bambi would be taken care of. Even Hughie didn't know about the trust. Eve had started it with a few shares of Intercon stock. It was her secret gift to Bambi, and if something did happen to her, she wondered who would oversee the responsibilities she'd carried for Bambi and Hughie.

Eve jabbed the canvas with a needle. She'd face medical problems later. Right now, she'd catch up with Hughie. She hadn't even spoken with him since she'd gotten home from Dallas.

Eve switched the phone on to the speaker system to free her hands. She moved to her dressing table and raised her arms, gathering her loose, silver-blonde hair as she launched into her daily beauty routine. 'I was just feeling a little down,' she said when she reached Hughie at Valeski's studio. 'How's Bambi? And how are *you*?'

Hughie was alert. 'Do I detect that the Magnificent Aunt Eve had less than a good time in Dallas?'

Eve laughed as she slowly began to plait her hair into a French braid. 'Dallas was fabulous. Even Fashdaggi was impressed. We visited with him and his new little girlfriend for one of those barbecues.'

'Ugh,' snorted Hughie. 'Burned cow on a spit and

enchiladas. No wonder you're under the weather. And how were all the Texas belles? Any up-and-coming stars I should scout as a Valeski model?'

'It's curious,' said Eve. 'The most captivating of all turned out to be that new young woman who works for Graham – the McBride girl.'

'The plain, dumpy one?' he asked incredulously.

Eve stared into the mirror. Were those fine lines around her eyes? The Texas sun was brutal, even when she wore a hat. 'You wouldn't have recognized her. It looked like she was wearing a couture dress. And that mousy hair was gone. You'd never call her beautiful, but still . . .' Eve dabbed cream under her eyes. 'All the men seemed to want to know who she was.'

Three lights flashed on Eve's five-line phone, but she ignored them. She'd told Cherie to tell anyone who called that she was out. She just didn't feel like discussing suppers for the Opera Ball right now.

'What did she do? Have plastic surgery?' asked Hughie.

'No, silly. I guess she lost some weight and decided to have a makeover. The men found her desperately attractive. But when she got up to dance with Michale Picol it was obvious she didn't know *what* she was doing. Yet everyone found *that* charming, too. Hmm!'

'What was she wearing?'

'It looked to me like a four-thousand-dollar Valentino.'

'What does Graham pay her?' asked Hughie, and wondered to himself what he paid her for.

'Oh, I don't know,' sighed Eve. She removed her blouse and looked at her small but still-firm breasts. She rubbed them with Elizabeth Arden's collagen cream, using upward strokes. 'Graham is so caught up with his Place in the Sun scheme, he's probably paying her a fortune. She must be the Place in the Sun girl.'

Hughie sat upright as if he was hearing the words for the first time. 'The Place in the Sun girl,' he murmured. As Eve talked about the barbecue and the beautiful Goya at the Kimball Museum outside Dallas, Hughie's mind was concentrated on Eve's words. 'The Place in the Sun girl.'

Of course! He'd been looking for the perfect showcase for Bambi. She was growing more beautiful every day – taller and more striking. She had a look all of her own, and his dream for her was a great dancer had disappeared when she had reached five foot eleven. Perhaps she belonged in the more lucrative world of modeling. He could even guide her career himself.

It was too difficult to promote his own sister to the great artist Valeski, who still liked to make his own discoveries. And Hughie had no interest in starting Bambi at the bottom, like thousands of other models.

The Place in the Sun Girl. Bambi could be the figurehead for the magnificent new resort Graham was planning. Surely, they'd do high-profile advertising for this place, and they'd need a fresh face, something that would lure every type. Plus, if he could convince Valeski to get involved, he'd get a commission as well. The Stuarts might as well get something out of Graham's scheme. If he had still had the family fortune, he could have just made this happen. As it was, he'd need Eve's support.

He would need to approach his plan gradually. He'd have to convince Valeski to take some test shots, then he'd show them to Eve, casually, and soon Eve would think the idea of A Place in the Sun girl was hers in the first place. He'd have to set just the right tone, since Eve would never agree to any idea that might be less than perfect for Bambi. And he'd have to get Bambi to go along with this. She'd always been too impatient to stand still in front of any camera, though this would be good for her. It was time she developed some new interests beside horses.

Hughie smiled. Valeski was summoning him from the set.

'Got to go, love,' he interrupted Eve. 'I'll come by the house tonight and bring you something. Big kiss!'

# 9

'I'll do this for one hour,' insisted Bambi, 'and that's it!'

Hughie grabbed her arm and shuffled her into a corner of the studio. 'Now calm down, Bambi,' he scolded, 'he'll hear you.' Across the room, two of Marshall Valeski's Oriental assistants padded silently on slippers, setting up lighting equipment and sweeps.

'No, no,' whispered Mikoto, one of the assistants, 'the umbrella must be much higher.'

'Hughie, how tall is your sister?' asked Kito.

'Five eleven,' shouted Hughie, and all the workers in the studio lifted their heads in surprise. No one, least of all Hughie, ever raised their voice in Valeski's atelier, where a hushed and reverent atmosphere usually prevailed. Bambi stood slumped sullenly against the wall, her arms folded squarely against her chest.

'This is dumb, D-U-M-B, Hughie. I'm not a model, I ride horses.'

Beads of sweat broke out on Hughie's forehead as he clenched his teeth. She was being impossible even after all he'd done to convince Marshall Valeski, the world's greatest fashion photographer, to take these pictures of his sister for a possible – not even real – portfolio! For as long and as well as he had known Valeski, Hughie knew this was a professional imposition. 'Trust me, Bambi,' he whispered, trying to regain his composure. 'It will be so easy. Just follow his instructions. If we get you this one modeling job, you can have your own horse.' Hughie never liked to discuss money with Bambi, but the fact was, he was worried about how he could afford to send her to college. The remaining money in his trust from the sale of his parents' estate barely covered their living expenses. Eve Donaldson gave them both an allowance that took care of all the extras. But Hughie was damned if he was going to ask Graham Donaldson for tuition money. The Stuarts did not beg. They used their resources. It was time for Bambi to learn this lesson.

Bambi cuddled up to him. '*And* dressage lessons?' She knew how to play her brother.

He threw his hands in the air. 'What am I going to do with you – dressage, horse, whatever. You can have it all. Just get back in there.'

Bambi wrapped her arms around her brother's fat little neck. 'I'll name him Hughie the Horse after the best brother in the whole wide word.' She kissed his ear.

'Just get back *in* there, Elizabeth Anne Stuart! And do whatever he says.'

'Okay, okay, I'm gone!' She loped onto the white seamless in her boots.

'No, no' admonished Kito. 'Take off the boots and get made up. Suki will help you now.'

Makeup, Bambi thought. Nobody had told her about makeup. She glared at Hughie for a moment, then smiled sweetly, remembering the horse. What a waste of a day. She should be finishing her homework and then going off for a ride instead of sitting here with junk on her face and people poking at her hair. Well, she supposed she'd do it for Hughie, though the idea of being a model was positively pukey. As the damp sponge approached her face, she closed her eyes. She didn't want to look.

Thirty minutes later, she stared into the mirror in horror. It looked to her like mud had been smeared on her face. Dark brown smudges were under her cheekbones and purple shadows over her eyes. Her eyebrows, thick as they were, looked like snakes. What had they done to her face? 'Hughie!' she called, tears starting to well up in her eyes.

'Don't worry,' he said, inspecting her hair as Suki brushed it out. 'Under the lights, we have to exaggerate.'

Flanked by the two Oriental assistants, Bambi moved onto the set. She hoped this would be over soon.

Marshall Valeski, wearing his trademark black, entered the room and went immediately to the camera. His slight, elegant frame darted swiftly about the equipment as he silently nodded approval or frowned disapproval. As long as Bambi had known him, his face had never changed. He had a timeless quality that would have marked him as uniquely handsome in any century.

Although Hughie had worked for Valeski since Bambi was six years old, she did not know him any better now than when she had met him. At first, she had wondered if he did not like her. But Hughie had explained that even though Marshall Valeski was a great genius behind the camera, he was very shy in public. He spoke through his pictures, Hughie had said.

'She looks very pretty,' Valeski commented softly, looking through the viewfinder of his Hasselblad. 'But were are her boots? She doesn't look like Bambi without her riding boots. And, Bambi, what's your favorite music?'

Bambi began to think that modeling for Valeski was not bad at all. He seemed awfully easy to work for.

When the first test Polaroid was taken, Valeski stared at it for a long time. 'This is very nice,' he announced. Everyone in the room knew that this was his equivalent of a great endorsement.

'Well, what do you know,' breathed Hughie, trying his

best to stay in the background. This was going to be a real shoot after all.

The next six hours seemed like six minutes to Bambi. From the time Hughie put on her favorite Fleetwood Mac tape, she began to relax and follow the lead of Marshall Valeski, who had suddenly turned into her personal Pied Piper.

The world's premier photographer's interest was aroused. After the Polaroids, he had come around the camera and sat with her and talked like a friend. He had asked her about her favorite horse, and to imagine all her favorite things. Bambi felt as though he was someone she could trust. He reminded her of the time Thumper, her pet rabbit, had baby bunnies, and she had given one to him. 'I still have him, out at my farm,' Valeski said. After three quarters of an hour, Bambi felt relaxed. When Valeski told her what to do in front of the camera it was easy. She hadn't even minded when he asked her to change into the long, Juliet-like dress and a pair of toe shoes. She found herself dancing as if she were alone in her room, choreographed only be Valeski's coaxing voice, and eyes. En pointe, she twirled, her long hair swirling, one leg extended up and back, feeling the leap and soar of her body.

It was like playacting, Bambi thought. She'd done this millions of times, when she'd ridden her horse into the forest and pretended she was a fairy princess on a white stallion, or Joan of Arc, riding to the rescue of her loyal followers. Here in front of the camera, she could be anyone. She forgot there was anyone else watching. Kito, Mikoto, Suki, even Hughie, all faded into the darkness of the edges of the room. Only she and the camera, and Valeski's soothing voice, existed in her world of make-believe.

She pirouetted on her red toe shoes in a black tulle wedding dress and veil, one arm in front and the other stretched back, her head arched, almost touching her spine, as if she were dancing a tarantella. With a giggle, she tossed the bouquet of blood-red roses over her shoulder as Valeski, hidden behind the camera, urged her on, applauding.

'Wonderful! Big smile, Bambi. Look up. Now look at me. Beautiful. Energy, Bambi, energy!'

She was barely aware of the commotion as she changed, as if in a dream, from dress to jeans to tank suit. And then it was over and everyone was hugging and congratulating her. What was supposed to have been a half-hour shoot had gone on to well past midnight. Still, she was not even tired; she felt elated.

In the dressing room, Bambi scrubbed off the makeup and combed through her hair, reemerging as the fifteen-year-old girl she was. Sitting in her cotton underpants, with no shoes and no bra or shirt, Bambi realized all her clothes were still in the studio. She'd have to go find them.

Suki, who had been helping her take off her makeup, looked around the room and grabbed something long, white, and wonderfully soft off the adjacent dressing rack. 'Here,' she said, wrapping the snow-white ermine cape around Bambi. 'This is for the Galanos shoot tomorrow morning, but Marshall won't mind if you borrow it for one minute.' Everyone was on a high. They could even allow Bambi to wear an eighty-thousand-dollar cape to fetch her jeans.

Walking barefoot back into the studio, Bambi called out, 'Who's seen my jeans?'

Valeski looked up from his conversation with Hughie. Then, without a word, he guided her back in front of the camera and motioned to Mikoto to reset the lights. He gently slipped the cape down her shoulders and spread it on the floor, turning for Hughie's nod of approval. Oblivious to baring her childlike breasts to the entire room, Bambi automatically snuggled into the fur, curling on the floor like a baby on a blanket. She felt only the luxury of the fur against her clean, near-naked body. If Valeski and Hughie thought this was right, it was, she told herself.

After a few minutes of shooting, Valeski himself helped her up, rearranged the cape to cover everything but her shining face and hair, slipped her arms back so that the cape covered her whole body, and said, 'Now, Bambi, look at me and fly.'

And, excitement tingling through her, she only asked, 'How high?'

# 10

*November 1967*

The shoot was a gentleman's sport, one that required skill, drama, ritual, and tradition, equally. And the Viennese family of Elizabeth Lintl Stuart practiced the sport according to every rule.

The first fifteen days of November were a tradition in the Stuart family. Every year, Elizabeth Lintl Stuart packed up her husband and their son Hughie for the annual hunting houseparty at her grandparents' ancestral home in Vienna. This year, Hughie was twelve and the newest member of the family, baby Elizabeth Anne, was present.

The long train trip to New York, the opulent ocean voyage on the Queen Elizabeth II, and the flight from London to Vienna was behind them as they relaxed with thirty other guests, many of them cousins, at Castle Lintl, a rambling, fifteenth-century fortress painted Hapsburg hunter yellow. It was filled with antiques, damask, ormolu, and hundreds of stag heads and sporting trophies. The guest list, as always, was carefully selected by the Lintls to include the crème de la crème of the world of international shooting. Elizabeth Stuart was, however, the only female shot in the actual hunting party. She had spent virtually all her childhood vacations at the castle. The fifteen hundred acres in the Vienna Woods had seemed magical to the young girl, who had been more of a tomboy than a debutante. At the age of seven, she had received her first gun, a miniature Holland and Holland, and by her teens she was a crack shot and a permanent member of the hunting party. Her marriage to Franklin Stuart, whom she met on a ski holiday in Switzerland, did not put an end to this tradition. In fact, shooting was a hobby they both enjoyed.

Elizabeth had quickly realized that her husband was still captivated by Eve Benton Donaldson. At first, Elizabeth had reacted by cooking heavy Austrian meals, spending hours rebinding old books in fine leathers and organizing sporting events that they could share together. But she had to sit by and suffer the humiliation of always coming up short in comparison with the perfect Eve Donaldson. Elizabeth Stuart realized, of course, that Eve had her shortcomings, but Franklin was blind to any imperfections. And, as the years went by, Elizabeth was more painfully aware that she had not been able to advance her husband's career the way Eve had Graham's. Frankin's family's fortunes had severely declined since their marriage, and her own family had for generations been land-rich and cash-poor. Even Castle Lintl was used by them only one month out of the year. The rest of the time it was rented out to automobile executives from Detroit and investment bankers from the Eastern Seaboard who wanted a taste of European aristocracy for even a few days.

She and her husband had found themselves floundering in a world not made for romantics. A couple who had started life together sharing a sensitivity for the finer things – like reading James Joyce by the fire, and sailing off the coast of Maine – they had prided themselves on charting their course by the stars. However, the stars were not enough in the fluorescent world of Benton and Stuart. Franklin found his responsibilities slowly eroding as his snobberies kept him from comfortably associating with people whom he considered to be crassly commercial, a roster that included clients and prospective investors. Graham Donaldson, on the other hand, was a go-getter who didn't mind rolling up his sleeves and who relished the excitement of working in a socioeconomic melting pot. The fact that the Stuarts had come over on the *Mayflower*, while Donaldson's grandfather had come via Ellis Island, meant nothing in the American world of finance.

It has been two years since Graham had taken the firm of Benton and Stuart, which he had been guiding so ably, and gone public on the New York Stock Exchange under the new corporate name of Intercontinental Minerals. Franklin's diminishing stock and importance in the company his deceased father had helped found left him powerless to thwart the steamroller tactics of Graham Donaldson. Wall Street referred to Donaldson as 'unstoppable,' 'a winner,' 'a man who never let emotion stand in the way of a good deal.'

Elizabeth had watched her husband's tall shoulders stoop as he weathered his loss of face, especially, Elizabeth thought, in front of Eve. Elizabeth found Franklin becoming increasingly isolated and emotionally remote. It seemed he always had a glass of bourbon or vodka in his hand. He rarely went to the office or looked after their investments. Instead, the couple drifted from hunting season to polo season to sailing season, becoming perpetual houseguests as their finances dwindled.

Graham Donaldson's rapid promotions only seemed to demoralize Franklin further, and, after each step forward for Graham, Elizabeth's husband seemed to sink into a deeper depression. During each down period, he paid less attention to his wife and son, who were constant companions, for as the gap between husband and wife widened, the relationship between mother and son intensified. Hughie in effect became her friend, ally, and confidante. He rarely left his mother's side, and, as she did not make friends easily, she was glad he was so dependent on her. His asthma allowed her a frequent excuse to keep him home from school, and they enjoyed making Viennese pastries together and poking fun at the absurdities of suburban life.

For a while, Elizabeth had tried to ignore her husband's situation by turning to Scotch herself. Her drinking and overeating had ballooned her weight to over a hundred and fifty pounds when she finally came to her senses. She was the kind of woman, she reminded herself, who could make the best out of anything.

A baby! She would have another child. This would keep the family together. It was the age-old European solution. And for a while, it seemed as if things were working. There was less drinking and more laughter.

And so Elizabeth Anne had been born. Her mother was certain that the baby would lift Franklin's spirits and that they could have, if not an idyllic, a very contented life. As determined as she was on the ski slopes, Elizabeth Stuart was even more determined when it came to her family.

Yet Franklin seemed inexplicably more despondent than ever. The baby, sweet as she was, seemed to get on his nerves. And Hughie, with his short legs and frail constitution, didn't measure up to his father's expectations.

Elizabeth could see that the business was slipping through her husband's fingers. He had been selling off huge blocks of Intercon stock recently to leverage some investments he had made on his own. He and Bunky Whittier, a polo crony, had invested heavily in a Virginia horse-breeding farm, against Graham Donaldson's advice. But Franklin had felt the farm was much more his style than oil and minerals.

The dispute was totally unimportant to Elizabeth, who knew that money had always come from somewhere when she needed it. If they could just move away from the trap of Eve Donaldson and Intercon, she was sure their life would improve. She would convince her husband that they should move to Europe, where their lifestyle would be considered a success because of their heritage, not their bank balance.

This fall was the perfect time for a visit to the Castle. They would take comfort in her family, and Elizabeth was determined to eliminate the competition once and for all.

Once they were in Vienna, surrounded by Old World elegance, culture and tradition, Franklin would see that the family belonged in Europe. Elizabeth planned to tell him her idea after the hunt ball that night.

It was a glorious fall day, and Elizabeth felt optimistic. It would be a splendid hunt. She joined the other guests promptly at eight for *petit dejeuner* in the flowered breakfast room overlooking the courtyard. Elizabeth wore the traditional tweed knickers, wool jumpers, and khaki, knee-high wellies – camouflage for the brush. The only colors in her outfit were her heavy fuchsia-and-canary-blue socks. Cheerfully kissing baby Elizabeth Anne goodbye, she handed her to her nurse. At 9.30, the Mercedes station wagons and Land Rovers took off, carrying the guns, shooting sticks, and ammunition to the day's site.

After the morning's shooting, luncheon was served outdoors on a long, linen-covered table under ancient acacia and maple trees. Hughie and his nanny drove out with the others who had not taken part in the hunting to join the group for goulash soup, brown bread, fruit, and cheese. They brought with them a telegram for Franklin, who had bagged several exquisite pheasants that morning. A fire blazed, and talk centered on guns and shooting techniques. Elizabeth, at her father's side, showed Hughie the birds, beautiful and still, paired according to type and outlined by a strand of pine branches. Hughie was especially fascinated by the spaniels and Labradors, anxiously awaiting the trumpet call that would announce the beginning of the afternoon hunting.

After lunch, Elizabeth and Franklin took to the woods again, and Hughie returned to the castle to nap before the black-tie dinner. There would be Viennese waltzing in the ballroom, and his mother had promised Hughie that he could join the party this year, since he was almost grown up.

In the fields, the beaters dispersed, clackers in hand, startling the birds into flight as the loaders took their places, each behind his hunter. Elizabeth and Franklin Stuart became separated from the group, but no one noticed until the sharp crack of a shotgun was heard, startling the hunters. All heads snapped to attention. The rules of the hunt were rigid, as defined by both tradition and the local warden, and were in fact solemnly recited at the beginning of each day's hunt so no precaution would be taken for granted. An unsupervised shot was no small matter in this tightly governed world. Then, with chilling shrillness, a second shot shattered the silence.

In a wooded bower, a half-mile away, shaded and lit only by the low, slanting rays of late afternoon sun, all was still. Elizabeth Stuart lay on the ground, a bullet in her heart. Her husband lay across from her, half his head blown away, his shotgun shoved into his mouth, his finger still closed around the trigger.

When the bodies were brought back to the castle, Hughie was inconsolable. He shrieked, howled, and kicked, demanding to see his parents, but his aged grandparents were in seclusion and no one would tell him anything, not even the nurse. Hughie, gasping for breath from an asthma attack, grabbed his baby sister and clutched her to him, not letting anyone touch her. He couldn't imagine what had happened, how both his parents could suddenly be dead. But no one, he swore, would take away his precious baby sister.

A week later, Eve Donaldson appeared. He ran across the room into her fragrant embrace, and she comforted Hughie and cradled tiny Elizabeth Anne. When at last the sobbing was over and Hughie was silent, she gently told him that his parents had loved each other and him very much, in spite of what had been a terrible, terrible accident. She promised Hughie she would care for him and his sister as if they were her own children. They would never be alone, never feel unloved.

Eve picked up baby Elizabeth Anne, only two months old and unable to understand. 'Look, Hughie,' she tried to divert his attention. 'Don't her eyes look like a fawn's? She's just like a little Bambi.'

Seeing the fear in Hughie's eyes, Eve soothed, 'Hughie, I know this is the worst thing that can happen. But you must be strong for your little Bambi. She needs you. You need each other. You and Bambi must grow up and be strong.'

This Hughie had understood, and from that moment, his life had been totally devoted to Bambi. The name Elizabeth Anne was gone, along with her mother.

Eve had wrapped the children in her arms and held them tight. She kissed the baby's dark, sweet head. This child would not suffer, she swore to herself. She knew that the bloodstained telegram in Franklin Stuart's pocket had informed him that Bunky Whittier had embezzled the money for the horse-breeding farm. But she also knew that wasn't the real, or at least not the only reason Franklin had killed himself and Elizabeth. Poor, dear Franklin.

She closed her eyes quickly, to shut out the memories and so that Hughie would not see her hot, remorseful tears.

# 11

*February 1982*

Catherine crumpled the interoffice memo into a ball and threw it into the wastebasket. She couldn't believe the nerve of Eve Donaldson. Socialite women were a pain in the neck and should stay out of the business world, she thought. The office was her territory.

The memo had been a three-sentence directive from Carla, forwarding Eve's request that Catherine see Vic Rose, Marshall Valeski's representative, regarding a possible photography idea for A Place in the Sun. Catherine hadn't even decided on a strategy for the creative program yet. She might use art work rather than photos in the brochures and ads. Catherine hated being backed into a corner like this, but she knew she had to humor Graham's wife.

Vic Rose, she had learned from her assistant, B.J., was known to be gratingly insistent and if he thought he had the go-ahead from Eve, Catherine would never be able to get rid of him.

At ten-thirty, Vic Rose appeared in the lobby. She had to see him, just to placate Eve, but she'd get rid of him as soon as possible. She picked up her phone and called her assistant. 'B.J., do you have a minute?'

'What's up?'

'Marshall Valeski's rep is here.'

'Oh, God, Vic Rose,' groaned B.J. 'I think I have to wash the cat.'

'Not funny. Come in to my office. We're talking an Eve Donaldson-ism here.'

'Oh.' B.J. instantly understood. Everyone still talked of the time the entire secretarial pool had to drop everything for a week in order to retype Eve's Rolodex and address her Christmas cards.

B.J. came into Catherine's office, shaking her curly head sympathetically, and dropped into a chair at the round table. At least it would look as if they were presenting a unified front. If B.J. was involved, Catherine could always tell Eve Donaldson that there had been a group decision.

B.J. *was* the perfect assistant, thought Catherine. She had come to her from J. Walter Thompson, a top advertising agency. She knew marketing, she did her work well, and Catherine never had to look over her shoulder. When she gave B.J. a job, it got done. And Barbara Jo, as she hated to be called, was fun to work with.

Her arrival in the department six months ago had caused a small uproar when, on the first Saturday after she was on the payroll, she painted her office neon yellow without asking permission. In the hall of the staid, conservative oil company, music from B.J.'s radio could often be heard. She also installed a small forest of plants on her desk and windowsill. Catherine said nothing, even under pressure from Ray Acconti. She reported to Graham Donaldson and he had no complaints. He seemed to like the crackling atmosphere that emanated from the activity around Catherine's growing department.

Sitting next to Catherine, her black suit giving her a professional look that was offset by her mischievous grin, B.J. caught sight of Vic Rose. He carried a small black crocodile case. After brief introductions he got straight to his point.

'Mrs Donaldson was in the studio last week having her portrait done for the Historical Society,' he announced, smiling smugly. Unlike most reps, he had the luxury of not having to sell and could chatter about anything. He merely had to display the work. Valeski's art did the rest.

Catherine nodded her head slightly, realizing Rose was about to propose Eve Donaldson's plan.

'She saw some pictures Marshall had just taken and thought they might interest you.' He unzipped the case and showed Catherine and B.J. the results of Bambi's shoot, handling each print like a priceless painting. He lined the prints in a row on Catherine's story board rail, until ten faces of Bambi, each more unique and breathtaking than the next, gazed at Catherine.

She glanced at B.J., whose eyes were glued to the photo of the nearly nude Bambi, her face shimmering without makeup, on the ermine cape.

'Gorgeous, aren't they?' Rose tapped a print with a manicured nail. 'That one is going to be the next Galanos ad. It will run in *Vogue*, *Harper's*, and *Town & Country*. And this one – ' he indicated a head shot. 'This is a possible cover for *Elle*.'

Catherine could hardly believe her eyes. The model was mesmerizing. She'd never seen anyone so naïve and sophisticated all at once. She was a woman yet still a little girl; dramatic, but not threatening.

But why would Catherine need a model? She couldn't just create a job for her. Assignments came first, then she looked for models. She wondered what Eve had been thinking and suddenly she understood. She'd take Graham's wife's idea one step further.

'Who is the model, Vic?' she asked.

'Bambi. One name only. She's fifteen years old.'

'Good God.'

B.J. rolled her eyes and asked. 'Does this baby have an agent?'

'Actually, no,' Rose said. 'She's just starting. These are her first shots, believe it or not. Between the artistry of Valeski and this girl, you're going to see some big-ticket chemistry. I'll leave these prints with you. Let me know when you're done with them and I'll have them picked up.'

'Thank you, Vic.' Catherine was still looking at the photos. 'Maybe there's an idea here.'

Rose flashed an unctuous expression. 'We'll have to do lunch.'

'Soon. Give me a call next week.'

When Rose was gone, Catherine and B.J. sat staring at the pictures. B.J. spoke first.

'Are you thinking what I'm thinking?'

'I'm thinking spokesperson,' said Catherine.

B.J. sighed audibly. 'What a face. If she weren't so young and innocent looking, you'd want to kill her.'

'Exactly.' Catherine knew that Bambi's innocence, the innocence only a fifteen-year-old could have, was what made her beauty both arresting and acceptable. Men would love her eroticism. Women would love the fact that she wasn't yet aware it existed. She was approachable, yet glamorous. She looked ageless, had universal appeal, and there was something special in her eyes – her expression – that drew Catherine in and held her there. She envisioned Bambi swimming, windsurfing, riding, diving, lounging elegantly on a terrace. She could be Venus on the half-shell, she could be Diana the huntress, punk or pretty, romantic or adventurer.

Catherine hated to admit it, but Eve Donaldson had an eye. And Catherine was intelligent enough to accept a good idea wherever it came from. She knew it was still up to her to form the concept into a useable context and make it work. The discovery of Bambi was just the beginning.

Catherine picked up the photograph of Bambi with the roses and her brow furrowed. Strictly speaking, this type of creative advertising promotion was not in her area of responsibility . . . yet. Catherine believed in taking the initiative and the responsibility and then asking for the official recognition. Taking over an area unofficially was often the best way to grow in your department, she knew. By pulling an advertising program together, she'd get involved in a total communcations package – everything from the ads and brochures to the promotional tie-ins to the overall image of the project. Communications was the visible end of a job, and this program would certainly help sell A Place in the Sun to the board.

Catherine took a last inventory. Graham Donaldson wouldn't object, if she kept him informed – after all, it had been partly his wife's idea. Ray Acconti would be a problem, but she could deal with him. Michael Picol couldn't care less about communications. She'd go for it.

'B.J.,' she said, 'what would be involved if we got the advertising agency involved in this on a spec basis?'

'They won't work on spec.'

'Right,' nodded Catherine. 'That's why we have to do this inhouse.'

'We might have to staff up.' B.J. figured they'd need at least two writers and an art director, just to get going.

'Call the headhunter in the morning. I'll clear it with management.' Catherine wondered briefly where they'd put these people. Well, she'd find a place, even if she had to stick them in the coffee room!

'We'll have to test this girl,' B.J. pointed out. 'Showing how people respond to her will help convince the board.'

'Right. Let's get together with research as soon as possible. Meanwhile, see if you and Melissa and Ted can squeeze some working ad and brochure layouts out of the art department.' Catherine winced. The Intercon art department was notoriously 1950s in its style. She'd have to get her own people on board fast.

Catherine counted on her fingers, ticking off what had to be done, as B.J. scribbled to keep up. 'Then we'll have to plan a promotional tie-in, probably with Air France, or one of the South American carriers. And let's be sure to get a reading on which agencies want this girl. We don't want her signing with anyone till we can get her signed. Maybe we can work out a holding fee until we get approval from Graham.'

B.J. was taking notes as fast as she could. 'What about Valeski?' she asked. 'I suppose he'll want to get involved.'

Catherine nodded. A world-class photographer would give the project status. 'No problem. He'll be perfect for the studio shots and the location stuff, too.'

'He probably won't do the test work,' B.J. warned.

'I know,' Catherine agreed. 'We'll just have to work from layouts till we can involve Valeski. But if we cover all our bases, we should be ready to get him under contract by the first of the year.'

Catherine stood up. 'Let's keep this quiet until I convince management,' she instructed. 'And put together a schedule, okay? I want to be sure of our timetables before we get too far.'

She glanced at her calendar. Lunch with Billy Wright was penciled in at noon. Part of her wanted to skip lunch and keep working on this new idea for the Place in the Sun girl. But she remembered the promise she'd made to herself after Dallas. She'd get out more, meet more people, stop skipping lunch, have a social life. The work would be waiting when she got back. It always was.

Catherine met Billy downstairs in the two-story granite lobby. As she came down the escalator from the upper level, she spotted him. Amidst navy and gray winter overcoats he stood out in his tan corduroy pants and a brown leather aviator jacket. His hands were jammed into his pockets as he leaned against the base of a ten-foot Brancusi sculpture. And he was still wearing the cowboy boots, noticed Catherine.

They pushed through the huge revolving doors and out into the shock of the Chicago winter. As usual, a glaze of ice covered the sidewalks, and the raw winds were especially bone chilling as they whipped around the downtown high-rises.

'Where should we go?' asked Catherine. She hardly ever ventured out of the office at noon, preferring to bring pitta bread with tofu spread and alfalfa sprouts from home.

Billy pointed north. 'The Goat. Where else?'

'What's the Goat?'

Billy stared at her in amused amazement. 'How long have you been in this town?'

Catherine shook her head. 'Seven months. But I don't get out much for lunch.'

'Well then,' said Billy. 'You're in for a treat. Billy Goat's is one of the top culinary establishments in the city. It's where all the action is. It's where the literary elite meet, you might say – all the newspaper people. And Mike Royko. Julia Child was even guest chef last year.' He pulled up the sheepskin collar on his jacket.

Catherine mentally tallied the contents of her wallet and frowned. 'I hope they take credit cards. I'm short on cash.' She knew the rules – when you went to lunch with a superior, he paid; when you went with a subordinate, you paid. Since she and Billy were equals, they'd probably split the bill.

'No problem. It's highly affordable.' He winked at her.

He took her arm as they pushed their way into the wind. After they crossed the Michigan Avenue bridge, he led her down a flight of stairs to a lower level of the city she never realized existed.

When they reached a beat-up red door decorated with the face of a goat, Billy bowed elaborately, and ushered her in to a hustling bustle of activity and the permeating smell of grease. The confusion was doubled by the noise, as people jostled each other, waiters with trays of beer elbowed their way through the crowd, and the white-aproned man behind the open grill shouted, 'Doobla-cheese! Doobla-cheese! Three doobla-cheese, two chips!'

'The Goat is an institution,' shouted Billy, pushing her to the end of a long line where everyone seemed to be ordering a 'Double cheese.'

'Remember the 'cheeseburger, cheeseburger, cheeseburger' skit on *Saturday Night Live*?' Billy asked. 'This is the place it's based on. Just relax and let the charm grow on you.'

'Doobla-cheese?' barked the grillman, jabbing a finger at Catherine.

'Doobla-cheese!' she shot back. There didn't seem to be any alternative.

They picked up their burgers, chips, and cokes, and Billy dashed to an open table.

'Now you can say you've really seen Chicago,' said Billy, as they finally settled down to eat.

The hamburgers were greasily delicious, Catherine had to admit. She hadn't had a cheeseburger since Dallas and Midnight the cat, who was now the undisputed ruler of her Hancock Building apartment.

'So what's the gossip down on seventy?' she asked Billy.

'It's all South American. Michael Picol is there right now laying the ground work for us to bring an engineering team into Venezuela.'

'Led by yours truly,' said Catherine, pointing at Billy with her hamburger.

'I suppose. And I'm really rooting for Picol on this one because that Bandera Roja makes me nervous.'

'He's got a pretty fancy track record,' said Catherine. 'Then again, Picol should have been a bandit himself – he's got the manners of one.' She silently ticked off the times he'd abandoned her or kept her waiting.

Billy waved across the room to someone. 'Well, maybe that explains why he made such points in Caracas. He fits right in with all those subversives. He speaks Spanish, English, Arabic, and Hebrew, so he can negotiate just about anything in any language. But,' Billy frowned, 'there's something about him that doesn't ring true.

'As I understand it,' explained Billy, 'Picol has worked out a program where our state department, backed by Intercon donations, will export excess food and produce to Venezuela.'

Catherine caught on immediately. 'Hmm. We scratch your back, you scratch ours. Is that the way he usually works?'

'You got it. Suddenly the Venezuelans reverse themselves and become very hands-off toward our dealings. Then doors start opening from my team.'

'What about the islands?' Catherine knew that Venezuela still controlled most of the islands surrounding A Place in the Sun.

'I don't think they really care about them much. It's just a boondoggle.'

She felt her face flush. 'How can you say that?' she said angrily. Belittling A Place in the Sun was undermining her whole job. 'You're hung up on the numbers. You only see one side to this business – yours!'

Before full-scale warefare could erupt, a man stopped by their table and shook Billy's hand. Billy introduced him. 'This is Dan Connolley, features editor at the *Sun-Times*,' he said, relieved at the distraction. It was obvious that Catherine had no sense of humor about her job. She was really looking good these days, Billy thought. If she'd take herself less seriously, she'd feel better.

'Congratulations on your poem,' said Connolley, glancing admiringly at Catherine as they were introduced.

'What poem,' asked Catherine.

Billy shrugged. 'Oh, I had something published in the *Paris Review*,' he admitted shyly. He quickly bent down to rescue Catherine's purse, which had slipped off her lap and landed precariously near a pool of ketchup on the floor.

'Really!' Catherine couldn't imagine an oil engineer who wrote poetry.

'Oil engineering is a pretty solitary job,' shrugged Billy. 'You have a lot of time when you're off in places like Addis Ababa.'

As the editor moved back to his own table, Catherine pressed Billy for more details about his writing.

'If you're interested, read the *Paris Review*,' was all he would say. 'What do you do in your spare time?'

'What spare time?' She looked at her watch. She'd promised B.J. she'd be back by one.

'Have you ever been ballooning?' asked Billy.

'Not since I watched the *Wizard of Oz*.'

'Well, here's your chance. How about coming up with me?'

'When?'

'Today. We can leave work early and be out at the balloonport by sundown.'

'It's freezing out.'

'You can change first. And I have extra parkas and gloves in the jeep. And it's a convertible. I haven't put the top up yet, so by the time we got there, you'd be used to the cold.'

'I can't get away today. You should see my desk. I barely made lunch!'

As they climbed the stairs back to Michigan Avenue, Billy persisted. 'How about a raincheck? I'm off for Venezuela at the end of the week if all goes well. But when I get back in a month, what do you say?'

'Sure.' But Catherine's mind drifted. She walked faster, hurrying to get back. The Bambi phase of her program was just beginning. Ballooning was the furthest thing from her mind.

# 12

Michael Picol nervously checked his watch and looked up the path leading to the flagstone terrace of the old colonial-style Caracas Country Club. Under the dark green awning, the atmosphere was tense. Six men had been gathered around the table negotiating for three hours. The sun was getting hot. Ambassador Diaz, in his white linen coat, smugly exhaled his cigar smoke. His brother-in-law, Romulo Perez, the minister of culture, glanced from person to person, trying to grasp what was happening. He stopped to stare briefly at Michael Picol's taut face and his brother-in-law's angry expression. Alexandro Navarro, key figure in the Ación Democratica political party, showed no expression behind his dark sunglasses.

In the middle of the table sat a platter of tequeños, crisp-fried white cheese wrapped with thin dough. Though none of the men would admit to hunger or fatigue after several days of tense dealing, the hors d'oeuvre platter had been replaced three times. General Mendez jabbed the air beneath Michael Picol's nose with a piece of fried cheese and raised his voice in a nonstop diatribe. '*Mira chico!*' he said. 'Look here, boy,' he condescendingly translated to emphasize his point. 'Fine, fine, fine. Not only do we share in the research and cultural funding, we get the food programs, the farm equipment. But I must have the airplanes and the artillery. It is only right.'

Michael Picol answered calmly. 'General, we are an American company, not a defense department or a dealer in arms. But I can assure you our report to the state department will accentuate your need for greater self-armament. After all,' he shrugged, smiling 'we are just an oil company. All we can do is try.'

On Picol's right, a young, meticulously mannered man in a tan summer suit and pinstripe shirt waved his hand as if to swat a fly. 'Gentlemen.' All conversation stopped. Even Michael Pcol listened carefully when Raoul Herrera, executive vice president of Trans-Oceanic, Inc., made a point. The huge international conglomerate sheltered more South American dollars than all the major banking systems combined.

'When Michael Picol makes a promise,' said Herrera, 'it is as good as done. And when he says he will try, that is as good as a promise.' He turned to his left. 'Romulo, you have cheese in your mustache.'

With a flurry of scarlet and pink, the flock of flamingos in the garden lagoon took flight, their long necks outstretched, and suddenly the clickety-clack of tiny spike heels broke the tension on the terrace.

Winnie Lifton, a petite pink-and-white confection, her long platinum-blonde hair bouncing as she walked, tottered in, navigating her way around puddles left from the early morning rain. Her tight pink silk halter dress revealed glimpses of enormous, alabaster-white breasts as she hurried over to the table. Every head turned to stare at the cherubic twenty-year-old who maintained Rubenesque proportions in spite of her five-foot-one-inch height.

'Michael! Hi, I'm here!' she bubbled. 'Look at me in Caracas! I hope I'm not late. It took forever on that freeway. The traffic from the airport was just like LA.' She batted her eyelashes under a fringe of fluffy bangs and all the men at the table leaped to their feet as introductions were made.

Michael Picol took a small, dimpled white hand and placed it in Perez's. 'Gentlemen, may I present Winnie Lifton, who really needs no introduction. I'm sure you've all seen her as the star of *Southwest*.'

'Oh Michael, I'm not the star,' she blushed, her cheeks getting even pinker. 'I only have a little part.'

Perez was enchanted. 'I try never to miss an episode of *Southwest*,' he enthused. 'You are the one beautiful flower in the whole television series.'

Winnie's aquamarine eyes grew wider. 'Oh, do you really get *Southwest* down here?'

Diaz pulled out a chair for Winnie and helped her into it, his hand unnecessarily assisting her.

'Thank you,' she breathed, straightening the bodice on her halter. 'I'm so flattered. But I must just look terrible. That highway is like a racetrack.'

The gentlemen all laughed. Ambassador Diaz bowed slightly. 'Yes,' he agreed. 'The *autopista* is very crowded at this time of day. You must be hungry. What can we get you to eat?'

'Oh, do they have tacos?'

'I don't know, but we shall order you whatever you like.'

'You know,' said Perez excitedly. 'As minister of culture it is my job to bring talented young people to the attention of the Caraqueños. We in Caracas love films. I propose that we have a Winnie Lifton Film Retrospective.'

The aristocratic Herrera took a sip of espresso.

Michael Picol's mouth turned up at the corners for the first time in days. Winnie glanced at him and then coyly admitted that she'd made only one feature-length film, *Halloween Chain-Saw Murders*.

'Does Venezuela have a Halloween?'

'No,' admitted Perez. 'But we do have All Saints' and Souls' Day. It's similar.' He had an inspiration. 'Ah! Instead we will have a retrospective of all your *Southwest* episodes. I will stage it at the Teresa Carreño, our most magnificent cultural complex.'

General Mendez nodded enthusiastically. 'Champagne for the table!' He called to a waiter.

'Miss Lifton is in town to unwind,' announced Michael Picol. 'She's had a very hectic schedule.'

'Do you like horseracing?' asked Navarro. 'We will take you to La Rinconada, our racetrack. They have a swimming pool for the horses.'

'I love to swim,' said Winnie.

All the men except for Picol and Herrera broke into laughter. 'Well, then we must take you to the sea,' said Perez. 'I keep a boat at the Carabelleda Yacht Club. We will go to the Los Roques Islands. I am taking a whole group of people this weekend. You must come, too.'

Winnie looked over her champagne glass at Picol, who rose. 'Gentlemen, it was a pleasure seeing you. But I have another engagement in Maracaibo this afternoon.' Though Caracas was the political and cultural capital of Venezuela, the men all knew that Maracaibo was the center of the petroleum industry. 'Take good care of Miss Lifton.' He put on his sunglasses.

As he turned to walk down the path, Winnie clattered after him. 'Michael, I came down here to be with you!' An edge of panic was in her voice. 'Where are you going? You can't leave me here all by myself with strangers!'

They were at the edge of the terrace now, entering the clubhouse. 'Look, baby,' he took her by the shoulders.

'I'm crazy about you. I'd like nothing better than a weekend with you in Caracas.'

'And I want to be with you. Why can't I come with you?'

'Look. This is a great opportunity for you. Perez will put together a festival in your honor. He's really a great guy.'

She looked dubious.

'I really want to see you, but Perez is more important. He'd be insulted. You know how Latins are.'

She pouted and looked at her shoes. 'How wonderful is he?'

He tipped her chin up with his hand. 'I know he had H. Stern make up something fabulous for you when I told him you were coming.'

She brightened. 'Oh, H. Stern! They're great jewelers.'

Picol looked her straight in the eye. 'Perez is important to me, Winnie. And he's important to you, too. Go on the boat. I'll try and join you.'

'But when will I see you?' She tugged at his sleeve, then glanced back to the terrace. The general caught her eye and saluted her.

'As soon as I'm done working so hard, you and I are going to have a nice, quiet week together, like we did in La Jolla,' Picol said.

'But that was three months ago. A girl can't live on that.'

Picol whispered under his breath. 'Baby, I'm *so* busy.' He sighed. 'You know, my friend Randy Cohen was going to cast you in the *Doll Machine*. When that happens . . .'

Winnie frowned. 'It hasn't happened yet,' she snapped.

'It will. Trust me.' He pushed her away. 'I gotta go to Maracaibo. I left you an envelope in the hotel.'

Winnie smiled petulantly. 'I really care for you.'

Picol smoothed her hair. 'Honey, you're a good actress. Put on a performance. I'd kiss you good-bye, but Perez wouldn't like it.'

'But how will I get in touch with you?'

'Just like Lauren Bacall said to Humphrey Bogart – put your lips together and blow.' He turned on his heel and disappeared into the clubhouse, leaving Winnie alone. She hesitated only a moment, then transformed her frown into a dazzling smile, as if she were facing the cameras, and bounced back to the table. The men jumped to attention, except for Herrera, who excused himself with a smile. 'I am due at Miraflores, the presidential palace,' he explained.

In the parking lot, Michael Picol slipped into a waiting Mercedes-Benz sedan. A darkly beautiful woman at the wheel greeted him with a kiss.

Herrera, standing under the columned portico, watched the car pull out.

Winnie Lifton sat on the kingsize bed of her duplex hotel suite at the Anauco Hilton blowing smoke rings with a cigar.

'Bravo,' applauded Perez.

'I knew you could do it,' said General Mendez. 'There's nothing like a good cigar after sex.'

They all giggled. Winnie's round, pink bottom and plump, white body sharply contrasted with the two naked and hairy men. Perez's rotund belly covered his genitals as he sat like a little Buddha with his legs folded beneath him. He took a large gulp of brandy and patted his mustache with the sheets.

'To a truly great lady,' toasted the general, naked except for his gold Rolex watch. 'But now I will teach you how a woman should light a cigar for a man.'

'Oh, show me, show me! Maybe they'll let me do it on *Southwest*.' Winnie sat straight up on her knees, her pink-tipped breasts inviting the general's kiss. He stroked each nipple with his tongue, teasing them into hardness before pulling back.

'Señorita, I know you will be a great star some day,' said Perez.

Under Perez's direction, Winnie gently bit the tip off a fresh cigar, then wetted it with her lips. She dipped the tip into the brandy, then slowly licked it again, holding it in her mouth and turning it between her palms. 'Like this?' she asked. Then she took the cigar out of her mouth and presented it to General Mendez.

'General, your cigar.'

Just then, the bathroom door burst open and Señor Navarro, wearing only a Fatima charm around his neck to ward off the evil eye, stood at the foot of the bed. He whipped a rolled-up, wet towel like a drunken matador, snapping it at Winnie's rosy bottom. She shrieked and leaped off the bed.

'In honor of your Halloween movie, we will now play *La Maluca*,' he announced. The men on the bed began to sing. *La Maluca* was a folk game played in one of the neighboring states on the night of All Saints' and Souls' Day. Navarro's variation on the game involved forming a circle around Winnie and snapping her with the towel.

She shrieked with laughter several time as the terrycloth whip slapped her bare flesh, but her cries only evoked more enjoyment in each of the men, who took turns hitting her. Finally Navarro grabbed her and held her hands behind her back as Perez stood in front of her. Perez's hands caressed her breasts as he rubbed his body against her, spreading her legs with his knees and forcing his fingers between her thighs. Winnie couldn't help leaning back against Navarro, whose wet lips nibbled her neck while one hand stroked the side of her leg. Next to him on the bedside table was a necklace of pink and yellow diamonds from H. Stern.

# 13

Catherine lay in bed at the Ritz-Carlton Hotel, propped up on pillows and looking out the window overlooking Embassy Row. Turn-of-the-century mansions, formerly residences of the very rich and now homes to foreign ambassadors, lined the street. In the park just beneath her room, cherry trees bloomed. The gold-wrapped Godiva chocolate the night maid had left was still on the pillow next to hers. She stretched languidly, then reached over to the room service cart for her vanilla yogurt and a copy of the *Washington Post*. She spooned the yogurt into a bowl filled with bran cereal and poured herself a cup of herbal tea.

Graham Donaldson's picture, taken yesterday as he testified before the Senate Interior Committee, appeared on page two of the *Washington Post*. Catherine gazed at his earnest face, at the authority in his features. She kicked off the covers and rubbed one leg against the other as she remembered just how glorious yesterday had been. She stared at the picture one more time, and reread its caption: 'Graham Donaldson, CEO of Intercontinental Minerals, testifying yesterday before the US Environmental Committee.' The article described why Graham and Intercon believed the mining of national parklands would not damage the delicate ecological balance of the land.

Catherine remembered her role at the hearing and was proud of the information she had culled for Graham. During the five-hour testimony, she had sat directly behind him and supplied the right notes at the right time.

They had worked together as a team; Catherine had never felt as synchronized with Graham's intellectual strategies as she did yesterday afternoon.

She pulled her T-shirt over her head and reached for her staid, simple navy suit and red silk shirt. It was boring, but right for a meeting with government people. She had noticed what everyone wore yesterday at lunch in the Senate Dining Room. Modesty seemed to be the rule of thumb in Washington. In between spoonfuls of her navy bean soup, she'd taken in the muted tones and low-key atmosphere. This was not a place for extremes. Even famous political adversaries, she'd noticed, had risen to greet each other like old friends.

She shook out her pantyhose and wondered what had gone on last night. While she and two young Senate aides had eaten dinner at a Vietnamese restaurant in Georgetown, Graham had dined privately in the family quarters of the White House with the President and First Lady, Pollyanne and Rex Savage.

Even though the Senate aides had imparted inside gossip about the Department of the Interior, Catherine had found the revelations about who was sleeping with whom less than fascinating. Her mind kept wandering to Graham Donaldson and what was happening in the White House. She had quickly decided that the two George Washington University graduates were incredibly naïve when it came to getting things done. They were consumed by detail, innuendo, and bureaucracy. By the time the enormous sea bass had arrived, stuffed from gaping mouth to tail with exotic Vietnamese vegetables and smothered in sweet and sour sauce, Catherine wanted to wind up this exercise in Washington Trivial Pursuits. She couldn't wait to get back to the hotel and brief herself for her meeting with the Secretary of the Interior. The Senate aides, she had decided, were so into the 1960s mindset that they failed to realize that if it weren't for the Graham Donaldsons of the world, there would be no free environment to protect. She had written them off.

She finished dressing and clipped on her cultured pearl earrings. Since Graham was always prompt she dashed down the hallway which was lined with Oriental rugs and Early American furniture. Although she was five minutes early, she located the Intercon limousine in front of the hotel. Graham was waiting inside.

'How did you make out with Washington's most eligible young men?' He smiled paternally.

'They've got the lowdown on French wines, Vietnamese restaurants, and who's sleeping with whom in Washington.'

Graham chuckled, 'Well, those three things happen to be very important in this town. What else did you learn?'

'Did you know your friend Secretary Henry Hudson has a few dissenters in his department?'

Graham looked at her. 'A lot of dissention?' He signalled her with his eyes to go on.

'Yes, apparently some people feel he's sold out to big business.'

'Bullshit.'

'That's just the gossip.'

Graham was always soft-spoken. 'How strong was the criticism?'

'They were very rough on him. Those guys have a lot to learn about a united front.'

Graham smirked. 'Maybe we should loan you to Washington for a few months to teach them. So wasn't there any good gossip? Who *is* sleeping with whom?'

'Not necessarily husbands and wives.'

'Well, you know, lots of these guys go in for that sort

of thing. I guess the power goes to their head – or someplace else.'

Catherine held her head and rolled her eyes. 'Ugh!' she laughed, as the car passed the Tidal Basin. She peered out and remembered the legendary Fanne Fox.

'Listen,' said Graham, 'we're running a little ahead, so I want to stop at the National Gallery of Art. I have a little errand to run for Eve. She's on the board of trustees, you know, and the director is a good friend of ours.' The car pulled up in front of the immense, white hexagonal I. M. Pei structure, juxtaposed with the row of neoclassical Smithsonian buildings lining the broad Avenue. Graham pointed to a small gift-wrapped box in the front seat. 'She asked me to leave this thank-you gift with him, for the flowers he sent to her in the hospital.'

Catherine nodded agreeably, but inside she felt a jolt. She couldn't believe Eve was using him as a messenger. Certainly other arrangements could have been managed since today was important for Graham and Intercon. He couldn't afford to be distracted by domestic chores! Catherine suddenly realized that her cheeks were flushed in anger, and she checked herself. This was not a good sign. She was actually resenting Graham Donaldson's wife and her infringement on their working relationship.

She focused on Graham as they walked into the atrium with its huge Calder mobile suspended from the ceiling. Even this massive, monolithic structure did not seem to diminish his sense of presence and power. She hoped Eve appreciated what she had.

As they went up the escalator, Catherine noticed proudly that people watched Graham. He moved with the grace of quiet authority, and his appearance was almost theatrically distinguished. They walked through a small room hung with early Picassos and into a large, cathedral-like room lined with unframed Rothko canvases, paintings of spectacular quality. Randall Hall, the director of the National Gallery of Art, was supervising the reinstallation of two of the massive exercises in color and space.

Hall extended one hand to Graham and greeted Catherine graciously.

'Good to see you. Two of our treasures are just returning from tour. They are so magnificent, we hated to have them gone. The blue one here is Eve's favorite. She's continually offered me a fortune for it, but nothing in this room is ever for sale.' Graham and Catherine stole a look at one another. Neither had the soul of an artist.

'The dark red one is one of the last created before the artist committed suicide. I think you can almost feel the sense of despair in it. Eve and I have spent hours at a time here in utter silence. It really left her faint. Very moving, isn't it?' The director paused. 'Now tell me – how is Eve recovering?'

'Very well, thank you,' said Graham. 'She wanted to make sure you got this gift and sends her apologies for not being able to make the board of trustees meeting today.'

'Is she out of the hospital yet?'

'Yes. I brought her home the day before yesterday, so she should be back to her garden and her music in a jiffy.'

Catherine stepped back to examine Eve's favorite painting, the one that left her feeling faint. She saw nothing but three muddy patches of color painted by a man who evidently couldn't deal with the real world. She stepped back into a second room where a more realistic picture of a sad-eyed harlequin caught her eye. She didn't want to hear any more about Eve Donaldson's illness. The office grapevine had been full of the details about the hysterectomy, and Graham had taken off two days to be at his wife's side during and after her surgery. Catherine was sympathetic. After all, a hysterectomy was traumatic at any age. She didn't understand why she felt so resentful about the time Graham spent with Eve. She had asked politely about Eve's recovery, but secretly she could hardly understand why a woman's gynecological problems should become a national incident. Catherine had never been sick a day in her life; illness was a luxury she couldn't afford.

She looked again at the Picasso and noticed that Graham had moved on. She hurried to catch up with him.

Without breaking his stride, Graham Donaldson watched Catherine out of the corner of his eye. He knew that this stop at the Museum had not been strictly necessary. He could have dropped off the package earlier, or sent it by messenger. But he was a man whose intuitiveness was the main reason for his success, and he was getting danger signals from Catherine – her willingness to work till ten or eleven at night without argument and the lack of reference to any young man in her life or personal plans were flattering to him and to Intercon, but definitely unhealthy. She was attractive, she had a brilliant, analytical mind, and they did work well together. But that was as far as their relationship could go, he reminded himself. He had to make sure Catherine understood that he had a life beyond the company and a wife whom he worshipped. Although Intercon often came first, his wife and daughter were firmly second. He was a loyal family man.

He looked at Catherine as she gazed up at him. During the last few weeks as they'd been working late preparing for this trip, her look of adulation had become familiar. He had noticed, too, how she would help him off with his jacket and smooth the pockets as she hung it up, her hands lingering a little too long on the fabric.

But then again, Graham thought as they pushed out into the spring air, she *was* open and earnest. Maybe he was reading a little too much into everything. Nevertheless, it never hurt to emphasize that he was very happy with Eve and intended to stay that way. He knew that only a fool would jeopardize a life such as theirs.

Once, fifteen years ago, when he'd spent months in the Middle East commuting between the Tehran Hilton and Chicago, he'd had a six-month affair with a stewardess. The sex had been hot and acrobatic, but that was the extent of it. He'd ended it abruptly after the Middle East negotiations were complete. In no way was Graham Donaldson going to let what happened below the waist interfere with his home life. The stewardess had pestered him for months, threatening to kill herself and even to tell Eve. But never for one minute, even in the height of climax and passion, had he put the woman in the same category as his wife. It had been insulting to his ego, but easier, to buy off the girl with a mink coat and a sports car. Somehow, after that, he had never heard from her again.

He turned to Catherine and unconsciously reached to put his hand on her elbow. It seemed so natural, but he abruptly pulled back and put it in his pocket. He wouldn't negate this allusion to Eve.

It took only fifteen minutes to drive from the huge, larger-than-life world of government-planned buildings and parkways to the quiet, historic Georgetown neighborhood, where narrow three-story red brick houses crowded the cobblestone sidewalks. Catherine wondered how people could actually live here. The homes were so narrow that they almost looked as if dolls or miniature people lived in them.

The car turned right at the end of the block. They passed inclined streets named after letters in the alphabet – R, M, N, and Q. She swung her head around to stare as Graham pointed out the house where young Senator and Jackie Kennedy had lived when they first moved to Washington. It was perfectly square and slightly rundown, with a few narrow stairs running up to the front door, and Catherine could imagine the elegant Jackie Kennedy pushing a baby carriage down the sidewalk in her short French dress and flat-heeled shoes.

'Does the Secretary of the Interior usually hold his meetings at home?' Catherine asked.

'Yes,' replied Graham. She noticed that he was preoccupied and uncharacteristically curt. 'Most of Washington's business that isn't conducted at the White House or the Senate happens at somebody's table.'

They pulled up in front of a wide, red brick Federal house covered with vines and set back by twenty or so steps. A houseman, anticipating their ring, answered the door and ushered Graham and Catherine through the flower-filled foyer, living room, and morning room, and then into the high, brick-enclosed garden.

Blossoming cherry trees, heavy green-painted lawn furniture, and noisy chirping birds did not seem to Catherine like an atmosphere for business. She glanced at the well-worn picnic table set with mint juleps, lemonade, sandwiches, and raw vegetables.

Graham nodded toward the table. 'Henry's been on the Pritikin diet for his cholesterol for years. He had a heart attack a few years ago, you know. Doesn't touch alcohol.'

Secretary of the Interior Hudson, slightly ruddy and

paunchy, and wearing a green cardigan and yellow golf shirt, descended the patio stairs.

'Graham, kiddo! Good to see you!' He nodded at Catherine. 'Hello.'

'This is my assistant, Catherine McBride,' said Graham.

Hudson ignored Catherine and directed his remarks to Graham. 'Twinkie won't be joining us today. She's playing tennis at the Vice-President's.' Twinkie, Catherine gathered, was Mrs Hudson.

Catherine was totally prepared with all the facts and figures to brief the Secretary on A Place in the Sun as the site of a designated undersea National Park and fish farming center. She was anxious to get down to business and begin her speech. She breathed in the spring air, heavy with the smell of dogwood and cherry blossoms. It was all so different from the stuffy offices of the Department of the Interior which, she had noticed yesterday, were filled with Indian memorabilia and buffalo heads hanging on the walls.

'Clayton, did you get the young lady something to drink?' Hudson gestured to the hovering houseman.

Clayton seemed to Catherine like a relic from the pre-Civil War days. He bowed at every opportunity, and Catherine thought it most ironic, to accept a mint julep from him in the world's capital of democracy. She also realized that she was being treated quite differently from Graham simply because she was a woman. She joined the men at the other side of the garden, where a heated conversation was beginning.

'Rhumbo Oil doesn't have a bloody shot in hell,' Graham pontificated. 'There's no legal precedent for their lawsuit. And they've been screwing the government for years with their crazy tax shelters. They haven't given back one dime. Those hotshots with the Justice Department will cut them down to size.'

An older man who Catherine couldn't quite place, but whose face was familiar from the news, frowned. 'No way in hell.' He lit his pipe, puffing a spiral of smoke into the clean spring air. 'Those fuckers have got such good lobbyists, and now they've got that big interest in Arabco Bank. They'll come out of this like two nuns at a church supper. And that prick Morton . . .' Suddenly he noticed Catherine at his elbow. 'Pardon my French, Miss McBride. He'd sell his mother for a favorable verdict.'

Catherine glanced at Graham. She wondered when the locker-room talk would be over so she could give her presentation.

Hudson spoke softly to Graham. 'You know, you'd better watch out for Morton's lobbyists. If you want that area declared a national park, you might have to play a little ball with old Morton.'

Graham blinked impassively. 'I can handle Morton. I hear he can be legally extradited in three states.'

'Maybe so,' Catherine spoke up. 'But he's holding a few aces and spades these days, Graham. My friends at Swift Guaranty tell me that two of his people are going over to the EPA. We don't want to lose out for good intentions.'

Graham nodded slowly. 'I hear you.'

'You got yourself one hell of an assistant there,' said Cobbs.

'Well,' Graham loosened his tie. 'I think she's headed for your department tomorrow morning. You might want to hear what else she has to say.'

Cobbs nodded. 'I'll make it a point to be there. It's a date, Miss McBride. Look forward to seein' you.'

'Thank you, Mr Secretary,' Catherine said. Graham,

she noticed, was glancing at her approvingly.

'Come with me, Graham,' interrupted Henry Hudson, as he hauled his old friend off to the toolshed to see his new fishing lure.

For the next thirty minutes Catherine chatted with Cobbs about his transition from big oil to government and how the wheels of bureaucracy seemed to roll so much more slowly than those of the private sector. He explained that instead of a handshake and a word of honor, he was subjected to a thousand levels of approval. She listened politely, but wondered when Graham would give her the signal to begin her pitch.

It never happened. Graham shook hands with Cobbs, and before she knew it, Catherine found herself back in the limousine. She sat there, stunned. She'd never lost her temper with Graham, but now she felt her face flushing, blood rising to her temples.

'Graham,' she said slowly. 'When exactly will I get to make my presentation, which has about thirty thousand dollars of research into it? Wouldn't it stand to reason that it would have made sense to at least give a partial talk when both the Secretary of the Interior and the Secretary of Energy were present at the same time?'

'You'll see them again tomorrow.'

'Great! They'll each stop in for three minutes. I'll get introduced to those kids five levels below the secretaries and then they'll split, and I'll be left with the day care group.' Her eyes were flashing. 'I want to do the best job that I can for you, Graham,' she continued. 'That lunch was just a garden party!'

Graham looked slightly annoyed. She had a lot to learn. 'Catherine, this wasn't the time or the place. The details do take place with what you call the day care set. And you're not exactly Aggie Palmer's contemporary yourself.' He shot a look out the window as they passed over the Buffalo Bridge and on to Pennsylvania Avenue. 'Today you made a *personal* presentation. Tomorrow you can give your briefcase presentation – to whomever. And you'll do very well.'

She looked down at her shoes, ashamed of her outburst. How could she have missed the point? Maybe she was under too much pressure. She patted her right eyelid, where she felt a tear starting to smudge, blinking furiously so Graham wouldn't notice.

But he did notice. One big tear was streaking down the right side of her face, falling into the hollow of her cheek. He didn't need to say more, he thought; Catherine was so hard on herself.

His voiced softened. 'You made a fine impression, Catherine. But understand that everything takes time. First you have to have a rapport, then, you can do business. People are important. I learned that from Eve. She's been a big part of my success, you know. She showed me how to temper my eagerness, and . . .' his eyes started to twinkle. 'I'll tell you what. I'll give you a real lesson of how business is conducted in Washington.'

She glanced up.

'I wasn't going to go, with Eve at home and all, but tonight there's a big state dinner in honor of the Venezuelan president. If Pollyanne can still fit us in, you can come as part of the Intercon contingent.' He thought for a moment. 'Just how spectacular is your presentation?' She ignored the question.

'The White House!' Catherine felt a chill run down her spine.

'I know your friend Picol's going, so you might even get a dance at the White House. Can you handle that?'

Thank God she'd packed the long blue dinner dress.

'Of course I can be ready.'

'I think you're supposed to have two ID's. One of them should have your picture on it. Other than that, it's just dinner at the White House.'

# 14

The ground-floor entrance to the White House was much less grand than Catherine had anticipated. A cacophony of Spanish and English filled the entrance hall as dignified guests in evening gowns and tuxedoes queued up to show their picture IDs which guards in business suits matched to their faces. Just ahead of Catherine, Graham, and Michael Picol, Barbara Walters, one of the most recognized faces in America, flashed her ID along with everyone else.

Graham led the way down the long corridor to the Diplomatic Reception Room. 'Rex and I can't figure out which of us has more security checks per day,' he joked to Picol as Catherine slipped her Intercon photo ID into her evening bag.

'I think we should hire marines in full dress,' said Picol, nodding toward one of the ubiquitous young men in a gold-trimmed uniform.

'Sure. They could stand at parade rest in the Intercon lobby. Except for when they salute you, of course,' Catherine suggested.

She found herself absorbed in the atmosphere of the White House. She focused on the wraithlike portrait of Jacqueline Onasis, painted soon after she became the President's widow, eerie and ethereal. The painting seemed like a portrait of a ghost, painted a whole lifetime ago, yet she so clearly remembered sitting on her father's lap, mesmerized by the funeral procession on television, watching the graceful Jackie Kennedy glide by in her black widow's weeds. Further along the hall was a multi-image portrait of Eleanor Roosevelt which showed her hands continually in motion. Interesting, Catherine thought to herself, how these women, who had helped shape this century, were relegated to the ground level where the coats were checked.

Henry Hudson stood in the doorway of the Diplomatic Reception room, but Catherine overheard Barbara Walters say she was going to the ladies' room, and she slipped away to follow her. She wanted to be absolutely sure she looked perfect for her first White House appearance.

Catherine felt very grand in the beautiful surroundings as she entered the Diplomatic Reception Room on the heels of Miss Walters, only to find the room almost empty. There was no sign of Donaldson, Picol, or the Secretary of the Interior in the homey blue and gold room ringed with eighteenth-century murals of people on horseback and ships at sea. However, before she could become alarmed, a tall marine offered his arm.

'May I?'

She smiled and allowed him to escort her up the marble staircase and into the Blue Room, where cocktails were being served.

Picol, Graham, and Henry Hudson stood under the elaborate chandelier suspended and entwined with satin ribbon that matched the silk upholstery on the gold-trimmed armchairs. Big bowls of Savage Roses were placed around tables on which, Catherine noticed, no one placed their drinks. The 'Blue' Room was another surprise to Catherine. It was not blue at all, but creamy beige, and trimmed with more gold than blue. Even the moldings were accented with gold medallions. The frieze-like painting around the ceiling was also gold and blue, and eagles perched at the top of nearly every gold-framed mirror.

A Viking-like, exquisitely beautiful blonde woman wearing a décolleté gown and a twelve-strand collar of diamonds and sapphires walked straight up to Catherine as if she'd known her for years. 'Helloo, helloo,' she chirped, in a heavy Swedish accent. 'I love your Valentino. I almost wore the same thing tonight, I had to tell you, Miss – ?'

'McBride,' Catherine filled in. 'Catherine McBride. Thank you very much.'

The Swedish beauty swung her heavy blonde braid to one side, and Catherine noticed that her earrings were seashells surrounded by diamonds. 'I am Britt de Jimenez.'

Catherine suddenly recognized the woman. She'd been profiled in the complimentary issue of the *Washingtonian* that she'd thumbed through in her room. Britt de Jimenez was one of Washington's great hostesses who crafted jewelry from seashells as a hobby. The Swedish-French former model was currently married to the ambassador from Argentina, who in his picture had looked light years older and a good seven inches shorter than his wife.

'You must meet my friend Mimi Dominguez from Caracas,' said Britt, leading Catherine to a petite redhead with a short-cropped hairdo and skin that looked as if it had never been south of the border.

'Caracas?' said Catherine, eyeing the woman's unfreckled, parchment-white skin. Clearly, South American women knew how to take care of themselves.

Mimi Dominguez slipped her arm through Catherine's.

'What part of Caracas are you from?' asked Catherine.

'All of it! Where are you from?'

'I'm here with Intercon Minerals.'

Both women traded glances. 'Oh,' cooed Britt. 'Then you must know Michael Picol. You work for a very good company. They always send such an eligible bachelor to our dinner parties.' Britt's catlike eyes scanned the room until they landed on Michael Picol. With a feline grace, she maneuvered to the edge of his group and stood at his side.

'Come,' said Mimi Dominguez. 'You must meet my husband.' She led Catherine to the adjoining Green Room, where cocktails were also being served.

'He is the biggest oil producer in the country,' chatted Mimi. A very handsome, thin young man with dark, wavy hair greeted her and Catherine with a smile.

'This young lady is with Intercon,' said Mimi. 'Catherine McBride, this is my husband Jimmy Dominguez.'

'Ah yes. I am due to come see you in Chicago soon. I think it is almost warm enough now.' He flicked an ash from his pencil-thin black cigar into an ashtray held by a passing waiter.

'My husband collects Duncan Phyfe furniture,' said Mimi. 'He loves the mahogany pieces in this room. The sofa and those drop-leaf tables are all Duncan Phyfe. Jimmy always tries to negotiate with the curator for them. He is so silly, my husband! I love him.' She blew him a kiss.

Catherine smiled, but she was wondering what had happened to Graham. For the most part, she noticed as she scanned the crowd of a hundred or so people, the guests had somehow segregated themselves into groups of either men or women. Even Elizabeth Dole and Barbara Walters were with groups of women. Britt de Jimenez was one of the few exceptions.

Catherine finally located Graham standing by the fireplace, reflected in the convex mirror that encapsulated the images of the entire room in miniature.

'Catherine,' he called out, noticing her. He moved over to escort her into his little group, which had by now been abandoned by Britt.

'This is Secretary Woods.' He introduced her to the Secretary of Defense. 'Catherine McBride is in charge of my latest Caribbean project.'

'A pleasure to meet you, sir,' said Catherine, shaking his hand. 'You know, I think you and I come from the same state, Mr Woods.'

'Do we? Are you a Pennsylvanian?'

'Yes.' She wondered what on earth to say to the Secretary of Defense. What was there to talk about? AWACS? Star Wars? 'And the first capital was in Pennsylvania, actually.'

'You're from Philadelphia?'

'No, I was born in the more industrial part. Pittsburgh.'

'Tragic what's happened to the steel industry there.' The Secretary pointed his finger as if teaching a class. 'It's always been my opinion that we should revitalize that steel belt and put in more ordinance factories.'

Graham interrupted. 'Arms,' he explained.

Catherine nodded, but wondered why he was so condescending. She hadn't spent time with Baron de Grunewald without learning an inordinate amount about ordinance factories.

'Well, hello, Graham!' A sandy-haired, very attractive man slung his arm around Graham's shoulders.

Catherine immediately recognized the senator from Kentucky. Recently divorced from a world-famous movie star, he'd been on the cover of *People* magazine, just two weeks ago.

'Congratulations, Jock,' Graham said. 'Catherine, Jock

Hooper here was just made head of the President's Commission on the Caribbean Basin.'

Jock chuckled. 'Oh, well there, I thought you'd be congratulating me on my colt, Kentucky Lady. We're running her in the Derby.'

He turned to Catherine, 'You like horses?'

'Actually, Senator Hooper, I love them if I don't have to sit on them.'

The senator looked at her approvingly. 'You can call me Jock. Ah raise a lot of animals. Which *do* you like?'

'I have a cat. It seems to have been abandoned.' She looked pointedly at Michael Picol, who had repeatedly promised to pick up Midnight, but never quite found the time.

The senator shook his head. 'Always judge somebody by the way they treat their animals. And I'm sure you treat your animals right. You know, I keep a few ostriches – hell of a good animal . . .'

The Marine Strings abruptly broke off the cocktail music and the conversation poised expectantly, waiting, as all eyes turned toward the reception area. Catherine followed Graham, Picol, and Senator 'Jock', and they waited outside the East Room. The band struck up 'Ruffles and Flourishes.'

President Tex Savage with the wife of the Venezuelan president and First Lady Pollyanne Savage on the arm of President Cistero descended the carpeted staircase. The First Lady wore a multicolored gown festooned with beaded parrots – her subtle homage, Catherine supposed, to the wildlife of South America.

'Oscar de la Renta,' murmured Britt, who had reappeared. 'A most suitable choice. Did you know he's from the Dominican Republic? We are friends.' She waved her handkerchief at the First Lady. It was scented.

Catherine was a bit overwhelmed as Graham ushered her to the receiving line. Rex Savage was in his seventies and one of the country's oldest Presidents, yet he had an incredible, magnetic vitality Catherine noticed up close. His heavily tanned face framed by curly gray hair seemed to have the gleam of good health. He took Catherine's hand warmly, as Graham prodded her. She shyly began to introduce herself. 'Mr President . . .'

Rex Savage cut her off. 'So this is your Caribbean consultant, Graham. I understand you're going to protect our interests in the South, Miss McBride.'

'We're going to try,' Catherine said with a smile, shocked that he had actually known who she was.

Catherine moved down the line and shook hands with the Cisteros. Pollyanne Savage stood at the end of the line. She wore no jewelry except for a simple gold wedding band, and the magnificent gown offset her tiny frame. Her handshake was perfunctory. She only nodded at Catherine before turning immediately to Graham.

'How *is* Eve? I'm having the entire dinner box-lunched for you to bring home to her tomorrow. I'm sure that'll cheer her up. I'll even slip in some of the Jefferson china, so you better hold it on your lap the *whole* way home!' She giggled a soft, Foxcroft boarding-school laugh, which Catherine recognized as identical to Eve's.

While Graham and the First Lady whispered cosily together, Catherine wandered off into the East Room, following Michael Picol and Senator Jock.

A dozen round tables flounced with pink Pollyanne Savage roses were scattered across the gleaming parquet floor. The cut-glass of hundreds of crystal chandelier prisms glittered in the candlelight, transforming the cold, stately room into a fairyland of feminine preparations. As she passed the tables set for ten, Catherine noticed that each was set with a different china pattern, giving an individuality and cozy touch to the grandly proportioned space, originally designed by Hobart to serve as a room for large audiences. The First Lady had recently been criticized by the press for her 'casual' use of antique presidential china and her mixture of periods and styles, but Catherine could now see that Pollyanne Savage had created a style all her own that was purely American, and that built on, rather than institutionalized, the past. The floor-length table cloths were alternately hydrangea pink, hyacinth blue, and Pollyanne pink, coordinating with the color of the china on each table. The Pollyanne Savage roses in the centerpieces were loosely arranged around chunks of minerals and rock crystal from which facets of amethyst, aquamarine, or topaz glittered. These were all gifts from the Venezuelan government for the First Lady, which had become part of the White House collection since no President could personally accept a gift worth more than two hundred dollars. Catherine felt dazzled by the splendor, beauty, and sense of history.

Picol walked up, carrying her dinner card.

'We're at the same table, McBride. But we're not seated next to each other. I'm next to your new friend Britt.'

'I thought she was *your* friend.'

He snorted. 'She's a good friend of most of mankind. Before she married Jimenez, she was a thousand-dollar-a-night hooker in Brussels.'

'You know, Michael, I'm learning to believe only one tenth of what you tell me. She looks more like a milkmaid.'

'Well, she's been milked plenty.'

With that, he pulled out the gilt-wood chair with a soft pink velvet cushion and seated her at her place between

Graham Donaldson and Senator Jock, both of whom rose as she sat down.

'It's moving, isn't it,' Graham Donaldson whispered to her. 'It sounds corny, but it *is* the White House. You're part of history when you're here.' He made no pretense at sophistication.

How like Graham, thought Catherine. Wealthy and powerful as he was, he was never jaded or pompous. It was one of the things she admired most about him.

Across the table, Michael slipped into his seat beside Britt de Jimenez with a dazzling smile and a quick glance at her décolleté.

The white-gloved waiters brought the wild mushroom terrine and Catherine found herself relaxing as if she were in someone's home.

The conversation turned to Michael Picol's recent return from Maracaibo, the oil capital of Venezuela, which Britt explained got its name from an ancient Indian tribe whose chief had been named Mara. As Britt haughtily described the native Indian tribe of the Mortilones as somewhat of a tourist attraction, Catherine felt her anger rise. Her days with Brian Thundercloud had left their mark.

Suddenly she broke into the conversation. 'Are any human beings really tourist attractions?' she asked softly, but all heads turned to see who dared to disagree with the wife of the Argentinian ambassador. Britt de Jimenez was known to have sent many an attractive woman who contradicted her squealing to the ladies' room. Senator Jock leaned back as if he wanted to disappear.

Catherine took a quick breath and continued. 'I think we're sitting in a city full of more engaging tourist attractions. Clearly the White House, and even your ostriches, Senator Jock, are tourist attractions.' She laughed as she teased the senator. 'You could probably sell tickets.'

'Well, that's an appetizing idea considering a senator's salary,' he nodded. 'We're the most underpaid men in America.' He glanced uneasily at Britt, still awaiting the poison arrows she was capable of firing off.

Yet Britt de Jimenez appeared to be conducting an in-depth examination of the ornate, geometric plasterwork on the ceiling.

Catherine turned in her direction. 'Flamingo tongues!' she exclaimed.

Everyone froze, wondering if a flamingo tongue was something akin to a motormouth. Was this the prelude to some sort of cat fight in the East Room?

'Those are very rare shells.'

Britt fingered her earrings and smiled, obviously flattered. She had spend hundreds of thousands of the ambassador's dollars in her efforts to become famous for her jewelry instead of her past.

'How clever of you to combine two natural elements – flamingo tongues certainly are the diamonds of the sea,' Catherine continued.

'How clever of *you* to know this, my dear,' she purred. 'I do feel it is an original concept. Very few women collect shells.'

'But almost all collect jewelry,' Catherine observed, lifting her glass in a toast to Britt's ingenuity.

Before Catherine knew it, dessert was being served: cold praline soufflé and fresh raspberries. Graham turned to Catherine.

'If I'm not careful,' he continued, 'I might just lose you to Washington.'

Her face flushed. 'Not likely,' she smiled.

After the toasts had been made, the two presidents and their wives began to dance.

When Senator Jock asked her to dance, Catherine instinctively turned to Graham.

'Do you mind if I whirl around the room with this pretty lady, Graham?' he drawled. 'Between the Senate sessions and getting my horses in shape this month, I think I need to hold a lady in my arms and move to the music.' He pushed Catherine toward the floor. 'Let's hope I remember how.'

After a few minutes, Catherine realized that the senator's good-old-boy antics were simply a cover-up for a very astute man. People in Washington, she was quickly learning, were often not what they appeared to be on the surface.

As the strings played 'Yellow Bird,' Michael Picol politely cut in.

'Do you mind, Senator, if I dance with my associate?'

'She was just startin' to learn my rhythm. But I hope to see you again, Miss McBride.' He turned and ambled off in the direction of the First Lady.

They had barely begun to dance when Picol ushered her off the floor.

'Hate to tear you away from your new beau,' he said, 'but Graham and I think it would be a good idea if you joined us for a few minutes of business.'

A marine guard was waiting for them at the columned entrance of the North Facade. They walked outside in the cool, fresh spring air along a short path that led to the West Gate. There a polite older woman standing in front of two large Secret Service men pleasantly checked their picture ID's once again and clipped a black-and-white plastic tag with a serial number to a chain. 'I'd hate to clip this on that beautiful dress,' she smiled, as she slipped the chain over Catherine's head.

'Nice to see you again, Mr Picol.' She clipped his tag to the pocket of his tuxedo.

They moved past a carpeted area with several desks and through a huge, ornate white door.

The marine guard closed the door behind them. Looking around the room, Catherine thought it reminded her of the former Trophy Room at the Intercon office. In contrast to the rooms of the East Wing, this section was very definitely men's territory. The bulk of the room was taken up by a dark, heavy oak conference table surrounded by oversize brown leather chairs studded with brass buttons. The salmon-colored walls were hung with paintings of men charging down buffalo and several large portraits of Presidents Theodore and Franklin Roosevelt. An enormous Remington bronze of buffalo surrounded by wolves sat imposingly on a massive credenza, just under a portrait of Teddy Roosevelt on a rearing horse.

Michael Picol leaned toward Catherine. 'In case you haven't guessed, this is the Roosevelt Room.'

'What are we here for?' she asked. Graham hadn't mentioned any meeting tonight. A hideous thought occurred to her. Maybe this was, at last, the moment of her presentation. She fleetingly wondered if anyone else had ever given a presentation in a ballgown.

Picol pointed to a door to the right of the fireplace. 'That's the Oval Office. Graham and the President are in there now.'

Just then a tuxedoed man joined them. Michael Picol introduced him as National Security Advisor Hank Mick. A gray-haired woman in a business suit followed him. Clearly, she had not been at the dinner, thought Catherine. The woman nodded perfunctorily and immediately sat in a chair alongside the wall directly in front of six large flagstands. She took a pad from a briefcase and started to write.

A marine lieutenant-colonel carrying a slide projector entered. He positioned the projector on the table and raised a screen at the front of the room.

Michael Picol stifled a yawn. 'Jet lag,' he murmured. 'How's Midnight?'

'Full-grown.'

'You must be feeding him then. Tell me what I owe you for the cat food. I didn't mean to do that to you. I've just been traveling so much, I don't have time to care for any living thing.'

Catherine found herself sympathizing. She knew his schedule *was* difficult. 'That's okay. Midnight and I have a pact.'

'Maybe I should leave you my plants, too.'

The door from the Oval Office suddenly swung open, and in marched the President, Graham, Henry Hudson, and Secretary of Defense Woods. Graham's face exuded confidence. He looked very much in his element.

The President spoke first. 'I know you'd all rather be dancing and enjoying Pollyanne's party. But I thought as long as we were all here we might break for a few minutes and take a quick look at what's happening in the Caribbean.'

He then spoke directly to the national security advisor, a serious man in his early forties, who looked barely out of his twenties. Catherine noticed how slight and pale he appeared, as if all his waking hours were spent under fluorescent lights.

'Oh, hello, Andy. Come on in,' said the President as the undersecretary of state in charge of the Central America Desk quietly took his place at the table.

'Mr President,' he nodded in greeting.

The President continued. 'Since Intercon is now involved in a commercial project in several islands off the coast of Venezuela, we have cleared Graham and his two top aides in this project so that they will have all the pertinent facts. And we're going to give them a full green light. Okay, everybody?'

The President loosened his black satin bow tie. 'Hank, we're going to talk for a few minutes, and then you can go ahead and brief them on the Grenada findings and make sure that their airstrip will be appropriately reinforced to handle our aircraft.'

Catherine sat straight up in her seat, her back not touching the leather. She could hardly believe that after one brief venture into the international world of high politics, she was now sitting in a room next to the Oval Office being briefed by the President of the United States. Not a word or gesture was wasted in this atmosphere, and despite the superficial friendliness, there was an undercurrent of tension and dead earnestness. Catherine glanced around the room. Everyone had a tight-lipped expression, and only Graham Donaldson seemed at ease as he puffed on a Havana cigar. But then, thought Catherine, Graham Donaldson had worked closely with more than one presidential administration. The other men in the room faded as Catherine realized that they held transient positions. When this President was gone, so would they be. But Graham Donaldson was different. He was beyond politics, a force in his own right.

Suddenly the President spoke her name. 'In a minute Catherine McBride here will fill you in on Intercon's plans for an island development. Henry, is that lease worked out?'

'Yes, Mr President. We have a hundred-year lease on

the main island and surrounding water from Venezuela.'

Secretary Woods broke in, 'This and the adjoining island Intercon is picking up gives us a good stronghold on the Caribbean basin off Venezuela.' He turned to the rest of the table. 'It will enable us to keep an eye on virtually everything that happens in the area. And a commercial venture down there will counteract the political activism in the area,' the Secretary continued. 'Henry feels we'll get ultimate protection and sea rights by declaring most of the area a protected US national park.'

The Secretary of Defense rose and pointed to the map. 'It's a logical reason, then, for us to keep naval equipment in this area.' He indicated a wide circle around the Intercon islands.

Catherine flashed a somewhat disturbed look at Michael Picol. Had he known all along that her hard-nourished resort and research center was going to basically be a CIA stronghold? She nervously fingered the two gold bracelets on her wrist and kept trying to read Picol's face, but he wasn't even glancing in her direction.

The President turned to her. 'Miss McBride, Graham said you might be able to enlighten us with an overview on your project.'

Catherine's mouth went totally dry. Her lower lip seemed stuck, frozen. This was it. Her presentation. Good God. Everyone was looking at her.

The President motioned her to stand. 'You might want to use Hank's map.' His eyes were encouraging, as if he were just asking her for her vote. Somehow, he had the ability to put her at ease.

She picked up the folds of her taffeta gown and smoothly walked to the map, her skirt rustling quietly, barely aware of her own actions. She even forgot that her plunging backline was now exposed to some of the most powerful men in the world.

Graham stood up. 'Miss McBride will give us a five-minute summary of Intercon's plans for the island development.' He leaned against the wall and waited for her to begin.

Catherine was buoyed by Graham's confidence in her. All her professional skills converged at that moment as succinctly and knowledgeably, she outlined the plans for A Place in the Sun: the airstrip, the resort, the research facilities, and three international banks.

'I like the banks,' said the Undersecretary of Defense.

'Yes,' said Catherine. 'Our plan does provide a conduit for South American and European capital.'

As the minutes rushed by, Catherine found herself concentrating totally on her presentation. She instinctively captured each person's attention by looking directly at him, while, out of respect, addressing the bulk of her remarks to the President himself.

At the end of her five-minute speech, the President asked a question. 'Graham, what's the emphasis of the underwater national park? Preserving existing marine life, or are you going to actually produce food underwater?'

Graham inclined his head in her direction. 'Catherine? You want to answer that?'

'Mr President, we intend to utilize aquaculture techniques that have been used by the Japanese for decades for food production.'

'Well, that's good for the balance of trade,' quipped the President. 'They've been "borrowing" our industrial technology for the past twenty years. It's about time we borrowed something back.' The tension was broken as the men broke into a polite chuckle. 'Continue, Miss McBride.'

She brushed a strand of hair off her forehead. 'We also hope to expand on their techniques. Our research has shown that we can produce millions of pounds of seafood per every five offshore acres. Our plan is to produce, in partnership with the government, a model to feed a world with diminishing resources. We feel we are in a position to turn the tide of oceanic exploitation.'

An idea occurred to Catherine. 'In light of the Kissinger Commission Report and more recent studies, Intercon also realizes the importance of increasing the opportunity of having American good will in the Caribbean Basin.'

'Well,' smiled the President. 'Then you're one step ahead already. You continue your briefing session, ladies and gentlemen. I'm going to get back to President Cistero. Pollyanne will be looking for me.'

The President, Henry Hudson, and Graham walked back toward the Oval Office. For a minute, as Graham passed her, she thought he was going to put both hands on her shoulders, but of course he did not. Still, she felt the unspoken praise in his eyes. He had to be proud of her. She hadn't stumbled once. In fact, she was quite sure she had won them over.

Catherine settled in for some serious briefing. The marine sergeant turned off the lights and showed them classified papers confiscated during a CIA intelligence raid. He also showed slides of weapons used by Central American rebels that bore Russian and Bulgarian serial marks.

After an hour of briefing, Secretary Woods adjourned the meeting. 'We have to work together on this,' he said. 'Thank you, everyone, for coming.'

As they left the room, Michael walked beside her. 'Not too bad, Catherine,' he murmured. 'What do you say I buy you a drinks at Pisces. Britt will be there, since the party's probably over by now.'

'Thanks, Michael, but why don't you just drop me off at the hotel. I'm pretty tired.' Actually, she had never felt more alive. But somehow she didn't want to come down to earth just yet. She'd had the President's ear tonight, and Graham's admiration, and she didn't feel like ending the evening sharing Picol's attention with the likes of Britt and Mimi.

They rounded a corner to the hall where the cars were waiting.

'Picol!' called a heavily accented voice. A rotund, mustached man approached them.

'Ah, my good friend, Romulo Perez, the ambassador's brother-in-law,' said Picol. 'You've got to come to Pisces. Winnie may stop by.'

'The lovely Winnie!' beamed the man.

'I hear you showed her a wonderful time in Caracas. She's very grateful.'

The man's mustache twitched. He spoke under his breath. 'Oh my God, she never leaves me alone about this film retrospective.' He laughed. 'I suppose I will have to do it!'

As the two men talked, a tall marine marched up to Catherine. 'Miss McBride? Mr Donaldson is waiting for you, if you'll please follow me. I'll take your tag, too, if you'd like.'

She waved goodbye to Picol, who was now engrossed in conversation. He rolled his eyes at her as she left. 'I have a ride,' she called.

# 15

'Well, Catherine,' smiled Graham as they settled back into the plush seats of the limousine. 'You've really had the insider's tour of Washington.'

'I guess *so*,' she laughed.

'You've won the respect of the President of the United States and compliments from the First Lady. Not bad for your first trip to the capital.'

Catherine was feeling giddily exuberant. The wine, the dancing at the White House, meeting with the President and making a presentation to him had her heart still racing. She tried to fold her hands calmly and hide her real feelings. What she really wanted to do was throw her arms around Graham's neck and scream, 'We've done it! We won! We are a *great* team!' Laying her head back on the neck rest, she smiled in the darkness to herself.

'How long have you known the President?'

'Almost thirty years. We've gone salmon fishing in Canada or Alaska almost every year since Eve and Pollyanne first got us together. Rex never was much of a fisherman, but he sure is one hell of a politician.'

'I think you would've made a great statesman.' Her flattery was sincere. 'Haven't you ever thought of running for office?'

'Catherine, I've been offered everything from secretary of the treasury to a run at the governor's seat. Rex wanted me to be Ambassador to the Court of Saint James, but I made my decision a long time ago.'

'What?' she whispered in order not to break the mood of his first real confidence to her.

'The work we're doing with the research could accomplish more than any five Presidents put together. When you're in public office you have to play games that waste time. I don't have to answer to anyone and that suits me fine.'

'But an ambassadorship . . . that's such a prestigious post,' she said.

'Right now, there are things that are a lot more important to me.' He looked uncomfortable with the subject.

'Toasts are in order,' announced Graham, changing the topic. 'I'm sure we have a bottle of champagne in here. These Ritz-Carlton cars usually have everything but a sunken tub.'

They touched the rims of their crystal glasses. 'To future projects with a very impressive lady,' Graham said.

Catherine had soon finished the entire glass. It felt good to finally relax. She held out her glass for a refill.

'To my next presentation,' she said as Graham poured. 'Which you will probably have me give on a space shuttle.'

'Well, that's the way it goes sometimes.' He was starting to relax himself. 'I knew you could handle it.'

'I'm glad you have such great confidence in me.' She couldn't hold back her grin.

'You've earned it.'

She laughed. 'For all you know, I could have been totally blitzed from all that California wine. What if I'd blown it?'

'Catherine, I know better than you at this point what you can handle.' And this time he did put his hand on her shoulder.

She stared at him, but he settled back into the shadows

of the car where she couldn't read his expression.

They drove past the Washington Monument, brightly lit from below, glitteringly reflected in a long, rectangular pool, and she gaped like any tourist. 'I still haven't seen the Washington Monument, Graham. Look! Isn't it beautiful?' She looked at him with pleading eyes. 'Let's pull over. Please?'

He glanced at his watch.

'Oh please, Graham!'

He chuckled. 'Whatever you want tonight. I thought you'd have seen all that. Doesn't everybody have a school trip to Washington in the sixth grade?'

'I was in the dry-cleaning business in the sixth grade.' She looked crestfallen.

Graham instructed the driver to pull over as he thought, it *was* still early. Just past midnight, in fact. And, now that he thought about it, he'd never seen the Washington Monument up close, either. He hadn't ever made that sixth-grade trip himself. Money didn't come easy in South Bend, Indiana. Especially for the family of a laid-off engineer at the Studebaker plant.

The champagne added to Graham's own pleasure at the success of his private conversation with Rex Savage. The deal was in the bag – Picol and Catherine only had to work out the details. He leaned forward. 'Driver, how well do you know Washington?'

'Very good, sir. I been here ten, maybe eleven years.'

'How about a little late-night tour then? We'll start here.'

The driver swung the car into the parking lot at the foot of the reflecting pool, and Graham helped Catherine out of the car. She picked up the heavy silk of the Valentino skirt, her bare back visible in the moonlight as they crossed the grass to the edge of the pool.

She perched on the edge of the rim and ran her fingers through the water.

She reached up and pulled out the two barrettes that held her hair up, shaking it down over her shoulders, turning her head slowly back and forth. Graham noticed the shininess of her hair against her neck.

'I was very proud of you tonight, Catherine,' he said.

Catherine couldn't believe that Graham Donaldson, the man she would give anything to please, was giving her an undisguised compliment.

'You made a very good impression tonight.'

They sat quietly for a few minutes, each lost in memories of the last few hours. Finally Graham helped her up, and she took his arm as they walked back to the car.

They stopped briefly under a cherry tree. A carpet of fallen blossoms covered the grass.

'I've relished watching you tonight as you turned a meaningless dot on a map into a US government-protected national park *and* incorporated it into national policy between the soup and the salad.'

'You don't miss much, do you?' Graham quipped.

'I am becoming an expert in the observation of the winning technique of Graham Donaldson.'

'How is that?'

'I was watching your mood. And I know when you're winning, because you look different.'

He couldn't help grinning. 'Henry Hudson will be flying down to the islands with us tomorrow morning. He wants to give the project his personal stamp of approval.'

'I expected as much,' Catherine replied.

Graham had never before found anyone who understood exactly what he wanted, who could read his moods, as easily and as correctly as this young woman. Not even Eve. In a short time, she had become an integral part of his life. He had known she would be able to answer the President's questions because they were beginning to think alike. Did she know that he suddenly felt like running his hand along her naked back and curling her hair around his fingers?

She stopped in her tracks and looked straight at him. 'We're alike, we really are.' She half closed her eyes. She was feeling light-headed.

He almost found himself reaching for her. 'We'd better be going.' They returned to the car and moved into the back seat, this time leaving less space between them.

Catherine pulled down the jump seat, hiked her dress to her knees, and propped her feet up as Graham poured them each a glass of champagne from the car bar.

'On to the Lincoln Memorial,' directed Graham.

The solitary white marble figure of Abraham Lincoln sat at the top of a flight of stairs, bathed in bright light.

'These stairs are *not* made for three-inch heels,' said Catherine, slipping off her shoes. She ran ahead of Graham up the steps. 'How fast can you recite the Gettysburg Address? Bet I can do it faster.'

Together they recited, 'Fourscore and seven years ago, our forefathers . . .' They rattled off the entire speech in unison before, laughing, they plopped down at the base of the colossal statue of Abraham Lincoln and Catherine's head fell onto Graham's shoulder. He gently, tentatively touched her face.

She turned and nuzzled her cheek into his hand. She had known he would feel like this. Somehow, she knew how every part of him would feel. He was made for her, couldn't he see? She closed her eyes and savored the thought, suddenly realizing that all those late nights and extra efforts were not just for herself and her career, but to earn his approval and his affection.

She moved both her arms around his neck and pulled him tightly to her, his face hard into hers, kissing him greedily, and for an instant he returned her kiss. For a few long seconds, she felt his reluctant body soften and give in to her.

He put both hands on her shoulders and firmly shook her loose, pushing her back until she was at arm's length. 'We're going back to the hotel now, Catherine.' His voice was husky. 'I think we've had enough sightseeing for one night.'

She searched his face. His expression seemed almost sad, but resigned. He quickly stood up and hurried down the stairs, leaving Catherine to gather up her shoes and follow him.

They rode wordlessly all the way back to the Ritz-Carlton.

Catherine bit her lip. Had she ruined everything, she wondered? What was happening? Had she been overwhelmed by the day? Her feelings for this man? The star-studded evening, the cherry blossoms, the champagne – had it all gone to her head? She had given him a long, passionate kiss that had shown him all of her emotions. But hadn't she felt him respond? He wanted her, she could tell.

She realized she was truly in love with him. She wanted to merge her very self with Graham Donaldson. He was the culmination of all her dreams and desires, and without him she knew she would only be half of what they could be together.

They walked into the small lobby of the Ritz-Carlton, each still afraid to speak. Graham was the first to break the silence. 'Are there any messages for me?' he asked at the desk. The clerk handed him an envelope with the hotel's crest and several pink slips. There was nothing for her. He unfolded the small piece of paper from the envelope and stared directly at Catherine.

'It's from Eve,' he said pointedly. 'If there's any more you think we need to discuss before tomorrow's meeting, we could have a quick drink here at the Jockey Club. But first I have to call home.'

His tone was unmistakably distant and annoyingly paternal. Catherine shook her head sadly, her throat tightening. This was reality. The Eves of the world had already laid claim to the Graham Donaldsons, and that left Catherine McBride clearly out of the picture. Graham was only placating her now.

'Well, it's getting late.' Graham wouldn't look at her. They both stared straight ahead as they rode up the elevator to the sixth floor.

Catherine slipped into her room and Graham passed on to his suite next door without a word.

Well, that's that, Catherine thought. She lay flat on her back on the king-size Colonial bed and stared blankly at the English horse prints matted in hunter's green hanging on the wall over the dresser. She kicked off her shoes and folded one arm under her neck. Her fingers drummed nervously on the bedspread and her eyes refocused on the brass chandelier.

She thought of the week ahead and sprang off the bed, yanking the Valentino off and kicking the dress into the corner as if it were responsible for her rejection. She brushed her teeth for a full six minutes, staring into the mirror at herself.

'Catherine.' She pointed at the mirror. 'You are a first-class fool. What makes Miss Dry Cleaners think one of the world's most powerful men would be attracted to the likes of you? Just because you were wearing a four-thousand-dollar dress doesn't make you a four-thousand-dollar woman!' Tears welled up in her eyes. What was the *matter* with her?

Maybe she should take a few lessons from Eve. Eve might not be able to give a presentation to the President of the United States, but she was elegant and refined and understood Rothko paintings, masterpieces that Catherine could only classify as muddy blobs. She couldn't see any beauty in those paintings.

Catherine understood balance sheets and budgets. She knew what it took to make A Place in the Sun financially feasible.

That was why Graham had hired her. No matter how many presentations she made or proposals she drew up, she was just an employee; his assistant. Since she'd taken that relationship one step too far, the consequences were not going to be pleasant. If Graham felt too uncomfortable, he could easily neutralize her position. She could spend the rest of her days at Intercon doing Mickey Mouse work, away from the real power, away from *him*, until the discomfort of the situation, or Ray Acconti, finally forced her out.

She turned off the faucet and went back into the bedroom. She flicked off the lights and waited for her eyes to adjust to the dark. On the other side of the wall was Graham Donaldson. She stood, naked, wondering if his bed was placed exactly against the wall next to hers. She moved her fingers across the white wood molding. There was such a thin wall separating the two of them.

She tried to tell herself it had been just a kiss. Michael Picol had kissed her, hadn't he? And he'd forgotten all about it.

She stared at the door that separated her room from Graham's suite. There was an overstuffed armchair in front of it.

She moved the chair as impulse, and instinct, took over. She unlocked the door, then turned on a bare heel. She slipped between the silky sheets which felt cool on her bare skin. She lay still, and listened.

For a few minutes, all Catherine heard was the ticking of the bedside clock and the sounds of the street below.

Then, suddenly, she heard a click. Was the door on the other side being unlocked? Would he come in, or was he just reaffirming that his side was secured, punctuating his rejection of her? She could hear her heart beat and felt as if no oxygen was getting to her head.

She heard her door creak. Catherine kept her eyes closed tightly until she was absolutely sure. When she opened them, Graham Donaldson was standing beside the bed, looking down at her, his gray hair lit from behind by the street lights. She couldn't make out his expression. Was it judgmental, inquiring, seductive? It didn't matter to her. She willed him closer and pulled the sheets down to her thighs, exposing the white skin of her firm breasts and gracefully tapered waist. Her soft thighs, lightly scented with baby oil, glistened. She saw Graham's gaze linger on every curve of her supple body, and in that moment she knew he wanted her.

She closed her eyes again thinking this could only be a dream, but then she heard the studs from his formal shirt dropping on the bedside table. The zipper of his tuxedo trousers came undone, and when Catherine again opened her eyes, Graham, too, was naked. She stared at his tanned body. It was as taut and as firm as that of a man half his age. The muscles in his chest heaved as he breathed deeply. Even naked, standing shadowed in the dim light, he exuded power and vitality. She watched him kneel in front of her on the bed and she sensed the restraint he exuded in that moment.

Her heart beat wildly, but she forced herself to lie as still as possible, waiting to see what he would do. She watched him pull the sheets down to her ankles, and the silky material trailing across her warm body made her yearn for his touch. Their eyes locked. Each hesitated, not knowing who should make the next move. Then Graham bent over her, lifting her from the waist, his lips gently moving across her entire face. Her arms entwined themselves around his neck as she pressed herself against him, eagerly returning each kiss. A shudder swept through her and she arched her back, trying to fit both their bodies together. Graham gently let her lie back on the sheets, the length of his body covering Catherine's. Again he kissed her lips, then her chin, and slowly he traced a moist path down her throat until his mouth rested on her shoulder. His hand caressed the back of her neck, his fingers gently rubbing the flesh in a circular, stimulating motion before moving to cup one soft breast. He stroked and then moved his head to her other breast. Catherine curled her fingers in his hair as she drew him nearer. Her legs wound themselves around his hips, moving beneath him, relishing his hardness against her.

As she ran her palm down his back and guided him onto his side, Catherine slowly kissed his chest; inhaling the musky, male scent of him. Her lips lightly flicked down his belly. When she boldly opened her mouth to receive him, Graham was unable to hold back. She sucked him until her own need was too great, and she lifted her head.

They faced one another on the bed. Once again Graham gently took Catherine's face in his hands, bringing her toward him as he whispered her name. They kissed and fell together onto the bed. Catherine now held herself just slightly above Graham, her breasts lightly grazing his chest as she moved over him. Opening her legs, she guided him into her for one long moment before slipping away and onto her side.

As they lay entwined, Catherine could hardly believe what was happening. Graham Donaldson, the man she worshiped, was running his hands over her body, pressing his hardened thighs against her own, stroking her hips, her legs, moving rapidly, his fingers entering her, playing with her until she cried out. She matched each touch, each kiss, each stroke with one of her own, reaching out for him, calling his name, guiding his hands. She wanted him everywhere at once.

For two more hours, during which Catherine felt herself spiral toward feelings she couldn't control and had no desire to, she responded to his every unspoken demand, turning and twisting as if caught in some furious dance. Their wants were equal and they glided together till the first trickle of sunlight started to shine through the windows. Graham Donaldson lay beside Catherine, quiet now, but still inside her, still hers. He gently cradled her in his arms, and Catherine knew a peace she had never before experienced.

He began to talk in the gentle tone of a lover, and Catherine felt that they had been moving toward this night since the moment they met. She listened apprehensively as he told her that their lovemaking had been incredible for him. She winced when he said in his most soothing voice, still husky with sex, 'happily married man.'

'I'm not a man driven by passion, Catherine. My emotions don't rule me. I make all my decisions with head. But tonight, I guess I wanted you more than even I could know.' He looked pale and shaken as if he had lost control and was unnerved by it. This leader of men, always so sure of himself, was now apologizing for touching her, yet one hand played with her hair.

He respected her, he told her. He was very fond of her. She was too important to him at work and as a friend to lose her after one reckless night. He had a home. A wife. A family. Eve needed him. Did she understand? They would have to forget tonight had ever happened. Okay? Okay.

Then he took her in his arms one last time and more gently than before they made love, surprising themselves with the intensity of their ardor. Then they fell into an exhausted sleep.

When the phone rang, it was still barely dawn. The third ring awakened her, and she noticed the empty place beside her.

'Morning, Catherine. I'm having coffee downstairs. Are you almost ready?' It was Michael Picol calling from the lobby.

'Ready?' Catherine propped herself up on her elbows in bed. Graham was gone. She nervously glanced at the door between their rooms. His was closed.

'Catherine,' Picol's voice persisted. 'If we want to get to Dulles on time we'll have to leave in twenty minutes, okay?'

'Okay.' Her voice was so soft she barely heard herself as she ran her hand across the musky sheets. She hung up the phone and glanced around the room. How could it look the same as it had yesterday morning? she wondered.

Then she rocketed herself out of bed, into the shower, her clothes, the elevator, and twenty-five minutes later, the limousine. For once she had kept Picol waiting.

She sat silently on the way to the airport while Michael Picol slumped in the seat beside her, napping, his feet propped up on the jump seat. She dabbed on a touch of lipstick and ran a comb through her hair, which was still damp from the shower.

*He respected her. He had a home. A wife. Eve needed him. Did she understand?*

Catherine's heart ached as she remembered last night. Yes, she understood. 'He'll be back,' she whispered to herself. 'I'll get him back.' Then she said it again, as if saying it would make it come true.

mopped up in the pump wear. She dashed on a touch of lipstick and ran a comb through her hair, which was still damp from the shower.

[illegible]

[illegible]

Catherine's heart ached as she remembered last night. Yet, she understood. 'He'll be back,' she whispered to herself. 'I'll get him back.' Yet she said it again, as if saying it would make it come true.

# PART TWO
# Girls in High Places

# 1

*We're crashing into the ocean!* Catherine was frantic as she realized she could be dead at any minute without having spoken or touched Graham one more time. She coughed and choked on the thick black smoke that poured through the cabin, her eyes searing as she blinked to clear them and find him. Tears streamed down her face; she knew she was losing him as the Intercon G-III careened toward the Caribbean. If they were going to die there was no need for formalities. She must get to him even though the smoke was so thick she could barely see across the aisle. She struggled with her seat belt in a desperate effort to free herself. It wouldn't unfasten.

Then the plane vibrated and pitched at such a wild angle that Catherine suddenly felt her spine pinned to the back of the seat. Her shoes flew off her feet and careened across the carpet. Her stomach dropped as if she were diving off the top of the world's tallest roller coaster. It was no use. Even if she tried, she couldn't possibly get to Graham.

'Puerto Rico Air Center. Gulfstream-three N-two thousand declaring an emergency.' The pilot, riveted to the controls, was oblivious to the mayhem in the passenger cabin.

The two stewards lay semiconscious, strapped in their seats, one bleeding from an ugly gash on his forehead. Orchids and broken china lay like flotsam in the aisle. Catherine and the others were following Graham Donaldson's lead, pulling on life jackets, and tucking their heads between their knees.

'We're one hundred twenty-five DME from you, Puerto Rico Center.' The copilot barked their position into the radio. 'G-three N-two thousand on the three hundred forty-degree radial at eight thousand feet. Descending rapidly and unable to hold altitude.'

Catherine's head was pounding, but she managed to check the location of the emergency exit. Out the window, she noticed a large body of land looming up ahead. She gritted her teeth, hoping they wouldn't go down too far from the shore. Her ears pierced with pain from the loss of pressurization. She doubted any of them would survive a crash at such a breakneck rate of descent. And if they lived through the crash, there was still the water. This was the Caribbean. There would be sharks.

In the cabin, the copilot barked into the radio as the pilot struggled with the controls. 'We've slowed down to VMC. We're still losing altitude, Puerto Rico. Please alert Coast Guard to pick up survivors. We have the Secretary of the Interior aboard. Alert appropriate personnel.'

The plane was diving more sharply now.

Who would take care of her mother? Catherine panicked. She had no will, no trust fund. She had a company insurance policy, but there was no one in her life who could execute it. Ironically, the only person who could possibly care whether she lived or died was in this plane. At twenty-seven, death had been the last thing on Catherine McBride's mind.

Dr Ray Acconti was out of his seat and shoving his way frantically back down the aisle from the cockpit, stumbling over the inflated orange raft, screaming. 'This is it! I just heard them – Mayday, the engine's out. Both of them! We're going down! Get ready to crash. Oh my God!'

'Asshole,' muttered Michael Picol. He bolted from his seat, pushing Acconti aside, and slipped into the cockpit.

She tried to unfasten her seat belt once more. It was jammed.

Moments later, the plane suddenly lurched to a forty-five degree angle and suitcases, boxes, briefcases, and blankets tumbled from the overhead bins. Catherine felt a jolt as something bounced off her back. Minutes moved like hours and then, somehow, the plane unsteadily rocked out of its dive. She lifted her head. The scenery outside the window was a nauseating swirl. Catherine gasped as the line that separated the horizon and ocean met for one frantic moment. Then there was a headlong, swerving montage of rushing green grass and ocean and black caddies and figures in brightly colored shorts scrambling for cover as Michael Picol set the plane down on the fifteenth fairway of the El Dorado Beach and Golf Club in Puerto Rico.

Hours later it was easier for Catherine to joke about the crash landing than tell B.J. what she really felt. 'Medical treatment?' She laughed into the phone in the VIP lounge at the Cerromar Airport. 'So far it's consisted of piña coladas and Ace bandages.' She didn't tell B.J. that the companion plane had exploded. From the security of the couch in the Puerto Rican airport, she assured B.J. that there was no need to panic.

'I think those golfers are in much worse shape that we are. When we barreled down the fairway, we scared the alligators right off their shirts!'

She stole a look at Graham across the room, wearing an arm sling and busily conferring with an FBI agent, several air force officers, and the governor of Puerto Rico. Michael Picol sat impatiently in the center of the group. A medical attendant was checking Henry Hudson's pulse, deeply concerned for the Secretary since he had only recently undergone bypass surgery.

Catherine hung up the phone and caught Picol's gaze as he rose from his chair and ambled across the lounge to her side. It was amazing, she thought, that he could look like a walking Ralph Lauren ad after a crash landing.

'I can't answer any more questions now,' he said, slumping onto the couch beside her.

'You could probably fly a cereal box, couldn't you, Michael?' She smiled, hoping he wouldn't see how nervous she was.

'To tell the truth, I was scared shitless.'

Picol stood up. 'I've got to get out of here. If anyone wants me, I'll be back in twenty minutes.' He turned toward the security exit, and Catherine noticed that the entire back of his jacket was soaked with sweat.

'Michael,' she called out. But he was already gone.

A pack of multilingual press was camped out in a small, hot waiting room. Straightening his tie and obviously ready to enjoy the limelight, Dr Ray Acconti strode briskly into their midst.

'Gentlemen,' he announced, 'I will give you a statement.' As the reporters angled for positions, Acconti read from a memo pad. 'Today, two Intercontinental corporate planes were damaged in midair for as yet unknown causes. The cargo plane carrying no passengers blew up, killing both pilots. The second plane sustained heavy damage, but was landed safely by a senior officer of the company, Mr Michael Picol. Graham Donaldson, chief executive officer of Intercon, Secretary of the Interior Henry

Hudson, and other passengers are all safe but grieved by the deaths of the two pilots.'

'Who planted the bombs?'

'Who was responsible?' The media hurled questions in Spanish and English.

Acconti shook his head. 'A full investigation is underway, gentlemen, and there will be no further statements at this time.' He strode back into the lounge, where two military men efficiently blocked the door behind him, shutting out the noisy mob of reporters.

As he passed, Acconti patted Catherine's shoulder sympathetically. 'Tough break for you, too, little lady. All that work gone up in flames. You look a little queasy. Why don't you go lie down? Everything's under control here, hon.'

Catherine grimaced. The man was a master of power games, poor taste, and obscene timing. She had duplicates of all her presentations, including a second full-scale model of the entire projected island development back in the office. Only a fool would neglect such a precaution.

'I feel fine,' she shot back. She stood up and snapped shut her briefcase. 'Too bad you didn't get to use your little inflatable boat,' she started to say, but didn't. She had more important things on her mind. She smiled confidently at Graham, hoping he could see what she was made of; how she hadn't lost control. Thank God her seat belt had jammed. 'Are you all right?' he shouted across the room.

'Yes, yes. I'm fine,' she lied.

She started toward the press conference at the end of the lounge. Come on, Catherine, she told herself. You've made it this far. Show them all what you're made of.

Suddenly the numbness left her body and all the pain, excitement, and horror of the day came rushing upon her.

Her mouth throbbed where she had hit her face on her knee. And as she ran her tongue across her teeth, she felt the jagged edge of a chipped tooth.

'You look like you could use this.' Billy Wright wrapped an ice cube in his handkerchief.

'Thanks.'

'So are you going to put a quarter under your pillow and hope that the tooth fairy comes by, or are you going to let somebody take a look at that?'

Her lip was starting to swell. She didn't even have a dentist in Chicago. She never thought of illness except in reference to her mother.

Billy held the ice cube up and pressed it gently against her face.

'It was a miracle we survived,' she said. 'Thank God for Michael Picol.'

'Yeah. For a flashy guy, he gave us a flashy landing.' She could tell by his tone of voice that Billy didn't like Picol at all. But Picol didn't thrive on friendship, but on control. If nothing else, he had earned the respect of everyone on the plane today.

Now that they were safe on the ground, all the rules were suddenly in place again. Who was in power at the moment was once more important, and the pecking order was reestablished. Even Ray Acconti, who had come totally unglued on the plane, reasserted his authority as he dealt with the press. Catherine felt as if no one recognized that they had just veered within inches of the brink of death; that none of these power plays mattered.

It was never more clear to Catherine that smooth surfaces were a farce. Now she didn't regret at all what had happened last night between Graham and herself.

She watched him across the room. He was looking at her, too.

Maybe, just maybe, both of their lives would change.

# 2

'Maybe I should get up,' thought Eve Donaldson, as she lay listlessly in her Porthault-linened bed, the semidarkness of her enormous bedroom lulling her into near-numbness. She stared out the sheer silk-curtained windows that overlooked her gardens and outdoor statuary. Beneath the coronet-shaped ornament that held up the heavy silks in shades of celadon and salmon, her new, fragile frame seemed rather insignificant beneath the mountainous backdrop of fabric. She pulled up the hem of her Lucie Anne nightgown and stared down again in horror at the six-inch scarlet gash that bisected her creamy white stomach.

It had all been for nothing. All those years, when she'd fought to have more children after Drucilla's birth, only to have a series of miscarriages and D and C's. All the waiting, all the heartbreak. She was a woman who loved children, who had wanted a big family. She and Graham had planned on at least four children. How disappointed he must have been in her, and how thoughtful to have never let her know.

Of course, Bambi and Hughie were like her own children. Hadn't she cherished them all the more because she couldn't have more of her own? Hadn't she made sure that when Graham sold off the Stuart estate there was enough money to put into a trust to keep the children secure and independent, so Hughie could grow up with his pride intact? Hadn't she kept them just close enough, in The Cottage, so she could keep an eye on them, giving in to Hughie's demand for independence even when Graham had insisted it was ridiculous? It was the one, the only, time Eve had defied Graham.

Of course, she had Drucilla, and Eve adored her only daughter. She'd given her every advantage, and indulged her whim to skip college and pursue gourmet cooking. Eve didn't consider that spoiling a child; it was nurturing her talent.

Still, with her womb intact, Eve had always felt that there was always a slight chance of having another baby if Graham really wanted to.

She knew that at her age she was probably being irrational. Yet she definitely felt that a part of her womanhood was gone – was she no longer a woman?

She ran her smooth hands down the ugly scar over her now-barren belly. A plastic surgeon had been called in to close the incision, but it looked as if it were beginning to keloid. Her hands began to shake. How long would it be before she would look pretty again? How long would it be before Graham would want her again? It had only been three days since he had left on important business for Washington, but suddenly she needed him more than ever. Was it a hormone imbalance, the sudden shock to her system, the hysterectomy itself – why was she feeling so cast-off and useless? She started to sob quietly.

'Now, now, what are we up to?' Thirty lights in the Venetian glass chandelier snapped on as Nurse Grupp bustled into the room, carrying a mug of hot ginger ale with a striped straw. Eve quickly smoothed her nightgown over her painful incision and slowly, tentatively, pulled herself up on the dozen or so pillows plumped up behind her. They must have cut every muscle in her stomach, she thought. The pain was unendurable every time she moved or took a breath. 'Isn't it time for my Demerol now?' she asked.

Miss Grupp gave her one of those seasoned nurse-patient looks that implied that all of this lady's pain must be psychological.

'Take some of this nice warm ginger ale, Mrs Donaldson, and I'll give you a nice back rub. And that will make us feel a lot better, won't it?'

Eve was convinced that nothing could make her feel better. But the bed would be so much more comfortable if Graham were quietly reading there beside her.

The insistent ringing of her private telephone line brought her slowly out of her languor. She opened the silver box on her bedside table that held her unlisted phone.

The cheery voice of Pollyanne Savage immediately made her smile in spite of her pain. Even when she was eight hundred miles away, Pollyanne somehow always knew just when to call.

Eve waited until the intrusive figure of Nurse Grupp had left the room before she confided in her oldest friend.

'I've never been depressed before, Pollyanne, ever. You know that. I know it's so silly – but I feel a part of my womanhood is gone. Of course it's foolish, irrational. I just feel like this is it, it's over. I'll never be able to bear another child. I don't even feel like a woman anymore.' She blurted everything out to Pollyanne. They had never had any secrets.

'Oh, Evie,' Pollyanne chided, but her voice was warm. 'If there's *anything* Graham wants it's another company, not another child. And, my dear Evie, you have already given him the company, if you recall. *And* a darling daughter. Now let's get into the important stuff. How much estrogen and calcium are you taking?'

Eve dutifully reeled off the prescribed doses. She sniffed back her tears.

'You're definitely taking the right amount of estrogen, but be sure to take gobs of Tums. It's loaded with calcium.'

A bemused look almost crossed Eve's face. When had Pollyanne become so interested in medicine?

'Darling,' Pollyanne continued. 'I know the pain is utterly awful but just remember – I'm sure it's on one of your pillows – "this too shall pass."'

Eve smiled genuinely for the first time since she had been wheeled into the stainless steel operating room of Rush-Presbyterian Saint Luke's Medical Center.

'The hysteria is natural, dear. It goes with the operation. Just give in to it. Throw something. Have a good primal scream.'

'I'm just feeling so lost and empty. Graham's been a lamb and adoring, but I've never felt less of a woman in my life.'

'Oh, Evie,' the First Lady was genuinely sympathetic. 'I never told you, but after my hysterectomy, I had a mini-depresh myself.'

'Really?' Eve was startled.

'Oh, I was a horror,' Pollyanne chuckled. 'I sat around for weeks in Rex's silk bathrobe – the one that said 'The Vice-President' on it – you know, it was during Buckley's presidency, and I watched soap operas and cried real tears every time anyone on one of those programs got pregnant, raped, had an abortion, got a brain tumor, or even had a bad day. Rex was convinced I was deranged and that maybe he shouldn't run for President with a perpetual tear duct standing by his side. But I got over it.'

The First Lady changed the subject to more pleasant events. 'Now, darling, I was *so* upset that you missed our little party last night. But let's look on the bright side. It's only six weeks till the dinner for the President of Egypt. I want you and Graham to come, and when it's over we can run down to Camp David for the weekend for a little girl talk. I want you to start thinking about it now so you'll be there in your best spirits and looking wonderful.'

Eve forced some enthusiasm into her voice. 'I can't wait, darling.' She picked at the ecru lace at the border of her pink pillow sham and half laughed. 'But God knows how I'll look. Anesthesia takes everything out of you that the surgeons didn't.'

'Well, I know the prescription for *that*,' gurgled Pollyanne. 'Secret, secret, just like in school?' she resurrected their boarding school vow of blood silence.

'Secret, secret,' promised Eve, 'just like in school.'

'Well, have you noticed,' the First Lady whispered, 'how in my pictures I am looking particularly fresh of face?'

'You had a face-lift?' asked Eve incredulously. She perked up.

'Nooooo, Evie. Remember when Senator Whiting was married to Lily Basset?'

'Broadway's leading lady.' Of course Eve remembered. Everyone did. Lily Basset had been in the news ever since she made her debut as the original Eliza in *My Fair Lady*.

'Well, do you know,' said the First Lady, 'that she's a good twelve years older than we are?'

'Impossible.'

'No, Evie, that's why Rex had to pull out his judge's robe and perform the marriage. We were the only ones allowed to see dear Lily's birth certificate.'

'No!'

'I mean, you wouldn't expect a President of the United

States to turn out to be a stringer for the *National Enquirer*, for heaven's sake.'

Eve started to laugh, but it hurt too much. 'There's a woman with a real secret secret.'

'But wait, one day after too many mint juleps she gave me her all-time beauty secret – are you ready?'

'Go ahead,' urged Eve. She took a sip of the ginger ale.

'Sperm.'

'*Sperm?* Whose sperm?' asked Eve, almost choking on the ginger ale.

'Yes, sperm, and it doesn't matter whose. She told me she applied fresh sperm to her face several times a week – like a masque – then let it seep into the pores. She swears by it. And her skin is as soft as a baby's bottom.'

'Are you trying to tell me – ' Eve was simultaneously blushing and dying to know more.

'Yes . . . but it can only be fresh – not more than two hours old – it loses something, I don't know what.'

'Wouldn't a face-lift be easier?'

'No, no,' said Pollyanne with authority. 'I'm trying to tell you I use the '"Lily Basset Balm".'

'You can buy it?' Eve was stupefied.

'No, it's got to be straight from the source and applied directly to a clean face.'

'If you're telling me you're using presidential sperm on your face . . .'

'Well, Evie, I'm not using vice-presidential materials. As I said – *straight from the source*. Why don't you try it when your darling comes back tonight? I sent him off with a doggie bag for you.'

Eve giggled, holding her stomach.

'But for God's sake, don't let them put the friggin' china in the dishwasher. And be sure to bring it back. *Wait* till you see what it is.'

'Pollyanne, you never change.'

'Neither does that dynamic man you're married to. He was *so* worried about you last night. Why he didn't dance once, it was all business, business, business.'

'I hope he wasn't a bore.' Graham was always lost without her. 'You know how he hates big functions. He told me he probably wouldn't go. I'm surprised you got him to show up.'

'Well, I did have to make room for that little girl who works for him. She chaperoned.'

'Little girl?'

'Senator Jock was quite taken with her. I think he took her number and everything. You know, she works for Intercon. She's in on that island business.'

It had to be Catherine McBride. At the White House? What was Graham thinking?

Pollyanne gurgled on. 'I understand she made a little presentation after dinner. Graham always gets the smartest people. I wish you could get him to join Rex's administration. Personally I feel Hudson is an embarrassment to Rex. Graham would be so much better in assuring Rex a good solid place in history, or Chief of Staff . . .' She droned on to deaf ears.

Eve felt suddenly weak again. Her muscles were tensed and pain washed over her. She knew Catherine McBride was harmless.

Graham had always been so devoted . . . except for that one, that *only* time. Graham had never suspected that she had known, because that was how she wanted it. A smart woman never acknowledged her husband's indiscretion. The surface had to remain smooth. He had never realized that she knew exactly what was going on in Tehran, or that he had told her everything when he, who never gave her frivolous gifts, arrived one day with pink and canary diamond earrings, too expensive, too valuable, and too ostentatious for Lake Forest. Something only Farah Diba, Empress of the Shah, would wear. She had accepted the telltale earrings with grace and feigned delight. Then she had put them away in the farthest reaches of her safety deposit box, never to be seen again. But she was foolish to even remember that. That had been long ago, when months had separated them and her devotion to their small daughter had kept them apart. She had never let distance come between them again. And she knew instinctively that he had never been unfaithful since.

Pollyanne's voice reached her ear. 'You know, Evie, I wouldn't feel too low too long. Not when there are assistants running around in backless dresses. Not to worry, you still drive Graham wild – but it's just never a good idea. Now hurry up and get well 'cause I'm going to put you on President Fabar's right. You're still the most beautiful roommate I ever had.'

No sooner had Eve put the phone back in its silver box than Cherie burst excitedly into the room. 'Oh, madam, a box for you. Max just dropped it off downstairs. It's from Mr Donaldson.'

Eve reached out eagerly for the heavy manila envelope. This must be Pollyanne's doggie bag. She opened it, smiling, and pulled out a large, flat black leather case with a monogram she recognized instantly. Harry Winston – written in gold across the top. She opened it and recoiled. Between the layers of velvet lay the most beautiful and romantic piece of jewelry she had ever seen. Seven heartshaped, multifaceted sapphires, sat in circles of pavé yellow diamonds evenly spaced in a three-tiered diamond necklace, shimmered extravagantly. It was obvious every stone was class A. The card read, 'To my Dear Heart.

You are always in my thoughts. Love, Graham.'

Eve did not touch the necklace, but Cherie, wild with excitement, threw up her arms. 'Madam! Look! Sapphires cut as hearts! I have never seen anything as beautiful. He must love you *so* much.'

This must be a gift of love to make her feel better, Eve told herself. It *was* truly magnificent. But the memory of those two ostentatious earrings whirled though her mind. This piece *was* different, she insisted to herself.

Cherie was practically dancing around the room. 'And you will wear the blue nightgown tonight that goes with the sapphires. *Quel cadeau!*'

Yes, it was quite a gift. A wave of nausea came over Eve as all color drained from her face.

Cherie looked concerned. 'Oh, this is too much excitement for Madame. Nurse! Nurse!'

As Cherie ran from the room, the walls seemed to spin. Eve's ears began to buzz, and pain washed over her whole body. Her head pounded and she felt perspiration soak her nightgown. She put both hands to her scar and fought off a sense of dreading panic.

She quickly swallowed the two orange pills the nurse held out for her and turned her face to the wall. When the phone in the silver box at Eve's bedside rang insistently she made no move to answer it.

After twelve rings, Cherie picked up the dressing room extension.

She frantically waved to the nurse. 'It's for Mrs Donaldson. From Puerto Rico. Mr Picol says it's an emergency. Something's happened.'

Miss Grupp firmly pulled the bedroom door shut behind her to keep her patient from being disturbed. 'I've just given her a sedative,' she shouted. 'She's got to get some sleep. I won't allow any phone calls.'

'But, Madame Nurse, this is an emergency. I am her personal maid, and this is a personal call from Puerto Rico.'

'I'm in charge of the medical condition of my patient.' As far as Miss Grupp was concerned, the case was closed. Her patient was resting comfortably; in other words, drugged into sleep.

'Oh, mon dieu!' Cherie picked up the phone again. 'Mr Picol, the nurse does not want Madame disturbed. She is like a *gendarme*.' Cherie tried to calm down enough to come up with a helpful suggestion. 'Drucilla is still at home. Perhaps you could call her?'

Cherie's hand trembled around the receiver. 'Yes, I'll tell her,' she repeated. 'Mr Donaldson is all right? Can he be reached? Is there a phone? Hello? Hello?'

Michael Picol had already hung up the phone.

Cherie gave Nurse Grupp her best French snub as she sailed out of the room. After all, she was practically an extension of the family. She and Drucilla would have the last word.

# 3

Bambi's huge brown doe-eyes were red and swollen. Tears rolled down her cheeks, and her shoulders heaved uncontrollably. She was curled up like a sullen six-year-old wrapped in a down-filled duvet, almost lost in the large rattan peacock chair. The room, like Bambi, was soft and gentle, with a soothing pattern of gray doves on white, mistily repeated on the walls and sheets. Sunlight streamed through the tall French windows, dappling the sheer white organdie curtains. At one end of the little room, an ornamental white birch tree seemed to have been transplanted from a fairy-tale ice forest, and at it's base, Beatrice, Bambi's dwarf white rabbit, twitched a pink nose at two pairs of sneakers before hopping under the bed. Normally, Bambi would have been in hot pursuit of her pet, but now she was too upset to notice. Her histrionics had gotten to the point where she was oblivious of anything but the tragedy at hand, which was that she would have to skip the Sophomore Prom. She would miss the big sleepover with her girlfriends the night before. She would have to call Jonathan and break their date. That in itself was no big deal, but the worst part was she would miss her only chance to be Sophomore Prom Queen. All for some stupid commercial. Every time she thought of it, Bambi sniveled some more.

'I'll do it another time. I promise,' she moaned. 'Please, Hughie? Another time?'

Hughie was almost as exasperated as Bambi was miserable. Were all teenagers like this? Did everything have to be a battle? He weakly wished he knew more about raising children. Maybe he should call Eve for advice. Usually, when Bambi cried, Hughie gave up. He hated to see her upset. Her tears wrenched his heart, but this time his business sense was stronger than his sympathy. He leaned forward in the white wicker chair and reached out to smooth Bambi's damp, rumpled hair. 'If it were up to me, Bambi, they'd arrange everything around *you*. But it's not up to us. The dates for the shoot have been set. The director has been hired. Money has been spent. Everything is lined up in France for that period, and believe me, they are not going to alter their plans just because the model will miss her Sophomore Prom.'

Bambi rubbed her eyes, making then even redder. 'Then I won't do it,' she sniffed.

Hughie strode across the room and looked at his beautiful young sister. He wanted Bambi to have all the fun of growing up like a normal teenager; he wanted to encourage her little social events. She had spent too much time alone or with adults or with her animals. But the fact was, college was on the horizon and, since Bambi talked of veterinary medicine, her education would cost a fortune. They were barely scraping by now on the interest from the money left from the sale of the house and property, Eve Donaldson's generosity, and his ingenious barter system. But the fact was, you might be able to trade a window display for a fall outfit, but this system was not going to hold up when it came to dealing with a university dean. Eve was a love and always so helpful with her time and money, unless she was preoccupied with her own problems. The recent terrorist attack on an Intercon plane in which Graham had almost been blown to bits had set her back in her own recovery.

But Hughie's intuitive feeling told him that Bambi had

the makings of a world-class model, one who could earn enough in a short time to put herself through college *and* veterinary school. He'd seen enough models at Valeski's studio to know that all Bambi needed was exposure. Test shots meant little – a model had to show that she could sell merchandise. The Place in the Sun contract was a start, a quality piece of work, but it wouldn't give Bambi mass consumer exposure.

Only a big-league, mass-merchandised product would accomplish that.

Hughie had heard through the grapevine that Al Cohen, the New York designer who was now calling himself Gianni Valeri, had signed with a major conglomerate that planned to launch a line of designer jeans. They had a sixty-million-dollar advertising budget. And they were looking for a model.

Hughie had phoned Al personally and called in his favors. He reminded Al of how he had gotten Valeski to use Al's designs in a cigarette ad ten years ago, a job that resulted in his first national exposure. It therefore didn't seem unreasonable to ask Al to look at Bambi's composite. Hughie didn't ask for promises; he knew one look was all it would take to secure Bambi's position.

Al had been more than impressed with Bambi's portfolio. He had been inspired. He told his ad agency that Gianni Valeri had to have Bambi for his new line of jeans. The concept was great. The idea of the old denim jeans was dead and overdone. Gianni Valeri was launching the dress jean, done in corduroys, velvets, satins and colors, and he wanted a whole new image for a whole new idea; a brand-new face for a brand-new look. How could Bambi cry over a school dance!

'Bambi,' Hughie said gently. 'You are going to do this.

It's your big break, believe me. We are not talking about a prom. We are talking about your future.'

She shrugged. 'Who cares? I want to be a veterinarian, not a model.'

'This contract will pay for two years of veterinary school. That's important to you, isn't it?'

Bambi still refused to look up. She pulled the duvet closer around her shoulders and pouted. The white cockatoo in the high brass birdcage ruffled its crest and peered down at her with a squawk. Her animals could always read her moods.

She blew her nose.

Hughie stroked her arm. 'Come on, honey. You want to be able to take care of yourself, and not marry some – some *accountant*.' His mouth twisted as if he were sucking a sour lemon. Then his voice changed, as Hughie described again his dream for her. 'Everything you do *you* will do. I want you to have every option, every possibility, so you can choose your own life. Do you really want to close doors at age fifteen? I'm sure that being Prom Queen is an honor, but it only lasts one day and the corsage will be dead in the morning. On the other hand, this modeling job will affect the rest of your life now.'

Hughie had an inspiration. 'You'll love the spots. You get to ride a horse.'

The first flicker of interest crossed Bambi's face.

'The theme is Buccaneer Jeans – for the woman who comes to her own rescue! They're shooting in the salt marshes of the Camargue, in France – you know, where they have the wild horses? You'll ride up on a wild white stallion, in slow-motion, soft-focus, wearing white Buccaneer Jeans and a swashbuckler silk shirt. You'll gallop across the marsh – they really need *you* because you're the only model they liked who can actually ride.'

Bambi sat straight. 'Really? They like my riding?'

'Love it. That's why you got the job – your riding is even more important than your looks. Who else could handle a wild stallion?'

'Most of those girls can't tell a pommel from a pomade,' Bambi giggled.

'And you have the *attitude*, too, Bambi.' Hughie could see he was finally winning her over. 'Buccaneer Jeans are for the new, independent woman who doesn't depend on Prince Charming. This is what everybody wants, and you have it. You won't have to play some bubblehead sex symbol. We'll be starting out with an image that's right for you.'

'What about being the Place in the Sun girl?'

'You'll still be doing that. We need a plan, Bambi. You'll be the Place in the Sun girl for the sophisticated consumer and the Buccaneer Jeans girl for the mass market.'

Bambi bit her cuticles. Marketing plans were of no interest to her. But she could see from Hughie's eagerness that this was important to him, and, she had to admit, he had a point. Veterinary school was expensive, and her new horse cost too much already. She knew they didn't have a lot of extra money for luxuries, even though Hughie made sure she always had anything she wanted. Her brother had worked so hard for both of them for years. He was constantly at the studio till nine or ten at night while she ate wonderful dinners at Aunt Eve's house. When she asked him what he'd eaten, he usually made a face, and she knew he'd had to order out for food, which he hated. She decided it was time for her to do something for her brother. After all, when Hughie was her age he had taken on the responsibility of raising her, a mere toddler. Bambi looked tenderly at him.

He was smiling encouragement at her, and she knew that if she didn't go along with him on this, he'd be very hurt. She couldn't do that to him. The Sophomore Prom was history.

'I'll show those guys what real riding is all about,' she said, her voice firm, a grin creasing her mouth.

Hughie beamed. 'That's my girl.'

# 4

*MEMORANDUM*

TO: G. DONALDSON
FROM: McBRIDE
RE:
- Attached promotional budget for condominium development
- Condé-Nast tie-in terms
- Inauguration of Baccarat glasses

Let's meet on all the above at 2.00 today

Catherine slipped the memo into an interoffice envelope and stamped it personal and confidential. Then she taped the envelope shut and dropped it on top of the pile in her out box.

She swiveled her chair and looked again at the blue box from Tiffany's and the bottle of champagne on her credenza. The box contained six Baccarat crystal champagne glasses and a congratulatory note from Graham for closing the deal with the Bank of France, and Morgan. Both banks had signed major financing commitments yesterday for A Place in the Sun. Catherine picked up the note that had come with the champagne glasses from her desk. It was handwritten on Graham Donaldson's personal stationery and said, 'A lot of people talk deals, some make deals, but only a few can close deals. Congratulations.Graham.'

She unwrapped one of the glasses and ran her fingers down the smooth crystal stem. Well, thought Catherine, this is what one might call a major mixed signal. Ever since Washington, Graham had studiously avoided her.

She had been so sure after that one passionate night that something was beginning between them. In spite of what Graham had said about being a family man, she had sensed that they would inevitably be together again. Her successful presentation at the White House and later at the Department of the Interior had only heightened her feelings, her certainty about their compatibility. Didn't they share the same goals, love the same business? She implicitly understood his belief in A Place in the Sun and wanted to make his dream happen as much as he did. Together, they could be invincible.

It had taken Catherine almost a month to pull herself together after that evening in Washington and the subsequent crash landing. The searing highs and devastating lows had pierced her normally armorlike emotional system. She had even taken four days off, reasoning that it would be good to think about someone other than herself. She decided to visit her mother.

Catherine took the train, which afforded her the luxury of staring out a window, admiring the scenery, and trying to make some sense out of everything that was happening. However, the many miles of rusty track and midwestern foliage did not diminish the overpowering image of Graham Donaldson. Memories of the hours they had spent working, dreaming, and finally making love only grew stronger as the distance got greater.

Even at Wickes Manor, she was consumed with the need to confide in someone. As she massaged the back of her mother's thin neck and brushed her gray hair, she told her entire saga of her romance in great detail. Her mother smiled blankly as Catherine ran the plastic baby brush again and again through her sparse hair. Finally, after the fourth retelling of the story, Catherine regained some perspective. She laughed aloud as she hugged her mother from behind. Well, if she did need a confidante, it was good to have one who would never reveal her dearest secrets! Her mother hadn't spoken for almost a year and was completely lost in her own world of fantasy and silence. Catherine soothed her cheek. She knew how hard her mother had tried, but in this world, she needed to fight.

Maybe it was what she had to do.

On the trip back to Chicago, Catherine resolved her mixed emotions. Aggie Palmer had the right attitude. It was okay to bend the rules a little bit as long as nobody got hurt.

Yet there *was* Eve – and Drucilla. Graham was clearly devoted to them. Catherine wondered if this was an obstacle beyond hope, though she decided that it was, in a strange way, good that he loved his family. She had met too many men who were ruthlessly one-dimensional. She remembered Graham at the National Gallery in Washington, carrying Eve's package like an eager puppy, and truly wondered if Eve knew and appreciated what she had.

Catherine realized she was suffering a classic dilemma: The reasons why she loved Graham were the reasons why she couldn't have him.

Yet she knew she had a chance. The proof was in her hands, in a blue box from Tiffany's. Champagne glasses were appropriate as a present, but a touch too personal as a business gift. They invited sharing, toasting together, romance. They said what Graham could not. Mixed signals meant conflict, thought Catherine, and if Graham Donaldson felt even mildly troubled about her, she had a chance.

At two o'clock, Carla called Catherine. Yes. Graham could see her now. Catherine walked toward the door of her office, but turned back, closed the door, combed her hair, and applied a dab of coral lipstick. Then she picked up her folders, smoothed her blue tweed skirt, and walked confidently through her department, which now ran almost the entire length of the hall to the executive offices. Carla motioned her in.

*Oh no*, thought Catherine, suppressing a frown of disapproval. Her private discussion had turned into an assembly. Ray Acconti and Michael Picol were already in the room with Graham, along with several junior executives from marketing. On the couch at the back of Graham's office Catherine noticed Ellen Louder, director of public relations, and Tim Cannell from finance. Catherine ranked meetings on a scale of one to ten, depending on the number of people and the weight of their importance. This looked like a six.

She took a place at the round table, and Graham greeted her with a glance. When everyone was seated, Graham stood. As he spoke, he looked from person to person, interjecting a casual tone into his voice that indicated this was a trusted group of close friends.

'I'd like to begin by thanking everybody for their efforts on A Place in the Sun. Each of you has played an important role. You've all worked hard on the outcome, and now I'd like to tell you, it's paid off. The Secretary of the Interior called me today to say that our undersea area is going to be declared a national park.'

A murmur went through the room. Ray Acconti beamed, as if the credit were all his.

Graham continued. 'And Catherine informs me that the Bank of France and Morgan are on board.'

All eyes shifted to Catherine.

'Ellen,' Graham looked at the gray-haired woman who was jotting down notes as he spoke. 'I think it's time to publicize the condo development. At lunch today, the executive committee of the board gave me the approval for a developmental program.'

Catherine knew that the word 'developmental' meant the board was still hedging. They must be scared of the stockholders, she realized. She should have known they wouldn't have the guts to put their money where their mouths were. What *would* it take to get this company into the 1980s? She fumed silently as she stabbed her pad with her pencil.

Ray Acconti cleared his throat and cleaned his glasses on the front of his shirt. 'I thought we'd eliminated the condo development, Graham,' he said. 'It's not consistent with our objectives.'

'It's consistent with making money for this company,' Catherine's voice snapped. 'You've seen the figures, Ray. Without the condo income, the project is a write-off.'

'Exactly!' Acconti leaped to his feet. 'That's exactly Intercon's role in this project. To provide a center for research, to fund discoveries the likes of which big business has never backed before. Permanent residency can only damage the environment. Air conditioning, sewage, detergents . . . we are there to do research, not exploit the environment.'

'I do not feel that Terry Skittle's plans exploit the environment,' Catherine insisted. She couldn't believe that he still didn't get the point. 'Considering current oil prices, this whole complex needs to subsidize itself.'

Acconti threw his arms up. 'I suppose you're going ahead with the airstrip, too.'

'Jetstrip,' Catherine corrected.

'Jetstrip?' Acconti rolled his eyes. 'A jetstrip takes up ten times as much land as an airstrip for prop planes and the only island big enough to accommodate a jetstrip is the big island, exactly where the reef is right offshore. You'd decimate the marine population.' He narrowed his eyes. 'No way.'

'Then you can write off the foreign dollar. These guys aren't going to row in on rafts.' She thought back to the White House briefing and her meeting with the Secretary of Defense. The jetstrip was to be long and strong enough to accommodate the possibility of military aircraft. Such information, however, could not be disclosed.

'Let's get back to the objective,' said Acconti, trying a different approach. 'They do not give a Nobel Peace Prize for the best three-bedroom bungalow. I suppose a Club Med is next!'

Graham lifted his hand. 'Nobody is ever one hundred percent pleased with any project,' he said. 'But everybody has to do his best to keep the wheels moving. This is business. Give and take is what it's all about.' He looked at Acconti. 'We need a jetstrip for access. It's imperative. Shipping everything and everybody in by boat is not efficient.'

Acconti squinted, but said nothing. He knew when not to argue.

'The jetstrip stays. Ray, why don't you help schedule landings and takeoffs so they are the least detrimental environmentally?'

Graham walked around the tables, stopping at Catherine's chair. 'As for the condo development, I've seen Skittle's proposal. He's innovatively designed his plans to work with the natural foliage and beach lines. And we can't make this work taxwise without the money the condos will bring in and the write-offs they'll provide.' He scanned the group in the room. 'Any objections?'

Everyone was silent. Ray Acconti merely smirked. Asking for objections, they all knew, were merely a polite shorthand for the fact that a decision had been made.

'Tim, before we all go, what does your pay-out plan forecast?'

Tim Cannell passed copies of his financial breakdown around the table. 'The bottom line is, we should be making a profit within twelve years.'

After the figures had been dissected, Graham ambled back to the chair behind his desk. The meeting was over and people filed out.

'Catherine,' called Graham softly.

She froze. Slowly, she turned and looked at him. He was holding her memo. 'About the last point on your memo. Can you handle five-thirty tonight? I can stop by your apartment on my way to Highland Park.'

'Yes,' she said, finding it difficult to merely smile when she felt like leaping into his arms. 'I can handle that.'

# 5

Eve gracefully hooked her elbows onto the ribbed edge of the white marble swimming pool and pulled herself out of the water. She shook out her long, silver-blonde hair and watched the tiny drops of stipple and cream, terra-cotta, and green mosaic scenes on the bottom and sides of the pool. Toga-clad figures and enormous urns of flowers, copied from Pompeiian murals, shimmered, danced, and then dissolved into hundreds of tiny spirals on the surface of the water. She lifted her face leisurely to the hot July sun, basking for a moment in the feeling of warmth and security. What a luxury it was to feel good again! The pool, the sumptuous English garden with its heady fragrances of mauve phlox, pink dahlias, paler Savage roses, and crowds of yellow and fuchsia snap-dragons mingled with locust and honeysuckle vines, and the view of carefully groomed topiary gave Eve a feeling of midsummer serenity. The dahlias had been planted in February, when fifteen hundred tubers had arrived from Holland, and the thought of their blooming had cheered Eve through the period of her recovery. She pulled her white Porthault terry robe off the stone lion guarding the pool and wrapped a matching towel around her wet head. Nothing felt as good as being back on her feet again. Her convalescence had made her realize more than ever that it was the simple things rather than massive houses and expensive jewels that were meaningful. If she didn't have her health, she couldn't enjoy life or take pleasure from doing things for the people she loved.

She walked to the edge of the frog pond, where she had dropped her Bernard sandals before plunging into the pool. Eve picked a small bouquet of Savage roses, then slipped through the gate that joined the Stuart property to hers and started toward The Cottage, where Hughie awaited her. She smelled the roses and smiled to herself. She had taken all Pollyanne's tips on a speedy recovery, including a few discussion sessions with Dr Corbett as well as a vigorous exercise program, totally mapped out by Pollyanne's personal trainer. The one formula that Eve had not followed was Pollyanne's recipe for youthful skin. Since her surgery, Graham had been treating her like a fragile piece of chinoiserie. That was natural, she supposed. Dr Corbett had explained to her that these adjustments were just as hard for the man as the woman. All thoughts of the sapphire and diamond necklace had been shoved to the back of her mind. As for her complexion, Elizabeth Arden's collagen treatments and Christiaan Barnard antiaging creme would have to do for now.

There was a lightness in Eve's step as she passed the large deer topiary at the edge of Hughie's lawn.

'Hellooo,' she sang out. 'It's me! I'm here!'

'Oh good. I'm on the sun porch. Come on in.' Hughie's head appeared from behind the forest green shuttered screen door. 'Don't you look wonderful. Wear just that to Ravinia tonight. You look great.'

She handed him the bouquet of roses and kissed him on both cheeks. 'Kiss-kiss,' she said, 'I feel great.'

'What's the program at Ravinia?' asked Hughie.

Eve settled into the floral chintz cushions of a chaise. All the furniture on the sun porch was made of Madeira wicker and looked as if it had had an earlier life on someone's summer lawn in Maine. 'Alexander Levin is conducting – Mozart, Beethoven, and for variety, a little Stravinsky.'

Hughie stuffed the bouquet into a copper ginger jar. 'What Beethoven? Not one of those late period *deaf* pieces, I hope!'

'Oh, Hughie. Those are very sophisticated tonal pieces. They're beautiful. It's going to be such fun. Dru is coming, plus you and Bambi, Graham and myself. Just the family.'

'Oh, you mean we're leaving out Michael Picol?'

Eve sighed. 'Yes, this is not a corporate event. Graham needs this break. I insist. He has been spending too much time at work.'

'I noticed you missed the Ballet Ball.'

She plucked a strawberry from a chipped china bowl on the table. 'Graham just won't let me commit to anything these days. The Place in the Sun business has just obsessed him. But tonight, I'm going to see that he gets some *real* rest and recreation.'

Hughie smirked. 'Why not invite the curator of the Art Institute to join us? He and Graham can discuss Cézanne's "Still Life with Fish"!'

Eve laughed, 'The menu tonight will be anything but fish. I'm so tired of hearing about aquaculture, hydroponics, marine biology. The goldfish had better stay out of my way.'

Hughie took a blue spatterware pitcher off a stripped-pine hutch lined with rows of Blue Willow china and poured three glasses of lemonade. 'It'll be good for Bambi to relax, too,' he said. 'She's been working fifteen-hour days. Ever since that shoot in France, she's been *so* busy. The pictures are *wonderful*. We can't wait for you to see them.'

'Can we see them tonight with Graham? He'll be so surprised at his little Place in the Sun girl.'

'Speaking of A Place in the Sun, I hope you won't mind if I talk with Graham for just a few minutes about Bambi's contract. We really should get it signed. It would be so good for Bambi to get everything off the ground.'

Eve never objected to things that were good for Bambi. 'Of course. Graham's just been too busy to think lately. Even Drucilla can't get through to him. But we'll put everything back on track tonight.' She smiled confidently.

'Perfect. Bambi has been dying for us all to spend some time together.' He called out to his sister. 'Bambi, Aunt Eve's here.'

Bambi was reading in the yard, sitting next to a vine-covered garden tool house that was so draped with greenery that it looked like another piece of topiary on the grounds. She was still dressed in her riding clothes and eating a ripe peach. At the sound of Hughie's voice, she looked up, tucked her book under her arm and dashed up to The Cottage.

'Why don't we do cold Cornish hens, pasta salad, marinated artichokes, and fruit-tarts,' Hughie suggested. 'I'll make the tarts – prune and raspberry.'

'Wonderful. I'll raid the wine cellar for Graham's favorites. Maybe we'll spike his wine with some of Dr Corbett's Valium – makes sure he has a *really* relaxing evening.'

They laughed conspiratorially.

'Well,' she shrugged. 'I've tried almost everything else.'

Bambi burst through the door. Her tall frame barely cleared the low-beamed ceiling as she entered the cottage. She flung herself into Eve's arms. 'Aunt Eve, I'm so happy to see you! Are we really all going out together tonight? Uncle Graham too? I'll wear my new Buccaneer Jeans.'

'I heard you did fabulously in the commercial. Hughie says you're going to be a famous model.'

Eve reached out and stroked Bambi's cheek as if she were a baby, although Bambi now towered over her. Regardless of what psychologists said, Eve knew for a fact that it was possible to love another woman's child just as much as her own. Bambi was different from her own daughter, who was much more like her. Every time Eve saw the resemblance to Franklin Stuart in Bambi, she felt an even stronger compassion for this girl. She was glad she hadn't followed Graham's advice and shipped Hughie and Bambi off to their Austrian relatives.

She knew the coach house arrangement was unconventional, and Eve wasn't blind. She knew Hughie had grown up gay, a fact that disgusted Graham. Yet there had always been a thick tension between Hughie and Graham and Eve had often tried to smooth things over. It wasn't up to her to change matter, but to make the best of any situation.

When Bambi was young and had crawled into Eve's bed along with Drucilla, Eve had hugged each girl equally. She knew Hughie had felt left out, and she had tried to compensate, but he had never been able to forget his parents, or completely accept Eve as a mother substitute. Hughie saw himself as Bambi's parent and brother in one. He was old before his time.

But now, looking at Bambi, she felt a strong maternal pride. Everything would ultimately be all right.

Bambi had always had a mind of her own. She was headstrong, and Eve couldn't help but smiled as Bambi launched into her latest diatribe.

'Modeling's the dopiest thing in the world and nothing

to be famous for. And that poor poor horse! I wanted to call the French ASPCA. I had to ride him until he was lathering before they got the right shot. And they lied. They said it would be a wild stallion, but it was some Hollywood horse. They even put on a fake tail!'

'But didn't you get to see the wild horses of the Camargue? Your father loved them.'

'We saw one herd in the distance, Aunt Eve. *They* were beautiful, but *they* weren't in the commercial. It was just me and the Hollywood horse.'

She flopped on to the faded rag rug and plopped a strawberry into her mouth.

The phone rang. Carla had tracked Eve down to tell her that Graham was running late. He had important meetings all day, but would she please go on to Ravinia without him? He'd catch up with her later.

'Oh, Carla,' Eve was frowning. '*Do* try to see that he gets out of there at a decent hour. I really want him to have a quiet evening for a change.'

Hughie and Bambi watched Eve put down the receiver, a little wrinkle crossing her brow. She said cheerfully, 'Well, let's try for six-thirty. Graham will have to meet us there.' She got up and kissed them both good-bye. 'I'm off. See you later!'

Hughie watched her disappear across the lawn and was certain she was headed for the music room. Damn Graham, Hughie thought. He hoped he would make it before dark so he would see Bambi's pictures in natural light. He was looking forward to talking to Graham and cementing the Place in the Sun contract for Bambi. There had been a lot of talk, but nothing on paper. Since the jeans deal had been finalized, Bambi's hourly rate had doubled. Graham had been unreachable, and that

McBride woman was dragging her feet. She was obviously a puppet.

'Why don't you take a nap, sweetie,' he said to Bambi. 'We're going to be up late tonight.'

# 6

Graham Donaldson drove from level to level at the Hancock Building garage, searching for a parking place. He had driven his own car today since Eve had made plans for Ravinia. As he circled the parking levels, Graham thought about what he would say to Catherine. The purpose of speaking to her privately was purely professional, but he suddenly realized that he hadn't been alone with her since Washington. Thinking about the hours they had spent together, of the white heat of his longing for her, made his whole body tense. He clenched the steering wheel and tried to push the thought of the two of them making love out of his mind. He hadn't been able to be alone with Catherine since Washington because every time he saw her the image of the two of them, naked in bed, was overpowering. He was not a man who felt comfortable losing control in any way.

He told himself that months had passed and that night in Washington was only a memory. He had made his position clear to Catherine, and she had accepted it. It had been a damn expensive few hours in terms of his own conscience, and in terms of time he lost whenever thoughts of Catherine had overpowered more important negotiations. And then there was the three hundred-thousand-dollar necklace for Eve, who deserved better than this. Eve was everything to him, he reminded himself.

Catherine was attractive, smart, and a business asset, but she was not Eve. Catherine represented his dreams –

A Place in the Sun, his lost youth, his vision of himself as a virile and uncompromising lover. She was a receptacle, a handmaiden. Eve was more – she was a partner. He had repeated this litany to himself often, until he was sure he believed it.

Graham prided himself on being a practical man. Catherine McBride was important to A Place in the Sun. She alone understood his vision, while Ray Acconti and Michael Picol only saw pieces of the whole. And she, he knew, was too smart to let personal business interfere with company business. A truce must be reached before things got so uncomortable that neither of them could work together.

He had decided that the answer was to promote her.

As he pulled, finally, into a parking place at the end of the sixth level, Graham reminded himself that her promotion was a necessity, since she had already been dealing with top-level government. And she deserved it. A vice-presidency would give her the clout and credibility she needed to get respect in the big leagues.

He had planned to tell her of the promotion at the office, but stopping by her apartment would give him a chance to really talk to her personally for a few minutes, without Ray Acconti or Picol interrupting. He needed to let her know they could continue to work closely together, and that they would put that night in Washington behind them once and for all.

As he stood outside Catherine's door he could hear the strains of rock music coming from her apartment. The intense, annoying beat reminded him again that she was of a different generation.

When Catherine answered, she glanced up at him with such an open, eager face that he wondered if she had guessed about the promotion.

Catherine, however, was totally focused on Graham. She sensed his ambivalence immediately and decided that he had probably made up an excuse to himself to come here. But she didn't really care. He was here. That was the first step.

'Perfect timing,' she said, trying to keep her voice even as she showed him into the living room of her small one-bedroom apartment. 'You're just in time for the sunset.' Two corner walls were completely made of glass. The sun cast ragged orange and red stripes across the darkening sky. There were no draperies or even blinds to block the view, although this was more due to decorating neglect than effect. Catherine had little interest in fixing up her apartment – and less time. The walls were basic white, the industrial beige carpet had been installed by the previous tenant, and her furniture consisted mainly of east-to-move and easy-on-the-budget pieces that she'd bought all at once at Conran's in New York. A simple modular couch was covered in oatmeal canvas, and her favorite place, a bright red hammock, swung in the corner. It had been a year since she had moved to Chicago, but Catherine still had unpacked boxes stacked under her bed. Domesticity was not her strong point.

Looking at Graham Donaldson sitting as elegantly as possible in a canvas deck chair, Catherine realized that there were probably Renoirs on the walls and fabulous antiques in every perfectly decorated nook of his home.

'I can't stay for long,' Graham said, shifting restlessly in his chair.

'I know,' she said, hoping he would change his mind.

'Eve and I are going to Ravinia tonight. But we have a few things we really should talk about.'

'Would you like a glass of something first? I've got a bottle of cranberry juice – Freixnet, that Spanish champagne, which would do justice to those beautiful glasses.' She didn't wait for him to answer as she stepped into the little galley kitchen.

'I guess I'll take some of that champagne.'

'Could you give me a hand here? I'm a disaster around corks.'

As he poured the champagne she couldn't help laughing a little sarcastically. 'Every time we get together, champagne seems to be pouring.'

Graham ignored her blatant reference to Washington. 'We have something to celebrate, Catherine.' He raised his glass. 'Here's to the newest vice-president at Intercon Minerals. And our first woman vice-president, I might add.' He waited for her reaction, expecting it to be ecstatic.

Instead, she looked quizzical. 'That's great,' she said softly. Was he buying her off? Promoting her to another city?

'You guessed.'

'No. I expected it.' She paused. 'I *deserved* it. I've worked hard. If I were a man, it might have come earlier. Exactly what does this promotion mean?'

He was confused. 'It means you're going up in the world – that's what it means. It means you can decorate this place. It means a twenty-thousand-dollar raise. You're my right hand. Without you, A Place in the Sun would still be a set of blueprints gathering dust. You made it work. We'll announce it tomorrow morning.'

Catherine walked into the living room and sat, expressionless, on the edge of a desk that was angled away from the windows. She ran her tongue back and forth over her newly bonded front teeth. She still couldn't get used to the fact that the gap was gone. Every nook held a special folder for her Intercon homework, except for one, which held her materials for Aggie Palmer's foundation.

'Aren't you excited?' asked Graham following her. 'I thought you'd be pleased.'

'I am.' She picked up a bulging envelope. 'The raise is certainly nice, but the title is a means to an end. Now maybe I can actually get some of these ideas off the ground.' She waved the folder. This was business as usual. Graham Donaldson was brilliantly putting her in her place and promoting her all at the same time.

'What's that purple folder?'

'Oh, just my crazy file. The home of all my wild and crazy ideas that I play with after hours.' She reached in and pulled out a plastic bag. 'Like these.' She shook out an orange and yellow T-shirt with the Place in the Sun logo on it.

Graham had never seen the logo before, much less on a T-shirt. He held it up. 'Now that's really clever. Nice, simple graphics. Clean. And leave it to you to put in on a T-shirt.' He was smiling.

'Take it. It's my present to you.'

'What else have you got in your grab bag?'

She spread a few more folders on the floor, and found herself describing the tie-in with Oscar de la Renta, a polo complex that the South Americans would love, and the underwater research habitat that could be cosponsored by other interested companies.

Catherine described how the underwater habitat could be the base station for aquaculture research. 'Almost like satellites are for outer space,' she said. 'Scientists would live underwater gathering data over long periods of time.'

She described in detail the possible plan for a marine farming project. 'Mankind depends on fifteen major crop plants,' she said, hastily scribbling a chart on a legal pad. 'Almost all of these are land plants that were domesticated thousands and thousands of years ago. So far, there are only about *four* domesticated marine plants – mainly kinds of algae. Opportunities in this field are just now opening, since we didn't have the technologies before. Or the awareness. It's a new frontier, and the Graham Donaldson Foundation can take the lead in new ways to feed the world.' She brought out another chart. 'Combined with the fish farming, this idea could be incredible. I've listed each species of fish, and the volume potential, on this graph.'

Graham was fascinated. 'How'd you get this information together?'

She laughed. 'From Dr Ishu, the Shedd Aquarium director, and Dr Epsom from the College of the Virgin Islands. I've spent some time on this.'

Graham and Catherine sat on the floor amidst the scattered papers as Catherine pulled more multicolored charts, folders, and printouts from her file.

'How many hours a day *do* you spend on this stuff?' Graham was impressed by her totally fresh thinking. She approached every idea as if there were no limitations and worked back from there, rather than boxing herself in on the front end with reasons why something *wouldn't* work, which was Ray Acconti's method. The sun had nearly set and the room was dusky. They sipped champagne and talked, each presenting ideas to the other. This was the real world; they were discussing real dollars, real power, and that was the most seductive conversation for them both.

Eve's picnic and Ravinia were receding further and further from Graham's mind. After the first hour had passed, he told himself he'd catch up with her after the first movement of the symphony. As he and Catherine discussed the pros and cons of the underwater habitat, he decided he'd attend the second movement. But the fact was, the symphony was not nearly as interesting to Graham Donaldson as the discussion in Catherine's apartment because, in reality, when he talked about A Place in the Sun, he talked about himself.

Catherine's plain little apartment with its drooping, neglected plants, lost its empty look. It seemed like a haven to him. She was actually a *living* poster of A Place in the Sun! There was no clutter, nothing eighteenth-century to be careful about breaking. This apartment was not designed to distract him from his work, as Eve's rooms were.

Night had fallen, and Catherine stood up to turn on more lights. 'So you think some of this could work?' She called over her shoulder, as she stepped into the kitchen.

'I think it's terrific,' said Graham. 'All of it.'

Catherine peered into her half-empty refrigerator. Tuna salad, alfalfa sprouts, and pita bread left over from yesterday's lunch. She stuffed the tuna and sprouts into the pita pockets and poured two glasses of cranberry juice, then carried everything out on a tray.

'I don't know about you, but I'm starved,' she anounced.

Graham couldn't remember when he'd had anything quite as delicious. The sandwiches tasted so simple and fresh – no sauces, no beurre blanc.

He felt relieved as he watched Catherine. He was glad that there had been no scenes or recriminations. It was back to business as usual. 'You're a smart woman, Catherine. Smart enough not to let what happened in Washington come between us.'

She stared levelly at him. 'I wouldn't want anything to come between us.' I want *you*, she said to herself.

He stared back and pushed the pipe he'd been fidgeting

with all evening into his pocket. 'It's really late. I'd better made a call. Where's the phone?'

'In the bedroom – on the table.'

She heard him call his home and leave a message about being detained. He requested that Mrs Donaldson be told he wouldn't make it to Ravinia, if she called.

Catherine couldn't let him go. They had shared so much in the past few hours and she couldn't revert to being just his employee again. And she knew he really didn't want to go. Tonight, they had reaffirmed their natural ability to work as a team. They were two people who wanted the same thing. She had felt energy between them that had been present from the beginning. She decided Graham was worth any and all risks.

In the other room Graham put down the receiver and glanced at himself in the mirror above Catherine's dresser. He saw a fit, middle-aged man who looked successful, though he was certainly not a sex symbol. He noticed some photos of Catherine tucked into the mirror frame. In one, she was wearing blue jeans and standing in a field with a group of Indians, looking comfortable and earthy. She didn't put on airs; she wore her feelings on her face, Graham thought. She was so different from Eve. Catherine was a burst of energy, ready to burn herself out for his dream. Beside her, Eve seemed cool and detached. His wife, he realized, lived in an ivory tower.

I'd better get out of here, Graham said to himself.

He walked determinedly into the living room, where he was surprised to find all the lights dimmed. He stood in the doorway, his eyes adjusting to the darkness. The files were still scattered across the floor and the tray of dishes was on top of the desk.

His newest corporate vice-president lounged in the red hammock, one arm behind her neck, her blue chenille shirt still tied in a large side bow and clasped primly at the throat with a gold leaf pin. Her meticulously tailored blue tweed jacket revealed a thin gold-linked chain that cinched at her waist. She looked like the perfect executive, ready to take on the board of directors, slash a budget, or call somebody on the carpet.

Except for the fact that she was naked from the waist down.

One long, shapely leg stretched out, her foot pointing directly at him, the other folded underneath her demurely.

He couldn't speak. He knew he should keep walking – out the door. But instead, he walked toward her, almost willing her to open her folded leg.

Catherine's hand dropped to her inner thigh, her fingertips curling upward, beckoning him. She uncurled her leg as he moved closer to the gently swaying hammock and kneeled down beside her. Catherine took his hand in hers and guided it to the tender pink flesh between her legs. She traced his finger there, telling him without words of her desire.

'Help me off with my jacket, Graham.' She stood up only inches away from him. He placed his hands on her shoulders and eased the jacket off her. He removed her gold pin, untied the silk bow, and let her blouse fall delicately to the floor. She wasn't wearing a bra, and for a moment Graham wondered just how often Catherine came to the office wearing nothing under her blouse.

She stood naked before him except for a strand of pearls that gently rested on her chest. He had dreamed of touching her breasts again, and now he placed both his hands on her soft skin, stroking, then pressing just his thumbs to each nipple in a circular motion.

Catherine unfastened his belt and pulled the strap all

the way through the loops before she unzipped his trousers and placed her hand on his erection. She stroked him and lifted her lips to meet his. When she kissed him, softly at first, then more insistently as Graham opened to her, she brought her arms up around his neck and held him close. Graham buried his head in her hair and encircled her waist with his arms, squeezing her so tightly she could hardly breathe.

'Catherine.' He kissed her neck under the strands of her thick hair. 'I'm losing all control with you.'

She slid her hands down his back and pushed his trousers to the floor. Then she entwined her arms around him and pressed his naked hips to hers.

'That's what I've been counting on,' she whispered.

He stepped back and let her remove his jacket and tie, and finally his shirt. He watched her as she pushed her coppery hair over her head, stretching her arms, then letting her hair fall playfully to her shoulders. Every move she made seemed instinctively sexual, her shy, sidelong glance incongruous with her naked pirouette. Wherever her fingers touched, he felt as if he were getting burned. And when she moved up and down the length of him, slowly tightening her thighs to grip ánd then release him, Graham raised his hips to match Catherine's every move. His hands held her buttocks, forcing her down on to him, and he heard her little cries of pleasure as they both climaxed.

Catherine lowered herself next to him, but Graham turned her onto her stomach. She propped herself up on her elbows and he pulled her hips into him as he maintained a rhythm between them. His hand moved from her hip, across her flat abdomen to cup one creamy breast, caressing it firmly as he bent over her back, kissing her shoulder blade and whispering words from far away, exotic and obscene things.

'Don't stop, Graham,' she pleaded as he thrust deeply into her and he felt her spasms of pleasure. He came into her again and then gently, slowly, his body stopped shuddering.

They turned and faced one another. Catherine once again took Graham's face in her hands and tenderly kissed him. He held her silky hair to one side of her neck as he carefully traced her face with his fingers, amazed at their love making, and his passion.

They lay beside each other for a long time, then Catherine found his jacket in the pile of clothes heaped on the floor and put it on, smiling coyly at him.

'Don't put that on,' he said, reaching out and pulling the jacket off. 'You won't be needing it.'

# 7

Catherine clung to the rim of the wicker balloon gondola and leaned over into the crisp fall air. She observed the golden colors of fall, which were spread out like a glorious patchwork below as she and Billy Wright drifted high above the country landscape. Red barns mixed with orange foliage, and the balloon cast a traveling shadow that startled the horses and dogs beneath. A kaleidoscope of ten other balloons drifted up and down around them, hanging in the sky like giant punctuation marks of yellow, green, and purple. Catherine, who had never been ballooning before, felt like Dorothy in *The Wizard of Oz*, as she was magically whisked across the farmlands and countryside of Barrington, Illinois. Their balloon was red, white, and blue, imprinted with the Intercon double-globe logo on the front. Catherine had expected to feel a dizzying sensation of moving up and down, but instead, the ground seemed to rush up and then pull away as they hovered, motionless. The only sound she heard was the hiss of the burner over their heads and the barking of dogs far below.

She was glad Billy had finally persuaded her to join him in the annual Barrington Balloon Rally, sponsored by Intercon. Fifty balloons from all over the country were entered in this meet, which had become a highly publicized fall tradition. Billy Wright, the only person at Intercon who knew anything about ballooning, was the favorite this year in the hounds-and-hare event, and a loyal contingent from the company had turned out to cheer him on. Billy had promised her that as copilot in the big rally her sole responsibilities would be communicating with the chase vehicle by radiophone and opening the bottle of Laurent Perrier champagne when they landed. He had surprised Catherine with a red satin team jacket, which fit perfectly.

Billy was preoccupied with controlling their altitude and the strategies of winning the race, while Catherine daydreamed. Billy had been a lifesaver, she thought to herself. They lunched together whenever possible and, although most of their conversation centered around work or the latest Intercon gossip, she felt she had a friend. He was a loner by nature, just like her, and they often understood one another in ways Catherine could not explain to Graham.

Her affair with Graham, she had to admit, had its disadvantages. Sundays always seemed particularly lonely for Catherine. She usually paced her apartment, unable to concentrate on even the magazine section of the newspaper for more than a few minutes. It was then she most vividly envisioned Graham with his adoring family, happily ensconced at the estate in Lake Forest. Billy had been a godsend when he had begun to monopolize her Sundays with trips to the Shedd Aquarium, the Field Museum, and playing tennis at the Saddle and Cycle.

So far, no one at work suspected anything about her affair with Graham. In fact, Catherine spent so much time with Billy that any office gossip involved him, if anyone. Catherine knew that Billy was handsome, fun, and successful – exactly what Miss Aggie called eligible. But Catherine saw no one romantically but Graham. She was glad Billy had a steady girlfriend, Lolly Bishop, who worked weekends at her Art Gallery on the shore of Lake Superior.

'Tell the chase crew we're coming down over the gray ranch house on the Lake,' Billy said, his voice breaking Catherine's reverie. 'They should ask for permission to land in the yard.'

'Roger.' She smiled up at him beneath her Cubs baseball cap and relayed the message as they drifted downward.

Graham would have loved this, thought Catherine. But it was Sunday, and Sunday was Eve's day. Catherine's time included hours stolen on business trips and at the company apartment Graham had rented in her building. They were always very discreet, for both were keenly aware of the consequences any scandal might arouse. She loved Graham too much to create any problems for him and had rationalized that it was better to have a little piece of someone brilliant and special than all of someone average and ordinary. And, after all, Eve was only his wife. She, Catherine, was his soulmate; the object of his passion.

Catherine was convinced Graham and Eve were sleeping in separate beds, and, even though he had never said it, she was certain Graham loved her. He often made excuses to stay late at the office, and messages that could have easily been telexed to Washington or New York were suddenly reasons for overnight trips on which her presence was required. Catherine often wondered how Carla, at least, could not see the truth. After all, when Carla couldn't find Graham, a single call to Catherine would result in a prompt return call from him. And whenever Carla made out-of-town arrangements for Graham, she duplicated them for Catherine. Carla merely looked the other way with unjudgmental eyes.

Once, when only she and Graham were working late at the office, he had come into her white Formica department and sat beside her as she studied various computer printouts. While she discussed financial plans Graham casually began to massage her calf. Holding her foot in his hand, he had placed it betweem his legs as he worked his finger up past her knee and thigh and then removed her pantyhose. Before she knew what was happening, her skirt was on the floor along with Graham's trousers and tie. They made love on the green couch, dressed only in their shirts, oblivious to the late-night cleaning ladies who could have charged in at any moment. That was the only time they had let desire overrule common sense, though every time she looked at the green couch, she remembered their passion.

Graham was the one person she had ever met who bettered Catherine at her own games. When he held her, she could feel all the power he controlled in his fingertips. A word from Graham could make things happen. One touch, and Catherine responded. She did not see a flaw in Graham Donaldson. Indeed, every decision he made reinforced her belief that side by side they could run an empire.

'Catch!' Billy's words caught Catherine off guard as she was suddenly called upon to help secure the ropes. Had they won? Was it over?

The balloon hissed and sputtered as Billy lowered it until they hung suspended at rooftop level. Just as they lightly touched the ground, he pulled the rope that released the air trapped in the balloon, causing it to deflate.

He climbed out of the gondola in one quick movement and helped Catherine as she jumped to the ground. She barely noticed Billy giving her a congratulatory hug because her eyes were focused beyond him on the cream-colored Jaguar with the vanity license plate 'Eve.'

She looked over Billy's shoulder and straight into the eyes of Graham Donaldson, followed by Eve, Drucilla Donaldson, and a thin, pale, pompous-looking young man. Graham's face looked pleasant enough as he smiled at Billy, but Catherine noticed a muscle twitching in his cheek.

'Hello, sir,' Billy held out his hand. 'It's only the third of five events, but I think Intercon did okay today. Next Sunday is the real contest.' He put his arm around Catherine, who felt like shrinking into the ground as she nervously smiled at Eve.

'Well, these young people make quite a team for Intercon, don't they Graham?' Eve slipped her arm through her husband's. Catherine wondered if she suspected that during the three nights a week when he wasn't home he was with her in the company apartment.

'With Catherine's help here,' Billy said, 'we made a pretty good landing.'

Graham stared at Billy's arm now around Catherine's waist. 'I noticed.' His face was stony. 'We just came out to present the trophy. I gotta go.' He avoided looking at Catherine's face, and his smile seemed frozen.

'Come on, Arnaud, let's go fly! Don't be afraid. The two of *them* just did it.' Drucilla Donaldson, in burgundy leather pants and a Fair Isle sweater, her long blonde hair caught up in a thick ponytail that hung halfway down her back, raced over to the balloon, dragging her reluctant date behind by the jacket. Two men started to ready the balloon for another lift as Eve turned to Catherine. 'Isn't it wonderful? Drucilla's just become engaged. She met Arnaud last summer at cooking school in Paris. He was giving a lecture on the de Cotrille family wines. He's visiting us in America. The wedding is at Thanksgiving.'

Drucilla had her arms around her fiancé's neck. She

stood almost a foot taller. 'This would be *perfect* for you. You could fly over all your vineyards and check out the grapes from the air in a great big balloon.' She lisped her syllables.

Arnaud nodded seriously. 'A very sound idea, my dear. Not unlike the Bombard Society, near my home.'

Catherine noticed Billy Wright roll his eyes, but she quickly looked down at a pile of leaves on the ground, trying to suppress a smile.

'The children want to be married in the very same place where Graham and I got married – the Fourth Presbyterian Church. And they'll have the reception at the Racquet Club, just like we did,' Eve was explaining pleasantly. 'We were *so* silly, weren't we, dear? We sneaked out before they even cut the cake. Remember?' She patted her husband's elbow.

Catherine wondered for whose benefit these remarks were being made. Eve must be desperate, she thought, if she had to dredge up memories from more than a quarter of a century ago. Still, she seethed inside at Eve's possessiveness. Seeing Graham's wife in person caused a pang of guilt Catherine had thought she was too sophisticated to feel. She *is* beautiful, Catherine admitted. Eve's elegant doeskin jacket, tied over a creamy cashmere turtleneck, made Catherine feel like a scruffy kid in her baseball cap and red satin jacket.

I look like a mechanic, Catherine thought, and she noticed that Eve's skin didn't have a single freckle or line. She probably didn't have a hysterectomy at all, Catherine speculated to herself. She probably had a face-lift. She'd seen Eve's picture dozens of times on the society pages and she had traveled to Dallas with her. But this was her first encounter with her *competition* – if she could call Eve that. Since she'd fallen in love with Graham and they had resumed their affair, there hadn't been a social gathering that included both Catherine and Eve. The thought of challenging Eve Donaldson was hardly pleasant. Catherine's palms began to feel clammy; she hoped she wouldn't have to shake hands with Eve. This woman was not some little suburban housewife who threw Tupperware parties. She was a woman who looked like a *Town & Country* cover, who played the piano, and who entertained the President of the United States. Of course, serving on a board of directors and practicing the piano could hardly be compared to working a sixty-hour week, but wasn't that exactly the sort of woman that men liked?

Catherine nervously glanced again at Eve. *Oh, God, she's speaking French to the fiancé*, she thought and wondered if there were anything Eve couldn't do. Graham looked entirely too right by her side. They were so graceful and easy together, as if they anticipated each other's every thought.

'How'd you like to go for a ride, Mrs Donaldson? It's not dangerous at all,' Billy asked. The balloon slowly billowed out with the air again as two men fired up one propane burner.

'No, no, let the children go.' Eve waved at Drucilla, who was searching for a helmet for Arnaud.

Eve looked over at Catherine's trim, youthful body. How long had it been since she had been able to stand in the brightest daylight with no makeup, in a pair of old jeans? She shifted her weight from one elegant foot to the other and slipped on a pair of sunglasses, suddenly wanting to hide behind something. She felt uncomfortable around Catherine. Even though her eyes were soft and clear, there was a smoky sensuality present which she found threatening. Her looks could easily convince a man that there was more to her than what really existed.

'Don't do that!' Drucilla Donaldson shrieked as a husky young man leaped from nowhere into the gondola with her and Arnaud. He reached out and grabbed Arnaud's wrist, tearing a lit cigarette out of his hand.

'If you don't want me to smoke, all you have to do is ask. You don't have to shove me around like a – a refugee!' Arnaud was indignant.

'Listen, Buddy,' said the crew member. 'Do you see that? It's a propane burner. Nobody puts a lit anything close to it. You were within seconds of becoming one big bang.'

'Why don't you have a sign posted then? Or tell someone – you know?' His French accent was haughty.

Billy Wright walked quickly over to the balloon. 'Everybody calm down,' he announced. 'No harm was done, and Arnaud knows the rules now.'

Graham looked very annoyed. 'Let's get going, everybody,' he said.

Eve put her hand on her husband's wrist and lifted it up to check his watch, although she was wearing a Piaget herself. 'It *is* getting late, darling.' The gesture was not lost on Catherine, who for no apparent reason felt compelled to give Billy a hug. Whether she did it to throw Eve off the track or make Graham a little jealous, even she didn't know.

'Catherine.' Eve was holding her hand out graciously. 'It was so nice to see you. And I'm so glad to see one of our women in the race for a change. Good luck next week.' Eve gave Billy a little peck, then turned again to face Catherine.

If this were a game, Catherine thought, she was at an unfair disadvantage. Eve Donaldson was wearing sunglasses, so she couldn't read her eyes. But there was something about her demeanor that bothered Catherine, in spite of all the polite social gestures.

*She knows*, she said to herself.

Arnaud strutted back to the car like a bird with ruffled feathers. 'You're going to love Daddy's wine cellar,' said Drucilla soothingly. She had clearly been reared in the Eve Donaldson school of bolstering wounded egos and making people feel comfortable in uncomfortable situations.

The four of them walked to the car, and as the Jaguar pulled away, Catherine stared after it, wondering what Graham was feeling. Seeing his family together had made her more uncomfortable than she ever expected. She couldn't wait to go home.

It took Billy only fifteen minutes to fold the deflated balloon, pack it in the gondola, and put it into the chase van. Catherine stuffed her hands into her jeans' back pockets and walked down by the small lake at the edge of the property until Billy called her back up to get into the jeep.

As they pulled onto the expressway leaving Barrington, Billy broke the silence. 'Are you going to sign on for next week? We have a shot at the trophy.'

'If you need me to.'

'How about a little previctory dinner at Ed Debevick's? Although we might be overdressed.'

'Do you mind if we skip dinner? I have a lot of work I'd like to get to tonight.' She seemed distracted.

'Catherine, do you mind if I put something right out on the table?'

'Shoot.' She was looking out the window.

'You've been spending a lot of time with Graham lately. And you wouldn't want anybody to get the wrong idea.'

'What do you mean, "wrong idea"?' Her back straightened.

'Well, you know how it is. Whenever a good-looking, intelligent woman and a good-looking, intelligent man spend hours together after work, there's going to be talk.'

'Whatever small, little minds say, I don't want to hear,' Catherine bristled. She hadn't heard such office gossip, but then it didn't surprise her that it existed. 'Graham is one of the most brilliant, powerful men in the country and people get jealous of my access to him.'

Billy was taken aback by her defensiveness. 'But other people have to be taken into account,' he said. 'I'm just telling you so you can take care of yourself. You're a big girl.'

'Graham and I have a beautiful working relationship and guys like Ray Acconti can't take it. Is he spreading something?'

'It's just a question, Catherine. Calm down.'

'Why don't they leave him alone? Here's a man who took this small, insignificant mineral company from Eve's family and turned it into Intercon, one of the world's largest corporations. People are just jealous. That's human nature.' Her voice quieted. 'And I'm the first woman vice-president in the history of the company. So I guess somebody was bound to say something.'

There was a long pause before she asked, 'What exactly have you heard?'

'Forget it. As you said, it's really unimportant.'

She hopped out of the jeep at the Delaware Street entrance to the Hancock Building.

In her apartment, she couldn't seem to do anything more constructive than make a cup of herbal tea and wait for Graham's call. Talking to Graham always put things in perspective.

She was sure the phone would ring any second, but it never did. She finally fell asleep during a rerun of *Roman Holiday*, stretched out fully dressed in the red hammock, the phone on the floor beside her.

'It's nice to have just the family for dinner.' Eve raised her glass of pear brandy and toasted the six of them, seated around the table in the yellow, blue, and white Portuguese-tiled sun room, where she liked to have informal Sunday supper. The warmth and intimacy of this room, just off the massive copper-countered kitchen with its industrial-style stoves and grills, suited the mood Eve was trying to create.

Alarms had gone off inside her head this afternoon when she saw Catherine McBride, and Eve's instinctive defense was to emphasize the closeness of the family.

'Well, I, for one, have never been bridesmaid, and I'm plenty excited,' Bambi enthused. 'Who's going to design the dresses?'

'Somebody French,' stated Arnaud.

Drucilla pulled her chair closer to his. 'Arnaud, you're such a patriot.' She gave him a peck on his cheek.

'I think it's wonderful, Arnaud, that you're taking such an interest in the wedding plans,' Eve laughed. 'I remember our wedding. Graham's only responsibility was to show up. Right, darling?' Her spoon pushed at the untouched chocolate mousse on her plate.

Drucilla put her napkin on the table. 'Well, everybody, sorry we have to run, but we're off to the city.'

'Dru, you're *not* going back tonight. The drive is too long.' Eve's voice was a command. 'And I thought Arnaud would show slides of his vineyard after dinner.' She watched Graham out of the corner of her eye. He seemed to be miles away. What could she do to bring him into the conversation? Good Lord, she was having to draw him out like a reluctant dinner guest. Conversation had always been so natural and free-flowing at their table, but he hadn't laughed once during the entire dinner. 'Graham, darling. Do you think we should let Arnaud in on a little family tradition? You know,' she turned to Arnaud. 'You're expected to honeymoon with your in-laws. Graham and I went to Wysetta with my parents.' She looked at Graham to see if he smiled, as he usually did, when reminded of their communal honeymoon.

'Luckily, I got along with my father-in-law,' Graham nodded.

'Too well,' Eve added. 'They spent the whole time discussing business.'

Graham pushed his chair back. 'Speaking of business,' he checked his watch. 'If you'll excuse me, I have to make a few calls before it gets too late.'

Eve caught up with him in the doorway of his study. 'Darling, don't you think you should join us for coffee in the library? This is Sunday night, Graham, and I'm sure everyone is with their families.'

He paced impatiently in front of the well-worn oak partner's desk. The phone was spotlighted by an antique brass lamp.

'I'll only be a few minutes.'

Her voiced was forced. 'No, darling. Let's go right now. This is a family night. I thought we might tell the children that we're going to give them a cruise on the *Lady Eve* for their honeymoon.'

He looked past her, staring at the sixteenth-century map of Amsterdam that hung over the door. 'They're not children, Eve. Dru's a grown woman.'

Her head snapped back in surprise. The fresh hysterectomy scar suddenly felt as if it were pulling. What was he telling her? That she was useless? Her role in life had always been to be a wife and mother. He'd always been so proud of that. She weighed her answer carefully, because she knew that whatever it was that they were not discussing was important. Then she took a graceful step deep into the room. 'Well, Graham, of course you're right. And this time *next* year you'll have your grandchild at the table.' She held out her hand.

He glanced once more at the phone, then took her hand as she led him back to the family.

# 8

Catherine picked up the phone and punched B.J.'s extension. 'Hi, it's me. Can you do me a favor? I need the Caribbean classified file from Picol's department. Can you track it down?'

The file would give Catherine all the ammunition she needed to handle Acconti's latest attempt to sabotage one of her ideas for A Place in the Sun. He wanted to replace her proposed polo field with a larger bird sanctuary. He insisted the thundering sound of horses' hooves would scare off the birds who would otherwise nest there.

While B.J. went to the sixty-eighth floor, Catherine opened a letter that had come in this morning from Agnes Palmer. She had just spoken to Aggie last week about their ongoing plans for the National Trust Museum, she knew that Aggie intended to make her a trustee of the foundation. Still, it was nice to see the official invitation to join the foundation board in writing. She was thrilled to accept. The billion-dollar Palmer Foundation was second in power and funds only to the Ford Foundation. It was a coup to be the youngest person by twenty years in the company of some of the most powerful people in the Southwest, an illustrious group that included several CEOs, patrons of the arts and prominent figures such as the attorney general-designate. She would be paid a fee each time she attended a meeting, all her expenses would be provided for, but the most important part of the appointment was the education that she was receiving from Aggie Palmer. One conversation with Aggie was like a year in the school of life.

B.J. materialized in the doorway. 'Picol's gone. Split for South America.'

'When?'

'Tomorrow. He won't be back in the office until next week. And he's got the file with him.'

'What about copies?'

'Locked in his private cabinet. Theresa can't give out the key unless he says so.'

'Great.'

'But here's his private number. Theresa says you might be able to catch him at home between six and eight.'

As she left the office after work, Catherine thought about swinging past her apartment, picking up Midnight, and finally giving the cat back to Michael Picol. But he hadn't asked about Midnight in months, and she had grown attached to him. It seemed just natural that one of Picol's selfish acts had later resulted in something Catherine could appreciate. His dumping of the 'Widow Palmer problem' in her lap had engendered a warm friendship between Catherine and Aggie Palmer, and even her place on the board of the Palmer Foundation.

It was only a five-minute drive along the lakefront from her office to Picol's apartment building, Lake Point Tower. The curved black glass building was set back apart from the rest of the city, a position that suited Picol perfectly. Catherine wondered what the inside of Picol's apartment would be like. As far as she knew, no one in the company had ever set foot in the private domain of the mysterious Michael Picol. Even his secretary had looked surprised as she handed Catherine two bound reports to take along to Picol's with her. She smiled to herself on the way up in the elevator, as she remembered how unexpectedly friendly Picol had sounded when she called him from the office.

Catherine wondered if he lived with someone and if so what she'd be like. The office grapevine said the only local woman Picol had been seen with was Drucilla Donaldson. More often than not a model from New York or an actress from Hollywood graced his arm. It was rumored that he had a valet *and* a Chinese cook who had been trained at the Pritikin Longevity Center in La Costa. He was obviously interested in self-preservation, Catherine thought.

Even though the doorman announced her, she had to lean on the buzzer for a long time before an enormous, swarthy man in a white coat and Indian turban answered. He silently ushered Catherine into Michael's cool, sterile living room. Everything looked so cold and uncomfortable that it was hard to know where to sit. So many of the walls were mirrored that she couldn't avoid staring back at herself whichever way she turned. The lights were dim except for a bright streak of neon light that stretched across the entire length of the living room wall. Catherine squinted as her eyes grew accustomed to the semidarkness. On one wall was a giant video screen. A Vasarely hung on the other wall, exhibiting the only touch of color in the expanse of gray, black and silver. Several pieces of antique pottery and stone sculpure sat on a stand subtly illuminated by an invisible light.

Catherine gingerly sat on the gray geometric couch that was built into the floor on a gray-swirl marble base. A chilling quiet prevailed.

'What can I get you to drink, please?' A turbaned giant, who looked more like a bodyguard than a valet, broke the silence and clumped a silver tray of sushi down on the gray slab of marble that apparently was the cocktail table.

Only the two onyx ashtrays at each end and a small pile of black paper napkins saved it from looking like a morticians's table.

'Nothing, thank you,' Catherine replied startled. 'Did you tell Mr Picol I was here?' Even her own voice held an unnatural echo in these rooms.

Just then Michael Picol emerged from beneath the arched doorway that led out of a darkened room. He was wearing a black velour jogging suit trimmed in gray and had a towel wrapped around his neck.

'I just did an hour on the Lifecycle,' he announced, breathing heavily. She couldn't see his face clearly enough to read his expression. 'Sorry to keep you waiting, but if you don't cool down slowly, you cramp up.' He mopped his forehead with his sleeve.

'Sorry to have to disturb your evening,' Catherine apologized, rising. 'I know you're leaving tomorrow but I really need that classified file. I won't stay any longer than necessary.'

He smiled at her and moved into the light. 'Don't be silly. I've imposed on you enough. Did Singh get you something to drink?'

'White wine would be fine.'

'Sorry. We haven't got anything alcoholic in this place. Singh does the shopping. He's a Sikh, you know. Used to be one of Indira Gandhi's bodyguards.'

Catherine's nervous smile was reflected a dozen times in the mirrors turning at every angle. Wasn't she murdered by one of her Sikh guards?

'Singh is very loyal to me. But some people have a hard time appreciating his charm. Ladies in particular.' He laughed.

'Michael, I'm anxious to . . .'

A communications console on the wall adjacent to the

TV screen started to light up in three different places. It looked like something from NASA Control. Three mini-televisions were built into a gray Lucite panel. Just above the TV panel was a shelf holding three gray Merlin telephones, banked by two professional-caliber reel-to-reel tape decks. The flashing lights were accompanied by a barely audible ringing.

'I gotta take this call. My briefcase is in the bedroom. Could you get it? The crocodile one.' Picol motioned toward an archway as he stepped over to the console, where he picked up the receiver and flicked a button, activating one of the tape reels. Then he began to speak in what sounded to her like Portugese.

Catherine remained on the couch watching. This Lucite console was obviously more than a bachelor's entertainment center – she'd rarely seen more sophisticated equipment in a recording studio, and wondered if he taped all his calls. She wanted to get this meeting over quickly, because Graham was supposed to call her at nine o'clock tonight. Deciding to speed things up, she decided to get the briefcase for him.

Her low heels made a heavy echoing noise on the gray marble floors as she followed the wide corridor. How could he live here, she wondered. It had to be fifty degrees in the tomblike apartment, because she was shivering. Midnight would have skidded across the over-polished marble floors and left cat fur on the impeccable gray suede couch. No wonder Michael had never retrieved the cat.

The bedroom was decorated in a warmer color and the temperature was higher. There were no lamps, flowers, books, or picture frames to detract from the clean lines and arches, and no personal touches indicating someone lived there, save a soft pungent odor that permeated the room. A platform covered by a simple cotton sheet was, she supposed, the bed, though it looked like something Gandhi might have slept in. Across the room, three arched mirrors lit by a peculiar pink fluorescence that emanted from three half-hidden wall sconces covered the window and reflected the bed and ocher walls. Between the bed and the mirrors, extending from wall to wall, was a raised travertine deck, the center of which was hollowed out as a sunken whirlpool tub. There was nothing in the room that could take place without being reflected back to you. Catherine mused, eying the tub.

There was absolutely nothing in the room that could reveal anything personal about the mysterious Picol.

She turned, looking for the briefcase. It was behind the bed, on a built-in marble shelf, leaning against a mammoth triptych painting of the Annunciation of Gabriel. The three-paneled painting looked medieval, as if it had come off the walls of a church in Ravenna, with its unsoftened colors and religious figures, stiff and uncompromising. The angel Gabriel was handing the Virgin Mary a dove. Catherine shook her head. She had thought Michael was Jewish. What bachelor would sleep with the Virgin Mary over his head, Catherine wondered, puzzled, as she bent down to pick up the heavy crocodile briefcase. But then again, she knew she could never expect anything typical from Picol.

She brought the briefcase back out to the living room and noticed dusk had fallen outside the curved windows. She could see the lights blinking from boats and the lighthouse far out on the breakwater of Lake Michigan.

Picol hung up the receiver and switched on one of the small TV screens to a Spanish news show. She handed him his briefcase, and he unlocked the combination, took out the file, and tossed it on the marble slab table before he left the room.

'Michael,' she called after him. 'I just need a few minutes.'

He returned, carrying a small line of powder on a pocket mirror. Cocaine, she thought. She'd never tried any. She felt genuinely shocked. He must be trying to prove something.

He inhaled the line into his nostril. 'I never do this,' he drawled. 'But I've got to be up for two days straight. I was already up all last night. And it's better than putting pills or cafeine into your system.' He poured himself a soda and dropped in a lemon slice. 'Want some?'

She shook her head. He must trust her discretion, she thought, to be doing this in front of her. Graham would die if he knew his legal counsel and right-hand man did drugs! Why did he seem so sure she would keep this secret? She suddenly became very wary.

'I hear you've got Donaldson by the balls,' Picol said. His voice was even, and his eyes were cold, like the room.

Catherine picked up the folder without a word and started to walk out.

He caught up with her at the door and apologized. 'I'm sorry, Catherine. I'm beat, jet-lagged. I didn't mean it the way it sounded. I don't know why I said what I did. Forget it. Come in and sit down.' He held her arm gently.

'I've got to get going,' she said curtly. 'Don't worry about it. We all get tired.'

'No, I have to explain, please.' His eyes were pleading. 'You really impress me.' He sat beside her on the couch, leaning back and rubbing his brow, his eyes heavy with exhaustion. 'I've watched you. You've got guts. I've never seen a woman get in there and hold her own before. You can play any hand they deal you. I heard how you put that ferret Acconti in his place.'

Catherine laughed in spite of herself. Acconti did look like a ferret.

'When I'm tired I strike out at whoever's on hand. That's probably why I'm always alone. Forgive me?' His little-boy smile seemed so innocently truthful that Catherine found herself feeling a little sorry for him. She decided that he was an obviously angry, hostile man who could only worship a Madonna on canvas in the bedroom. He had no relationships, no warmth in his life. Maybe the office rumors were true, and only starlets and stewardesses passed through his lonely rooms on a one-night basis.

She looked at Picol. His hands were trembling and she felt a rush of sympathy. Sitting beside him alone, in his apartment, he didn't seem like a tough corporate genius. He, too, was vulnerable.

'When you're working at this kind of pace, sometimes you have to realize you're only human. Sometimes it's okay to be just a man, a person,' she said.

He shivered. 'You're right. I'm too hard on myself. Two, three, four days without sleep. Caracas on Monday, Curaçao on Tuesday, Chicago, New York, Geneva . . .' His voice faded for a moment.

'Listen, hon, would you mind? Singh's gone for the night. Do you think you could brew me a cup of tea? That's better than coke any day.' He grinned and put the hardly-used white line of powder down. Catherine wondered if it had been just for show.

It took her only seconds to pour the boiling water from an instant hot-water spout into a cup and locate the caffeine-free teabags in a glass canister.

'I think you understand me. Everybody thinks I'm an

iron man with no feelings. Is it my fault women act like they do with me? They don't want me. They want what I can give them.'

Catherine had a feeling she was going to hear more than she wanted to, but her curiosity wouldn't let her leave just yet. He was confiding in her, despite his comment about Graham.

'I understand women,' he said. 'They all either want something from you, or they have a cause. Like my mother. She had her cause. She had to save the world. So she left me alone when I was eight to join a kibbutz in Israel. She devoted herself to teaching a bunch of strange kids, but she wouldn't give me the time of day. I stayed home with my dad, who didn't like kids much. Especially me.' His eyes searched hers to see if they were making some connection.

Catherine listened as Picol told how he had grown up, the son of an Italian grocer and a strong-willed Jewish mother who taught in the public school system on Chicago's Southwest Side. Luigi Picolini swore that no son of his would ever be a Jew, which only made tension unbearable at home.

When Israel became a state, Ruth Picolini bought a one-way ticket to the new country. She had promised to send for him once she was settled, Picol said emptily, but it didn't happen for seven years. His father couldn't stand to look at him after Ruth left because he looked too much like her. Picol touched an old scar on his forehead, and rolled up his sleeve to show a twelve-inch indentation running up his inner arm. In a whisper, he described the horrible beatings at the hands of his hard-drinking father and the countless hours spent locked in a dark, airless broom closet where, lying on the floor, he had realized that he would never belong to anyone.

Catherine reached out and gingerly touched his arm. Different as they were she realized they were also alike. Both of them had been abandoned; both were still fighting for their place.

Picol continued. Just as he was on the brink of becoming a statistic in Chicago's gang wars his mother sent for him. Israel changed his life, he told Catherine, for it was there he realized he could make his aggressions pay off. Trained as a fighter pilot at an age when American boys were learning to drive cars, he later enrolled in the Israeli Defense Force.

'Why did you become a lawyer, then?' asked Catherine.

'I didn't like to share,' he said. 'I loved the adventure, but look at this place.' He grinned at her. 'Can't you see communal living isn't my style?'

'Yes, I can see you like your privacy, Michael. But,' she hesitated to make a personal remark, 'aren't you ever lonely?'

He turned to Catherine, and she caught the sweet, musky scent of his cologne. His gaze was intent, almost sorrowful.

'Yeah, I get lonely.'

Then, without warning, he pulled her mouth down to his in a tender but forceful motion. For a split second, Catherine found herself responding, as she had that night in Dallas. He pushed her down, onto the marble table. She felt papers sliding underneath her, the chill on the back of her legs, Michael's hands moving quickly on her body, his teeth on her neck.

Her senses returned to her in a rush and she pushed against him, fighting him off. Yet this seemed only to excite him, and she could feel the strength in his body increase, the more she resisted.

He pinned her down as she struggled and screamed,

'Damn it, Michael, stop! Cut it out! Just leave me alone.' His teeth bruised her throat as she pounded his back with her tightly clenched fists. He was so heavy, she could barely breathe.

She made a desperate grasp for the nearest object – anything for self-defense. She grabbed something and smashed it squarely on his head. It shattered and a large chunk fell to the floor, where it lay splattered across the marble.

Picol jumped up in a fury. 'What the hell do you think you're doing?' he shouted, grabbing her wrist. 'Don't you know what that was worth? That was a statue from Macedonia! From Alexander the Great!' He was staring in disgust at the fragments on the floor. 'It was priceless, you bitch! What's the matter with you? Shit!' He got down on the floor and picked up the damage.

'You're a disgusting *animal*!' Catherine said, and pushed her skirt down. Picol rubbed his head as blood trickled across one eyebrow and onto his workout suit.

They exchanged glances.

'Listen, baby, don't blame me if I tried to see what's got Graham Donaldson so pussy-whipped.'

She spun on her heel just as three lights on the phone panel lit up. Picol ambled over to pick one up, and before she could reach the door, he called out, 'Get me some ice for my head before you go – will you?'

She couldn't slam the door hard enough behind her.

# 9

Catherine tipped her baseball cap to shade her eyes and waded into the turquoise sea, wearing only her Place in the Sun T-shirt over a bikini. She spotted a pink and yellow shell lying in the foam at the shore of the white sand beach, carefully picked it up, and studied it. Catherine smiled up at Graham. In her bare feet, she seemed much smaller than he.

The surf kicked at her heels. She was glad she hadn't mentioned the Michael Picol incident to him. It would have served no purpose, and both she and Graham needed Picol to complete this project.

Catherine was finally on location at the island supervising the first shoot for a promotional package that it was hoped would attract foreign investors in both the banks and the condominiums. Bambi was due to arrive tomorrow with Valeski for the fashion shots and ads. Valeski's assistants were already here, setting up and shooting interiors. Graham had flown down at her special request because after three months of background work she was finally ready to unveil her two surprises to him.

She looked around. The beach was deserted. The crew must have gone up to their cabins to clean up for dinner, Catherine thought with a smile. She didn't want any cameras or jealous busybodies around. She would have Graham to herself tonight, but tomorrow, once Bambi arrived, she knew they'd never have a moment alone.

Graham had been carelessly showing her affection in the open lately, and, in spite of her better judgement,

Catherine couldn't force herself to do anything but welcome his touch.

They made love on the beach and in the warm, shallow water. Moonlight shimmered on the waves as they touched each other with a tenderness Catherine treasured. Afterward, she had curled up in his arms in the sand, and as they counted the stars in the sky, Catherine had wished for them to be together always.

They then spent the night together in her cabin, and the next morning, as they breakfasted on her thatched terrace, high on the crest of the hill, they surveyed the entire Sound. 'It looks pretty good, doesn't it, Graham? Our dream is really coming true.' Six flights of stone steps below, the photography crew was already at work. A few of the assistants were trying out the new windsurfers. She and Graham lazily watched the brightly colored sails skimming across the cerulean waters. Palm fronds on the roof of the terrace rustled softly, like a taffeta dress, while they ate their fresh pineapple and corn muffins. A tiny yellow and olive-green bird landed on the table, and Catherine fed it sugar from her hand. Across the bay, she and Graham could see the long island where the jetstrip was under construction. She still thought of that island as Aggie Palmer's. Yet even in this tranquil setting there was still work to be done. Dr Io was waiting for them.

Catherine took Graham by the hand, and they walked to the marine biology research center. She had managed to set the center up on her own, circumventing Ray Acconti, with Dr Io's expertise, and this was, to her, not only a completion of part of their project, but a gift of love to Graham. Eve might be able to give him diamond cuff links from Cartier's but only she, Catherine, could give him his life's dream, his Place in the Sun.

Hand in hand, they walked down to the building made

of native stone which literally hung over the ocean. As she led him through the construction site, Catherine finally announced the results of the center's first two experiments. 'Catherine McBride, Dr Io, and the Graham Donaldson Marine Biology Research Center now present to you their first scientific breakthrough, The Bionic Fish!' She looked on proudly as Dr Io explained how the center had crossbred until they had created a more resilient and faster-growing fish. Io had also found that by accelerating the tidal action he could speed up the entire development of the marine food chain and was able to cultivate fast-growing algae and seaweeds in one fifth of the normal time frame. These advances in aquaculture would offer food potential for underdeveloped nations that had never been realized. Graham was enthralled, and his face glowed as they walked to the pier. He examined the specimens in the open-sea holding tank, each separated by nylon screens and wire-net compartments. The Graham Donaldson Center was barely under construction, yet it had already achieved great success.

Catherine pulled off her cap and bowed as if she were on center stage. 'But! Behind Door Number Two, we have what promises to be the money-making machine to cover all the center's expenses. Follow me.' They walked down a tangled path, weaving around a thicket of sea grape plants and ducking beneath hanging tendrils of frangipani. Pushing their way through the newly landscaped hibiscus bushes, which already sported a fiesta of scarlet, pink, and yellow blooms, Catherine picked a flower and tucked it behind her ear.

'And what is this?' joked Graham, as they stepped into a bulldozed area with two-foot-high stakes stuck into the dry ground, ropes strung between. He climbed into one of the roped-off squares. 'Knowing you, this is where you've invented hydrophonic pineapple.'

'I'm afraid you're standing in the middle of the black-jack table.'

'Blackjack?' A sudden frown crossed his brow.

'I've done all the advance planning, and I've worked out our preliminary licensing. Graham, we can totally underwrite the research center if we establish a gambling casino as part of the resort. Terry Skittles and I have worked it out. The whole area here,' she pointed at the large groups of roped-off ground, 'is based on the one at Paradise Island in Nassau.'

'Casino! Honey, you've gotta be crazy. Intercon is not in the casino business. I can see the board of directors now.' He frowned again.

'So can I. And they'll never go for the Graham Donaldson Research Center if it costs them one cent over the bottom line. Darling, it makes *sense*.' Catherine couldn't understand why he wasn't more excited. Her plan was brilliant, but Graham's face remained clouded. She couldn't understand it. She'd just handed him the money on a silver platter with bougainvillea and passion fruit, and he was worried about the board. Nor could she understand what was so wrong with casinos. Baron Grunewald owned two – one at the Cote d'Azur and one in Baden-Baden, and he was one of the most respected businessmen in the world.

Graham shook his head. 'I don't know, Catherine. Casinos are a pretty dirty business.'

She shrugged her shoulders. 'They're *big* business, and legitimate ones. I've got the figures back at the cottage.'

'I don't care about the figures. You know this is my gift back to the world so why put price tags on it?'

'But, Graham, sometimes you have to compromise to

make gifts come true.' She reached into his pocket and pulled out a book of matches so she could light his pipe. The cover was printed with the insignia of the Onwentsia Golf Club in Lake Forest – Eve's club. It seemed like a million miles away. She lit his pipe for him and tossed the matches into a steel bin.

'Well, if it makes you happier we'll only have chemin de fer. It's very classy and the house always wins.' She smoothed his hair behind his ears. 'You're getting sunburned,' she whispered, letting her hand linger on his cheek.

He took her in his arms and brought her face to his. 'You funny thing, you know I adore you!' He kissed her on both cheeks and then on her mouth, both of them totally oblivious of the camera crews and construction workers nearby.

'I hope you like my presents,' she finally said. 'They're everything I have to give. It's all I have – my ideas and my work. Please accept them.'

'Oh, honey, I'm so proud of you. I've never had anything better – even under the Christmas tree.'

All of a sudden, the sky was dark with fat, gray rushing clouds, and a sudden warm barrage of tropical rain began. Every morning, it seemed to shower for fifteen minutes or so.

Graham put his arm across Catherine's shoulders to shield her from the rain, but they did not rush as they climbed the hill back to their cabins.

Her hair was wet and stringy, her T-shirt plastered to her body and his clothes were soaked by the time they got inside his room. She started to unbutton his shirt. 'You'd better take off this shirt or you'll catch cold, Mr Chairman.'

She dropped the shirt onto the lacquered wood floor and pulled her T-shirt over her head.

Graham slipped one of his hands inside her bikini bottom where the flesh was so lean it was almost boyish and pressed the other to her sunburned face. 'Catherine, I've been waiting for this all morning.'

The rain had darkened the turquoise sky to a dark blue with streaks of pewter and lavender. It beat a rushing pattern on the thatched roof and tiled terrace, and poured down like a curtain around their private bungalow, obscuring the rest of the world.

They were moving toward the bed, but she stopped on the bare wood floor, rivulets of water trickling down their legs and forming tiny puddles at their feet.

'Graham, I want you to do something for me.'

'What, honey?'

'I want you to dance with me.' She walked backward to the bamboo console and pushed a compact disc into her portable Sony. To the sultry tones of Sade, she put her arms around his neck and began to sway her hips against his. 'I'll lead,' she said.

Graham smiled into her damp hair. He'd never had a woman take control as often as Catherine did, and sometimes he felt as if he should be the one to lead her. After all, *he* was the man. He pushed himself harder against her and moved as she did. 'What do you call this step?'

'Come closer and I'll tell you,' she whispered.

'Any closer and we'll be inside each other.'

'That's just the point.'

As if they were part of the tropical storm, their feelings and passions merged together, as consuming as the rain, the sky, and the sea. Catherine felt a new lushness in her body as Graham kissed her neck and bare shoulders, teasing her skin with his teeth.

She slowly dropped her bikini bottom around her ankles, tugged his suit to the floor, and stepping out of their clothes, they again moved in a slow dance. Catherine led, but Graham was now inside her, pushing himself deep within her. His hands clasped her buttocks as they both stood watching themselves in the floor-length mirror across the room. Catherine was transfixed by the reflection of their bodies fusing into one erotic form. Through half-open eyes, she saw them come together and pull apart to the rhythm of the rain. Over and over, she reached out to caress him, to pull him back as he moved away, to press herself against his suntanned skin.

Gently, Graham reached down and circled Catherine's waist with his hands and pulled her up until she brought her knees beneath his arms and firmly wrapped her legs around him. She let her head fall forward over his shoulder, her hair tumbling onto his back. They stood, drenched in their salty sweat, both feeling a shortness of breath that made their hearts beat rapidly.

Graham moved them over to the bed, bent Catherine over backward, and laid her on top of the batik cotton spread. With her breasts and face pressed against the pillows, she hooked her legs around him and pulled herself to him. Taking her hands and clasping them behind her neck, Graham pushed within her until he lost all control.

Later, Catherine turned and again lowered herself over Graham's body. She held him tightly between her legs, barely moving, knowing the pressure would slowly stimulate him into a shattering climax. Graham tried to move, but he could only hold her hips firmly against him as they pressed together, then apart, in a building passion that left them both spent.

As Catherine later dozed in his arms, Graham stared at the ceiling fan. He felt as if he were eighteen years old again. And she, so wholesome and innocent looking, was more daring and adventurous in the bedroom than he could have imagined. Catherine was neither shy about her body nor coy about her open desire for him. She was always ready for him with a sexual hunger that alarmed yet stimulated him.

He kissed her head as it lay nestled on top of his shoulder. She needs me, he thought. And more than anything in the world, he wanted her to be safe and make her happy.

# 10

Should I tell her or shouldn't I? The Greeks used to kill bearers of bad news, thought Hughie as he held up the C-print color enlargements he'd ordered on rush from Astra Photo. All the photos from Bambi's Place in the Sun shoot had turned out brilliantly, as expected. The combination of Valeski and Bambi together was magical. Hughie had been annoyed when he was told he wouldn't be able to go to the island shooting session and had blamed Catherine McBride for not letting him attend his sister on her first trip to the Caribbean. She had orchestrated the whole shoot from her legendary white Formica dictatorship and had refused to write him into the budget. Two hair and makeup stylists were all she would spring for. Since Bambi was underage Hughie felt he should have been there. What if Bambi had needed him, or felt homesick? She'd never been away without him before. But Valeski had thought it would give Bambi an opportunity to spread her wings and had promised to look after her, so Hughie had agreed.

He pulled his photographer's loop out of the pocket of his Armani jacket and peered more closely at one of the pictures. No wonder Catherine McBride hadn't wanted him there! Since she wanted to play dictator in her banana republic among the sea grapes, Hughie thought to himself, then she could fall from her tropical paradise just as easily! Dictators never lasted long, he reasoned.

Hughie had caught Graham Donaldson in living color, embracing the McBride bitch. His hand was firmly entrenched inside her bikini top, and she had an expression of concentrated seduction on her face. Serves the old bastard right, Hughie told himself. Graham would get what he deserved with this Lucrezia Borgia. He examined McBride's eyes more closely. If Graham was so interested in his fish research, he had certainly caught himself a barracuda!

He shut the heavy library door so he wouldn't be distracted. Valeski and his crew were trying to make the athletic Drucilla Donaldson look fragile and patrician enough for a *Town & Country* cover. The task was impossible.

Hughie sat down at his desk, trying to decide what to do. If he showed the photo to Eve she would be devastated. Seeing her husband in the arms of a woman years younger, would cause Eve unbearable grief. And from the expressions on the faces of Graham and Catherine, Hughie knew they were not having a casual fling.

Garham's behavior over the last six months had been puzzling, but this photo explained everything, and although Hughie didn't want to hurt Eve he knew she would find out sooner or later. Hughie loved Eve, but Graham had made a lifetime career of acing people out of what was rightfully theirs. And now, true to form, he was going to cheat Eve out of the happiness she deserved. At this stage of her life, Hughie thought, a beautiful, sensitive woman like Eve Donaldson should not have to fight for her husband.

Eve had always been strong and resilient. Her ethereal appearance was deceiving. She'd come to his and Bambi's rescue when their parents had been killed and taken them both under her wing. And she had also survived his affair with the stewardess in Tehran. She had wisely handled that situation by ignoring it until it disappeared.

But McBride was different. She was also creating obstacles between him and Bambi. She never returned his phone calls, and Hughie always had to work through her vapid assistant, B.J. He'd seen her type before. As soon as she got a taste of power, she didn't care who or what she destroyed. She was, Hughie realized, just like Graham Donaldson. They probably deserved each other.

If Eve were smart, she'd let him go. Even at forty-eight, she turned the heads of men half her age. At Ravinia, she had dazzled the young conductor who had joined them after the concert as they waited at the orchestra party for Graham. Eve had not taken her eyes off the door, hoping Graham would make a late appearance. But the conductor, Alex Levine, had not taken his eyes off Eve. Yes, she could survive without Graham Donaldson.

Hughie picked the photograph up from the framed-birch inlaid mahogany card desk and took a deep breath, stuffed the picture into an envelope, and entered a flurry of activity.

In the two-storey foyer with one entire thirty-seven-foot-high glass wall overlooking the Oak Street Beach, Lake Michigan, and miles of the Outer Drive, Drucilla Donaldson was posed in a Regency chair, her white silk strapless ballgown carefully billowed around her in a swirl. This casual arrangement had taken Valeski almost an hour to perfect and light so that the girl, the dress, the jewelry, and the Chicago skyline were all in focus at once.

Drucilla and Lolly Bishop now lived together in the seven-thousand-square foot duplex. It had originally been the pied-à-terre of Eve's parents, the Bentons, and then had been sublet for many years.

Bruce Gregga had gutted the gloomy space and turned it into an eyrie of bleached woods, hyacinth and mauve when Dru decided to move into the apartment. Pastel dhurries tossed on the floor lent a casual feeling, and the apartment had quickly become the clearinghouse of social activity for anyone under age thirty-five in Chicago. An endless stream of visitors came up the private elevator with its green leather couch. Ski instructors, local socialites, fringe royalty, emergency gynecologists, and John Lanzendorf, the wizard hairdresser, were all regulars. Twice a week, Ann Lombardi, who ran a popular nail emporium in Oak Street, broke her rule of never making house calls to shape and mend the girls' fingernails. Everyone loved to visit Dru and Lolly. It was such a good place to catch up on gossip and find out who had married, who had divorced, who was in, who was out.

The apartment had even been in the headlines when one of Drucilla's ex-boyfriends had been refused admittance and slashed his wrists on a broken wine bottle in the entrance hall. The girls had had to call Dr Corbett, the family psychiatrist, and Channel 5 minicams had recorded the entire event as the young man was carried out of the lobby. Drucilla had been shielded by Dr Corbett, and Michael Picol had handled the press. After that the Donaldsons had been concerned about the girls' security and paid the doorman handsomely to screen their visitors, but the building staff had given up on identifying every face in the constant parade of assorted visitors. They couldn't remember who went in at three in the afternoon and who went out at three in the morning.

At the engagement party Lolly had thrown for Drucilla and Arnaud, they had had a Ferris wheel hoisted to the penthouse duplex by two helicopters. The lawsuit papers filed by the tenant in the apartment below now lay on a desk at Intercon.

Thirty people were jammed into the apartment. The

*Town & Country* spread would appear just after Drucilla's wedding to Count Arnaud de Cotrille, eighth-generation vintner whose family château, Chenomme, was called the Versailles of the Médoc. It had originally been a hideaway for one of Louis IV's mistresses, and the young couple planned to honeymoon there, not on the *Lady Eve*, as Dru's parents had suggested; Arnaud confessed that even sitting in a bathtub made him seasick.

Arnaud stood on the sidelines sulking as the camera focused on his fiancée. He hated publicity, but if Drucilla had to be photographed, *Town & Country* was the one publication he found suitable for a de Cotrille. His family had kept people on salary for generations to keep the family out of the press, except for an occasional approved story on the vineyards. Now that the de Cotrilles owned a California winery, he and his family had decided that a rich American wife and a little controlled American press coverage would be in the family's best interest. His mother had felt it time for a bride who could bring her own finances to the family fortune, and Arnaud hoped that Drucilla would bring healthy American bloodlines to his aristocratic family. And, to the Europeans, the Donaldsons were royalty of a sort.

Just as Valeski was ready to begin shooting. Arnaud stepped up to the camera.

'You don't mind if I take a look at my fiancée and how she will appear in the magazine?' He held his head back haughtily, exposing a prominent Adam's apple.

Valeski, his face frozen, took a step back and made a mocking bow. 'By all *means*. Be my guest. Have *several* looks.' His eyes telegraphed to Hughie that in a few minutes this person would be absolutely intolerable and they would have to leave. Valeski had been patient and polite with him all afternoon, but now he was poking his nose into Valeski's camera.

Arnaud snapped upright from the Hasselblad. He was even paler than usual. 'This will not do! There is entirely too much décolleté in this picture. This is the future Countess de Cotrille, not a Manhattan model!' He sniffed disparagingly. 'She will have to change her dress.'

The assistant who had spent the last hour arranging the folds of the dress looked as if he wished murder were legal in Illinois.

Hughie sensed that Valeski was about to call it a day, and his professionalism took over. He dashed to the sideboard table, which held an array of jewels from Tiffany and Cartier, and picked up a diamond-and-pearl brooch. Then he walked back to the setup and pinned the bodice of the dress together until it was as prim as Drucilla's Alice-in-Wonderland hairstyle. 'There, that should fill in nicely.'

Arnaud nodded a curt thank you and Valeski returned to the camera.

Calm had barely been restored when Dru's mother tiptoed into the room, mouthing a silent hello to Hughie. Eve carried two big bags from Elizabeth Arden under her arm. For weeks, she'd been caught up in the excitement of the wedding plans, shopping for lingerie and trousseau items for Dru's honeymoon. She had bought everything in her daughter's favorite colors, mauve and pink. Hours had been spent choosing the clothes for the wedding party. Becky Bisoulis was making up a special lace suit for Eve, and Scarron was doing the bridemaid's dresses, all in the hyacinth shades. The wedding dress was a closely guarded secret.

Arnaud greeted his future mother-in-law with a dry kiss

on each cheek as Hughie took her packages and set them down at the foot of the stairs.

Hughie decided what he would do. She *had* to know. Knowledge was power, after all, so he'd be doing her a favor. He hated to be the one to tell her, but it was necessary.

'Eve,' he said determinedly. 'Come upstairs with me for a moment. There's something I have to tell you.'

'Okay.' She smiled in anticipation, draping her white lynx coat over the bannister. She always loved Hughie's surprises. But his news sent her reeling to the nearest chair, pictures clutched in her hand and then, silent during the long drive back to Lake Forest and still visibly trembling, Eve Donaldson climbed the stairs to the tower music room where she handled every crisis in her life.

# 11

Catherine put down her second glass of carrot juice. She'd been waiting at the juice bar of the East Bank Club for almost half an hour, dressed and ready for her regular Wednesday night racquetball game with Graham. She had beaten him the last two games, so maybe he was afraid to show up, she joked to herself. Ever since Graham had given her a company membership at the East Bank Club, she'd been swimming, jogging on the indoor track, and had even embarked on a weightlifting program. Catherine could actually bench-press fifty pounds and she'd never looked trimmer or firmer. Her hips and legs had slimmed down and didn't look half bad to her or to the men who approvingly glanced Catherine's way. In her size-six white shorts and pale blue T-shirt, surrounded by all the eighteen-year-old girls who were strutting around in their high-cut spandex and Day-Glo leotards, Catherine's firm, self-confident figure and aloof air caught the eye of even the most jaded of the city's cruise crew, as she jokingly referred to the legion of men who seemed to hang out at sports clubs to add luster to their social calendars. She wished Effie could see her chocolate-chip-filled little girl, who was now half the size she had been at age fourteen! Even Baron Grunewald wouldn't recognize her at a hundred and six toned-up pounds. Catherine had always hated appearance-conscious women, but she had to admit looking good was no sin, and taking care of her body was an investment in herself.

She looked through the glass partition down at the

tennis courts a floor below. At this time of the evening, every court was filled with young working people ridding themselves of the day's aggressions through their favorite sport. The club was always so crowded that no one ever looked twice at who was with whom, and so it was the perfect place to meet Graham. After-hours workouts had taken the place of the five o'clock cocktail hour for business associates. Consequently, a distinguished-looking company chairman sharing a racquetball court with his pony-tailed vice-president never even raised an eyebrow.

Although Catherine and Graham made sure they arrived separately at the East Bank Club, they had a routine. They would generally play an hour of racquetball, shower, change, and go back to her place or the company apartment. If he was much later this week, Catherine thought, glancing at her watch, they'd end up losing their court time. She wondered if a crisis had arisen and if she should try to call him on his private line.

She was just getting up and checking for change when Graham arrived. He was still wearing his charcoal and white pinstripe suit and blue and white fine-lined shirt.

'Hi. Oh – you're not ready. You'd better hurry.' She smiled. 'We only have twenty minutes of court time left if you want to hit some balls.'

She read his face. He looked serious. Something *had* gone wrong at the office! If he hadn't been so tan from their last trip to A Place in the Sun, she'd suspect he was turning pale.

'Listen.' He pulled her over to a bench near the entrance to one of the locker rooms, a little removed from the crowd. 'Honey, we can't play tonight.'

'Well, fine time to tell me. You mean you want to rush straight home tonight?' She looked up playfully from under her thick, sandy eyelashes and bumped at his ankle with the rubber sole of her tennis shoe.

'No, honey.' His voice was quiet as he edged her into the corner. 'The thing is – there's a problem. I can't spend Mondays and Wednesdays in the city anymore. It's Eve.'

'What about Eve? Is she sick again?'

'No. But somehow she's found out.'

Catherine's face was beginning to flush. She could feel her pulse get faster. 'Found out what? That we work together?' What was he telling her? This couldn't be, she told herself, but somehow she knew what was coming. She could feel it. You didn't make love to a man and work with him day and night without sensing what he was thinking. And what he was thinking frightened her. 'What are you trying to tell me?' she asked. All her own feelings of guilt as well as her own anger at being the 'other' woman were welling up, almost choking her.

His eyes looked very distant. 'What I'm doing isn't fair to Eve. I'm insulting her. She doesn't deserve it. She's the mother of my daughter and I have great respect for her. I would never hurt her.'

Catherine felt her heart sink into her tennis shoes. 'I didn't think we were hurting Eve. How could she know anything?'

Graham shrugged. 'Somebody must have told her. I don't know who or how exactly. She gave me an ultimatum. The family or you.' He paused and would not look at Catherine. 'My family is very important to me.'

'What about *me*?' Catherine was getting angry; her body tensed. 'Aren't I important to you? Or can you just call up Katie Gibbs tomorrow and replace me?' She managed a brittle laugh. 'What should I do? Join a sorority with Fanne Fox and Elizabeth Ray?'

Catherine felt tears brimming in her eyes. She could

take a lot of things. She could take fourteen-hour days, nights without sleep, coming and going at Graham's beck and call, feeding him healthy food to reduce the cholesterol of Eve's sauces, even sharing him. But she could not sit in a sweaty health club and listen to Graham tell her he had to protect his wife from her. She was being thrust into the role of femme fatale, an enchantress – yet she was a driven career woman who worked as much for *him* as for the company. This wasn't fair.

'So,' she finally said, feeling a sudden pang of loss. 'You mean we can't see each other any more? I love you, Graham. We're in love, aren't we?'

'We'll still see each other.'

'When?'

'On trips. In Washington, the island – just like before.' He reached out to touch her. 'It just can't be *here*. You do understand that I can't hurt Eve?'

'No! Of course you can't. You can't hurt Eve, but you can hurt me,' Catherine said, shaking her head. Where did he get off, anyway? she asked herself. He must think she was a jerk. Catherine stood and backed away from him.

'Catherine . . .'

'I'll turn in my resignation tomorrow morning. You won't have to worry about hurting Eve anymore.' She turned on her heel and raced up the staircase to the indoor jogging track.

Tears streamed down her cheeks as she started at too fast a pace around the padded rubber track, sprinting past all the steady runners. Maybe if she ran fast enough, she told herself she'd just faint on the floor. Then maybe Graham would sweep her in his arms . . . carry her away . . . rescue her from the despair she felt spreading through her. No, he admired her strength. She'd survive.

But Catherine instantly realized that she'd gambled and lost everything. She couldn't imagine getting up in the morning and not seeing Graham each day at the Intercon office. What was she going to do now? Didn't he know she loved him? That they were a team? Didn't he know what he was throwing away? Had *she* miscalculated *him* all along?

She pounded around the track, breathing hard. Maybe she would calmly walk into the office in the morning and set her files on fire. Catherine knew that without those files A Place in the Sun would never happen.

Maybe she should call Eve herself. Tell her to give up while she was ahead, that it was about time she did more with her life than run opera balls and write place cards in her famed calligraphy!

Or maybe she should just go home and wait for the phone to ring. He would plead with her. She would stay calm, unmoved by his tears. She'd find another position somehow, one more grandiose than her job at Intercon. Maybe with a competitor. She'd show him. He'd come pleading to get her back. And she wouldn't take his calls. The faster she ran, the harder the tears ran down her face. Who was she kidding? She loved him, and he had just told her good-bye. The runners around her dissolved into blurred patches of color, and she stumbled into the next lane, bumping a young girl almost off balance.

And then she heard him call her name. 'Catherine!' She blotted her eyes with her terrycloth wristband and looked over her shoulder. Graham was running after her, still dressed in his business suit and Bally loafers, his tie flapping.

Catherine sped up.

A uniformed attendant was waving at Graham, trying

to get him off the track, but Graham merely brushed him off and raced after Catherine.

It was her third time around the track, and she was getting tired, more from emotion than from physical exertion.

He caught up with her at the entrance, after another full lap. She was ready to drop, but she kept running. He ran alongside, his pace uneven in his street shoes.

'Catherine, I don't want to hurt you.'

'Remember, it's Eve you don't want to hurt. Go back to Lake Forest. There's more room to run out there.'

He was out of breath. 'Listen, are you going to talk to me, or are you going to kill me here?' He feigned a smile.

She managed one, too. How she wished he would just take her in his arms right here, in front of everyone, and let the world know how much he loved and needed her.

She trotted to a stop and turned to face him, her blue eyes raised hopefully.

He took her by the shoulders. 'Catherine, you're the most beautiful, talented, brilliant woman I know. You think twice as fast as any man. I've never worked with anyone I admire more.'

Catherine stared back at him. What was this, a performance evaluation?

'Any man, any single man, younger than I, would be luckier than hell to have you. You're too good for me.'

'Graham,' she began.

'No.' He interrupted her. 'You're upset. I'm upset. You knew what you were getting into from the beginning when we began this affair. You knew I was married. I'll tell you what. Let's let things cool down before we decide anything. Why don't you take a week off? I refuse to accept your resignation. You've been working too hard; a vacation is the only sensible thing to do.' His face was resolute. 'Maybe we both just need a little time apart.'

'What about Eve?' she whispered.

'Eve is my wife.' He looked at her evenly.

'And what am I?'

'Don't get emotional. It's only a week.'

*Emotional?* What did he think this was, a relationship or the Pillbury Bake-Off? Catherine couldn't believe what she was hearing. Where was that Alexander the Great statue when she needed it! She could use it to knock some sense into Graham's head. Eve, the beautiful, the accomplished – Eve the insipid – had won, Catherine told herself. And as her mother had always promised, she, Catherine, was left alone.

She took a deep breath. 'Well. I'm giving you an ultimatum, too. If it's me you want, it's got to be only me.' Her voice rose. Runners stretching their hamstrings on the sidelines turned to look in their direction.

'I will not have a scene in here, Catherine.' Graham turned and walked hastily off the track and through the door.

Catherine couldn't believe her eyes as she watched him leave. He didn't want a *scene*? Was that all this man really cared about? His appearance to the outside world? Maybe he was better off with Eve.

Somehow she got off the track, somehow she found her way home, and somehow she didn't die when she took too many Valium in her apartment on the ninety-first floor of the Hancock building.

# 12

Outside the Art Deco lobby of Claridge's Hotel, a gray Daimler waited. A pale, thin Catherine McBride stepped into the damp, gray London chill as the young man behind the wheel jumped out and came around the car, his hand extended. Before he could reach her side, she motioned him away, opened the door herself, and slid into the back seat. 'Never mind,' she cut him off. 'I'll do it myself.' Somewhat taken aback, the driver got back behind the wheel and turned to face her. 'I see you're one of those independent American women,' he said. His accent was impeccably upper-class British and his look slightly amused, but Catherine did not seem to notice.

'Just a tired American woman,' she answered. She kept her gaze averted.

He watched her in the rearview mirror, but it was obvious she didn't want to engage in conversation, let alone reminisce. Her expression was vacant, her eyes listless, and her hollow cheekbones gave her face a haunted, elusive look.

Catherine turned her head and stared at the stately stone buildings through the gray drizzle. She supposed she ought to at least take in the sights – this was, after all, her first trip to London – but she felt no sense of excitement or interest.

Catherine was surprised she had gotten to London at all. It had been an enormous effort to walk through the madhouse of the international terminal at O'Hare and board the British Airways flight to Heathrow Airport.

She had slept during the entire flight, the first real, natural sleep she'd had in a week. She had thrown out the bottle of Valium after that first night when she almost overdosed on too many pills. When the drug hadn't put her to sleep right away, she had taken several more, and then lost track of how many she had taken. She had slept sixteen hours the next day, until the faraway ringing of the buzzer had finally roused her out of her stupor. She remembered getting to the door somehow, and then B.J. walking her around the room. B.J. had pulled open all the narrow windows and made a pot of coffee while Catherine had mumbled something about having the flu and taking too many antihistamines. B.J. had been worried about her because it was so unlike Catherine to miss a staff meeting and not call in. Catherine had thanked her for her concern and, with a weak smile, accepted her gift of two cans of Campbell's chicken noodle soup and her offer to tuck her back into bed. Both women knew what had really happened.

After that Catherine had aimlessly roamed around the apartment for days, wearing one of the undershirts that still carried the scent of Graham's pipe tobacco and the smell of her lover's body. Over this she wore his plaid wool robe, and a pair of his argyle socks. He never wore cologne so the smells of Graham Donaldson were the natural, musky smells of a man. Catherine could conjure up his smell on a moment's notice and then feel a tension travel up her body.

She had tried over and over to call him on his private line, the number of which only she, Eve and Drucilla had. For three days it was constantly busy. Catherine assumed it was off the hook. Please let him answer, please let him want me back, she would say three times before each call as if the tautology of the number three would be magic and then he would suddenly pick up, answering the phone in that soft, husky voice that spelled out power, security, and love to her. On the fourth day, utterly exhausted and miserable, she got a recorded message telling her that number had been changed to another unlisted number. When she hung up, Catherine had sat stunned and shaken, bleakly wondering what to do. The week was almost over, and she knew she couldn't call him at home over the weekend.

She had thought about going to see her mother, but this time she needed someone to comfort her – a real mother, or a real man. She needed Graham.

Finally, she put ice cubes over her swollen eyes and called the regular number of Intercontinental. She went through two secretaries before she had heard Carla's friendly voice over the phone.

'Hi, Catherine,' she said. 'How's your flu? You better hurry back. We miss you around here.' The flu was it? Good old B.J. 'Just a second,' she said. 'I'll put you through to the boss. This is a good time to catch him.'

Catherine's heart had fluttered in anticipation and excitement when Carla told her this was a good time. Everything was going to be fine. Why hadn't she called Carla before? She quickly rehearsed in her head what she'd say to Graham, but her mouth suddenly went dry. What if she couldn't get any words out? She should have practiced something before calling. Her heart was racing and beating so hard she could hear it.

'Graham?' She finally got the word out in a burst of courage when somebody came on the line. But it was Carla again, this time the maternal tones sympathetic and slightly puzzled.

'Listen, Catherine, I'm sorry,' she said. 'My fault. He's in there with some people and I didn't even know it.'

She'd paused, and the pause said it all. 'He'll have to get back to you.'

Catherine barely managed to hang up the receiver before she let out a cry so desolate and anguished that it didn't even sound like her own voice. She couldn't remember how long she'd screamed until, suddenly, she stopped. Nothing came out of her throat.

Catherine felt that at least Graham could have spoken to her himself, and his rudeness was the last indignity she would tolerate. Letting Carla run interference for him was nothing short of an intentional insult – a casual acquaintance was treated better.

That weekend she had made one last effort to reach him by breaking the rules and dialing his number in Lake Forest. Eve had answered and she swiftly hung up. After that, Catherine had taken her own phone off the hook and continued to pace throughout her apartment.

By Sunday, she had somehow mustered the energy to go to the building commissary and buy some groceries. She hadn't eaten for days, and she filled her cart with chocolate chip cookies, milk, and yogurt. For good measure, she grabbed a bouquet of flowers.

She plopped the flowers, still wrapped in their rubber band, into a drinking glass, then settled on the couch with a yellow legal pad in her lap.

She wrote 'Priorities' at the top and then divided the page into two columns: 'Good for Catherine' and 'Bad for Catherine.'

The Bad for Catherine column was easy to construct. She wrote Graham's name down seven or eight times.

The Good for Catherine column consisted of Aggie Palmer and Effie, the only people in her life who had never let her down, though even Effie couldn't help her now. She called Aggie Palmer. The houseman told her

Mrs Palmer was visiting friends in Cuernavaca.

Catherine thought of her old boss at Swift, wrote his name down, but decided not to call him. She was beyond his help, and she could never go back to being a small cog in a big machine after having total control of her own department.

She briefly considered Brian Thundercloud, but as a lawyer immersed in Indian affairs, he now lived in a different world. And he was from a different part of her life. She could hardly call him and say, 'Hi Brian. I just broke up with a married man. Let's talk.'

Well, where did that leave her? Catherine had sat very still, fingering the gold charm that had hung on a chain around her neck since her Neiman-Marcus makeover. She traced Baron Grunewald's crest over and over as she sat in the living room, staring at the incongruously cheerful bunch of flowers. Where was the baron when she needed him?

Yes, where *was* the baron? She'd left him off her list because she hadn't actually seen him for eight years, and, except for Christmas cards, her last contact with him had been the note she'd sent after she joined Intercon.

He had replied with a brief note of congratulations and had suggested she keep in touch. He was always interested in his Grunewald Scholars. Catherine went into the kitchen and ate some chocolate chip cookies. They always made her feel better about anything.

By the time she finished the bag of cookies, Catherine had decided to call the baron. *He* had been her first mentor, not Graham. She wasn't positive the baron could help her, but he would at least point her in the right direction.

Once Catherine made her decision there was no limit to her enthusiasm. She would go to Europe and meet with the baron in person – a phone call was not enough. The baron was her one real hope, and she wanted to make sure he understood what she'd been doing for Intercon. She wouldn't tell him about Graham, since the baron didn't have to know everything. She'd just let him know she needed some career counseling. No one knew more about careers than Baron Eric Grunewald, owner of six banks, an international transportation conglomerate, and automotive, munitions and publishing empires. Graham was successful; the Baron *was* success. She was sure that if she met with him everything would fall into perspective. Maybe he would even help her find a position in Europe, since no place in the States could be far enough removed from Intercon Minerals, and Graham Donaldson.

Catherine had quickly calculated the time difference. It was almost four o'clock in Munich. She had pulled the baron's last letter to her out of her desk file, checked the number of Grunewald International, and dialed it direct.

The baron's administrative assistant politely took down her request for an appointment. Baron Grunewald, he informed her, was out of the country. He would relay her request and get back to her. Catherine had spent enough summers interning for the baron to know that her name would be fed into the computer, her past and present record checked, and what relationship she had with the baron established before any decision would be made to actually contact him.

Two hours later, the baron's London office had returned her call. She spoke to Cicely Timbelton, who informed her that the baron would be delighted to receive her in London two days from now. Catherine confirmed a two-thirty appointment, assuring Miss Timbelton that two-thirty would fit in perfectly with her plans. She tenderly touched the gold Grunewald charm. The baron to the rescue again!

Catherine realized she had made no plans beyond trudging through her apartment, wrapped in Graham's robe. She picked up the phone and charged all her arrangements to her Gold Card. She would fly a commercial airline for the first time since she'd joined the inner sanctum at Intercon. But she'd get used to it; she was on her own again.

Catherine had done some last-minute shopping, packed a bag, and called B.J. She said she'd be out another week with 'the flu.' B.J. had sounded concerned as she told her the department was a mess, and they needed Catherine. 'Don't get into that medicine again,' she'd warned.

'Don't be silly, I'm fine.' Catherine had tried to keep her voice light. 'I'm just taking a little trip. I need to get away for a few days. Chicago is getting to me.'

'What if I need you to make a decision?'

'You can handle it.'

When she was leaving for O'Hare, she checked the apartment one last time to be sure all the lights were off and her résumés were packed. The bed was still unmade, but that didn't matter. Then she noticed Graham's plaid robe, hanging on a corner of the bathroom door. She yanked it down, picked up the undershirt and shocks that were lying in a heap on the floor, and shoved them all unceremoniously into the incinerator.

Once in London and on her way to see the baron, Catherine realized she could be headed for anything from a ten-minute tea party to a possible interview.

She sighed loudly enough that the driver looked at her again in the rearview mirror. This time he caught her eye. He wasn't dressed in Baron Grunewald's usual livery – a loden-green-and-gunmetal-gray uniform – Catherine thought to herself. His suit was an expensive, tailored Savile Row. But then, the baron usually had aides of all sorts doing all sorts of things. For all she knew, this guy could be a Harvard MBA and a Grunewald Scholar, sent on an errand by the baron. He looked about her age, and he was actually quite handsome in a cool English way. The baron always liked to surround himself with attractive people.

The car pulled up to a weathered stone row house that bore no identifying insignia. The small lobby had only a desk, manned by a guard wearing the baron's uniform. He rose and stood at attention as they went straight to the Victorian-looking lifts. Two of them were open and waiting, but the young driver took out a key that opened a third brass door. They rode in silence up to the top floor, and he used another key to open the door. They stepped out into a world for which Catherine was totally unprepared. An expansive, high-tech rubber floor in loden green spread out for thousands of square feet in a space that bore no resemblance to the small, elegant building they had entered. Of course, Catherine thought. The baron must own the whole row of houses on this block, and had opened them up into a huge, loftlike space. Desks in shades of red, yellow, green, and blue were scattered across the enormous area, occasionally divided by low metal screens. On the dark, lacquered, navy blue walls hung pieces from the baron's world-famous art collection. The Grunewalds had collected art for the last two hundred years and owned some Flemish masterpieces, Catherine knew, but these were large modern canvases of violent colors and figures.

'Are you interested in art?' asked the driver, noticing her curious expression.

She nodded. 'I thought the baron collected period pieces.'

'These are his latest acquisitions,' he said. 'From the new-wave German school. Most of these enormous monstrosities came straight from the Art Fair at Basel. Rather gruesome, aren't they?' He indicated thirteen feet of three shadowy figures plunging a knife into a fourth, with rubber face masks sutured onto the canvas. 'Our curators tell us they're a good investment, but I find them quite hideous.'

Catherine looked around to see if anyone else had noticed these sacrilegious comments. In her days with the baron, no one ever dared to make negative comments on *any* of his choices. Her chauffeur must be either very new or very secure in his position, she concluded.

They walked through another room filled with computer equipment and CRT screens, until they came to two huge lacquer doors that led to the private offices of Baron Eric Grunewald. The young man inserted a card into a slot, and the doors swung open. He moved with authority as they walked in.

Three women sat at highly polished burled oak desks.

'Hello, Cicely,' nodded Catherine's driver.

'Good afternoon, sir. How are you today?'

Catherine looked at her precocious driver. It was obvious he was more than an ordinary employee. Who was he? Did she recognize him? She'd brushed off his introduction and now she couldn't even remember his name. Catherine hoped she hadn't offended him.

'He's expecting you,' said Cicely. The young man turned to leave.

'Both of you,' she added.

He pulled a gold pocket watch from under his coat and frowned.

'*Both* of you,' she repeated. 'Sir'.

Behind one more massive wooden door on which was carved the familiar Grunewald falcon crest was the baron's private office. The crest gave Catherine a sudden burst of confidence. She and the falcon were old friends.

She straightened her short wool burgundy spencer jacket and adjusted the black velvet cuffs. She checked the dozen black velvet buttons that ran down the front of the jacket to make sure none had come undone. The baron had always noticed the smallest detail.

An enormous green table occupied almost a third of the room, which in itself was a good thirty by forty feet. On the table was the most intricate, elaborate toy train set Catherine had ever seen. The baron's aristocratic figure, in shirtsleeves, was bent over the miniature landscape of turrets, trestles, signs, and bridges, over which two tiny trains rumbled over crisscrossing tracks, narrowly missing each other as they careened around a corner. All the cars, from the engines to the wagon-lits, bore miniature Grunewald crests.

'Ah, it works *perfectly*,' the baron exclaimed as he simultaneously manipulated the dual control systems. 'This is revolutionary! Alfred, come here. All our trains will carry this safety system. It is brilliant.' He turned around and held his hand out to Catherine. 'Catherine McBride you have turned into my most glamorous Grunewald Scholar. You remember Alfred? You and he must be good friends by now. He makes friends easily, especially with attractive women. It runs in the family.'

With a jolt, Catherine realized that the young driver she had so cavalierly dismissed was the baron's son, who ten years ago had caught her eating the baron's tea chocolates. He was about five years older than Catherine and tall like the baron – over six feet – and he had the same warm, indigo eyes and aristocratic nose as his father. The baron at seventy-three had the physique of an athletic fifty-year-old. Only his deep, ruddy complexion, heavily lined with a fine network of creases earned over decades of sun and yachting off Marbella, Corsica, and Sardinia showed his age. His thinning, snow-white hair contrasted with his son's, which was thick and brown, and so fine that it kept falling over Alfred's broad forehead.

The baron took her hand. 'Yes, my dear. I always make time for my Grunewald Scholars. And especially those who have achieved so much in a short time.'

Catherine smiled. 'You were so good to see me on such short notice.'

'Unfortunately, I don't have as much time as I would like. Alfred is receiving an award for his newspaper editorials, and I am taking the afternoon off to attend.'

Catherine cringed inside, remembering how she had ignored the Baron's son and treated him like a chauffeur. 'How very exciting. Of course you must go.'

'But we will spend a little time today and then, if you are in town for a while, perhaps dinner tomorrow?' The baron was as charming as she had remembered.

'Oh, I really won't take that much of your time,' Catherine began to protest, but the baron pressed on.

'We will not take no for an answer,' he said in a curt Teutonic manner. Then he smiled. 'You will get a tour of the offices here today, and tomorrow after Alfred's award, we will all celebrate with a dinner at the Connaught. It is settled.'

Catherine wondered when she would have a chance for serious discussions with the baron. 'How generous of you,' she said. Obviously, there was no arguing with him.

'You are still at Intercon, are you not? I hear great progress of your work. You have tremendous responsibility, I understand.' The baron walked over and put on his jacket. 'I have shot quail with Graham Donaldson, but I do not know him all that well.'

Catherine evaded the issue of Graham Donaldson. She moved over to the train set. 'This is wonderful,' she said. 'Did Grunewald Metals custom-make these for you?'

The baron laughed, his thin lips showing his yellowed teeth. 'No, this was fabricated to our specifications by Marklin in West Germany. Every detail is exact to the actual construction.' He handed her one of the miniature cars to inspect.

'I'll look forward to our conversation,' Catherine said. 'Your advice is very important to me. After all, you've been molding my career since I was thirteen.'

'I'm delighted to continue the relationship. I'm only sorry you didn't come sooner. Why, a person with your background should have limitless opportunities. Is that not so, Alfred?'

Alfred, sitting in a Milanese leather chair, glanced appraisingly at Catherine. 'Of course,' he nodded.

She suspected Alfred was laughing to himself and didn't think she was quite as astute as did his father.

'I understand that you are working in the highest of circles,' the baron continued, 'and I'm proud of you. I think you will see that even we have grown since you were involved with us. I am anxious to show you.' He opened the door and barked out, 'Cicely, Cicely! We are ready now to give Miss McBride the tour.'

Cicely materialized at his side in less than a minute.

'You will show her please the Bavarian Airways case history, and also everything on the American companies in which we have controlling interest.' He turned to Catherine. 'I think there will be some surprises for you in here.'

With that, he motioned to Alfred and briskly stepped out the door.

'It was nice to have seen you again, Catherine.' Alfred offered his hand.

'I'm so embarrassed,' she said. 'I was just so preoccupied.'

'So you seemed.'

She blushed. 'I may not have recognized you, but I did notice – you were the most attractive chauffeur that has ever driven me.'

'In that case, I forgive you.' His expression was earnest and open, his eyes warm and without deception. 'After all, appearances are deceiving. You, for instance, look like neither the shy, bookish girl I encountered ten years ago, nor the important businesswoman my father assures me you are.'

'What *do* I look like?'

He grinned. 'Like a person who could still put away five pounds of chocolate if she put her mind to it.'

She laughed for what must have been the first time in days. Watching Alfred go, Catherine remembered all too vividly the day, years earlier, when Alfred had rescued her from a most embarrassing situation.

Clutching the stack of manila envelopes, seventeen-year-old Catherine grabbed the side of the swaying train car for balance as she pushed through the door inset with an etched-glass panel bearing the Grunewald crest to the library car of Baron Eric Grunewald's private train. She had only been in three of the five cars, but this was by far the most splendid. Dark, burled wood covered the walls, and the sunlight that filtered through the half-drawn green shades threw spotlights on the paisley carpet, dimming the light from the glowing brass sconces with their tasseled silk lampshades.

Catherine had won the Grunewald Senior Scholarship, a four-week student internship in Germany working for the baron's parent company. It was the coup of her senior year, for during previous summers, she had been required to spend hundreds of hours researching and writing papers in the local library. But the scholarship for seniors included a foreign exchange program. Catherine had been assigned as an apprentice assistant to the associate comptroller, who always traveled with the baron.

Dieter Schidor, the comptroller, had explained that, although the baron owned an airline, he found traveling by train far more comfortable. They were spending a week touring the Grunewald vineyards and factories along the Rhine, and Catherine found herself running from car to car carrying messages, taking notes, and writing conference reports as the train traced the terraced hills and poplar-and-willow-lined river.

It had been an incredible experience for a girl who had never gone farther than Maple Street. When she traveled to Phillips Academy as a student three years ago she had been overwhelmed, and there had been nights when she had felt so alone that all she could do was cry herself to sleep. Yet the harder she worked the more she seemed to excel, and in her senior year she had at last earned an opportunity that even her wealthy classmates from privileged families could not share.

If her father hadn't abandoned them and if her mother hadn't been in an institution, Catherine realized, she would probably still be in Maple Hill High, going to dances and taking gymnastics. Although she had never been to a dance, she had now been to Germany.

Catherine gingerly placed the envelopes on a marquetry

desk, which she assumed to be the baron's. Usually, his private secretary took the papers, but there was no sign of him. The compartment was empty, except for the Art Deco glass bookshelves holding hundreds of leather-bound volumes and a white-clothed tea cart holding an elaborate array of sugary Austrian pastries. A brace of plump chocolate porcupines with raspberry eyes stared up at her, nestled beside a four-foot-high marzipan basket filled with fruit. Mounds of marrons glacés, tiny pinched tarts, mille-feuille layered with custard, charlotte aux fraises, and a peacock with a tail made of exotic chocolates beckoned from Meissen and silver platters. Catherine knew she was overweight, but eating was the only way she could indulge herself. She couldn't afford many clothes and luckily Phillips supplied uniforms. Her very plain sweaters and skirts were so basic that she seemed in uniform even outside the Academy. The baron insisted his employees wear neutral colors that wouldn't clash with his corporate loden green, and Catherine had no difficulty complying. She had no dates or life outside her studies. It was almost as if her weight were a wall between herself and the rest of the world, protecting her from having to even try to do the things other seventeen-year-olds did.

She eyed the chocolates. As long as she was alone, no one would know if she ate just one. Catherine's hand reached out and plucked a large, dusted chocolate truffle from the peacock's tail, causing a domino reaction as dozens of little chocolate balls rolled across the table. For a moment, she wondered if she should eat them all or stuff them back into the hole.

'I see you've discovered the Cave-In theory,' a proper British voice startled her, as Alfred Grunewald emerged from behind the ornate brass bookcases. Alfred was interning in his father's company at the collegiate level.

During this summer he supervised the communications center and wrote daily briefings for the baron.

Catherine and he had never spoken. Alfred was not only disarmingly good-looking, with his wheat-colored hair, patrician features, and cleft chin, but he was thin. She was always intimidated by thin people, and Alfred was the baron's son as well. What would she have to say to him? Her words were stilled. 'The Cave-In Theory? Our group hasn't gotten to that yet.'

'Yes. If you take a chocolate, don't take it from the middle, or the whole thing caves in.' He took a truffle and popped it into his own mouth. 'Well, we might as well destroy the evidence.'

Catherine started to smile, but self-consciously covered her mouth with her hand. She hated the gap between her front teeth. 'I-I'm sorry,' she stammered.

He scooped the entire peacock tail into a serviette. 'Nonsense. They'll never know what they missed.' He offered a chocolate to Catherine. 'The Cave-In Theory is followed by the Cover-Up Theory.'

He seems so self-assured, she thought, yet he is only a few years older than me. Feeling like an overstuffed American turkey, she tried to say something witty. 'I don't know why I'm eating these. I never really liked peacocks.' When Alfred didn't laugh she polished off another truffle. 'Have you ever heard the sound peacocks make? It's revolting.'

He nodded. 'We have them on the grounds in England. They do screech somewhat.' He pointed to the window. 'Quite unlike the siren song of the Lorelei. Look – there are the Lorelei rocks; you know, the ones where the sirens lured sailors to their deaths with their songs.'

She put both elbows on the window ledge and pushed aside a paisley drapery as the train made a turn approaching Bingen. 'I think the myth was wrong,' she said. 'The sirens lured people with pastries.'

The door between the cars hissed open. 'Quick! Wipe your mouth,' Alfred whispered, laughing. 'You've got the evidence all over your face.' He stuffed the napkin-wrapped chocolates behind a shelf of bound magazines.

It wouldn't have mattered if they'd been caught hoarding every chocolate and pastry on the cart. The woman accompanying the baron was so arresting that she instantly became the focal point of the room. Her presence overpowered even the baron and another woman whose face was hidden under a large fedora.

Alfred walked over and kissed the beautiful woman at the spot she pointed to on her cheek. 'Mother.' Then he nodded to the fedora woman. 'Sybil.' He turned back to Catherine. 'This is – '

She cut him off with an airy wave of her hand. 'Are you doing research, darling, or are you joining us for tea? Sybil is going to read her new poem. Your father has other plans.'

The Baron seated himself at his desk, and began opening the envelopes Catherine had delivered.

She started to back unobtrusively toward the door. Mr Schidor would be furious if he knew she was breaking the ironclad rule of never interrupting the baron's private circle. Suddenly she felt something under her foot. It was the heavy boot of the woman wearing the fedora, who sneered at Catherine.

The baroness, however, gave her a grand and sweeping smile when she left the compartment as hastily as possible.

This was clearly not a place for a scholarship girl from Pittsburgh.

* * *

The baron's party of six was seated around one of the secluded banquette tables in the Connaught Grill. The baron and numerous other celebrities as well as members of the Royal Family often ate here because they knew they would not be recognized, or disturbed if they were. The baron preferred to use the top-floor, gabled penthouse apartment suite of the Connaught as his pied-à-terre in London, rather than make the long drive back after late dinners and meetings to his country estate in Windsor. The Grunewald grounds bordered Windsor Great Park on one side, and the vast house was a masterpiece of Victorian architecture, but the baron often found himself unable to commit himself to the country lifestyle for more than a few days at a time.

He had ordered Catherine the famous Connaught trifle for dessert, telling her, 'When in England . . .' and she finished the sentence, 'Do as the Germans do.'

The baron threw back his huge white head and roared with laughter, bringing his brandy glass down on the table with a thud. 'Catherine, Catherine,' he chortled. 'You certainly have changed from the timid young student we had working for us all those summers.' He leaned closer. 'But truthfully, you don't remember Alfred?' He gestured toward his son. 'He worked in the office with you that summer. He wrote all the copy for the Air Bavaria brochures, while you outlined our strategy. You know, you were only two young people, but both of you had good instincts.' He held his cigarette between two middle fingers that had a hint of nicotine stain. 'Really, I adore young people. I am stimulated by them. One must always keep the mind young.'

A black-coated waiter served Catherine a creamy plate of trifle. 'Did Alfred tell you I thought he was the chauffeur? I'm ashamed to say I didn't recognize him.'

She shot a glance across the table, where the baron's son was apparently engrossed in conversation with Lady Camille Farnsworth, an old family friend of impeccable lineage and translucent complexion who had previously been romantically linked with Prince Andrew before his marriage. Alfred sensed her look and turned to face her for an instant, his eyes mischievous, showing he had overheard Catherine's conversation.

'I thought I passed my chauffeur's test with flying colors,' he broke in.

'I only hope I haven't alienated Alfred,' Catherine sighed in mock resignation to the baron. 'It's always a negative move to get on the wrong side of the press.'

The baron nodded fervently. 'I couldn't agree more. That's why I approve of Alfred's career. Although I would have preferred to have him work for me in Munich.' He wadded up his napkin, dropped it on the table, and leaned back in the over-stuffed leather chair. 'Speaking of negative press, did you get a chance to look over the Darco Coal file?'

Alfred turned back to Lady Camille. He knew when his father was closing in on serious business.

'Yes. How are you going to counteract those accusations?' Even though she'd once worked for Grunewald, Catherine hadn't realized until yesterday that the baron owned the controlling interest in the largest coal company in the United States. Darco was currently under suit by the Environmental Protection Administration. They had shut down production in several major locations, and the loss of revenues had to be crippling. 'How are you going to handle *your* negative press?' she asked again.

'I'm not.' The baron emphatically crossed a fork with a spoon. 'I *never* talk to the press, unless it is one of my own newspapers, edited by my own son.'

'Very wise of you,' Catherine commented. She polished off the last of the trifle. In the past two days, both her color and her appetite had returned.

'Well,' she continued. 'You certainly should be able to work out something with the EPA. Henry Hudson's a very reasonable man.'

The baron's eyes narrowed. 'I understand you know the Secretary of the Interior quite well.'

She wondered for an instant how the baron knew this, but she wasn't surprised. He was meticulous about his background checks. 'Well – I've met with him a few times while in Washington.' Something was coming, Catherine sensed, and it wasn't exactly a job offer.

The baron lit another Gauloise. 'Curious to find you on the board of the Palmer Foundation at such a young age. You certainly are a girl in a high place.' He took a sip of coffee. 'Randy Powell is on that board, is he not?'

Catherine shook her head. 'Not any more. He had to resign. He's due to be sworn in as the new Attorney General in a week or two.'

The baron waved his hand absentmindedly. 'Of course. Now. Do you think my Grunewald Scholar can set up a very private meeting between your new Attorney General, Henry Hudson, and my Darco board? And myself, of course.' He stared at her directly.

Catherine knew the suit must be costing him millions of dollars a week. 'I'm sure if you called them they'd be happy to talk to you,' she demurred.

'No, on the contrary. They're being most unreasonable. After all, I am a foreigner – and of course my family did supply arms to our country in the war. People do not forget this in Washington. Look at that damned Bitburg incident. But perhaps an associate who knows all parties might be able to set up a private, civilized meeting at which we could come to some agreement.' He leaned forward and put his bony, liver-spotted hand on her arm. 'I would be *most* grateful.'

Catherine stirred her tea. What the baron was asking for was beyond what money could buy. Evidently, expensive lobbyists, lawyers, and legitimate and illegitimate means had been applied and failed. And she knew she was in a good position to expedite matters for the baron. It would only take a few phone calls and perhaps a quick trip to Washington. She had a good working relationship with both men. If she were successful, Baron Eric Grunewald would be in her debt. And he had many companies in Europe for which she would have then demonstrated unique qualifications. But now was not the time to mention that. And it was, in fact, unnecessary. They both knew where they stood. The contract the two made with a glance was unspoken, but perfectly clear. 'I will certainly try for you, sir.'

'I'm confident you will.' He refocused his attention on the rest of the group and stood up. 'Now! We are done. We will go to Annabelle's and we will dance. I have been sitting all day, and for once I have a beautiful partner.' He offered Catherine his arm.

'You'd better not humor him,' Alfred warned her, leaning across the table, 'unless you know all the latest steps.'

'But I don't.'

'Good. I won't be the only one sitting on the sidelines then.' Alfred had a way of making her feel uncomfortable, she thought, taking the baron's arm.

The sound of the phone ringing reached Catherine even through the heavy wood door. It had the annoying tinny ring of European phones. The brass key felt clumsy in her hand as Catherine tried to juggle a dozen Beauchamp Place and Bond Street shopping bags without dropping them or the new Burberry raincoat slung over the crook of her arm. The phone was insistent. Ten, fifteen, twenty rings, until, finally, the latch caught and she flew for the phone, leaving her packages in a heap in the hall.

'One minute, please,' said the British operator,' for a person-to-person overseas call for Miss Catherine McBride.'

'This is Miss McBride.'

Who could be calling from overseas, thought Catherine, as she plucked the card from an enormous bouquet of country flowers that had evidently been brought into her room during her shopping spree. On the card was written: 'Enjoy your London visit. The Grunewald Boys.' Catherine had to laugh at this Americanized reference to the imperious seventy-year-old baron as a boy.

She tossed the card down on the dresser. Overseas. It was probably the baron calling from Munich. The only other people she'd given the number to were B.J. at the office, and, of course, Wickes Manor, her mother's nursing home.

Catherine froze.

As she stared at the large floral arrangement, Dr Gresham told her how Elaine McBride had quietly passed away during the night of a heart attack. She had felt no pain, he assured her, and she had had no awareness of who or where she was.

'Are you sure?' Catherine wasn't certain whether she was asking if her mother was really dead, or whether there had been no pain.

No pain, thought Catherine as she hung up. And no joy, either. Having suffered the pain of losing Graham Donaldson, she now understood so much better what her mother had gone through when Ed McBride had left her. The difference was, she, Catherine, had survived, while her mother had really died fourteen years ago. Ed McBride had forced Catherine out into the world and her mother to retreat from it. What a very sad life Elaine McBride had led, and now there was only Catherine to mourn her.

After she had made what perfunctory arrangements she could over the phone, and had called and left a message for Effie, Catherine called Cicely at Grunewald headquarters to let her know she was leaving, and why. Ten minutes later, the baron himself called from Germany. He wished to express his deepest condolences. She was not to worry about a thing. His car would pick her up, and his personal Boeing 727 would fly her directly to Pittsburgh. What else could he do for her?

Standing quietly with her bags at the discreetly placed front desk in the lobby she looked up with surprise to see Alfred Grunewald walk through the door wearing a worried expression.

'I had hoped we might spend more time together. But as long as you are leaving, and under such sad circumstances, I thought you might like your regular chauffeur.'

'Thank you. That's very kind of you.'

This time she sat beside him, in the front seat.

On the way to Heathrow, Catherine sat quietly until Alfred said, 'I hope you will not have any more unhappiness. I could see how sad you were, in the car, when you came.'

'It's all right,' Catherine answered. 'My mother has been sick for a long time.'

Alfred shook his head slowly. 'I'm sorry to hear that. But it doesn't help, does it? I know. When my mother died, she had had – problems. As you saw for yourself, she was very beautiful and very accomplished. And very troubled. Yet she was a wonderful mother. When my parents were divorced, I moved to London to be with her. When she died, it was very difficult for me.' He looked at Catherine. 'I hope you don't mind my telling you this.'

'No, I'm glad you did. It's funny how you can love someone so much, even if they've not made your own life easy.' She told Alfred the story of her mother's interminably long disintegration.

By the time they reached the airport, Catherine felt purged, as if a weight had been lifted from her shoulders. It felt good to share her emotions rather than hide them. Alfred seemed so kind and understanding.

As she handed him back his monogrammed handkerchief, damp with her tears, he folded it back into her hand. 'Oh no,' he said, pressing her hand for just a minute. 'I want this returned in mint condition, in person.'

Catherine waved good-bye through the plane window, the handkerchief still clutched in her other hand. Since she was the only passenger on the enormous Bavarian Airways 727, redesigned for the comfort of just twenty people, she was free to slip through the club room and into one of the sleeping compartments. There she lay on a large bed, a gray-and-green plaid cashmere blanket woven with the Grunewald crest tucked up under her chin, and slept all the way to Pittsburgh.

The burial was short and anticlimatic. She and Effie were the only mourners. They stood on opposite sides of the open grave as an unfamiliar priest spoke about a woman he had never met. And then it was over. Catherine had hugged Effie close, but she knew that this part of her life was over forever. She spent the night at Effie's house, where she found herself comforting the old woman even more than Effie could comfort her. And when

Catherine left the next morning, she had no one. She knew it was time to face reality, to go back to the office, clean out her desk, handle her business in Washington for the baron, and make her plans for the future. Alone. Somehow coming 'home' had crystallized everything for her. She had struggled out of every difficult situation in her life – there was no reason she couldn't pull herself together now.

As Catherine let herself back into her own Chicago apartment, she thought about how much had happened since that night at the East Bank Club less than two weeks ago. It seemed as if months had gone by since she had left.

She put her bags down and realized the lights were on. She had been in such a state when she'd left the apartment that she was amazed she had remembered her passport and had left a key downstairs so B.J. could come in and feed Midnight.

Suddenly she was aware that she was not alone. Someone was in the bedroom. As she stood, unable to move even one foot forward, Graham Donaldson came down the hall.

'I've left Eve,' he said. His face was unshaven. 'I'm all yours.'

# 13

'From dressage to dresses. Some comedown,' whistled Bambi. She would have thought that on her sixteenth birthday she'd have better things to do than go shopping for a dress to wear to an old people's party. The Deerpath Riding Club Show was a week from Sunday, and she needed all the time she could get to practice her dressage exercises.

Harmony, a chestnut mare with a white blaze on her forehead, was Eve's birthday present to Bambi, and since yesterday when Eve had led Harmony on to the front yard, a saffron ribbon tied around her neck, Bambi hadn't been able to think about anything else. The horse was schooled in dressage, but still faltered in some of the *haute école* moves. But she was a beautiful mover, a much more sophisticated horse than 'Hughie,' her brother's namesake, and with hard work and a good trainer, Bambi was sure she could ride her at the Olympic level. That was her goal.

'What a waste of time,' she called out to Hughie. She was standing on a bale of hay impatiently braiding Harmony's mane into tight little coils and then binding them with heavy white tape.

'I can wear my prom dress. I never got to wear that, remember?' It was lying crumpled up in a ball in her hope chest.

'Bambi, this is Aunt Eve's first time out in public since the separation, and she needs the whole family around her. We're all she has now.'

'Uncle Graham will be back . . .'

Hughie leaned against the stall. 'Look, humans are a little bit more complicated than horses.'

'I know. That's why I prefer the company of horses.' She smiled over her shoulder, then patted Harmony's neck. 'There. How's that look?' She jumped down to survey her morning's work.

'A model who has appeared on the cover of *Vogue* does not appear at a major charity event at which there will be photographers from national publications wearing a seventy-five-dollar sale dress from Marshall Field's. Especially if that model is a Stuart.'

'Okay, but only for Aunt Eve.' Bambi tossed a white saddle blanket onto Harmony's well-groomed back. She sniffed and tossed her heavy hair over her shoulder. 'I think it would be much more fun if I rode in naked on Harmony's back and gave those old hags something to talk about other than the fact that Uncle Graham is sleeping with that girl. I mean, like who cares?' She heaved the well-worn Hermès saddle that had been her own mother's off a high peg on the wall and positioned it over the saddle blanket.

'It's not easy for Aunt Eve,' Hughie said. 'She's hardly left the house since Graham moved in with the Barracuda. This is like her second debut. It will make her happy to see you in a new dress. Rodney and I will take you down to Ultimo and it won't take any time at all – they're holding some special things for you. We've all got to wear black or white, you know. You can try them on and come right back on the train.'

Bambi yanked on the cinch. 'Only for Aunt Eve. But,' she shot Hughie a look, 'I love my Uncle Graham, too, and I don't want to hear any more bad things about him.' She turned to her brother. 'This must be what it's like when your parents get a divorce. I refuse to choose sides.' She backed the horse out of the oversized stall and into the meticulous, paved aisle. 'We've got to practice for just a little while,' she said. 'Then I'll go.'

Hughie followed her outside to the practice ring. It was obvious that dresses were the last thing on Bambi's mind. It was better to let her ride for half an hour, put the horse through its paces, and then go shopping rather than to drag her, petulant and whining, through the stores.

She swung onto the horse's back and trotted up to the fence, where Hughie waited. 'Now, we're going to do the extended trot and then the canter pirouette. Watch, will you, and tell me what you think?' Her eyes were excited.

They were quite a pair, thought Hughie. Bambi's thick hair swung down past her waist and contrasted with her white over-sized Irish sweater and white jeans. Suddenly she and the horse were streaking across the hedge of yews clipped into a geometric series of arches and planes, the horse's taped legs a white blur as they tore across the fall landscape. She and Harmony came to a stop, and then her hooves kicked out into the extended trot, seeming to march in slow motion with one straight leg balanced in midair at each graceful step.

Bambi subtly flexed her little finger against the reins as they moved together in the pattern of a figure eight. Yet it was difficult for her to concentrate because she was worried about her Aunt Eve. She had depended upon her aunt her whole life; she was the closest thing to a mother Bambi would ever know. Now she had taken to her bed and slept till eleven every morning, when she had always been up at six. Drucilla had told her that her mother was usually up half the night, playing the piano for hours on end. Everything was topsy-turvy – all on account of sex.

Sex must be it, Bambi thought as she tensed the muscles

in her calf, urging the horse to the center of the ring. Graham was having sex with Catherine, and an entire family fell apart. Drucilla certainly acted as if somebody had just died, and although Bambi wanted to ask her what was *really* going on, she didn't feel right about it. Bambi had always hoped Dru would be like a big sister, but Dru never seemed like anything more than a piece of ribbon and taffeta, a decoration one encountered in the hall or at the dinner table with a wave and a kiss. That was about it. Of course, Hughie was the world's best brother, but she had long ago given up hope that he would marry and give her a sister-in-law, nieces, and nephews. Hughie's friends who padded down the stairs after a night of whatever went on, nice as they were, had names like Terry and Rodney.

She shifted her weight, pressed one leg in and gave the signal for a canter pirouette. She needed to pay attention now. Bambi knew that she couldn't let herself be distracted if she wanted everything wonderful in this world – like a horse farm and an Olympic medal. She had to give those goals her full attention. Love, romance, and especially sex just got in the way and caused more problems than they were worth. No boy she'd ever met gave her the same feeling of excitement and belonging that she got from being with her horses or in front of Valeski's adoring camera.

Sex. What a dumb thing it was, she told herself. It certainly couldn't be worth driving Aunt Eve into the dark recesses of her house and Uncle Graham, with his bags packed, downtown somewhere like an uninvited houseguest instead of a husband.

Dismissing her crazy thoughts, she concentrated on getting her next move right. They were almost finished, and Harmony's reactions were in total syncopation with her own. Together, they were like a big wheel, turning, one fluid motion from arms to reins to the horse's mouth, head, and neck, through to Bambi's body and legs.

She reined Harmony to a slow walk and circled the track four times. 'All done,' she called out to Hughie, tossing him the reins. 'Here, Hughie. You cool her down. I'll go change.'

Bambi, Hughie, and Hughie's best friend, Rodney, trooped up the narrow, charcoal-gray steps of the African-patterned, paisley-shirred shop on Chicago's Oak Street where a series of chic boutiques and hair stylists' salons were huddled together with small eateries and ice cream parlors.

The Hollywood-style Esquire movie theater monopolized the middle of the street, and although it was glittery and showy by night, it was seedy and dreary in the day. Marilyn Miglin's townhouse, where cosmetics were custom-blended and her special fragrance Pheromone sold for $300.00 an ounce, stood on one side of the shop with a dimly lit hamburger spot reminiscent of the city's Prohibition era speakeasies on the other.

Ultimo, its clientele exclusive enough to be a private club, advertised itself simply as haberdashers for men and women. Of course, the trench coats were unobtrusively lined with sheared sable, and a depressed socialite could meander into the cinnabar-lacquered foyer contemplating opening an artery and emerge two hours later – and ten thousand dollars lighter – with a spring in her step that breathed new life into the adage, 'When the going gets tough, the tough go shopping.' The salespeople all seemed to have degrees in psychology and a diplomatic touch that proved itself necessary when the soft-spoken staff simultaneously tended to the needs of the wife of a leading

Chicago entrepreneur *and* his mistress as they both searched for a gown to wear to the same event. Gigi and Patrick graciously juggled the charges, which would both coincidentally go to the same gentleman's La Salle Street Office. This, however, was nothing compared to the ingenuity and technical engineering of the staff when a certain handsome banker and his boyfriend were shopping for sweaters on the first floor while upstairs his wife and girlfriend – both identical sizes – were vying for the same Azzedine Alaia leather coat. Within this magical cocoon of chic comfort, Chinese vases, and renewed self-esteem, little people grew taller, shy people became self-confident, and most important, the unhappy were made ecstatic. Salespeople and customers kissed and exchanged compliments in private rituals before any merchandise changed hands. And if someone didn't know the salon etiquette, she was immediately suspect.

Hughie was immediately greeted with open arms, as he'd been more than an habitué of the store, having arranged the windows on a free-lance basis since the day the doors opened for business. But it was Bambi around whom everyone clustered, and she instantly found herself attended by two salespeople.

Within fifteen minutes, Bambi had tried on black or white gowns by Bruce Oldfield – one of Princess Diana's favorite designers, she was told – Norma Kamali, and Valentino, but everything seemed too stiff, and the discomfort showed on her face. One dress was particularly beautiful – a strapless white satin Ungaro with an enormous black satin bow at the hip that reached a width at each end of almost four feet.

'My God, she's gorgeous,' Rodney said. 'If I were straight, I'd be worshipping at Bambi's feet.' He fell to his knees.

Bambi giggled. 'Oh, get up, Rodney. It's a great dress everyone, but how can I sit down?'

'Well, it's an entrance maker,' explained Gigi, adjusting the tight-fitting bodice.

'Well, I don't want to stand up all night. Hughie?' She turned to her brother.

'Right,' he said. 'We wouldn't want Bambi to miss her birthday cake while she's standing in the middle of the room.'

'Can't I wear a pants outfit?'

'It's a ball, Bambi,' Hughie explained. 'All the girls have spent weeks getting their ballgowns ready. We want you to really stand out.' He held a white tulle dropped-waist dress by a new young French designer at arm's length and shook his head emphatically, 'Too demure. She'd look like a debutante in this dress.'

Bambi agreed. 'Nobody likes those kind of dresses except boys' mothers.' She stood in her white cotton panties, holding her undershirt to her chest and staring glumly at the pile of dresses that was being carried away by Gigi, while Patrick disappeared into the back room to forage for other possibilities. Hughie sat on a paisley-covered stool wondering what they would do next. He and Rodney and even a woman who had come in to pick up a silk blouse were all tossing out ideas for what Bambi should wear.

'No bows or frills,' Hughie proclaimed rejecting a lace ballerina-length skirt.

Patrick emerged from the back and with a secret smile dropped a white dress over Bambi's head.

He adjusted the white silk, one-armed Karl Lagerfeld, shimmering with ice-cold cut beads that looked like snowflakes, stood back, and surveyed his choice. Gigi tucked a gold cord under Bambi's long hair and laboriously plaited the cord and hair together into a French braid. When she was finished, everyone was nodding enthusiastically, except for Rodney, who cryptically dashed out and down the stairs. Two minutes later, he returned with a small shopping bag from Marilyn Miglin's next door, from which he produced a container of iridescent gold powder, a huge puff, and an atomizer of perfume. He lightly powdered Bambi's bare shoulders and neck until she seemed to shimmer from within and, as a finishing touch, he sprayed Pheromone perfume just over her head and allowed it to drift down, as Bambi stared into the communal dressing room mirror.

'Rodney, you are a genius,' said Hughie. 'Let's look in the right light,' he commanded, with a nod to Gigi.

The lights in the main room were instantly dimmed, candles appeared as if by magic, and Bambi was led out for the whole shop to admire, and to step into three-inch white satin Walter Steiger sandals, trimmed with crystals.

The dress hugged her well-toned body and she looked like a Greek statue made of marble, come to life.

The room was hushed, except for Bambi's voice. 'These shoes don't fit.'

The shoes were whisked away and lined with two pairs of foam pads, while a tailor nipped and tucked before their very eyes.

The small room crowded with people suddenly became quiet with the realization that a blue-jeaned teenager of less than an hour ago was a world-class beauty.

'*Isn't* she dazzling?' A man who had come in to shop with his wife broke the silence as he stared.

With her hair swept back off her face, her fine features rather than her overwhelming mane of hair demanded attention, accentuating her enormous eyes, full lips, and delicate bone structure. Her gleaming, gold-dusted body was now over six feet tall in the spike heels as she stood, staring at herself in the mirror, turning and turning.

Bambi was not sure. She looked old, like Drucilla, she thought. But Hughie seemed so excited, and maybe he was right. Maybe her face did look better without all that hair.

Then she heard a whisper. 'My God, she's not human. She's an ice princess.'

She felt frozen to the spot, as if she *were* an ice princess. Role-playing for the camera was one thing, this was another. This was real life. Would her whole life turn into play-acting as she pretended to be someone else?

'That's enough for now,' she said, unzipping the dress.

But no one seemed to hear her.

'Bambi, let's go, The car is here.' Hughie paced around Bambi's bedroom. What was taking her so long? Her French braid was perfect, they'd worked out the entire outfit that afternoon at Ultimo, and there was nothing for her to do except slip on the dress.

'In a minute, Hughie. I'm in the bathroom,' she called through the closed door.

'Don't put on too much makeup. You look fine.'

Bambi sat perched sideways on the old pedestal sink and peered into the mirror. Her new three-thousand dollar gown, a bargain price negotiated in return for Hughie's promise of her modeling services in the next Valeski ad for Ultimo, was carelessly slung over the shower rod.

She tugged at her still-damp hair and hacked at it some more with her cuticle scissors. The sink was full of hair, as was the floor. Hair seemed to be everywhere, except on her head, which was now covered with inch-long, irregular, spiky curls. She looked like Tadzio in Thomas

Mann's *Death in Venice*, the young boy who held such a sensual yet mysterious appeal for both men and women.

She wondered what Hughie would say. Oh well, it was done. She felt free. Not like an ice maiden, but like herself. She tousled her hair one more time, dabbed Vaseline on her lips and thick eyebrows, and stepped out of the bathroom.

'Oh, Jesus,' her brother gasped. 'What have you done?'

Drucilla Donaldson had a problem. The yardage of her ecru silk taffeta Emanuel ballgown billowed up almost to her shoulders as she twisted first to the right, then to the left, attempting to negotiate a trip to the ladies' room without crushing the organza roses that cascaded down the back and sides of the dress. Fourteen yards of material stuffed into a four-by-six ladies' room stall was not an easy maneuver. She stretched her arm up and over the stiff hem of the skirt, reaching under four layers of flounced taffeta petticoats for her pantyhose. It was a feat that required almost Olympic-level agility.

She was oblivious to the chatter and gossip outside the stall until she overheard her father's name.

'I hear she's fucking his brains out,' said a voice she recognized as belonging to none other than Wilhelmena Huntington, one of her mother's closest friends.

'Well, *I* saw them having dinner at Gordon's one night, and it looked like *she* was the dessert. They left the restaurant so fast, I think they went straight to a hot sheet motel.' Emily Horst's voice piped up over one of the stalls.

Drucilla froze. She shoved all the fabric of the skirt back over her head, slammed down the toilet seat, plopped onto it and dropped her elbows to her knees, her bare shoulders quivering with anger and humiliation.

She and Arnaud had been trying so hard to bring her parents back together. They had even taken their father to lunch and implored him not to break up their family. Dru had always counted on Graham for stability, but suddenly her world was rudely and radically changed. There had never been a divorce among the Donaldsons, and Drucilla was worried about the embarrassment it might cause the de Cotrilles. She fretted over who would sit where at the wedding and whether or not her father would want his girlfriend in the receiving line.

Since her engagement to a Frenchman, Drucilla considered herself a worldly sophisticate at the age of twenty-four. Hiding out on a toilet set listening to the Lake Forest locusts discuss her father's orgasms was too déclassé for a future de Cotrille, and at that moment she resented her father for imposing such disgrace upon his only daughter just before her marriage.

'Shit,' she said aloud, as Pinkie Berman launched into a detailed narration of how she and her husband, who probably hadn't been able to get a hard-on in seven years, had pulled up alongside the dynamic duo at a stop light and caught Graham and Catherine in flagrante delicto.

'Shit!' she said it again.

If there were bigger charity parties in Chicago, there was none more competitive than the annual Black and White Ball at which Chicago's social elite raised money for the worthy cause of mental health and vied for the spotlight in an extravaganza of black and white formal wear in every conceivable variation of silk, satin, taffeta, organza, velvet, lace, and chiffon. Each costume, rendered more luxurious and sophisticated by its monochromatic shades, was traditionally showcased under the fifty-foot-high stained-glass rotunda of the Chicago Cultural Center.

Round, white-clothed tables were arranged on either side of the rotunda and were framed by vaulted ceilings and white marble archways outlined in green-and-white floral mosaics. Floor-to-ceiling arched windows on two sides of the room reflected the light of hundreds of candles, the shadows and shapes of whirling dancers, and the warm glow of dozens of ornate bronze-and-glass Victorian sconces. The rotunda had been the architectural highlight of its day when the building had served as the city's public library, and its splendor had not diminished.

At table number two on the edge of the dance floor, Eve Donaldson was glowingly serene as one couple after another came up to admire her Yves St Laurent ivory sequined, hip-length sweater and chiffon ballerina skirt, to exclaim over her Fabergé egg, which hung from a chain of diamonds around her neck, or to inquire about Drucilla's wedding plans. No one, of course, mentioned the real reason for their solicitous cheek kisses and encouraging hugs. Eve's social appearance without her husband for the first time in years did not, however, go unnoticed.

It was common knowledge that Graham had moved out of the Lake Forest house, and it was no secret that he was openly seeing Catherine McBride. Even those not attuned to the city's gossip had recently seen pictures of them accompanying an article on A Place in the Sun in the newspapers' business page. *Crain's Chicago Business* had even run a story about the Donaldson's separation and its implications for Intercon. Catherine now traveled with Graham constantly and, when they were in town, they were seen having dinner together several nights a week at the Mid-America Club, The Palm, or Les Nomads. Eve and Graham's friends were waiting to see how the situation would resolve. Most felt sorry for Eve, but no one would alienate Graham Donaldson, chief executive officer of one of the country's most powerful companies and perennial fundraising benefactor.

Eve hadn't wanted to attend the ball tonight. She still felt too fragile and abandoned to put herself in the center of a public event. But Dru had convinced her mother that unless Eve went, she would nag her unmercifully and stay home herself.

It was time, Eve had finally decided, to stop being selfish. She and Graham had been separated three months and she couldn't let Drucilla, Bambi, and Hughie worry about her forever. She wanted to hear music and laughter again, to dance and do something totally frivolous. She had grown weary of examining and reexamining her life.

Pondering her future was something in which Eve Donaldson had absolutely no experience. Her life had been set before her like a luxurious roadmap from the time she was born. She had taken only one detour – when she married Graham Donaldson instead of Franklin Stuart. She had always assumed that after Drucilla had grown and Graham's business became a success, she and her husband would use their latter years to rediscover each other in a reaffirmation of their love.

Even after she had learned the truth, Eve had been certain that the drifting of Graham's affections was temporary. Every marriage had its times of crisis, and when she gave Graham an ultimatum, he had, as she expected, returned dutifully to her side. For two weeks everything had seemed superficially correct, flossy in fact. The flowers were in order, the guests in their places, Graham once again sat at the head of the table. But they were never alone. Eve always made sure that Drucilla, Arnaud, or Bambi was always at dinner.

Her revenge for his betrayal was subtle, if unconscious. Eve quietly made sure every minute of his life was accounted for by calling the office to see if he had arrived safely, and twice during that week she drove down to lunch with him at the Tavern Club. For the first time in their marriage, Eve found herself checking his pockets and his calendar when he set them out at night and picking up their private line without waiting for Cherie to do so, pitching her cheerful tones to purposefully discourage any unwelcome callers. Their private line had been one source of anguish to Eve. After the second time that she picked it up and heard a receiver drop back into its cradle, she simply had the phone disconnected. She explained to Graham that no man should have to bring his business home from the office and that they were being unnecessarily interrupted. It was not critical that the chairman of the board be reachable twenty-four hours a day by anyone who knew his private number. That's what Michael Picol and the rest of the staff was for, wasn't it?

Eve slowly and subtly found herself becoming more Graham's jailer than his wife. Any mention of A Place in the Sun or the Caribbean filled the atmosphere with tension. At night, when they were finally alone together, she talked about plans for Christmas at Wysetta, where they had spent happy Christmases together with the children in hopes of rekindling the spark of their life together.

But with each step Eve took forward, Graham took two back.

When she tried to sit down and discuss their relationship, his eyes looked past her and focused at some point outside the window, beyond the yew hedge.

She had done her best to bring him back into the fold, even to the point of serving his favorite veals and lambs, sauced to perfection with recipes of her own creation. But when Graham had pushed the food aside, muttering 'Don't we have any alfafa sprouts or tofu in this house?' she had stared at him in alarm, realizing he did not want to return to the past.

Since Graham seemed to show such a sudden interest in cardiovascular fitness, Eve had called in Bruce Gregga to design an indoor lap pool off Graham's dressing room. This was to be her gift to him. But he had embarrassed both her and the interior decorator by walking out of the room when they showed him the plans, saying, 'I have the East Bank Club now.'

Finally, in a last effort, Eve had decided to make a truly symbolic new start by replacing their bed of the past twenty years. The old, king-size bed in which she had conceived her child was hauled out unceremoniously, and in its place was installed a new, smaller, queen-size bed that ensured less room between them. She had hung the bed with box-pleated, quilted canopies and curtains heavy enough to shut off the outside world and the memories that belonged to it.

After one restless night in that bed, Graham had moved out of the house, out of Lake Forest, and out of their marriage.

Now Eve glanced at her left hand, which for the first time since her marriage displayed neither her wedding nor engagement rings. Her hand had felt strangely naked at first, but, tonight, she had put on her mother's twenty-five-carat sapphire solitaire, and the heirloom gave her confidence. The Bentons had done pretty well on their own before Graham Donaldson had come into their lives; Eve would do so again, though it wasn't what she wanted.

Living without Graham was cold and empty. All his clothes were still in his closet, his glasses still rested on the night table. Everything was ready for his imminent return, yet she wasn't really sure if she would ever take him back. Every day that passed took her further and further away from her charmed life with Graham. He had taken their priceless relationship and consciously smashed it. He had taken her joy, her love, their family and tossed them aside for a greedy, twenty-eight-year-old company assistant. Eve wondered what Catherine wanted with a man old enough to be her father. Graham had never been all that sexy and must seem practically geriatric to a woman in her twenties.

How could he move in with this childish creature? What would they be like in twelve years? Was she planning to push his wheelchair into the sunset? Eve took a deep breath. Oh well, she thought, if she could get angry at Graham and find fault with him maybe she was starting to let go. Dr Corbett had told her anger was a good sign. Graham must have lost his mind. Eve had done her best to hold things together. She'd reasoned with him, pleaded with him, cajoled him, demanded of him. But she wasn't going to beg. The pride and self-restraint she'd been bred with resurfaced and saved her from that. Eve Donaldson was not a beggar, she told herself. And anyone, even Graham, who reduced her to that could never be a part of her life again. Her sessions with Dr Corbett had helped her realize that no matter what happened to her marriage, she herself was worth saving. She was Eve Benton Donaldson. Perhaps that was enough.

Yet after Graham had moved out, Eve had been unable to go to Owentsia and the Winter Club. Whenever she was around their old friends, she didn't feel the usual warmth and rapport, but pity. Some of her lifelong friends showered her with attention until their husbands appeared. Then they turned their backs on her. How strange, Eve thought. Here she was utterly miserable and alone and *they* were jealous of *her*!

It had taken every ounce of Eve's wavering self-confidence, however, to make an appearance at tonight's ball with a man who was not her husband. Cary Leggett was the elegantly popular New Yorker of impeccable lineage who had himself never married but had made a career of sorts out of squiring prominent ladies to parties, the ballet, theater, and dances when their husbands were unavailable, out of town, or disinterested. Since President Savage was constantly busy attending to affairs of state, even Pollyanne often pressed Cary Leggett into service as an escort. The society columns called him a walker, a Stepford escort who was respectable, socially acceptable, and safe from innuendo. When a woman appeared on the arm of Cary Leggett, her relationship with him was never questioned. He was simply a human accessory.

It had been Pollyanne's idea to ask Cary to escort Eve to the Black and White Ball. Pollyanne had been supportive, Eve thought, as she watched her daughter and Arnaud walk among the other couples in the room. Every couple had its ups and downs, Pollyanne had reminded her. This had to be a temporary result of male menopause. When Eve had told Pollyanne that she wasn't sure she wanted to reconcile with Graham, her friend had been uncharacteristically silent. Finally, Pollyanne had said, 'You must do what is best for yourself, darling.' And Eve *would* understand, Pollyanne had silkily purred, if she and Graham received separate invitations to next month's dinner at the White House. Of course, they were *both* her dear friends. Eve had declined that invitation. The Black and White Ball was one thing. A White House dinner, with a possible public encounter with Graham and his little friend, quite another.

Eve, Cary Leggett, and Drucilla and Arnaud had all arrived early in the navy blue, stretch limousine Leggett had rented for the evening. She and Graham would have come in her Jaguar, or in one of the company cars. In the limousine she felt so public, so vulnerable. The media was fully visible tonight – the eager young girls from the *Sun-Times* Page Ten section; the all-seeing reporter from *Women's Wear Daily* and her ubiquitous photographer, Flash, and the old-guard society editor from *Townsfolk*. A special crew from French *Vogue* was there to cover Comte Arnaud de Cotrille and the future comtesse, Drucilla Donaldson. Governor Bob, the mayor, Bob Hope, John Travolta, and other notables supportive of the National Mental Health Association had inspired *People* magazine and *Entertainment Tonight* to attend.

Bambi and Hughie were late, Eve noticed as the cocktail hour was about to end. Hughie had earlier phoned to tell her how dazzling Bambi was going to look. Eve didn't doubt Hughie was planning a spectacular entrance – that was his style. He had described the white-beaded snow goddess gown in such detail that even Eve was anxious to see Bambi create her own show.

Eve glanced at her own daughter. Pretty as Dru seemed to her, she did not have the spectacular looks of Bambi. Perhaps that was a blessing, since her life would therefore always be more traditional. Eve considered it healthier for a woman's life to be focused on love, marriage, children, and possibly a career. She lowered her eyes. Divorce and heartbreak were also part of that package, she now knew too well. This was territory Eve herself understood, and she knew it was the only world Dru could comprehend.

But Bambi was breaking away from such a life. She was developing that intangible air of aloofness, of inaccessibility that Eve had witnessed in many great personalities of the theater and politics. Pollyanne Savage had it. It was a quality that made certain people stand out and seem invulnerable amidst the ordinary. Thus isolated, their presence seemed to say 'Look – but don't touch. I am larger than life, a public person outside of and beyond your experience. Give me important things to do, put me on a pedestal, but never get close to me.' Eve frowned slightly and Dru put a reassuring hand on her mother's arm. She smiled back, but her concern continued to tug at her.

She had so hoped Bambi would be able to lead a normal life after such a tragic beginning. Hughie had tried, as had Eve, to lessen the blow of not having real parents, but there was only so much they could do for the young girl. And now Bambi's beauty would most likely preclude a normal adulthood. At least she had enjoyed her horses as a child, Eve thought, and sighed.

A beaded designer gown and stiletto heels were hardly right for a young girl celebrating her sixteenth birthday. Maybe Eve should have a talk with Hughie and suggest not rushing Bambi too quickly into the adult world.

'Good lord, Mother, look,' Drucilla gasped. 'Is that Bambi?'

Bambi strode up the Cultural Center stairs and straight into the marble ballroom, but there was no sign of the stiletto heels and ice princess gown. Fresh-faced, eyes brilliantly twinkling and with short, soft hair barely brushing her ears, Bambi looked more like an insouciant Greek boy than a Greek goddess. Hughie, his hands stuffed into his tuxedo pockets, walked nervously behind. She *had* followed the black and white dress code. She wore a pair of black velvet, jodphur-style Buccaneer Jeans and an off-white lace shirt that covered her long neck and cuffed delicately at her wrists. Eve recognized the lace shirt as one of Bambi's grandmother's, a Stuart heirloom, tied at the neck with a jabot and caught with a pearl and diamond brooch.

'Gosh, Mother, look what she's done to her hair – that gorgeous hair. And she's wearing slippers!' Dru was practically stuttering now. On her feet, instead of the too-high heels, Bambi wore a pair of black velvet gentlemen's evening pumps appliquéd with deer on the toes. She looked happy, unmade-up, beautiful in the refreshingly natural style of a sixteen-year-old.

Everyone in the room watched as this sparkling creature rushed over to Eve, hugged her, and burst out with a barrage of apologies for being late.

Drucilla and her friend Lolly Bishop traded glances at the table.

'I think we're overdressed, Lol.'

Lolly swallowed a glass of champagne. 'But look at your mother. She's laughing. She's loving it.'

'Well, if that's what it takes to get Mummy to smile these days, then who cares what Bambi looks like.'

The video-tape crew from *Entertainment Tonight* abandoned Bob Hope and rushed across the room to capture the excitement of Bambi's entrance.

The fashion editor of the *Sun-Times* turned to Hughie and crowed, 'For once Chicago one-ups Paris. Whose outfit is it? Who's the designer?' Her pencil was poised.

Hughie thought for a moment and announced proudly, 'Why, it's a Bambi original.' He hesitated a moment. 'From the new line she's working on.'

'Of course,' said the editor. 'I love the deer on the shoes. Who's carrying the line? I want to be the first to know.'

'I promise you, Pat,' he said. 'You'll be the first to know. After me.'

Arnaud narrowed his eyes and grumbled, 'The press. They're like dogs after the rabbit.' He turned to his fiancée. 'Don't ever cut your hair like that. *C'est laide* . . . absolutely hideous!'

Eve felt a tap on her arm, and she gracefully rose to let Cary Leggett lead her to the dance floor. He whirled her around the room, and she found that her legs did not crumble, that everyone in the room did not stop and stare. Back at the table, flanked by Drucilla and Arnaud, Eve mustered up the courage to make a small announcement to her family.

'I've been meaning to tell you that I've just been accepted in Alexander Levin's master class, and I am now enrolled in the Music School at Northwestern University.' Her voice wavered softly. She hesitated a moment, as if expecting some member of her family to object because she had made this decision without consulting Graham, probably for the first time in longer than any of them could remember. It was the first time she was doing something just for herself. Her new life had begun; she was proud that she had been accepted into the music program.

Alexander Levin had given Eve a serious critique of her music. He was very young – less than thirty-five years old – but he had enjoyed a brilliant season last summer as the guest conductor at Ravinia, and he was now being compared to James Levine and Seiji Ozawa, both of whom had also begun their careers there. Levin's enthusiasm delighted Eve, for this was the first time anyone had ever taken her music seriously.

'It was uncanny,' she told Dru. 'He seemed to sense what I was going to do before I played a note. He actually said that with enough practice and knowledge of basic theory, I might have a recital!'

Drucilla stood and raised her wine glass. 'Here's to my mother, the concert pianist, and her new, brilliant career!'

Eve's cheeks flushed with pleasure. She knew that going back to school would be a lot of work; she had so much to learn. Yet that was the wonderful part! She had something to look forward to again. For the first time in months, she actually felt like more than half a woman, Yes, things were looking good again. Hughie was right. There *was* life after Graham Donaldson.

As the last of the dancers took their seats for a midnight dessert of pears poached in amaretto on a bed of raspberry purée, Hughie Stuart stood on the far side of the room, arms folded, surveying the scene with satisfaction. Most of the younger women and girls were wearing Scarlett O'Hara-type gowns, overdone in ruffles and frills. They looked as if they belonged on top of a wedding cake, Hughie snorted to himself. Drucilla and Lolly Bishop, in their *Town & Country* dresses, were a cut above the crowd, but still, nobody could compare with Bambi. If he himself had a sense of style, his sister had an innate feeling for what was right for her. He watched her fluid movements as she walked off the dance floor with a first-year attorney from one of the larger law firms, and twenty cameras, it seemed, followed her.

The decision to crop her hair and wear the jodhpur jeans had been right, Hughie thought. In this outfit, one noticed the girl, not the gown. Next to Bambi, most of the other girls loked foolish and decked out to distraction. He felt proud of his sister, who after all these years had come into her own tonight. The ice princess image was *au courant*, but it was wrong for Bambi, and she had sensed it. How smart of her to realize her own special appeal!

Bambi had achieved the ideal look for herself, ideal because it was uniquely her, not a copy of a fashion dictate. She had an aura of independence, needing neither man nor woman, somehow spanning both femininity and masculinity, and an unthreatening, fresh appeal. It was the kind of appeal that millions of girls would pay to copy, he thought.

Hughie sauntered over to the table to join his sister. The time was almost right to begin his secret dream for Bambi. She was too special to be just another model.

Dessert had just been served when Hughie gave the signal to the orchestra leader, and a grand drum roll heralded the entrance of a huge antique cage containing six white doves, carried aloft by two waiters in tails. Intertwined in the white scalloped bars were dozens of white cymbidium orchids, and a clutch of sparklers glittered at the top. The orchestra struck up 'Happy Birthday,' and everyone in the room sang to Bambi as she smiled and laughed unaffectedly, throwing her arms first around Aunt Eve and then around Hughie. All the guests applauded wildly when Bambi opened the cage door and flung her arms wide as the doves burst into the air and fluttered toward the rotunda. Photographers captured the picture that would adorn the next issue of *W* with the headline: 'Bambi – Buccaneer at the Ball.' As of that moment, Hughie's sixteen-year-old baby sister no longer needed so much as a last name. She was a personality in herself. She was Bambi.

# PART THREE
# A Place in the Sun

# 1

In a town accustomed to assassinations, parades, and motorcades, the shrieking siren of an ambulance, careering around corners, tearing through red lights, and weaving in and out of traffic still stopped spectators in their tracks along the Washington streets.

Inside the ambulance, Catherine crouched in a corner, pushed almost flat to the back of the driver's seat by two white-coated attendants hovering over the inert body on a stretcher covered by a tangle of wires and monitors.

'Everybody clear!' yelled one of the attendants, shoving Catherine even further into the background as she nervously bit her lip, thinking she'd never seen a man so close to death. His face was milky gray, when, only a few minutes ago at lunch, it had been suntanned and animated. Even his lips were cracked and chalky. Now his features stretched across his face like a death mask, and the corners of his eyes and mouth, which had tilted so warmly up, were suddenly loose, as if the wire holding his face together had been cut. His lips pursed in pain as his body jolted from the electric shock that was restarting his heart.

The ambulance screeched to a halt, the doors crashed open, and doctors and nurses materialized, rushing to fold out the legs and wheels from the collapsible stretcher and roll it into the emergency entrance of George Washington Hospital. Graham, so ashen-faced it looked as if he himself might be ready to collapse, raced alongside his longtime friend. Catherine was left to climb out of the ambulance alone and rush behind them, carrying the Secretary of the Interior's jacket and tie and Graham's briefcase.

Graham and Catherine had been having lunch at Sans Gregoire with Henry Hudson. She and Henry had been making progress on acquiring national park status for A Place in the Sun. The meeting that he helped her set up between Baron Grunewald and the Attorney General in Nassau had been the beginning of the solution to the Darco Coal problem. But Hudson had been under extreme pressure from the media recently, lambasted by *The New York Times*, and attacked by the Sierra Club for his 'reckless' environmental policies, particularly his latest antiwilderness bill. Graham had commiserated and offered support, and he and Catherine had been in the middle of a debate on the irresponsibility of the press when Hudson became strangely quiet. A forkful of his Spanish omelette had dropped into his lap and he had stared straight ahead, drooling from the right side of his mouth. Graham had immediately leapt up from his chair and taken charge, ordering the ambulance and loosening his friend's tie as Catherine helped him lower Henry to the floor between two tables. The waiter and maitre d' hovered over the table, a look of professional concern on their faces as if the omelette had been at fault. It wouldn't do the restaurant any good to have a cabinet member fall dead into his plate.

At the hospital, Graham demanded the top cardiac man, supervised the paperwork, and rattled off his friend's medical history to the four young interns on duty. Hudson had seemed fine after his bypass surgery last year, he told them, but this last barrage by the press seemed to be pecking him to death. Catherine and Graham had had dinner last night with Henry and his wife and the President and Mrs Savage and he had seemed agitated all through the meal.

There was only one phone in the emergency waiting room, and a line of several anxious people waited to use it while an overweight woman rattled hysterically in Arabic, waving away anyone who dared approach the phone. Catherine had quickly appraised the situation and approached the nursing supervisor.

'This man is the Secretary of the Interior. Could I please use your phone?' The startled nurse ushered her into a private office, where she finally located Twinkie after her third call to the pro shop at her golf club. Catherine got the feeling from Twinkie's voice that she was almost as upset to get a call from the young woman she had cold-shouldered only the night before at dinner as she was to hear the news of her husband's heart attack. Twinkie was one of Eve's friends.

Graham hurriedly entered and grabbed the receiver just as Catherine hung up. First he called Dr Denton Cooley, who had done the bypass surgery, and arranged for him and his team to fly to Washington on an Intercon jet, if Henry passed through the critical period. As Graham ran back and forth between the telephone, the doctors, and Henry, Catherine situated herself on an orange vinyl sofa in the waiting room. She'd be there if Graham needed her.

After a while she looked at the clock. Five o'clock. She'd been waiting almost four hours, but she didn't dare approach Graham. Twinkie Hudson was with him. When Twinkie had arrived, Catherine had offered her sympathy, but had been brushed off like lint on a sweater, and she'd quickly decided to stay out of her way.

By the time they moved Hudson to the intensive care unit, six hours later, Catherine had read the paper that lay on the table at least six times. She had been startled to see Graham's and her faces staring up at her from the front page of the Capital Life/Metro section of the *Washington Times*. First she had been amused and delighted – they both looked wonderful. Was she really as pretty and refined as the girl in the photo gazing adoringly at Graham? Pictures didn't lie, did they? she asked herself.

Catherine had only recently learned that Eve had learned of her husband's affair through an incriminating photograph, taken at the island, which had caught them off guard. She sighed to herself. Even though this wasn't the most opportune time for national exposure, there they were for all the world to see. They had been photographed in the forefront of a group of a dozen people, including Henry and Twinkie Hudson and the King of Jordan. The combination of one of the country's most powerful CEOs, who had recently left his wife and now escorted his assistant, and the controversial Henry Hudson was evidently an irresistible photo opportunity. She studied the newspaper picture for the tenth time. Even in the presence of royalty, she and Graham seemed to monopolize the photo – both gazed happily at one another. 'Oh God,' she whispered as a thought crossed her mind. If Hudson dies, this picture will be picked up by every news service in the free world! She ripped out the page and tucked it into Graham's briefcase.

A folder on the top of his papers caught her eye. It was labeled 'Place in the Sun.' Well, maybe she could catch up on the latest reports while she waited. There was one from Terry Skittle, a copy of which had been sent to her, some interoffice memos, and a letter from Arnie Welles, Aggie Palmer's geologist. It was marked 'confidential,' and although it had been opened, it was still in its envelope.

She settled in as comfortably as possible on the hard, vinyl banquette and pulled out the letter. Catherine hadn't been in touch with Arnie Welles since the testimonial dinner in Dallas and she wondered what he could have to say.

Catherine's eyebrows drew together as she tried to understand the letter. She read it twice, once quickly, then slowly, word by word. It was dated a week ago, and, although the language was highly technical, it was full of references to a seismic report detailing the existence of oil in the undersea area surrounding Palmer Island. So that was why old man Palmer hadn't wanted to sell, Catherine realized. She had studied the maps and elevations and there was no mistake. The area to which Arnie Welles' report referred was specifically Palmer Island and, speculatively, the entire area of A Place in the Sun.

Catherine unfurled a large black map heavily peppered with gray spots representing underwater oil deposits. Catherine folded the report back in her lap. Why hadn't Graham told her? Why hadn't she been even copied on the letter?

Then she knew. Graham must have known about the oil report all along and had camouflaged the incredible find so Intercon could acquire the islands, in a package, and then procure the hundred-year lease from Venezuela and the reappropriation of the government property. She shut the briefcase and walked around the table. Graham was a bloody genius, as the baron would say! Yes there would be the undersea park, and of course the research center, but now a major oil reserve would be discovered as well.

She sat down. What could this mean? Were the plans compatible? Could they go full steam ahead on A Place in the Sun in light of this report? It was unlikely that the preserve and research could coexist with undersea oil drilling. Why hadn't Graham discussed this with her before, she wondered. Didn't he trust her enough? Well, she rationalized, such information as this had too many ramifications. The smallest leak would send the stock sky-high, and of course, the South American government might yank their lease before the papers could be signed. She wondered how many people besides Welles knew, and *when* had Graham planned to tell her about the oil. They would need to plan everything entirely differently, and Catherine would have to readjust all her ideas. Hundreds of thousands of dollars and hundreds of hours had already been spent on A Place in the Sun, but Catherine knew this latest development would more than pay for any lost expenditures. She couldn't wait to discuss it all with Graham.

'You're still here.' Graham walked in slowly, as if every one of his muscles was in pain. 'I thought you might have left. I'm glad you didn't.' His shirt was rumpled, his tie awry.

'How could I? How's Henry?' Catherine made room for Graham to sit beside her.

'It's touch and go. Looks like a stroke. They won't know for several days how bad his condition will be. He can't talk. There is partial paralysis. That's all they're certain of right now.'

'Will he – '

Graham sighed. 'Too soon to tell.' He shook his head and dug his fingertips into the vinyl as Catherine covered them with her hand. 'Poor Henry,' Graham half whispered. 'When we were at Notre Dame together, he was like a light source. Everybody wanted to be with him. The kind of guy you expected to be important. Not like me.' He smiled weakly.

She moved to kiss his forehead.

He waved his hand. 'Henry Hudson dedicated himself to his work. And look what he got. It killed him.'

'But he's not definitely going to die, is he?' Catherine asked.

'Well, let's hope to God he doesn't. But his work and the press killed him all the same. They stabbed him again and again until he had to bleed. Everybody's a critic when you're in the public eye, Catherine. You can't please anybody. Ever. And they ultimately kill you for it. That's why I'm getting out.'

Getting out? What was he talking about, Catherine wondered.

Graham pulled her head to his shoulder. 'Catherine, thank God we have A Place in the Sun. It's a chance to do something good for the world, and for us. It's more than that.'

Her eyes lit up. 'Yes! I just read the letter from Welles.'

Graham didn't seem to hear her. 'I won't go out like Hudson.' His voice was still soft, but fierce. 'I'm not driving myself into intensive care. I'll be able to slow down, relax.' He smiled at Catherine. '*We* will. Thanks to you, we'll end up in paradise, honey.'

Catherine wondered if he could have opened Arnie Welles' report without reading it, but she didn't want to interrupt his reverie. It seemed therapeutically calming for him.

He held her and stroked her hair. 'I see this as a sign that A Place in the Sun was meant to be for us. Our retreat from this world, where people are hounded into oblivion. I don't like this life anymore, honey. I'm tired of oil, drilling, chemicals, minerals. We're going to do significant humanitarian research – if Henry gets well, we'll make a place for him.' His tone changed. 'You're so young.' He took her face in his hands.

'I'm almost thirty,' she mumbled.

'I don't want you trapped in the treadmill, like I was. We'll have A Place in the Sun together. We'll have our dream. We're the lucky ones.'

Catherine pulled back slightly, so she could pick Welles's letter up from her lap. 'Look, Graham, it's going to be so incredible. You have to read this letter from Welles.'

Graham glanced at the letter. 'I read it last week.'

Catherine tossed her hair and it fanned out around her face, shining even in the cold, fluorescent light. 'I knew it. You're right. We have the opportunity of a lifetime. Why, within fifteen years we can build a new Intercon empire in the Caribbean. That *was* your plan, wasn't it?' Her words rushed out.

'Catherine, that's just another oil geologist's report. I get hundreds of them, and they never change a thing.'

'It sounds like a major find to me.'

He shrugged wearily. 'What's major? Major is lying in a hospital letting a machine breathe for you. I've been drilling for oil for over twenty-five years now. That's enough.'

Catherine wasn't sure she'd heard him correctly. She was tired, and he was probably still in shock. That must be it. Catherine held up the letter. '*This* is our future, Graham, but we'll talk about it later.'

He took the letter from her and shoved it into his pocket. She reached across and plucked it out again. 'When were you going to tell me?'

He didn't answer.

'You *were* going to tell me.'

Still no answer. He slumped back and rubbed his

temples. 'We'll discuss this later. My friend is fighting for his life. I can't deal with you, too, right now.'

'*Deal* with me? What am I? I thought I was part of your life.' She paused. 'You weren't *going* to tell me, were you?' Her spine stiffened, because she knew the answer.

'We'll talk about it later.' Her voice was soft again. 'But we *will* talk about it, won't we?'

'There's nothing to talk about.' Graham closed his eyes wearily. 'Forget it, honey, it's not part of the plan. Once you get started on something like this, there's no end.'

'That's the point.' Catherine persisted. Was he actually going to walk away from this find and turn into some sort of executive beachcomber? Would Graham Donaldson turn his back on discovering whether or not there was a billion dollar deal here?

Catherine stared at Graham. For the first time, she realized they were not on the same wavelength. She wasn't even getting through to him.

'Come on, Graham, you've been in here for hours. Let's get you something to eat and some rest. We can come back later to see Henry.' She turned to face him.

He looked old, she noticed. There were dark circles under his eyes, and a pinched look to his mouth. In the intensive care unit of George Washington Hospital, Catherine tried to focus on the most dynamic man she had ever met, but it suddenly seemed impossible. All she could see were his socks.

# 2

'This will be a take,' Bob Bacardi said with a nod to his assistant director, and his words triggered a flurry of frantic activity. As if mobilized by electric shocks, the assistant director began flailing his arms like a traffic cop, barking rapid-fire commands into a walkie-talkie that emitted periodic bursts of ear-piercing static. He signaled the prop men to activate the fog machine that would blur any hard edges of the block of downtown Los Angeles that had been chosen for its resemblance to New York, so that when the scene appeared on film in the comercial, it would look like Metropolis as seen by Renoir.

The advertising agency producer, a white-haired man in pastel plaid pants, stepped to the director's side for a whispered conference, and with seven terse words communicated the seriousness of the situation; 'We are into Golden Time, you know.' Golden Time, a financial nightmare to be avoided at all costs, meant that the shoot had gone on longer than the two-hundred-thousand-dollar budget allowed, and twenty technicians, fifteen extras, a team of hair, makeup and wardrobe stylists and an animal handler were now being paid triple-scale overtime every minute the clock ticked. The agency producer and the frowning gaggle of account executives knew that getting into Golden Time meant they would all be called on the carpet by their client, Premier Stores. Premier had agreed to the six-figure shoot cost above the seven-hundred-thousand-dollar contract fee for obtaining the exclusive rights to launch the new line of sportswear that bore

Bambi's name. In addition, four million dollars were being spent for magazine ads and air time for the television roll-out in a test market.

The commercial featured Bambi, wearing different outfits from her line in a series of quick cuts, dancing down the city street with her pet fawn at her heels. As the agency creative director had explained to Hughie, this commercial would showcase Bambi as she really was – unspoiled, natural, and romantic, but contemporary. The fawn had been Bambi's idea, to tie in with her own deer logo that would be tastefully appliquéd to every piece of clothing. 'The deer will be the alligator of the Eighties,' Hughie had told the marketing group at Premier, which he knew had been casting envious glances at Sears' successful Cheryl Tiegs line. The fact that Hughie's first meeting with Premier coincided with Bambi's inside front cover spread in *Glamour* for Buccaneer Jeans was certainly not the result of luck, but of careful planning. When Hughie had unfurled the magazine pages and then played a video tape of Bambi's Buccaneer commercials, he had noticed the marketing team lean imperceptibly forward, nodding their heads in a gesture that, in the boardroom, was equal to a burst of applause on a fashion runway. Within weeks of that first meeting, Hughie had found himself signing a contract as Bambi's legal guardian and vice-president of Bambi Enterprises, Inc. Bambi was the president of her company, and insisted that her personal approval of every design should be written into her contract. She had learned her lesson from Gianni Valeri, whose merchandise often seemed to her to be constructed of Handi-Wipes, pressed lint, or Naugahyde, depending on the item, and she refused to have her name on anything that she did not feel was of sufficient quality.

Gianni Valeri had been furious when he learned Bambi

was marketing a competitive sportswear line, and he had immediately made threatening phone calls and sent several legal letters, all of which proved meaningless. Bambi's contract with Valeri had been for three commercials and one print ad. Having fulfilled those obligations, she was legally free to direct her career as she wished. Both Bambi and Hughie knew the Bambi line of clothing would probably cause the downfall of Buccaneer Jeans, but neither of them were particularly disturbed. That was business, Hughie rationalized. They would take their opportunities when and where they arrived. Besides, it certainly was not Bambi's fault that Valeri's product was less appealing than Premier's. If it hadn't been for Bambi, Buccaneer Jeans would never have sold at all. The model's fashion line would feature quality merchandise made from fabric Hughie would personally inspect. The clothes would have simple, coordinating designs, clean pastel colors, and, most important to young women in their teens and early twenties, a reasonable price tag. Bambi was beautiful, but Hughie had always known that the key to her brilliance as a model was that her look was not so threatening that it seemed out of reach. Achievable beauty was what Bambi offered the camera, and achievable style was what her clothes would offer Premier's customers. The ad agency had touched this hot button when they came up with a slogan that said this in double-edged words Hughie considered, if less than Proustian, commercially descriptive: *Bambi becomes you.*

Today's shoot had actually begun with a crew call at two o'clock in the morning. Bambi had to be on the set by three-thirty for hair and makeup, which took place in the special luxury motor home that was provided for her. Bob Bacardi was known for some of the most beautiful fragrance and cosmetic advertising, and he specialized in a back-lit, soft-focus, romantic look. Such an achievement, according to Bacardi, was impossible in the glaring light of midday. Bacardi shot only at sunrise and sunset, and those who did not care to rise before the sun and then wait patiently for it to set could not be accommodated by Bob Bacardi.

The assistant director consulted with the script girl, replaying the last take on a black-and-white video monitor that was hooked up to a generator by a tangle of inch-thick black cords. A six-by-six image of Bambi appeared on the tiny screen, dancing gracefully down the center of the street. Stunt drivers in carefully choreographed cars screeched to a halt inches from Bambi as she sashayed down the street with the fawn on a leash, while drivers in special color-coordinated pastel cars stopped to gape on cue.

'Put on TV cutoff and run that again,' ordered Bob Bacardi, and a black cardboard mat with a television-screen-shaped cutout was affixed to the monitor screen. Bacardi peered at the picture and frowned.

The script girl scribbled on her pad. 'That's NG. The fawn's head went out of frame.'

'One more,' shrugged Bacardi.

'I need Bambi and the fawn,' the assistant director said, as if he were ordering a tuna on whole wheat for lunch. 'And all the drivers.'

He raised the walkie-talkie closer to his mouth. 'Security, please hold traffic.' Two pairs of off-duty policemen at each end of the street replaced the yellow barricades.

Bambi climbed down from her motor home, trailed by her makeup and hair stylists, who stood by in case a stray curl or smudge needed attention. She took her starting position, which was marked by a strip of white masking tape at the far end of the street. The trainer, a husky, bearded man in a baseball cap, ran up with the fawn and handed her its leash, then positioned himself just out of camera range, where he would coax the fawn with morsels of food. Bambi reached down and stroked the fawn's quivering ears, and it looked up at her with eyes as soft as her own.

Two four-hundred-pound camera dollies wheeled into position, looking strangely festive under orange-and-green striped beach umbrellas that shielded the huge lenses from reflections. Behind Bambi, six technicians wrestled with a swimming-pool-size square of white parachute fabric stretched on a tubular steel frame to buffer the sunlight.

'Very quiet, everybody,' shouted the assistant director. 'Nobody walks, nobody talks!' He rushed up to Bambi and held a light meter to her face, then raced back to the cameramen for a frenzied conference.

When the wardrobe woman had basted a thread to hold down the pocket flaps of Bambi's pink-and-white striped oversized gauze shirt, the sound man taped a tiny microphone to her skin just under her breastbone, and they were ready.

The assistant director nodded to the sound man, who was almost hidden behind a nest of cords as he monitored his equipment. 'Roll sound!'

'Speed!' called out the sound man.

A black-and-white striped clapper snapped under Bambi's nose. '*A* camera mark!' The second clapper snapped. '*B* camera mark!'

The script girl looked up. 'Apple up, Bob,' she said, indicating the *A* camera.

Bacardi squinted at the scene. 'Stand by. Camera ready. And . . . action!'

Bambi felt silly, pirouetting down the street by herself,

but her ballet training made her every move look natural. As the music blared out from the speakers, she strutted and twirled, her arms and hands emphasizing the pockets, the collar, and the flowing line of the clothes so casually that it seemed as though any woman who wore these clothes could look as good as Bambi.

The fawn stared at her, frozen to the spot.

'Cue the fawn!' Bacardi yelled.

The trainer waved the treats with more gusto, and the animal sprang into a light trot at Bambi's side, seemingly oblivious to the pink and yellow cars that crisscrossed their path. The music blared, 'I'm a Bambi girl, Bambi gets you there in style, Bambi girl . . .' Finally, at the end of the street, the director called, 'Cut!' Bambi stopped and cuddled the fawn for a close-up and her one and only line, which consisted of two words.

She ruffled her short hair and leveled her gaze straight at the camera. 'Know what?' she whispered.

'Bambi becomes you,' shrieked the music in answer.

'Playback,' ordered Bob Bacardi, and everyone gathered again around the video monitor for an instant replay of the scene.

'Perfect, print it,' he proclaimed. 'On to the next scene, please.'

Bambi retreated to her trailer. They wouldn't be needing her again for at least an hour. She'd learned that on the Buccaneer Jeans shoot. She thought she'd go back to the trailer and call Aunt Eve, until she remembered what time it was in the real world. It always took forever to reset the lights and cameras, and then there was her makeup, which was touched up after every take. She shivered in the thin cotton outfit. The most strenuous acting she'd have to do today, she decided, was pretending it was a tropical heat wave in the middle of November, which was chilly and damp at sunrise even in Los Angeles.

Hughie was waiting for her, flipping channels on the color TV set in the trailer. 'My God,' he yawned, wrapping a blanket around her and rubbing her shoulders as he had when she was a little girl, bundled in a towel after a bubble bath. 'It feels like the middle of the night. I wouldn't have left Valeski if I'd known the hours I'd have to keep managing you. What time is it?'

'Six o'clock.'

'It *is* the middle of the night.' He hugged her close for a few seconds. 'How's my girl holding up?'

'No complaints.' Bambi flopped into a swivel chair in front of the makeup mirror.

The hairstylist sprayed water from an atomizer onto Bambi's inch-long curls, then fluffed them with his fingers. 'The less I do, the better you look,' he said.

'But *I* need you, I really do,' Bambi smiled at him. 'Moral support.' In fact, Bambi liked Kim because he did so little to her hair. He didn't try to tease it or set it or change her look, as some others had. She insisted on Kim at every shoot and always got her way, even though he worked out of New York and had to be flown to all her locations. This morning, he had half a tissue hanging out of each nostril to absorb some of the aftereffects of a night of too many West Coast indulgences. Everyone ignored this idiosyncrasy. They were used to seeing strange things on shoots.

Hughie dropped a sheaf of papers into her lap. 'Here's something that'll warm you up, Bambi.'

She put the papers on the counter. 'I'll read these later. What is it?' The best thing about having Hughie with her all the time wasa that she knew he'd take care of all the details.

'You know the Farrah Fawcett poster? The one that

made her a star. Well, what do you think of a Bambi poster?'

She didn't answer right away, so Hughie went on, leaning close to the mirror to examine his face as he talked. 'We have an offer from a poster company. You keep twenty-five percent of the profits. This kind of thing can be *very* lucrative, you know.'

'What would anyone want with a poster of me?' Bambi asked, and giggled. She knew her breasts were so tiny that a bathing suit poster would be a joke. 'What would I do for this poster?'

'They'd like to do a series, I think. A close-up of your face in one, then maybe you in toe shoes for another. Whatever. We'd have approval.' Hughie unscrewed the cap froma bottle of Visine, pulled down one eyelid, and squeezed in some drops.

'What did you tell them?'

'That we'd talk about it. But really, Bambi, it seems like it has potential. Not much work and a lot of money. And think of the visibility! I'd make them guarantee high-quality outlets, of course, like bookstores . . .' He squeezed some liquid into his other eye.

Bambi looked at her brother in the mirror, her jaw firmly set. 'Bambi wouldn't do that,' she said softly.

'What?'

In the past few months, Bambi had come to think of herself as two people. The first Bambi, the real Bambi – Elizabeth Ann Stuart – loved horses, the outdoors, and sipping hot chocolate in front of the fire. The public Bambi, the nearly famous model, wore ropes of pearls with both bathing suits and furs, lived in the glossy pages of the fashion magazines, and had spiky, short hair that made her appear as you wanted, boy or girl. Being a model was not all bad, she had to admit. She'd already saved enough money to pay for veterinary school, and she'd be applying to colleges right after Christmas. But she wasn't going to go off to college and face all those new kids and have them laugh at her because some stupid poster of her in lip gloss was in the campus bookstore. Besides, it didn't feel right, just as the fancy dress hadn't seemed right for the Black and White Ball. Bambi was definitely not a poster, she decided. She had better ideas of her own.

'I've been thinking, Hughie. What about a doll? A new kind of Barbie. It would come with clothes from the Bambi line. And then the girls would want to buy our Bambi clothes for themselves.'

Hughie nodded thoughtfully. His little sister was definitely not so little anymore, and he was grateful that she was caring about something other than horses. At first, she had always sat on the fringe of meetings, not daring to speak, relying totally on his judgement. But, more and more, she was getting involved, giving opinions, saying yes and no, having ideas of her own. And they were surprisingly good ideas. Her instincts were uncannily correct. The Bambi doll made sense, because it was more attuned to her image. Bambi's appeal was too asexual for a poster. Hughie had to concede that nobody understood Bambi's image better than Bambi.

'And what about a Bambi perfume? It could smell like fresh-cut grass and lilies-of-the-valley. We could put the fawn on the bottle, and . . .'

Hughie was wide awake now. He grabbed a pen and started jotting down notes. 'Absolutely. A Bambi perfume is a very big idea.'

Bambi smiled sweetly, but she didn't really care about big ideas. She cared about what was right for her, and if it was a big idea, great.

She glanced somewhat guiltily at her French textbook, which had lain unopened on the couch for two days. She was supposed to read the rest of *Chanson de Roland* by Monday. It seemed like a big waste of time. Conjugating French verbs was not going to help her be a better veterinarian, or even a better model, so she wasn't going to kill herself to please Mrs Aronson, that stringy teacher who looked at Bambi as if she were gross or deformed, or in some other way not good enough for her stupid French class.

School just wasn't important anymore, except as a means to becoming a veterinarian and breeding her own horses. She knew she would have to pay attention to anything that was really going to get her someplace. She'd pay attention to Bambi. She didn't need hype, she only needed Hughie and herself. Somehow, Elizabeth Ann Stuart knew that the glamorous Bambi would take care of herself, and Hughie, too. Bambi could do things that Elizabeth Ann could not. She could take off her clothes in front of the camera, stand for twelve hours under hot lights without complaining, and, most importantly, provide a safe harbor for all the worries and insecurities of a girl who had lost both her parents the year she was born.

Hughie had taken care of her then and Eve had been like a mother. But Bambi would take care of her now. And when the short era of the tousle-haired, androgynous free spirit was over, and another model photographic-type took over, Bambi would have set Hughie and his baby sister free from financial worry. They'd be free to do whatever they wanted.

She sensed that she would have to move while she was hot. Television commercials, fashion lines, dolls, and perfume were all getting her what she eventually wanted.

Elizabeth Ann Stuart had big ideas for Bambi.

# 3

October 15

TO: ALL INTERCONTINENTAL MINERALS PERSONNEL
FROM: GRAHAM DONALDSON
RE: CATHERINE MCBRIDE

This is to announce that, effective immediately, Catherine McBride has been appointed a senior vice-president of Intercon. I'm sure you all join me in congratulating Catherine for this well-deserved honor.

---

October 16

*CONFIDENTIAL*

TO: ALL INTERCONTINENTAL EMPLOYEES
FROM: HARVEY MCINTOSH
RE: CORPORATE SECURITY POLICY

It is one of my less pleasurable but most important duties to reiterate company policy concerning kidnapping and threats of extortion, since the Bandera Roja, a Venezuelan terrorist group, kidnapped Guillermo Hawks, vice-president, South American Oil Exploration. He was held ransom for six million dollars. Fortunately, due to bold intervention on the part of the Venezuelan military, Guillermo has finally been released unharmed.

However, we all must be aware that Intercontinental Minerals cannot and will not give in to threats that would essentially make us all victims. Ransom will not be paid under any terrorist circumstance, for the common good. There are no exceptions to this policy.

The company applauds Guillermo Hawks's bravery and loyalty to Intercon. We hope the need to enforce this stringent company policy never again arises.

# 4

Whenever a department-head meeting was called in the Intercon auditorium, a current of excitement flowed through the entire staff, because such meetings were not held unless a major announcement was to be made. Such events caused great anxiety since everyone there wondered how this new information would affect their own position. The State of the Corporation Address, for instance, which Graham Donaldson gave once a year from the auditorium podium, showed slides and bar charts that indicated profits or losses in various divisions. Afterward, every person in the room could make an educated guess on the amount of his or her bonus.

An assembly like this could change the entire corporate balance of power in five minutes flat. Everyone still remembered the meeting at which Michael Picol's appointment to the company was announced, the silence that followed the slide diagramming his position in the hierarchy just beneath Graham Donaldson, and the fact that, as a result, fifteen résumés discreetly hit the street by lunchtime.

Even Catherine was not sure what this meeting was about. Even though they were virtually living together, there were some business decisions, like the oil find, that were clearly Graham's territory.

Graham still hadn't given her all the details about the oil find. Nor had she been able to impress upon him the opportunities it afforded. She tried reasoning with Graham, explaining to him, and she even appealed to his sense of duty to the stockholders, but the result was always the same: a weary wave of the hand, a tightening of the face, and a patient dissertation on the fact that an oil find, however major, was inconsequential compared to the opportunity to do something of lasting worth. You couldn't put a price tag on things like that, he'd insisted, ending the discussion every time Catherine brought it up. During the past week, he'd been especially irritable, ever since *Time* magazine's People section had picked up the picture of them at the White House. Henry Hudson and the others had been cropped out of the photo and it seemed as if Catherine and Graham were having a romantic rendezvous in the East Room. That picture had received more attention than Henry's stroke, although he was recovering rather well and was now in physical therapy.

As she saw Graham step up to the podium and join Michael Picol, Irv Turner, Harvey McIntosh, and Guillermo Hawks, Catherine felt an irrational sense of pride, as if a part of her were also there with him, in command.

The lights dimmed.

'The Intercon family is delighted to welcome back Guillermo Hawks. Guillermo's bravery is an inspiration to us all, and, luckily, his story had a happy ending.' Graham turned to Hawks, who looked thin and undernourished, as if he had not fully recovered from his ordeal, and his tan somehow seemed artificial.

'Guillermo, in recognition of your unswerving loyalty to the company and your country, we'd like to present you with this plaque and our heartfelt appreciation and compassion for what you went through.' The audience applauded as Guillermo and Graham shook hands. The rumor had already been circulated through the interoffice network that Guillermo Hawks had been presented with a check for over one hundred thousand dollars this morning by the board of directors. Although the corporate position dictated that terrorism was not to be pandered to, bravery and loyalty were well rewarded.

Guillermo briefly addressed the assembly to express his thanks. 'I must tell you,' he began, 'that even a few months of incarceration makes the Intercon cafeteria something to dream about.' Laughter and applause erupted again.

When Guillermo had taken his seat, Graham again stood at the podium.

'This is an unofficial meeting, but I'd like to share with you some exciting news. When the final reports are in, this will be the highest earning quarter in the history of Intercon Minerals.'

More applause.

'It is due,' he said in his gentle, soft voice, 'to the people of Intercon. People like Guillermo Hawks, who suffered the horror of incarceration by a terrorist group determined to obstruct the free enterprise system. And that's just the beginning!'

He adjusted the microphone. 'I'm not saying you have to endure kidnapping to get recognition in this company. Our success is also due to people like Tommy Scoggins, from our mail room. Today is his twentieth anniversary with the company. He runs a mail department that's as big as a small country's postal system with efficiency and professionalism.'

There was polite applause.

'Then there are newcomers to the Intercon family,' Graham continued. 'Like Catherine McBride.'

The applause was even politer, as Catherine shifted uncomfortably in her seat.

'She is among the newcomers who have moved swiftly

up the corporate ladder due to their energy and contributions.'

*What could he be getting at*, Catherine wondered.

'I would like to stress that her recent promotion to senior vice-president was due, as all who work with her would attest, to her excellent capabilities, and not to any personal favoritism, real or imagined.'

The room seemed to buzz, and Catherine tried to grow invisible in her seat. Was he trying to make fools of them both? That picture in *Time* would only cause a ripple, but this would create a maelstrom.

She tried to look neither right nor left, but she sensed every head turning in her direction. Graham was still talking, and as words drifted through the thick fog that seemed to have surrounded her, she frantically thought of ways out of this mess.

Billy Wright had warned her about office gossip, and so far she'd been able to simply turn her back and ignore it. Her relationship with Graham had never been openly referred to, and the last person she ever suspected to broach the subject was Graham. Catherine knew he had just totally undercut her authority. What *could* he be thinking? Catherine asked herself. This was not the Graham Donaldson she loved and respected.

The lights came up, and people started to file out of the room. A small crowd surrounded Graham as he left the stage, congratulating him on his speech, but the rest of the group avoided Catherine as if she carried the bubonic plague. B.J. leaned forward from the row behind her. 'Methinks he protests too much,' she whispered, and Catherine nodded wordlessly as her throat tightened.

'What are you going to do?' B.J. asked.

Catherine glanced at Graham again. He was beaming confidence, and she could see he was pleased with his morale speech. He caught her eye and strode up the aisle to where she was sitting. 'Well, that's history,' he announced. 'Now maybe we can get on with running this business.'

Catherine was furious. 'We'll have to discuss this later.' She got up to leave. 'I can't believe you did this without telling me first.'

'If I had told you, would you have agreed?'

'Of course not. I wouldn't dignify the gossip.'

'This should end it. Don't worry. It was all part of my strategy.'

'And if it backfires?'

'It won't. I've dealt with the issue, and that's it.'

They rode up the elevator together in silence, though Catherine would have loved to tell Graham just what she thought of him at that moment. Carla was waiting when they reached his office. 'There's a reporter on my line, trying to get through to you,' she said to Graham as he went to take the call. She turned to Catherine sympathetically. 'Don't let it get to you,' she said in a low voice. 'I know jealousy when I see it. Some people just can't stand to see a young, pretty girl get ahead.' A touch of bitterness crossed her face. 'I know.'

'Thanks, Carla. I can handle it.' Catherine's knees felt weak as she walked back to her department. She'd have to formulate a plan right away, since the story was bound to be all over the news by tomorrow.

Turning a corner, she collided with Ray Acconti.

'Well,' he said, smirking. 'This explains a lot of the decisions that have been made in the past few months. It's hard to get your point across during business hours when the winning arguments are being presented at night. After White House dinners, of course.'

He had clearly seen the picture in *Time*. Spiteful,

insecure reptile, Catherine thought as she brushed past him without turning back. 'You're obviously over-wrought, Dr Acconti,' she said, her voice icily precise.

Back in her office, she dialed Graham's private line. 'It's impossible,' she said. 'Acconti's already all over me. And the press is going out of control.'

He was so cool. 'Allow me to handle something for once, Catherine. Have some faith in someone else for a change. You have made A Place in the Sun possible. It's going to happen, and you have a new promotion because of it. Those are the issues here. Focus on them. You should feel great.'

'I don't know what I feel. We're supposed to be a team, aren't we? But you've just taken it on yourself to announce to the world that we're sleeping together.'

'Catherine, I *denied* it. There are other people to think about besides ourselves. I've put everyone off until the divorce is final.'

'If you believe that, you're so naive it's incredible.'

His voice softened. 'I did it for *you*,'

She sighed. 'I know. It'll be okay.' She hung up and wished she could believe that for even a minute.

Absentmindedly, she sifted through the inch-thick stack of phone messages on her desk. There was one from Alfred Grunewald, with a local area code. Was he passing through town? she wondered. She decided to call him back. Maybe he had news from the baron.

'Hello, Catherine McBride,' his elegant voice came on the line. 'I'm here overnight to give a publishing speech at Northwestern. We're giving a journalism scholarship as part of the Foundation.'

'What a wonderful idea.' It felt good to think about something other than Intercon for a few minutes.

Alfred came right to the point, sensing the hurry in her voice. 'Are you free for dinner?'

She really should stay late at the office, in case Graham needed her. But then, he could always meet her later. And right now her presence would only add fuel to the fire. Besides, just talking to Alfred made her smile, and she needed a break. Seeing Alfred would be a perfect way to end an otherwise unpleasant day. Tonight, for the first time in weeks, she'd leave at five and meet Alfred for dinner. 'I'll be sure I'm free,' she heard herself saying.

Over dessert at Spiaggia, Catherine found herself telling Alfred her problems with the press. 'I don't know,' she said, ignoring the skyline view of the Magnificent Mile and nervously crumbling her torte instead. 'It's a real problem. And so unfair to Graham.'

Alfred leaned back and put his arm over the back of the banquette. 'No. Actually, I'd say it's unfair to *you*. But the press isn't really to blame, Catherine. You have to look out for yourself.'

'What should I do? Hire a press agent?' she asked sarcastically.

'Be your own press agent. If you put as much effort out for yourself as you did for your company, and for your friend Graham Donaldson, things might look differently.'

'I thought it was all the same thing,' she murmured. But Alfred was right. She never made decisions based on what was best for herself, but what was best for Intercon. Anything else seemed so calculated. 'Are you a fan of Machiavelli?'

'No. Just a fan of yours.' He smiled at her in the conspiratorial way she remembered from their pastry cart caper, years ago. There was still a lot of little boy in him, Catherine thought as she smiled back and began to relax for the first time all day. It was really too bad Alfred lived in Europe, for she sensed that they could be great friends. After dinner, he'd be gone, and she would again face the real world on her own. Catherine didn't know how Alfred understood everything she was going through, but she read the empathy in his eyes.

'I'm just a phone call away, if you ever want to talk,' he said. It was not an uncommon thing to say, but she knew he meant it. He scribbled something on a card. 'Here. This is my private line at home.'

'Thank you.' She wondered how many friends she really did have to call. Graham? Billy? B.J.? Miss Aggie, perhaps? Everyone she met was also a business associate.

Except for Alfred. He was a friend, and she was happy. There *was* life beyond Intercon, she told herself.

Going down the lobby escalator in the mauve marble foyer, Catherine found herself slipping her arm through Alfred's, her hand brushing his cashmere overcoat. It seemed like the right thing to do.

Even though it was only a block from the One Magnificent Mile building to Catherine's apartment, they managed to stretch it out to a thirty-minute stroll. On the corner of Walton and Michigan Avenue, the light turned from red to green ten or twelve times as they stood inches apart, their breath a frosty cloud between them in the subzero Chicago winter, as they talked, not even realizing the time or the temperature.

'I must have left my gloves at the restaurant,' Catherine finally noticed.

'Here.' He took both of her hands in his and tucked them into his pockets.

She felt his chest press into hers, and then they were kissing, her fingers rubbing slowly, involuntarily, up and down his back underneath his coat. She lifted her face and turned it slowly, oblivious to the icy wind beating against them in gusts as she felt his lips kissing the corners of her mouth, moving tenderly down to the mink collar of her coat and breathing softly against her throat. They stood under the streetlight as the traffic signal changed four or five more times and snowflakes whipped in a vortex around them.

Somehow the snow, the wind and the cold conspired to bring them together against her will. Something was happening between them. Something had always been happening between them.

'We shouldn't be out on a night like this,' she whispered as she held him.

'No, we shouldn't.'

'I think my teeth are numb.' She tried to disentangle her fingers from his. 'I'd better give you something warm to drink.' They ran across the street to her apartment building, bracing themselves against the gusting wind.

The John Hancock is one of those buildings that seem to have been designed by Daedalus to thwart entry – a labyrinth of seemingly endless lobbies, elevator banks, and travertine barriers that twisted around and around in a most disorienting fashion. One bank of elevators took Catherine and Alfred to the forty-fourth floor, where they took another elevator to the residential floors.

She pushed the button for her floor – ninety one.

If she was supposed to be so much in love with Graham, why was she wishing that she was still outside so she would still have an excuse to put her hands inside Alfred's pockets? Was this a reaction to the press conference? Was she getting even for something? Or were her feelings for Alfred just totally confused? Or was something happening to her love for Graham?

Before she could wonder any more, Alfred stepped closer, and she backed into the control panel, lighting every button for every floor. Alfred took both her wrists in one hand and raised her arms over his head, pinning her to the wall as he kissed her and slid his other hand underneath her coat. Then he unbuttoned her coat and pressed himself against the silk of her dress. He had taken off his coat in the lobby, and Catherine felt his hardness grazing her.

A wild thrill went through her. She felt reckless, and she didn't care. The elevator stopped jerkily at every floor, the doors constantly bumping open and shut. Anyone could come in at any time. But no one did. If someone had, he would have been met with the sight of Alfred Grunewald taking the hem of Catherine's dress in his hand and lifting it to her waist beneath her heavy coat.

He ran his hands across her thighs. She wanted him to continue, to slip his hands underneath her pantyhose. She wrapped one leg around his, her shoe falling to the floor. He picked her up and held her inches off the floor, one knee on each side of his body as she wrapped her arms around his neck.

He opened the snaps along the back of her dress and reached around under the cotton camisole, stroking her bare breast.

She no longer cared about propriety.

Catherine reached out and opened his shirt one button at a time, gliding her hand against his taut muscles, etching her fingers across the light blond hairs on his chest.

Alfred hooked his thumbs under her pantyhose. Suddenly she wanted to be free, to be naked, to be everything with him. She stepped out of the pantyhose and left them in a heap on the elevator floor.

As they reached the seventy-fifth floor, they were twenty times more out of control, each panting into the other's mouth, each fingering the other's body. He pushed hard against her, and Catherine thought they would soon be making love right there, for everyone in the building to witness.

Her hips were moving against his, and her face, round and serious with her high cheekbones and large, clear eyes, stared back at him, open and ready. She edged her hand between their waists and across his chest, and he backed away slightly, relishing the feel of her hand under his belt, her small fingers grasping as he sucked in his breath with a sharp gasp.

I want this man, she thought. I want him right here, in the elevator, Catherine told herself as she unbuckled his pants.

And they probably would have made love right then and there if Mrs Shapiro hadn't gotten in on the eighty-seventh floor with her miniature poodle.

Catherine casually closed her coat, Alfred stepped away, and they walked out on the ninety-first floor with the utmost dignity while Mrs Shapiro continued to the roof, where she would undoubtedly walk her dog.

They stood for a moment looking at each other, jolted back to reality in front of her apartment. Catherine's cheeks were flushed bright red from the combination of subzero cold and the red-hot elevator ride.

'I'd ask you in, but I think I live with somebody,' she whispered.

He pulled her pantyhose out of his pocket in one aristocratic motion. 'Well, then you might be needing these.' There was nothing more to say.

Catherine closed the door behind her, still breathless. She hadn't betrayed Graham, but she had wanted to. Was that the same thing, she wondered as she stepped out of her clothes and slipped naked under the sheets.

Hours later, when she was still lying awake in the dark, her cheeks still burning, Midnight the cat purred contentedly across her legs. She heard Graham's key in the door and she closed her eyes, turned over, and pretended to be asleep.

# 5

With a certain undulation of syllables and caressing of phrase, Michael Picol communicated what was on his mind as clearly as men of less finesse might have said 'Let's fuck,' but Catherine was oblivious to his signals as she sat nervously in his hard-edged living room.

She had sworn she'd never again set foot in his apartment, and only desperation had driven her here. She was on the brink of losing both her professional credibility and her emotional symbiosis with Graham. The fallout from the *Time* magazine picture and Graham's subsequent auditorium announcement had been horrendous, ranging from snide looks from the secretaries to a picture in *Persona* magazine, cropped to look as if the two of them were alone and gazing adoringly into each other's eyes, captioned 'The Bedroom and the Boardroom.' In fact, the board had received several anonymous, obscene, and threatening letters, which, since he was chairman, had gone directly to Graham. Catherine had only looked at one, which, between scrawled biblical references, spelled out explicitly how the author proposed to burn her all over her body with lit cigarettes. Graham had assured her that she need not worry about the ravings of a lunatic, but she had also received so many nerve-wracking, heavy-breathing, obscene phone calls at home that she had been forced to change her phone number and keep it unlisted. 'There's no place in our kind of thinking for small minds,' Graham had said, brushing aside her horror, and he had taken both her hands in his and assured her that together nothing could touch them.

Nothing could touch *him* was more like it, Catherine knew. A socially prominent man who had been chairman and CEO of a Fortune 500 company for twenty years and a close friend of the President of the United States was not exactly in the same position as a twenty-eight-year-old woman in her second job. Graham's relationship with her, she knew, would be a nonentity on his record, a little afternoon delight to be viewed with, if anything, envy by the code of double standards. But her relationship with Graham would be positioned exactly as Ray Acconti had seen it: Catherine McBride got to the top on her back. The prime-time soap operas were just the appetizer for real life, Catherine knew. People were greedy when it came to gossip and scandal. The Graham Donaldson Undersea Research Center might one day win the Nobel Prize, but she and Graham would be thought of not as the team that brought new hope to the hungry, but as the couple who were doing it behind the copying machine.

The oil find was therefore very important to both of them personally and to Intercon. It dealt with the one issue that commanded absolute attention and universal respect. News of such a find held international implications and could affect global economies. She and Graham could be heroes, returning with their shields instead of on them. If only she could get Graham to understand this, she thought as she listened to Picol mumbling pleasantries next to her.

Since the development of an undersea oil field would most likely mean the end of all marine research, Graham had decided not to jeopardize his dream. Catherine had suggested the possibility of relocating the site of A Place in the Sun, but Graham had pointed out that it had already taken a decade to coordinate each element as it now stood, and he didn't necessarily have another decade. Look at Henry Hudson, he'd grimly reminded her.

Graham further complicated matters by steadfastly refusing to explain Arnie Welles's findings in detail to Catherine, saying only that they were irrelevant since 3-D seismic studies were nothing to get excited about. It was always possible that her suspicions were off-base, that this find was really not in the big leagues and therefore not worth pursuing. Catherine just didn't have the technical background to understand all the implications herself, and she needed help. Billy Wright would have qualified the report in an instant, but he was unreachable in the field, and he was the only person she could really trust.

She certainly did not trust Michael Picol, Catherine thought as she moved as far away from him as possible on the couch. The memory of the cold marble slab table pressed against her bare thighs still made her shudder. Because she was catching him between trips to New York and Venezuela and he therefore wouldn't be back in the office for weeks, she had to see him at his convenience. She needed his input and she knew that sometimes even enemies are allies, if the purpose suited both sides. She had never mentioned that night in Picol's apartment to Graham, so perhaps Picol owed her for that.

He reached for the raw pea pods that Singh had placed on the table. 'So,' he said, 'is this visit a business meeting, a peace offering, or should I call my insurance adjuster again?' His eyes followed the curves of her body to her ankles, then back up again. His shirt was open halfway down his chest, the lights were dim, soft music played, and Singh was nowhere in sight. He clearly had set the stage with some care for an extremely warm reconciliation.

Momentarily unnerved, Catherine didn't answer.

'You *did* call me,' he reminded her. 'If you don't want to talk, you can always come in the bedroom – to watch me pack.'

She set her briefcase on the table and opened it. This was clearly business. 'What I'm here to discuss with you is what Arnie Welles has to say.'

'Welles?' Picol was instantly alert.

'What I'm going to show you is totally confidential. Even the executive committee hasn't seen it. I'm sharing it with you because I know you are on Graham Donaldson's team.'

'So?' Picol leaned back and touched the cleft of his chin with his knuckle.

'I know he gave you your start in this business. *Both* of us owe Graham a lot,' Catherine said. 'Which is why we have to be careful to keep this information to ourselves.'

Picol shrugged. 'As far as I'm concerned, you were never here.' He paused. 'You were never here before, were you?'

She glared at him.

He tossed her a lazy grin. 'Client confidentiality is my specialty.'

She handed him a copy of Arnie Welles's report. He skimmed it quickly, and Catherine started to ask his opinion. 'Michael what . . .'

He raised his hand and cut her off. 'Hold it. Let me read.' Picol took fiften minutes to reread the report, weighing each word. This incredible attention to detail, Catherine realized, the studied conclusions and analytic assessments were what Graham referred to when he called Michael Picol the one man you'd want on your side if you wanted to shoot down anyone from a threatening union official to a sleazy bureaucrat on the take. Michael Picol was famous for stepping in, taking control, and eliminating the problem.

Finally, Picol swung both legs heavily on to the coffee table and pushed himself back into his seat. 'What the Venezuelans wouldn't do with this,' he said under his breath.

'Such as?'

'Such as give us the gate, lock up their leases till infinity, and gold-plate the slums of Caracas with the spare change.'

Her hunch had been right! 'You're sure this report isn't too preliminary to be conclusive?'

'Talk English, McBride. Graham's up the creek. He could lose his ass right here. And it explains a lot of things. Such as why Agnes Palmer's husband asked her on his deathbed never to sell. He had Welles in his pocket. Probably would have cashed in himself if he hadn't been ready to kick off.'

'Why didn't he tell Miss Aggie?'

'The Southern ethic. Didn't want her to worry her pretty little head, no doubt.' Picol chuckled. 'And the minute the old Colonel died, Graham Donaldson put Welles on his payroll.'

'So how big do you think we're talking here?'

'According to this . . .' he slapped the papers with the back of his hand. 'We could activate some semisubmersible rigs on the Cay Vega Block and within two years have three platforms set, seventeen to twenty wells drilled, and flow rates of a hundred million cubic feet a day. Let me see.' He took out a pencil and scribbled on the back of the report. 'Mineral, you're talking – thirty thousand barrels a day, net crude production.'

Catherine couldn't help but notice the difference between Graham's elegant demeanor and Michael Picol's cold, ruthless approach. 'Michael, legally isn't he under an obligation to release this to the entire board? Shouldn't it be a group decision?'

'Your boyfriend could go to the slammer, if that's what you mean. Now who else had this information?'

'As far as I know, just Welles, Graham, and myself, and I just found out by accident.'

'Was that pillow talk, or were you just prowling through his papers?'

She grabbed the report. 'I can deal with this myself.'

'No, Catherine. You did the right thing coming to me.' His tone softened sympathetically. 'We'll be partners in this conspiracy to make Graham see the light.'

'I don't know how we're going to do it. He's got his heart set on A Place in the Sun. He's talking about a Nobel Prize. He's not interested in money anymore. He's into humanitarianism.'

She chose her words carefully. 'I'm not sure Graham thinks now is the time to make this information public.'

'Well, he'll have to move soon. You can't just ignore something like this.'

She shook her head. 'I think he's going through with A Place in the Sun.'

Picol jumped up from the couch. 'That asshole, going for the Nobel Peace Prize when he's sitting on the biggest oil find of the century. He's losing it.'

'Maybe he's got some plan nobody knows about,' she said loyally.

'No he doesn't,' Picol muttered. 'I just drew up Graham's new will and a trust when I was handling the divorce decree. His secret plan is retirement. Soon. He's going to sit down there and be King of the Islands, sort of a preppie Emperor Jones.' He spit out the words with a bitterness that took Catherine by surprise.

'Come on,' she scoffed. 'You can't believe that. He's not retiring. He probably just wants Eve to think so.'

Picol turned around, his back to her. 'Why, then?'

She rallied to Graham's defense. 'It's strictly a matter of a value judgement. His judgement is that the research center takes priority.'

'Profits take priority. This *is* America.'

Of course Picol was right. If only Graham saw the issue in these terms. 'Help me, Michael,' she asked, nervously pacing the marble floor. 'I know we can bring him around on this. We owe it to him to work out this thing logically. We've got to help him save himself from this.' She ran her hands through her hair. 'I'm so worried about him. It's not like him to throw away everything he's ever done for his company.'

Michael Picol watched her tirade impassively.

'I don't know whether it's because of the divorce, or Henry Hudson, or what . . .' her voice became more shrill. 'He just seems so easily distracted by personal things. It goes against his grain.'

'Take it easy, Catherine. Nothing is ever decided in an emotional state.' He was only half listening to her. Catherine could tell he was thinking about something. Good, maybe he had a plan, she said to herself.

'Are there any copies of these papers floating around?'

'No, these are the only ones.'

'Let me keep them.'

She hesitated for a moment. She knew she was making a decision of whether or not to trust someone and that Graham would have been able to make it in three seconds.

He seemed to read her thoughts. 'Well, do you want me to help or don't you?'

She couldn't answer. Had she done the right thing?

Would this destroy Graham's trust in her, or his love? She had to risk it. She couldn't let him ruin his career; she would save him. She bit her lip. 'Keep them.'

He nodded, watching her chin start to tremble. 'If this oil find ever came to light in the wrong way, you could be in as much trouble as he is. It's a public company. The shareholders don't care who's sleeping with whom, but they certainly care if somebody's screwing around with their money.' He stood up and squeezed her shoulder reassuringly. 'Don't worry, Catherine. Legally, you've done the right thing. We'll work together on this.'

'You'll get back to me then?'

'I'll keep you posted every step of the way.'

'He won't go to jail, will he?' she whispered. She'd never imagined it would be so serious.

'Maybe I can save his ass.' He glanced over at her with a half smile as she stood up. 'Hey, try not to throw anything on your way out.'

# 6

'The people from Neiman-Marcus are on their way up with the bras,' shouted Lolly Bishop, but no one could hear her over the din.

Both doorbells and the telephone seemed to ring continuously, and the penthouse doorman called up again and again to announce the arrival of the wedding photographer and the delivery of flowers, telegrams, and dozens of bridesmaids' shoes that had been dyed the wrong color.

The manager of Tiffany's Michigan Avenue store hurried down the penthouse hall carrying a baby-blue shopping bag. 'Oh, Foppy!' Lolly greeted him with a kiss. 'I didn't hear you announced.'

'I think your doormen have given up announcing,' he said, passing her the bag, which was filled with small baby-blue packages.

Drucilla Donaldson's seven bridesmaids were scattered across the girls' massive dressing room, which had three times the hanging space of the Ultimo boutique. Each bridesmaid wore a turquoise satin combing coat with her own monogram, a gift from Eve Donaldson. Hanging on two rented chrome racks were the seven voluminous bridesmaids' dresses, stuffed with tissue paper so stiffly that they looked as if they had a life of their own, a forest of fall colors, each silk moiré gown ombréd from light to dark like an autumn leaf, one amber, the next burnt amber, and then cerise, marigold, tangerine, apricot, and hunter green.

Arnold Scarron, the designer of these breathtaking

dresses, had flown in from Paris to supervise the final details. He was in serious discussion with the bridal consultant from Neiman-Marcus over his dissatisfaction with the hosiery.

'What color would you call this – puce or vomit? These are couture dresses. We need *silk* stocking in the colors I specified when I sent you the samples.' He threw three pairs of pantyhose up into the air with such force that one pair caught on the bedroom chandelier and hung like some dismembered erotic mobile. '*Silk stockings!* Not nylon support hose,' he snorted.

'But Mr Scarron, none of these girls wears a garter belt.'

'Well, *get* them, my dear, get them. What do you think you're here for! This is the wedding of the year, not the grocer's daughter marrying the plumber's son.'

'M-Mister Scarron,' the girl was almost in tears. 'Do the bras have to match too? These were all we had.'

He rifled through the bag. 'Just so they're strapless. I can't have *straps!*' He spit out the word as if he were describing chewing gum on the sole of a shoe.

'Girls! Girls! Girls!' Scarron's assistant clapped his hands together like a ballet master assembling his students, but none of the bridesmaids paid the slightest attention, as they squealed with delight. Each was totally preoccupied with ripping the blue wrappings off their gifts from Drucilla Donaldson.

'Oh, it's the most beautiful thing I've ever *seen!*' Gabby Von Austen, Dru's former classmate, gasped as she pulled a twisted freshwater pearl choker from the tissue paper. The clasp was garnet, to coordinate with her dress, and the other bridesmaids' necklaces sported clasps of tourmaline, aquamarine, citrine, amethyst, and blue and smoky topaz, depending on the hues of the dresses. Even

Diane de Cotrille Chaumet, Arnaud's disapproving sister, stared wide-eyed at the opulence of the scene. She herself had been married in the Normandy Chapel built in 1552 on the family grounds and, even at this moment, felt a reception in a public hotel to be hideously vulgar.

Bambi's long fall lay on the floor beside her like a dead lap dog as she tried on her necklace. Like her dress, the pearls fit perfectly. Each girl's neck, bust, waist, and shoulders had been measured at least six times in preparation for the grand march down the aisle, and all the bridesmaids had been flown to Paris on the Concorde for a long weekend of fittings.

The hair stylist turned to her. 'Here, let me help you put your hair on.'

'I don't see why I have to wear that mangy thing. Do you suppose it was somebody's real hair, or is it dynel?'

The stylist twisted some dried heather into tiny braids on the side of the fall. 'Think on the bright side,' he said. 'All the other girls had to sit there for hours while I wove maple leaves and heather into their hair – I can do yours without you.'

'Nothing to eat, nothing to drink now,' someone called out as the girls took their last bites of cold shrimp and rye crackers.

'Just step into your dresses, don't touch! Marielle will zip you up,' ordered Scarron.

'Lolly, we need the maid of honor!' somebody called.

She was in the bathroom, smoking a joint with Pemberly Bracket. 'I don't get to marry a count,' Pemberly complained. '*I* have a past.' She had had three fiancés to date. She fanned the telltale smoke toward the air-conditioning vent.

'So why don't you get a job instead? You should think about a career,' Lolly said thoughtfully.

'Well, Bishop, dating *is* a ful-time job.' Pemberly passed the cigarette to Lolly and pushed her sleeve up to her elbow.

'Dating is divided into three stages. Getting it together, getting it on, and getting it in.'

They slumped on to the side of the bathtub, shrieking hysterically.

There was serious knocking at the door, so Lolly put the joint out with her fingers and stuffed it into an empty Benson & Hedges box, to be slipped into her evening bag before she left.

At last, all the bridesmaids were lined up in the front hall for a final inspection. Their dresses were adjusted off the shoulder, from which each sleeve ballooned out dramatically, the waistlines narrow and tapered, Diane Chaumet's an illusion created by a boned waist cincher. Cheryl Lincoln, the seven-year-old daughter of Chicago's second black mayor, smiled an angelic, toothless smile, her flowergirl basket brimming with orchids and rose petals. The bridesmaids' skirts flared out to ballerina length, and each pair of silk stockings, after three frenzied trips back to Neiman-Marcus, now shimmered in the appropriate autumnal hue.

Louis, the ancient Donaldson gardener, tottered down the line, handing each girl a slightly varied bouquet of grapes, heather, clipped lavender, and fall leaves. The last bouquet, wrapped in lavender tissue paper, was for the bride; the Royal Bride, as she had been referred to by the press.

'Now remember, girls,' Scarron instructed, 'pick up your skirts before you climb into those carriages, and then again as you climb the stairs to the church. This will give the most graceful look for the photographs. And ladies, you look as if you've all just stepped out of a Renaissance garden.'

As if on cue, a barrage of flashes heralded the opening of the huge double doors from the library, and the bride, serenely followed by her mother, stepped out to join her attendants.

A spontaneous burst of applause and admiring sighs greeted her as the bridesmaids broke out of their formation and jostled around her to get a closer look at the dress that had been such a closely guarded secret.

Three thousand seed pearls, hand-applied by La Sage, the world-renowned beading specialist, glimmered on the tight-fitting ecru satin bodice. Huge Elizabethan sleeves ballooned out to just below the elbow, where they narrowed to a close fit, encrusted with gold beads, tiny rhinestones, and hundreds more pearls. The billowing fourteen-foot train was looped over Drucilla's arm, and her sheer organza, cathedral-length veil was held off her face by a pair of enormous diamond filigree sunbursts, de Cotrille family heirlooms which had been lent to her for the occasion. The entire effect was so spectacular that Drucilla's three-thousand-dollar satin shoes, with their mother-of-pearl and gold beads, went completely unnoticed.

'Here comes the dress,' hummed Lolly Bishop.

'Don't be nasty, Lolly,' countered Bambi. 'You're just pissed because Billy Wright won't pop the question.' She turned to the bride. 'Now, we have something old.' She handed her an antique handkerchief. 'Something borrowed.' She pointed to the diamond sunbursts. 'Something new.' Drucilla fluttered her fingers and flashed her ten-carat yellow diamond.

'Don't blind us! What about something blue? Blue! You've forgotten something blue.'

'I haven't. I've got my blue contacts in.' Dru blinked her eyes.

The house phone rang for the thousandth time, announcing that the father of the bride was waiting downstairs to escort her to the church.

'It's going to be fine, Mother,' Dru reassured Eve, who suddenly stepped quietly back into the library. Graham's insistence on inviting Catherine McBride to the wedding had caused hours of arguments until a compromise was finally reached. Catherine would attend the church ceremony along with twelve hundred other guests, but for the sake of the mother of the bride, she would not be included at the reception.

Dru hugged her mother one last time and then turned to Louis to receive the trailing bouquet, splendid with a potpourri of orchids from Eve's greenhouses, the sprays of oncidium reaching the hem of her gown.

The bridesmaids were ferried two at a time down the leather-upholstered front elevator, while Drucilla, whose train was too billowy, was carefully maneuvered into the freight elevator, which had been lined with bed sheets.

Eight antique horse-drawn carriages, festooned with flowers, were lined up in front of the building and, one by one, they clattered down the block and a half from the apartment to the gray Gothic Presbyterian church on Michigan Avenue, passing hundreds of gawking spectators and five mammouth swan-shaped ice sculptures that were being unloaded from a hearselike van for the reception at the Drake Hotel.

The bridal party climbed up the few flights of steps and past a cordoned-off crowd of press photographers whose motor-drive flashes whirred frantically to capture the arriving dignitaries, who included everyone from the lush-lipped rock star Mick Wintersting, a close personal friend of Pemberly's, who arrived in a leather tuxedo with a bandana as a cumberbund, to the First Lady of the United States.

Catherine McBride observed the bridal procession from her seat at the back of the church, where, she noticed, she'd been unceremoniously dumped with the Intercon office contingent. She'd seriously considered skipping the wedding altogether, but Graham had insisted that she attend, since he'd made such an issue out of it with Eve. In his mind, he had won the argument. But Catherine could see, as she watched Eve being escorted up the candlelit aisle by Hughie Stuart, there was no real place for her at this family affair except as an employee. She bit her lip as she rose with the crowd while Graham majestically escorted his daughter to her fiancé's side. He didn't glance in her direction, but sat next to Eve, in the family pew.

Catherine sat down shakily, trying to hide her feelings, but unable to stop staring at Eve Donaldson, the woman who had lived with the man Catherine loved for almost as long as she'd been alive.

She told herself that she would get used to it. She knew Graham loved her; she'd adjust to everything else. Adaptability was, after all, her specialty. Leaving Graham to his family tonight would be her private wedding present to Drucilla. Catherine wondered if Dru knew how lucky she really was, not to have this lavish wedding, but to have her father there at her side.

Catherine held her head high as she noticed Mrs Ray Acconti turning to stare at her from the next pew. Who cared what a woman who was stupid enough to marry the likes of Ray Acconti thought? She'd get through this, Catherine silently repeated.

After the thirty-minute ceremony, which was conducted

in French as a gesture to the groom's family and therefore understood only by the foreign guests and Eve's fellow members of the Alliance Française, the Count and the new Countess de Cotrille led their guests across Michigan Avenue in an open carriage. Even though the Drake Hotel was only a block away, the streets were cleared for the bridal party by a succession of yellow police barricades, and mounted policemen allowed a steady stream of limousines to make a series of round trips from the church to the reception and back.

The highlight of the reception was not the bride and groom, nor the eight-thousand fresh flowers flown in from Singapore, Thailand, and the Netherlands, many of which ringed the ceiling of the Gold Coast Room of the Drake Hotel to form a fragrant floral molding, nor the silk moiré tablecloths ombréd in slate grays and ambers, but the hundred-foot-long dessert table. After a dinner of trout and mushroom mousse followed by Cornish hens and wild rice, the Donaldsons' guests were directed to an extravaganza of all the bride's favorite desserts – everything from bowls of Oreo cookies and chocolate mousse to tarte de fraise du bois, bûche de Noël, crépes suzettes, taffy apples, wild raspberries, strawberry shortcake, and birthday cakes.

In addition to this, an eight-foot chocolate wedding cake dominated the dance floor.

As the fleet of uniformed waiters carried in one hundred and eighty bottles of champagne from the de Cotrille vineyard, Arnaud stiffly rose to toast his bride. His eyes swept the room and focused not on Drucilla but on his widowed mother, who sat between Graham and Eve Donaldson. Like her son, she surveyed the opulence of the room with the cold fish-eye of a banker checking credit references, which was only natural since the Donaldson fortune would be augmenting the de Cotrille vineyards. Marie Thérèse de Cotrille was descended from Belgian royalty on her mother's side and was a distant cousin of the Bourbon pretender to the throne of France – 'what-if royalty,' as Hughie called them.

The music and laughter died as Arnaud cleared his throat and tapped his glass. 'Mesdames et messieurs – Madame Savage, my mother, the Countess, Mr and Mrs Donaldson, and honored guests. Our family château, as you may know, is one of the finest in all of France. And now it will be graced with the great beauty of my bride.' He gracefully bowed in her direction. 'She will be my *châtelaine* – the mistress of my château. In homage to my cherished Drucilla, I am now giving her, as her very own, this seventeenth-century woodcut of the château, which has been in the family for centuries.' His brother-in-law, Philippe, stepped forward with a flourish, brandishing a small framed sepia drawing, and presented it to Drucilla, who had grown up expecting jewels or French Impressionist watercolors as tokens of affection.

At the bridesmaids' table, Pemberly Bracket groaned. 'In this case, I'd rather be the bridesmaid than the bride.'

'Hush!' hissed Lolly Bishop. 'That happens to be an early drawing by Louis Le Van, one of the architects who designed Versailles.'

'I hope the blueprints come with that,' said Pemberly, ''cause Dru's going to get Bruce over there to rip everything out and put in central heat and air.'

The first dance began, and across the room Hughie Stuart spotted the editor of *Paris Match* and moved subtly to his side.

After Drucilla had danced with her father, and then Graham with Arnaud's mother, the rest of the guests waltzed in one elegant direction. Everyone except B. B.

Bruce from Texas, one of Graham's business associates, who stampeded his new twenty-year-old wife, a former Dallas Cowgirl with breasts of rubber cement, in the opposite direction to the edge of the bridal table to say his howdy-dos. With a forecful two-step, the lively septuagenarian galloped past the country's leading gossip columnist and her partner, Father Reilly, a best-selling novelist-priest, misjudged the distance, and crashed into the table putting his foot through the antique woodcut of the château, which Philippe had propped against the bottom of the tablecloth after the toast.

'Pardon me,' he barked out, 'but Jo-Belle here won't let me wear my glasses at parties. I have to pamper my new bride.' Jo-Belle panted under the weight of her jewelry.

Arnaud stared aghast at the wreckage of the woodcut, which now bore a distinct imprint of B. B. Bruce's heel.

'We oughta get these girls together, don't ya say, Arnod?'

'It's Arn*aud*.'

Drucilla leaned forward and peered over the table. 'Oh, Lolly'll know how to fix that. There's a great restorer right here at the Art Institute,' she soothed.

'Never! This is too priceless to leave in America.' Arnaud skirted the table and swept the woodcut under his arm. 'Come cherie.' He looked at his watch. 'Let's leave these guests to their – exuberance – while we change for the – .'

'The going-away,' she filled in. 'Lolly's expecting me to pitch the bouquet right at her.' She noticed her friend was dancing with Michael Picol.

Arnaud guided Drucilla through the crowd, his lips close to her in what appeared to be whispered endearments.

'*Quels cochons!* What pigs!' he was hissing. 'When we get back to France, I promise you, people will know how to respect fine things.'

Hand in hand, they crossed the indoor passageway from the Drake Hotel to the Drake Towers next door.

As Drucilla started to change into her pink Chanel suit, Arnaud alternated between inspecting the latest gifts and lamenting about the woodcut. 'We could have sent out from *Au Pied de Cochon* for that assemblage.' The Parisian brasserie where onion soup was served twenty-four hours a day was always as crowded and hectic as the reception they'd just left.

Drucilla impatiently searched for an appropriate hanger. Where were Scarron's assistants? They should have followed her up to help her.

Arnaud finally opened a gift that met with his approval, a blue-and-white lily-pattern Limoges soup tureen which, from its hallmark, appeared to be late eighteenth century. 'Ah, Drucilla! Look. I can't believe this. This is from the chairman of Tarkon Oil Company. These people must have taste. Too bad I did not meet them tonight.' He joined Drucilla in her bedroom.

'Oh, Arnaud, you did meet them.' She gave up her search for a hanger and draped the dress across the bed, pushing aside a crumpled cascade of tissue paper. 'Where are those people from Scarron? That must be them.' The house phone was ringing.

Arnaud picked up the phone and shrugged at Drucilla. 'Not yet. More flowers coming up.'

'Do you want to get them?' Dru was in her camisole now. She pulled back her waist-length hair and clasped it in her favorite sterling silver barrette.

Her new husband stroked her breast. 'No. Let them rot. The front door is unlocked – they can leave them in the foyer. I have *my* flower right here.' He slipped both camisole straps over her shoulders and they fell together on to the bed, on top of the nine-thousand-dollar wedding dress, Drucilla giggling, 'Oh, Arnaud, you're so passionate. But what about throwing the bouquet?' He was slipping out of his pants.

Drucilla bent to unhook her garters as Arnaud reached for her breast.

Suddenly she felt something frightening, cold, and metallic punch into the small of her back. With a gasp that was part confusion, part terror, she felt her head yanked back by the hair until she thought her neck would snap.

It was so fast and disorienting, Drucilla could hardly make sense of what was happening. There was the quick, absurdly colorful flash of a ski mask, covering a face she couldn't see, and the steel glint of a pistol, then a machine gun. There were strange uniforms, harsh sounds. Drucilla wrenched to free her head, and she felt her hair tear out at the roots by excruciating handfuls.

'Drucilla!' she heard her husband scream, his voice a quavering falsetto. Where was he? What was happening?

It seemed as if men were descending from every direction. Burglars? Guerrillas? Terrorists? She couldn't reason or think; her breath was coming in shallow gasps as she hyperventilated, struggling for air as a huge, calloused hand clamped over her mouth, smashing her lip.

She sank her teeth into the hairy flesh and promptly tasted blood as the hand jerked away.

'Get out,' cried Dru, kicking and biting wildly. She swung her arms and felt a hard crack as her diamond ring connected with the bridge of a nose. 'The ring!' she gasped. That had to be what they were after. That and the wedding gifts. Mustering new strength, she shrieked, 'Arnaud! Arnaud! Get them off me.' She jabbed out with both elbows.

Arnaud cowered on his knees, curled his body into a ball, and started to roll under Drucilla's bed.

'Hit him with the tureen!' she screamed. Since there seemed to be four attackers, Dru reasoned that if they both fought they'd have a slight chance. She jackknifed her hockey player's knee into the closest groin.

A heavy boot crunched into the base of Arnaud's spine. He threw up hands, wailing 'I surrender! *Je me rends! Prend tous!*'

'Fight, Arnaud, fight!' Dru shouted, grabbing one of the three-thousand-dollar satin shoes. A shower of mother-of-pearl beads burst into the air as she nailed her attacker's head with a spike heel.

'Take the ring,' Arnaud pleaded. 'Take the tureen! We are very rich. I will fill it with gold!' As two of the thugs moved menacingly toward Drucilla, Arnaud scurried half on his knees toward the door, then catapulted down the hall, his tuxedo shirt flapping over his bare behind, and locked himself into the hall powder room.

In the bedroom all four men descended on Drucilla as her fight became more frantic. 'Hold her down! Shut her up!' a harsh foreign-accented voice commanded, as one of them shoved her down on the bed.

If they were going to rape her, she'd go out fighting. Drucilla used her last ounce of energy to knock the biggest one across the room with a hard kick to the stomach.

They were pinning her down now, one at her hands, two holding her legs. She closed her eyes and expected the worst. A hand grabbed her cheeks and squeezed her mouth. 'You're going to talk now,' he said. She opened her eyes and saw a small tape recorder inches from her face.

'Say these words.' One of them held a piece of paper in front of her eyes.

No, she wouldn't. Once she did what they said, they'd kill her. She froze, immobile, defiantly clamping her mouth shut.

'Say them! Say. These. Words.' The voice was threatening.

She shook her head.

He turned to one of the others and snarled out, '*Ves y trime*.'

If only she could reach the panic button in the bedside bureau, she could set off the security alarm. Where was Arnaud? He could distract them.

Suddenly they pulled her to her feet, pinning her arms in a body lock.

The big one unscrewed the top off a metal can. Acid! That was it. They were going to pour acid on her face!

But no, he was heading toward the bed. He splashed something all over her wedding dress. Now she could smell it. It was gasoline.

There was the bright flick of a flame, and then, with a burst, the entire dress ignited. Twenty-five thousand dollars worth of lace, pearls, satin, and rhinestones incinerated. Orange tongues of flame consumed the pillow shams and bedspread and leaped toward the ceiling.

They were going to burn her alive.

No, they were grabbing her again. They dragged her, still struggling, down the hall. With two short, swift kicks, the powder room door caved in.

Arnaud was crouched, cowering on the onyx floor.

'Don't kill me! I am a French citizen,' he pleaded.

With a slap of adhesive tape, Arnaud's mouselike

squeals were silenced. His eyes and mouth were taped shut and his wrists bound to the lapis Sherle Wagner sink. He gagged into the tape, hunched froglike over the shell-shaped pedestal. His bare buttocks quivered as he made one last uncontrollable flutter, like a trout flopping out of water. Then Arnaud fainted.

She saw the can again. The one with the handgun drenched Arnaud's limp back with gasoline.

'Do what we say,' one spit into her ear, 'or he's a French fry.' He snapped on a lighter under her nose.

There was the tape recorder again, and the piece of paper. She'd have to do it. She smelled smoke coming from the bedroom and heard the sharp beep of the smoke alarm. As if in a trance, she read a message to her father, word for word, until she saw a glistening hypodermic needle come closer. She watched it sink deeply into her arm, and then everything spun out of focus.

When she was finally silent, Drucilla's unconscious body, still in the cerise satin-and-lace camisole, was carried down the floral-carpeted steps of the duplex and dumped unceremoniously into a laundry cart waiting in the same service elevator in which she had regally descended only hours earlier.

The four men stripped off their ski masks and florist uniforms and tossed them over her into the laundry cart. They wore dark green overalls which had block-lettered 'Lake Shore Linen Supply' printed on the back. They spread a sheet over the top of the cart and casually strolled it out through the service entrance.

'Does this mean I'll have a *record?*' Pemberly Bracket sobbed uncontrollably as the plainclothes policewoman pressed her manicured fingertip into the ink pad and then rolled it onto the fingerprint card that was carefully positioned on top of the Louis XVI boulle marquetry commode. She and all the bridesmaids except Lolly Bishop, who was also missing, and Bambi, who had been released when Hughie lashed out protectively that she was a minor, were ashen-faced, their dresses crumpled, hair fallen, makeup streaked from tears. A team of rubber-coated firemen, detectives, uniformed police, and FBI men with squawking walkie-talkies conferred with Pete Connolly, Intercon's head of security, while lab technicians swarmed through the smoky, water-soaked penthouse.

The detective looked at the living room parquet which had been sprayed when the smoke sensor set off the ceiling's automatic sprinkler system. Wet tissue paper, plastic bags, soggy silk stockings, magazines and over-turned ashtrays were strewn all over the floor.

'You're lucky this fire alarm system is hooked up to the police station,' said the detective. 'The fire was confined to the upstairs bedroom.'

Connolly looked at Graham. 'I mean lucky for your son-in-law. He was covered with gasoline.'

'You're sure my daughter's not somewhere in this apartment?'

'Yes, sir. We've searched the premises.'

'Why don't you tell them to just *find* her?' Eve's voice was shaky. 'Can't they do something? Shouldn't they be out looking for Drucilla instead of fingerprinting these bridesmaids?'

Graham's face was taut. 'Eve, I think the best thing we can do right now is cooperate. These young ladies are her friends. They won't mind.' He gently guided her into an armchair.

Arnaud, wraped in a silk maroon robe, sat on the bottom step of the curving staircase. His hair was disheveled, and there were red marks around his eyes and mouth where a layer of skin had peeled when the adhesive tape was removed. 'They did this to me!' He pointed to his swollen forehead. 'One of them clubbed me. They were armed. There were seven or eight of them!' He coughed. 'My lungs!'

Dr Corbett, the family physician, still in his tuxedo, dabbed the purple hematoma above Arnaud's eye with antiseptic. 'This will sting a little bit, but it's really nothing serious. Your pupils aren't dilated, so it doesn't look like a concussion. Maybe a little smoke inhalation. But mainly it's just shock. You'll be okay.'

'What exactly did they hit you with, sir?' asked one of the uniformed policemen.

'With everything they had. There were at least ten of them, swinging at me. Look!' He pointed at the long-stemmed flower boxes on the foyer floor. 'That's what they carried the machine guns in. I know guns. They were Uzis. These people are professionals. I had no chance.' His voice was shrill. 'I was suspicious from the beginning. I was helping my wife out of her bridal gown. We were changing to join the guests.' He twisted his tasseled sash nervously. 'I fought furiously for my Drucilla,' he choked. 'If only I had my gun, I would have killed them. I would have killed them with my bare hands, but the barbarians were armed.'

'What did they look like?'

'Look like! They looked like kidnappers! Terrorists! They had ski masks on. I tried to rip off their masks. That's when they hit me – here.' He gingerly touched his forehead. 'Do you think I have brain damage?' He turned to Dr Corbett.

'No, no, Arnaud. But when the officers are finished, I have some pills for you.'

'They have the Countess! You must get her back!' He leaped to his feet. 'Get Interpol!'

'Exactly how tall were they?' asked a detective.

'When you are fighting for the life of your bride, you do not use a tape measure.' He sobbed into his hands.

Graham Donaldson leaned over the banister. 'Arnaud, isn't there anything else you can tell us?'

'They wore workmen's clothes with the name of a florist printed on the back.'

Arnaud shook his head sadly. 'Mr Donaldson, I fought furiously for your daughter. It took all of them to tie me up. There was no escape from these thugs. What do you expect? Two terrorists can hijack an entire plane. A dozen were here and there was only me to fight them.'

'Did you see Lolly Bishop after you left the reception?' the chief of police asked.

'How many times must I tell you,' Arnaud wailed. 'No. No. No! It was just the two of us, against these – professionals.'

'Did your wife say anything at all?'

'She called my name. And then she fainted.'

Graham looked askance. Drucilla had never fainted in her life, not even the time her knee had been slashed open and they sewed it up without anesthetic. When she had broken her nose playing hockey she had insisted on finishing the game.

Just then an FBI agent walked up carrying a tape recorder in a plastic evidence bag.

'Mr Donaldson, this cassette recorder was playing next to the sink.'

'To burn alive is a horrible death,' shuddered Arnaud.

'We played this tape,' continued the FBI agent. 'I think you should hear it.' He pushed the button with the tip of his pen and Drucilla's voice, trembling but controlled, silenced the room.

You must help me. Do whatever they say. I am a prisoner of the Bandera Roja. If you ever want to see me alive again, you must remove all Intercontinental capitalist activity from Venezuelan holdings and remove all interest in Venezuelan commerce. They will tell you what to do. When you receive instructions, you must follow them or I will be dead.

Then there was nothing except the drone of silent tape.

A chill went through the room.

Eve stepped up behind Graham and he put his hand on her shoulder. He looked toward Pete Connolly. 'Please get Picol immediately.' Graham addressed the FBI agents. 'Michael Picol is a brilliant negotiator, and he has dealt with the Venezuelans. He has connections with Perez.'

Connolly shrugged. 'I'm sorry, sir. We're already trying him everywhere we can think of. He must have left the reception just before this happened.'

Eve tightened her lip. 'We must find her.'

'We've been calling Picol's private line since midnight,' Connolly said.

Graham stroked Eve's arm reassuringly as Arnaud sat quivering like a trapped animal. 'We'll do everything they want. We'll get her back. I promise.'

Eight blocks away, there was no other light in the room as two naked figures on the twelve-foot video screen flickered erotically. A man lay in the marble platform tub, while a blonde head sporadically disappeared under the water. The man grasped her wet hair and pulled her face down below his waist, and a glimpse of the bridesmaid's bouquet perched on the side of the tub was visible in the background.

Dru's best friend, Lolly Bishop, nude, straddled Michael Picol's waist and massaged his bare legs with musk oil. A few hours ago, she had been a demure maid of honor. Now she watched a home movie of Michael and herself cavorting in color, reliving a scene directed by Michael and inspired by glasses of de Cotrille champagne served at the wedding. Lolly stared wide-eyed at the screen. She could hardly believe that was *her* in the film. She hoped Drucilla wouldn't be too upset that she hadn't stayed to catch the bouquet, but Michael had hustled her out of the reception and up to his apartment in such a rush. 'God, look what you're doing to me up there. I could have drowned.' She giggled. 'What do you suppose the Count and Countess are doing now? If I were her, I wouldn't let that frog touch me.'

'Move your head, baby. I can't see the tape.'

The light panel on the bedside phone blinked incessantly.

'Are you sure you don't want to answer that? It hasn't stopped for three hours.' She kneaded his inner thigh. 'What if it's important?'

'What could be more important than you rubbing my legs? Do my calves now.'

# 7

A personal catastrophe had never before disrupted the daily functioning of Intercon. The efficient operations of administration, finance, research and oil exploration discovered that memos were too frequently unanswered, expense accounts were not quickly reimbursed, and vital strategies remained unapproved. Top management was paralyzed while Graham Donaldson dedicated himself to finding his daughter. His search became a mission that consumed all his physical and emotional energy.

Since his son-in-law was nearly catatonic with fear and refused to leave the confines of the Donaldson estate, it was Graham who led the countless meetings, briefings, and discussions with police and FBI agents. Michael Picol was usually at his side. At first, Graham had agonized over whether or not he would follow his own Intercon policy of withholding ransom if the kidnappers demanded money. He honestly did not know whether his duty as a father or as chairman of the board should take precedence. But the Bandera Roja did not contact Graham or anyone else. Graham therefore concentrated his organizational skills on the search process, insisting, to the unbridled disagreement of the FBI, that Intercon Security and Michael Picol play key roles. Although such interference in an FBI investigation was normally not tolerated, Graham Donaldson was not an ordinary citizen. He was a close friend and associate of the President of the United States. Rex Savage had personally called Eve and Graham to offer his full support immediately after he learned of the kidnapping. The national security advisor, the special advisor to the President on South America, and even the director of the CIA had been in contact with Graham, and a special task force of guerrilla warfare specialists had been activated as part of the search for this one man's daughter.

As time passed and no one was any closer to finding Dru, Graham became more obsessed with finding her. To him, his daughter's kidnapping was more than a tragedy. He saw it as a retribution, a blow he had been dealt as punishment for leaving his wife and family.

Nobody recognized this better than Catherine McBride.

'I don't know,' she said to Michael Picol as they waited in the hall for the management meeting to start. 'After three weeks without word from the kidnappers, I'm not too optimistic. Graham won't sleep at night, he's on the phone constantly to South America or Washington.' She dug her toe into the gray carpet. 'I'm as concerned about Drucilla as anybody, but somebody's got to run this company.'

'Graham's always run this company out of his back pocket. It's the biggest one-man show around,' Picol stated.

He seemed almost angry, and although everyone had been under enormous pressure, Picol had been on twenty-four-hour duty ever since the kidnapping. He constantly shuttled from Chicago to Miami, New York, and South America as he attempted to locate the kidnappers or their intermediaries. He had that same hungrily drawn, intense look on his face that he wore just before closing a deal that consumed every nerve ending in his body. It was also evident whenever Michael Picol was in search of prey. 'Today's meeting will finally bring a solution,' he said tersely. 'Remember, we're both working for Graham's welfare. You'd better get some rest yourself, because I'm counting on you. Go on in.'

She walked into the executive conference room, and Catherine noticed her reflection in the mirror over the bar. She, too, had a lean and hungry look, accentuated by her high cheekbones and the slim, long lines of her Norma Kamali gray wool jersey dress, strong shoulder pads, and low-slung leather belt.

Irv Turner was already at the table. Catherine had always found him pleasant enough, perhaps even intelligent, but distinguished mainly by his golf handicap. He had been in Graham's shadow for so long that no one knew what he could really do, although he made it clear by his posture and attitude that he felt he could step into Graham's shoes at any time.

Harvey McIntosh, head of the International Division, was pouring himself a tomato juice at the bar. Harvey was obviously confused. His eyes darted around the room as he moved away from the bar. It was clear that a new pecking order was in the wind, and McIntosh, a political animal, was obviously wondering which side of the table to sit on – Irv Turner's or Michael Picol's, the two most likely candidates to head up a crisis regime.

Sam Adams, chief financial officer, was seated on Irv Turner's right, picking the raisins out of a Danish. Ray Acconti was putting together a pile of handouts for Irv Turner, to whom he had obviously swung his allegiance. He chirped a bright hello at Catherine, confident that her power was on the wane now that Graham was backing out of the picture. However temporary, Acconti viewed the situation as an opportunity to regain the foothold he had lost to Catherine.

The private door to Graham's office opened and he walked in with Michael Picol, who took the empty chair beside Catherine. Standing at the head of the table, Graham was stony-faced, fatigue shown in every movement, and his eyes were listless. Everyone shifted in his seat at the sight of this calmly controlled man so clearly in anguish.

'Thank you all for coming.' His voice was emotionless and to the point, as if even this one meeting was an intrusion on his time. 'I suggest that we form a special executive steering committee that has the power to run this company on a day-to-day basis, for interim purposes.'

Ray Acconti scribbled a note and silently pushed the paper in front of Irv Turner.

'Due to the suddenness of this crisis, it would be unfair to turn over all the responsibilities to Irv – or any one person. I think it would be better for the running of the company and the stockholders if there were shared responsibilities. So I'm appointing a triumvirate.'

Catherine put her hand on her chin and leaned forward on her elbow. Graham hadn't mentioned any triumvirate. But then, he hadn't mentioned anything about business since the kidnapping. Maybe it would be a good thing. With a new group in charge, she might be able to take him down to the island for a few days, away from the constant calls from Eve and the FBI. A week after the kidnapping, the security people had demanded that he move into the corporate apartment. And since an atmosphere riddled with wiretaps, hidden microphones, and panic buttons was not exactly conducive to relaxation or romance, Catherine remained at her apartment. Graham had actually volunteered to move back into the Lake Forest house, but Eve had turned down the offer. It seemed to Catherine that Eve could only handle one emotional crisis at a time.

Suddenly Catherine heard her name being spoken.

Good Lord, he was putting her on the executive steering committee!

'So,' concluded Graham, 'Irv Turner, Michael Picol, and Catherine McBride will be in charge of all day-to-day decisions and operations, and are able to make any legal decision normally made by the CEO and are now acting as temporary chairmen of the board. Thank you.' He turned to leave.

Ray Acconti and Irv Turner both leaped to their feet, but Graham interpreted this as a sign of respect. 'Thanks for your support, gentlemen,' he said, and before anyone else could speak, Carla rushed into the room. After a whispered conference, he walked out hurriedly.

Ray Acconti picked up his papers and left without further discussion.

Harvey McIntosh and Sam Adams exchanged glances and without speaking sealed an agreement. They would roll with the punches. After all, *this* was only temporary.

Irv Turner sat down at the table and folded his hands. 'I think Graham's decision is a good one, and I'm sure we can work well together in this *temporary* troika.'

Everyone then turned to look at Catherine, as if they assumed she had had advance notice of this news, but she said nothing.

Michael Picol took charge. 'Everyone, I have an agenda here. We might as well turn to it.' He looked at Catherine. 'We have to decide whether or not to expand the groundwater protection program we've begun downstate.'

'We gotta do it,' Irv said. 'It's a good program.'

'Catherine?'

She nodded. She knew nothing about this program.

Picol continued. 'We'll start a timetable. Next there's the Place in the Sun budget. Where do we stand?'

'That's important to Graham,' Irv said, and sighed.

'What are the dollars on the construction costs?'

'Five point seven million to begin,' Catherine answered. She stood up, as she always did when she had an important point to make. 'Our plan calls to be in major construction by June. The casino project will follow the residential work.'

Turner nodded. 'Casino.' He shook his head. 'As I said, I know this is important to Graham, but I don't think we belong in that business.'

'That's not the issue,' Catherine countered. 'The point is, this is one area that we need to know more about before I'd recommend going ahead. The research center is holding its own according to plan. I'd say we should table any further activity until we know more. I'm planning some quantitative research that will be back to us in twelve weeks. At that point, we can make an informed decision.'

Turner looked at her with surprise. Usually, she railroaded through anything having to do with A Place in the Sun.

Catherine remained calm. Turner probably thought she was carrying out Graham's wishes. Actually, she was buying time. It was the least she could do to protect Graham.

Suddenly the door banged open and Pete Connolly leaned in. 'Everyone clear the floor. Use fire procedures,' he barked, and then disappeared. The meeting disbanded as the new triumvirate joined the other employees who were walking to the fire stairs as they'd rehearsed many times. Some people were laughing and joking, convinced this was another drill. Security measures had been incessantly dramatic since the kidnapping.

Catherine caught up with Carla. From the expression on her face, she could tell this was not a false alarm or a drill. 'There may be a bomb,' Carla whispered. 'In the mail room. Bandera Roja.'

Catherine swerved out of line and rushed back into the hall to find Graham, but one of the security men blocked her way and pushed her into the stairwell.

In the mail room on the ninety-first floor where a metal box addressed to Graham with the Bandera Roja mark had been found, everything was eerily quiet. Graham refused to leave and asked again and again the exact details of how the box had been found.

The bomb squad was gingerly opening the package as the canine unit circled the perimeter of the room with dogs trained to sniff out explosives.

When the mysterious metal box was finally opened, eighteen inches of golden blond hair held by a sterling silver barrette initialed 'D.D.' lay neatly coiled.

Graham broke out in a profusion of sweat as he automatically reached out and tried to touch his daughter's hair and the barrette that she had worn since she was thirteen years old.

An FBI man gently caught his arm. 'I'm sorry, Mr Donaldson,' he said. 'Fingerprints.'

The sun was sparkling on the waves as the water lapped gently against the hull of the sixty-foot Hatteras cruiser. It was warm and balmy outside. But inside the closet that had been her home for the past three weeks, Countess Drucilla Donaldson de Cotrille saw nothing but darkness. Drucilla knew she was on a boat – she could feel the humidity, smell the fuel, feel the rocking. The whole effect was like being in an immersion tank, being brainwashed. She was no longer panicked; she felt as numb as her arms and legs. Her ears rang from the tapes blasted through earphones whenever the kidnappers came into the room, released her briefly to push her, blindfolded, about a tiny cabin, lead her three steps to an ice-cold shower. Then they would tie her hands and tape her mouth again, and shove her back into the closet.

She touched her face and what was left of her hair. Yesterday, when she thought she was being taken for her daily shower, blindfolded as usual, she was suddenly grabbed from behind and felt the heavy weight of her hair – her pride and joy – being sheared off. The loss of the hair that had not been cut since she was nine years old was as great as if the scissors had cut into her flesh. Standing naked in the cold shower, she shook with rage, humiliation, and futility. In the pitch-black closet, she twisted her engagement ring, which now hung loosely on her finger, and wondered if they would be back to cut off more parts of her body. Since they had not taken the ring, she had to believe they had torture, not money in mind.

Where was her Mummy? Her Daddy? The police? Why didn't Arnaud come? She lost track of time, and of the useless questions, and cried herself to sleep.

# 8

'Where is Picol?' The voice was smooth, with an elegant exotic accent.

'He's in conference right now.'

'This is Raoul Herrera from Caracas. It's important that I speak with him.'

'Caracas.' Michael Picol's secretary, Theresa, became instantly alert. Perhaps this man had news of the kidnapping. She quickly slid out the shallow drawer where she'd taped an index card with a list of single-spaced names that Michael Picol would speak with at any time. Raoul Herrera, executive vice-president of Trans-Oceanic, was one of them.

'One moment please. I'll see if I can interrupt him, Mr Herrera.'

Across town in the Irena's Skin Care Spa, soothing music was being piped into the cool, blue-and-white facial room. It was dark except for a small, dimmed wall lamp that allowed the facialist some working light while the client relaxed in the shaded cocoon-like environment. Swathed in a soft blue towel, hairily naked to the waist, Michael Picol was having his weekly facial. His private hour was four-thirty, and he never missed it unless he was out of town. The regime was always the same: the relaxing twenty-minute facial massage, the deep-pore cleansing treatment, the peel, the warm collagen mask, the seaweed-lotion wrap, and the finishing application of specially blended creams. This was his secret weapon against jet lag and too many hours in the sun. It was also why people often said that Michael Picol must have a Dorian Grey-type painting in the closet that aged and wrinkled, leaving the real man with no signs of overwork or overindulgence.

Hot and cold towels were applied alternately to his face. Then the Viennese facialist worked on his chest and neck with her heavy hands as Picol lay back on the white leather chaise with scented cotton pads covering his eyelids.

'I have something new to try today,' Rose said in her Viennese whisper. She took a tiny vial of cream that had been blended especially for Picol at two hundred dollars an ounce from her Formica worktable.

'Yeah? What's it for?'

'This is a blend of rare oils, collagen, embryonics, musk, and crushed violets. The musk and violets will make it pleasant to smell, no? It is a secret formula only for you. Use it very sparingly on the face, just a little and a little more around the eyes and mouth.' She patted the cream on with her fingertips. 'See, it is like a special flight cream for you. The airplane takes all the moisture out of your skin. This will put it back in like a tall glass of water. With this cream,' she promised, 'you will never need a face lift.'

After applying the cream she wrapped his face with a damp linen towel. Just then the salon manager knocked softly at the door and came in carrying a princess phone. 'I'm so sorry to disturb you, Mr Picol. But your secretary insists.' She plugged the phone into the wall jack and put the receiver in his hand.

'Mr Picol?' Theresa's voice was always upbeat and competent. People wondered how a brusque individual like Michael Picol could hang onto such a jewel, a woman who was not only capable of making decisions in his absence but who was probably capable of running her own corporation. It was not known, however, that even though Theresa was one of the highest-paid secretaries at Intercon, she was also paid an independent bonus directly by Michael Picol. With his personal bonus, she was making as much as some of the managers.

'Mr Herrera is trying to reach you. I placed a conference call like you always ask,' she said. 'I'm patching him directly through.'

'Good girl.'

'I'm sorry to get you out of a meeting.' Raoul Herrera's voice was cool.

'No problem, Raoul. I'll always talk to you. These other people can wait.'

'You have any more information for me?'

Picol put his hand over the receiver and pulled the linen towel from his face. 'Excuse me, Rose, do you think you can get me a glass of iced tea?'

'Of course.' She disappeared.

'I've put out a few feelers for us. Just let me say this should be the biggest oil discovery since 'The Elephant' in the North Sea. It's a monster.'

'Does three billion barrels sound right to you?'

'Yeah. It sounds right to me.'

There was a pause and some static on the line.

'That should do nicely. When can we take possession?'

'It shouldn't be long now. We have to be real close-mouthed about this. I don't want OPEC's raiders bidding against us. With the market the way it is, we can pick this up for just what we want. With you in control . . . right?'

'Well, we shall work together, of course.' Herrera's voice left no doubt that he could make Michael Picol his errand boy with the flick of a finger.

Suddenly Theresa clicked back onto the line. 'Excuse

me, Mr Picol. They're waiting for you in the meeting. What should I tell them? They say it's urgent.'

Now Herrera was acquiescent. 'It sounds like you have important business, my friend.'

'Is Miami still good on Thursday?'

'Ideal. And you'll have the written reports?'

'Yes, everything.'

Herrera clicked off the line.

Theresa was guarded. 'I'm so sorry, Mr Picol, but I have Winnie Lifton on the line and she's saying she'll call the police if she doesn't talk to you.'

'Thank you, Theresa.'

Hiccuping and hyperventilating, Winnie Lifton spoke in gasps. 'Michael?'

His voice was frigid. 'Honey, this had better be important.'

'Oh, Michael, I think he's dead! He's not breathing!'

'Who?'

'Perez! Romulo!'

'What makes you think he's dead?'

'He's just hanging there and I can't see his eyeballs.'

'He hung himself? Where?'

'In the bathroom.' Her voice tumbled on hysterically. 'You told me to do anything he wanted, and I did. Romulo is a very kinky man. But he is – was – so sweet,' her sobs poured out. 'He was going to put the film retrospective together, we were working on it . . .'

'Get to the point. What about the bathroom?'

She took a deep breath. 'Well, it was his idea. He's done it before. He likes bondage. We had the leather collar around his neck, with a towel, and we looped it around the shower door. It was just a game, and he was fine when I left him.'

'You left him hanging on your shower?' Picol propped himself up on his elbows.

'I had to go take off one of my false fingernails.' She was sniffling again. 'And when I came back . . . Michael, help me! What'll I do?'

'Yeah, then what?'

'When I came back, he just wasn't breathing anymore.' She coughed uncontrollably into the phone. 'Help me!'

'Does it look like he coulda had a heart attack?'

'No, it looks like he was hung! My show! The sponsors will have a fit!'

'He had a heart attack. Are you listening?'

'Y-y-yes,' she whispered. 'Oh, Michael. Can't you come out to Los Angeles? I need you.'

She was more trouble than she was worth, he thought. But if she got hysterical, she could implicate him and make a mess out of everything. 'I'll be on the next plane out. I'm leaving right now. Don't worry about anything.'

'Thank God!'

'You just have to take him down, put him in your bed, and call the police. Say he had a heart attack.'

'I can't do that! The sponsors! *Southwest* is a family show.'

'I'll get you new sponsors, a new show.'

'I won't call the police!'

Picol changed his tactics. 'Listen, baby, just get rid of him.'

'How?'

'You'll think of something. Don't call me again about this. It's too dangerous. I'll call you. Do you understand?'

'But I need . . .'

He hung up.

Still sobbing, Winnie ripped off her chiffon robe and threw on a turtleneck and jeans, raced into the kitchen for a pair of poultry shears, then rushed into the bathroom, hacked through the leather collar, and cut down Perez, who fell into the bathtub with a thud.

'Oh migod, oh migod,' she was stamping her feet and clapping her hands. 'Romulo, I think you're dead.' She frantically wondered what to do.

He was inert in the tub, his eyes rolled back in his head. 'Okay! Okay!' she told the body. 'I'll get you dressed.'

It took every ounce of strength in Winnie's five-foot frame to dress Perez. She remembered everything except his socks.

Grabbing his shoes, she dragged him by the heels to the front door, creating a wake in her white shag carpet. At least the foyer hall was marble and wouldn't leave the same path, Winnie thought. God, what if somebody came into the hall! She punched the elevator button frantically.

'Oh migod, you forgot your hat!'

She was panting and shivering as she raced back into the apartment, then made it back just in time to see the elevator door open. It was empty!

She punched in the 'Hold' button, yanked Perez in by his underarms, balanced him standing up in the corner, jammed his hat over his head, pulled out the 'Hold' switch, jumped out, reached in, and slammed her fist on 'Down.'

# 9

'I just can't seem to get the right shadings on this.' Eve Donaldson ran her fingertips lightly over the keys of one of the twin grand pianos, going through the adagio of the Mozart fantasia for the tenth time that morning. 'Oh, Alex, it's not working, is it? I'm so – clumsy!' She dropped her hands into her lap and stared helplessly at the perfectly simple arrangement of notes on the sheet music.

Alex Levin leaned over her shoulder and made a pencil mark on the page. 'I think the problem is right here. These notes should be played in quick succession.' He played the phrase himself to demonstrate. 'Your attitude is what's important here. This part is *scherzo*, it has a gaiety.'

She stood up, walked over to the leaded window and leaned her head against the frosty pane. Outside, everything looked barren and bleak, as only a midwestern winter can. It was almost Christmas, and the one snowfall of the season had turned slushy and gray, mimicking her mood. At the edge of the garden, it looked as if one of the old elms was dying. She'd have to tell Louis. 'I just can't bear the thought of Christmas without Drucilla,' Eve whispered.

'Eve.' Alex was beside her. 'I can't get over how brave you are.' He put his arm around her waist. 'If you can't feel the music, it's impossible to play, of course. Zubin Mehta said, "Musicians are like birds. If the weather is not good, they don't sing as much."'

She turned her head. It was amazing how he was always

able to express exactly what she was feeling. His dark eyes were so black that the pupils and irises seemed to blend. His wavy dark hair was always going off in a direction of its own, unlike his meticulous, mathematical, and musical mind. There was a softness about his mouth that had nothing to do with effeminacy, but reflected his sensitivity. She moved her hand as if to organize his undisciplined hair, but then decided she really liked it as it was, curling over his ears and collar. 'You've been so patient to work with me these days,' she said. 'But sometimes I don't think I have any life left inside.'

Alex took both her hands in his and faced her. 'I don't believe that. I don't believe you're capable of giving less than your best or feeling less than alive.'

She looked at him curiously. He was young, at least fourteen years younger than she, and yet he seemed in some ways to have so much more understanding and wisdom. His seemed like an old soul, Eve thought.

He smiled at her, and she sensed his empathy. 'If you peel away a little of the despair and sense of loss, underneath there is a seventeen-year-old girl, full of life and spirit and with a tremendous capacity for love.'

She dropped her head to hide the tears she felt welling up, not from sadness but from the sense of hope that he seemed to give her whenever he was around. Her long hair fell forward around her face, like a curtain.

He picked up one of the silver filigree frames that held Drucilla's wedding portrait. 'Let's anticipate her coming back. You must be strong for her. She'll need you.' He paused. '*I'll* be there for *you* in any case.'

Alex was so different from her son-in-law, Eve thought. Arnaud seemed to have not only given up all hope of ever seeing Drucilla alive again, but viewed himself, rather than Drucilla, as the victim. He'd been staying at the house with Eve ever since the night of the kidnapping, and of course she sympathized with his tragic state, but he was making things increasingly difficult for the rest of the family, who were trying their best to be optimistic. I'm getting tired of being the supportive one, Eve thought to herself. It feels so comforting to have Alex to lean on, to be able to tell him my fears.

There was a light tap at the fruitwood-paneled door, and Cherie flurried in. 'Mr Donaldson is here,' she started to say, but he was right behind her.

Graham strode into the room as if he still lived there. 'Oh, sorry,' he said, noticing Alex Levin. 'I didn't realize you were having a piano lesson.'

Eve suppressed a smile. How typical of Graham to relegate a musical genius like Alexander Levin to the ranks of a piano teacher. 'Graham,' she said. 'You remember Alexander Levin. He's the guest conductor at Ravinia.'

The two men shook hands, and Graham was polite, but it was obvious he had something else on his mind.

'Excuse me, then,' said Alex, and he started to move toward the door.

Eve shook her head. 'No, no, Alex. Please stay.' She glanced imploringly at him, and he walked back to her side.

Graham frowned. This was family business. He examined Levin a little more closely, concluding that he was probably one of Drucilla's friends. He dismissed him and turned to Eve.

'I have some news.'

Eve stood absolutely still. In her heart, she knew Drucilla was still alive, but there was always a shred of horrible uncertainty since the incident with the hair. Eve herself had not been able to put her own hair in a bun or a chignon since.

'The kidnappers have made contact through Picol's South American connections.'

'Who? When will we get her back? How?'

'An intermediary. Picol's been using an underground network. That's the only kind of mentality these people understand. He's going down to Miami.'

'What do they want?'

'We may have a compromise. They want some benefit from Intercon's Venezuelan oil profits.'

He looked terrible, thought Eve. Wasn't that girl taking care of him?

He ran his hand back and forth over his eyes. 'They want us to give money, food, and transportation to the guerrillas. They're using Dru as some sort of political pawn.'

'Can't Rex do anything?'

'Rex would love to stop this, but there are other diplomatic considerations.'

He pulled a piece of paper out of his pocket. 'These rebel guerrillas kidnap or hold for ransom between a hundred fifty and two hundred Americans a year, and most of them are oil executives.' He didn't tell her that they murdered another hundred every six months. 'Rex has to go through channels. We don't. We're working directly with Picol's task force.'

'We should tell Arnaud.' Eve motioned to Cherie, who hurried off, and three minutes later, Arnaud came in, carrying his coat.

'Ah, Mr Donaldson. I'm glad to see you in person. You should know I am returning to France.'

'Maybe you should stay a while. We're negotiating with the kidnappers.'

Arnaud threw up his hands. 'Who can take the word of a barbarian? I saw them. They were maniacs.'

Eve put her hand on his arm. 'Arnaud, we know what you've been through, but Graham says negotiations are going to begin.'

His voice rose an octave. 'It is settled. I am going back. They know me. They will find me. You know what has happened – they have strangled their own minister of culture, Romulo Perez, a very fine man. He was murdered in an elevator in Los Angeles. Perhaps he was negotiating, too!'

'You're overtired, Arnaud,' glowered Graham.

Arnaud clenched his fists until the knuckles were white. 'My face is all over the American press. I am like a common entertainer. My family's name is dragged through the mud. Everyone knows what I look like, who I am. *I* am in danger. My family insists I return.'

'What about your wife?' Eve tried to feel compassion, but it took all her composure.

'I can do more good through my international contacts.'

'What contacts?' Graham asked in disgust. 'You have a responsibility to Drucilla.'

'As my mother reminded me this morning, this marriage was never consummated.' Arnaud's voice was haughtily precise.

A shocked silence fell on the room.

Arnaud started to shake as he lit a cigarette. 'I'm sorry. I do not mean to be cruel. But I cannot take any more of this. I have been tied up, beaten, vilified. I fought to the death for my Drucilla, but she would want me to go on.' He inhaled nervously on his Gauloise.

Graham stalked out of the room, and Arnaud looked frantically from Eve to Alex as if to try and dredge up some shred of sympathy. The man was clearly on the verge of a nervous breakdown. He was starting to break out in a rash, his hands shook wildly.

'I'll call Dr Corbett,' Eve offered.

'No, no. Just send my luggage. Drugs cannot cure heartbreak. I am going home before they assassinate me. Don't forget, they have seen my face!'

'You're always welcome anytime, my dear, but I understand. Everyone should be with their families at times of crisis.' Eve's tone was distant and polite, but her eyes were fixed on the doorway where Graham had left.

They kissed perfunctorily on both cheeks, and Arnaud made a regal exit.

Eve turned to Alex. Neither of them spoke for several minutes. Then he said, 'Poor Arnaud. He's not strong enough.' He paused. 'Eve?'

'Yes Alex?'

'Are you still in love with Graham?'

She felt as if all the breath had been knocked out of her. The two of them stood there and stared at one another, Eve behind an elegant fauteuil chair, holding onto it as if it were a shield.

# 10

'Knight to queen's pawn two,' intoned Baron Grunewald, peering at Catherine with a sly grin. He loved games of strategy.

Catherine cupped her chin in her hand as she studied her next move. She ran her finger down the smooth copper cone that served as her queen. She found the copper and gilt chess pieces distracting. Every time she looked at one of the abstract shapes she had to think again to make sure it was what she thought it was. She had never played chess before on a work of art. The surrealist chess set had been designed by Man Ray on a bet with the baron, to appeal to his sense of whimsey. The knights were stylized horses' heads, the rooks hexagonal towers, the pawns balls, the kings pyramids, and all elegantly protruded from a pine laminate board with a white border on which was painted a hand-written quotation from Man Ray, who had played with Picasso on this very set.

Catherine contemplated her possibilities. She knew she could never outwit the baron, to whom winning was never as important as playing the game, but he seemed to be amused by her competitive tenacity.

'Take your time,' said the baron. 'It will make no difference.' He exhaled a cloud of smoke.

'It's not over yet,' she countered, pushing her rook into position to challenge his bishop.

'Catherine McBride never gives up, Baron,' Billy Wright said from across the gallery as Lady Camille

Farnsworth handed him a cup of tea. Catherine and Billy had joined the baron at Audley Hall, his sixteenth-century English estate a few days after Christmas.

Graham had been too preoccupied with the kidnapping to think about the holidays, so Catherine had spent Christmas Day with Aggie Palmer. She had welcomed the respite from the overly burdened schedule she'd been keeping, and since Graham's divorce would soon be finalized, she needed the time to reflect upon her future with him. Their relationship had become a sub-paragraph in every business story involving Intercon, and Catherine knew she felt too young and driven to retire to A Place in the Sun by Graham's side once Drucilla's kidnapping was resolved.

The baron had offered her a position in Darco after she helped him save the company, and although she hadn't accepted the job, she had agreed to spend part of the holiday as his guest in England. When Billy Wright informed her of his decision to leave Intercon, Catherine had persuaded him to join her in England for a couple of days. Her instincts told her that Billy was the perfect candidate for the Darco presidency, and so far she had been right.

The baron was committed to turning his sleepy coal company into a springboard for American acquisitions. He always responded well to young people with initiative, and so, as Catherine had suspected, he immediately took to Billy Wright. Billy had grown tired of the inner politics at Intercon as well as the company's stagnation, and he needed new challenges in an aggressive organization. Billy Wright and the baron had spent no more than two hours together before it was clear that Billy would fit in very well with the baron's plans for Darco.

Alfred and his perennial girlfriend, Lady Camille Farnsworth, and her parents, Earl and Lady Farnsworth, were spending the holidays at Audley Hall. Lord Harry Harcourt, the uncle of the late baroness, was also there. So far, Catherine hadn't seen Alfred alone, and she was glad. She didn't know how she'd react – or how he would.

Uncle Harry was famous among the country house set for his legendary practical jokes. Alfred had told Catherine how, a few Christmases ago, upon finding the fur hat of a houseguest particularly offensive, Harry had it shaved, set on fire, and carried on a stick through the portrait-lined gallery to the accompaniment of his bawdiest off-color, off-tune ballads. This year, his antics had been more restrained, and, in deference to Lady Camille, he had confined himself to one mild-mannered short-sheeting of Billy Wright's bed.

Catherine knew it wasn't right to feel a small twinge of disappointment when she learned of Alfred's imminent engagement to Lady Camille, but she had blanched when the baron had confided in her. She had a commitment to Graham, and her feelings for him, although less passionate than at first, were still strong, so why did she care if Alfred married? Wasn't she supposed to rescue Graham, to help him? Wasn't that what lovers did for one another in crises? She'd convinced herself that what had happened that night between her and Alfred in Chicago was a fluke. She'd been upset, Graham had been busy, Alfred had been lonely . . . Catherine had a list of reasons and rationales for her behavior. Alfred had called her several times after that, but she'd kept their conversations short. She couldn't quite imagine Alfred and Camille – one of the Sloane Rangers – in an elevator together. A smile crossed her face.

Everyone was gathered in the library, which had been renovated in 1647 by Inigo Jones. The twenty-five-foot

Christmas tree was ringed by an antique miniature of the baron's private train that wove through a scale model of the Black Forest. Distributed throughout the forest was an opulent array of packages wrapped, by the staff of seventeen, in green-and-gold wrapping papers that bore the baron's crest. The small group was scattered comfortably around various overstuffed damask chairs and tea tables. One entire wall was devoted to the baron's collection of leather-bound rare books, and an ornate marble fireplace humorously decked out in wreaths and garlands, blazing with a welcoming fire. On each side of the fireplace hung two small Van Eyck portraits of the baron's ancestors and two massive tapestry cartoons by Raphael, rumored to have been part of a selective cache that had been looted from the mansion of a wealthy Jewish banking family during the German invasion of Italy.

Lady Camille pulled her needlework from a quilted Laura Ashley bag, leaned over, and whispered something to Alfred, who was engrossed in reading the editorials from fifteen different newspapers, all of which were speculating on his suitability for a seat in the House of Commons.

Lord Harcourt served himself some potent hot punch made of Chinese tea, ginger wine, and whiskey from an ornate silver cistern. 'House of Commons,' he snorted derisively. 'There's never been a Harcourt in the House of Commons. You'll be my successor, Alfred, and your son after you, if you and Camille do what I didn't and get married before it's too late to perpetuate.' He let out a simultaneous laugh and a wheeze. 'Unless you don't think it's too late for me, that is.' He brushed a shower of powdered sugar from his sweater and winked at Lady Camille, who blushed under her sidelong glance.

'Uncle Harry, I have no fear,' Alfred retorted. 'You're an institution.'

'Just like Harrods,' chimed in Lady Camille.

'Check, my dear,' the baron announced, sliding his bishop into place.

Billy got up and stood behind her chair. 'Might as well concede the South, McBride.'

'Well.' She pushed back her chair. 'You should always play for time.'

The baron cocked his head. 'The secret of the game is simple. You must understand who the other person really is – not who you think he is.'

'I'm a pragmatist, Baron. I deal with reality.'

He adjusted the paisley ascot around his neck. 'But you're playing on a surrealist board – and not just in this room.'

'You've trained me well. I've learned from the masters.'

'Yes. You have been under the tutelage of the Grunewald philosophy. But then lately, you have been influenced by other techniques,' he said, emphasizing his last word as if he were describing a hard-edged crustacean. 'Remember . . .' he pointed to the handwritten words that rimmed the chessboard. 'The king is a pyramid, the queen is a cone, the bishop is a bottle, the knight is a bone, the rook is a castle, the pawn is not alone. My dear, the object of the game is never to be the pawn. Now.' He turned to Billy. 'Perhaps you will join me in my study for a few minutes.'

Catherine walked over to Lady Camille. 'Would you like to go for a run with me?'

Lady Camille looked startled, as if Catherine had suggested a game of leg wrestling. She sat sedately in her tweed skirt and Pringles sweater, her Welsh corgi flopped at her feet, its ears pricked and slightly pointed, its foxy face squinting at Catherine. 'Not just now, thank you,' she breathed, 'I've got this whole background to fill in.' She spread out the half-finished needlepoint canvas for Catherine to see. 'Plus, isn't it snowing? You American girls are a rather hearty lot. I really don't care to run in the snow.' She uttered each word politely, but with a decidedly aloof air.

Cathering stuffed her hands into her green sweater dress.

'I think I feel like a run myself,' Uncle Harry piped up, dragging his three-hundred-and-fifty-pound frame up from the floral chintz couch by the fire. 'A run up the stairs and straight to my bed for a nap!' He walked unsteadily over to Catherine and leaned on her arm for support. 'I'll escort you up to change, Catherine.'

They arduously mounted the stone steps to the West Wing, the only part of the house that was fully centrally heated, where Catherine went into her suite and laughed to find her Nike jogging suit hung in the massive wardrobe on a pale-blue padded hanger and stuffed with tissue paper. One of the upstairs maids had unpacked her clothes as if they were all couture originals from the Faubourg Saint-Honoré rather than off-the-rack merchandise.

She unbuttoned her dress and unbuckled her Barry Kisselstein-Cord belt with its sterling silver concho clasp. She'd bought it for herself in a fit of self-indulgence after the senior vice-presidency promotion, and she wore it with almost everything. She kicked off her boots, changed, and in minutes reemerged. She trotted downstairs and grabbed a tweed cap off the guest rack that the baron kept by the side entrance and tucked her hair under it. Catherine jogged away from the soaring towers, turrets, chimney stacks, and domes of the manor and onto the broad drive already lit by lanterns.

Snow began to fall as Catherine ran past the frozen pond and down the sloping grounds of the park. Even though the ground was frozen and the trees dusted with snow, Catherine could picture the beautiful landscape. She could see each bridge and the gatehouse. Everything was so artlessly placed that the atmosphere was one of timeless beauty. Lord Harcourt had told Catherine that the parkland had been laid out by Capability Brown so that every structure or planting was mirror-imaged and repeated in the many lakes and ponds. The three arches under a Palladian bridge became full circles in the stream underneath, and a garden maze became twice as mysterious by its reflection in the joining ponds.

Catherine ran past a flock of sheep, reciting to herself the name that had become a mantra accompanying the beat of her feet: Capability Brown, Capability Brown. She guessed that the Capability Browns of today were occupied with corporate headquarters, the modern citadels and castles. They were designing golden arches for hamburger chains instead of Palladian bridges and parks for dukes and duchesses.

Suddenly Catherine felt lonesome. Everyone seemed to be attached to someone else. Lady Camille and Alfred looked very content in their proper English love for each other; Lord Harcourt had Serena Castilla, the grand master bridge player who had been his constant companion for the past thirty years. Lady Camille's parents were the epitome of marital contentment. Even the baron and Billy Wright seemed to have found each other and were enthusiastically plotting Billy's first acquisition plans as Darco's new president.

Last night, she had awakened and touched the empty

spot beside her. She missed Graham's arm slung over her body in their familiar sleeping position. But, she thought as the snowflakes became thicker and seemed to hang suspended in the air like a world under a Christmas bell jar, nothing really seemed to be right with the two of them these days. In the beginning, they had shared every decision, plan, and dream. Now the only thing they shared was the bed. Graham's preoccupation with Drucilla's kidnapping had limited all their conversations to 'who called' and 'Catherine, cancel this meeting for me.' She had even given up briefing him on the executive committee's decisions, as no business details seemed to interest him.

He was clearly caving in under the stress. These days, she felt more like his nurse than his lover, mixing Maalox into his Perrier, spending the early morning hours rubbing his back and suffering along while he passed kidney stones. Hopefully Drucilla would be found safe and they could get on with their lives again. Otherwise she could not imagine the consequences for Graham. He was already confusing the company with the kidnappers, pulling further away from Intercon with each passing day.

Her running pace was strong as she passed a cluster of small outbuildings and jogged up into a thicket of trees. She heard the barking dogs ahead. The main house was far down the hill below her. It looked like one of the baron's toys, a miniature manor in an expansive valley.

Cathering stopped to catch her breath before returning. She brushed the snow off her cap. The snow was heavier now, falling in huge, wet flakes. She hadn't run three yards down the hill when two snarling black dogs came charging out of the woods at her. She tried to outrun them, but they cut her off. One nipped at her jogging shoes while the other blocked her path, baring a clenched mouthful of sharp teeth.

Catherine froze, and both dogs held her at bay, growling menacingly. Staring at the thick-necked, muscular animals, Catherine shivered, but she didn't dare extend her hand. These dogs looked as if they would attack at the slightest provocation.

'Heel! Lotti! Günther! Heel!' Alfred Grunwald called as he hurried up, his Purdey sporting gun held under his arm, and the dogs instantly drew back two steps and calmly sat at his command. He turned to Catherine. 'Who's there?'

'Alfred, it's me. Catherine!' She pulled off her cap and shook down her hair. 'I – I was just out for a run.'

'This is five miles from the house – hardly a jog around the garden.'

'I always do ten miles.' She glanced apprehensively at the two dogs, who were now licking Alfred's hand. 'What are these? The Hounds of the Baskervilles?'

He laughed. 'Their manners are terrible.' He rubbed Lotti's loose, floppy ears. 'They are rottweilers.'

'I've never heard of them.' She still didn't trust the strange-looking dogs.

'There aren't many in America. They're German dogs – ancestors of the Doberman pinscher. A very old breed. They were used to carry money belts during the Middle Ages.'

'I'm sure nobody tried to rob them.' Günther looked like he could rip out a cow's throat for an appetizer.

'They sleep at the foot of my bed,' Alfred said. 'But they're in exile. They don't get along with Camille's Ladykins.'

'Who's Ladykins?'

'The corgi. Every time Camille brings Ladykins along,

she tries to attack Lotti and Günther. So I have to exile them to the falcon house.' He gestured up the hill. 'I drove up here in my Range Rover to take them for a walk. You actually ran all this way?'

'It wasn't exactly a marathon.'

'Well, perhaps you'd accept a ride back from your former chauffeur.' He held out his hand.

It was almost dark. 'If I take your hand, please tell Lotti and Max, or whatever their names are, that I'm on *your* side.'

'They like you,' he said with a grin.

'I'm not so sure.' She took a tentative step.

'If they don't like you, they eat you.'

They walked together back up the hill, the dogs trotting behind. 'I'll just feed them and then we can join the others. Father won't want dinner to be late. He's showing *Modern Times* afterward.' Neither one had ever spoken about their last meeting in Chicago, and they both evaded the issue now.

The small brick falcon house was empty, except for two dog beds on the floor, a bench in front of a stone-hearthed fireplace, and rows of empty cages that looked centuries old.

'Do you still keep falcons here?'

'My father never cared about falconry. It was my mother's sport. She used to come here all the time.'

Catherine walked across the stone floor and opened a heavy wood door. Some furniture was draped with tarps and sheets. She closed the door again. 'I only saw your mother once. What was she like? Was she as fascinating as the baron?'

'Some said more so. She was a Harcourt, and Harcourt women have always been the most beautiful in England.

*And* they produced sons, which made them even more desirable.'

'Sounds more like horse breeding.'

'Hardly. Brilliant, gifted, and debauched. That was the Harcourts, since the thirteen hundreds.'

'Debauched? Is that what it says on the family coat of arms? I can't believe that elegant woman I met on the train was *debauched*.'

He set bowls of food down for the dogs and joined Catherine on the bench. 'In my mother's case, the words were brilliant, gifted, and *passionate*. But sometimes passion can bring unhappiness. And tragedy.'

Catherine's clothes were damp, and she was shivering. He looked up at her. 'Here, we'd better have a fire. You look chilled. It won't take long.' The logs and kindling were already set, and Alfred struck a match and touched it to the crumpled paper under the logs.

Catherine leaned forward and warmed her hands over the flames. 'She must have been an incredible woman to capture the love of someone like Baron Grunewald.' She looked at Alfred's face, seeing traces of the baroness there. The cleft in the chin, the unexpected dimples when he smiled, the thick, dark lashes, were all Harcourt features.

'She was independent and aloof. Held herself apart. My father could never own her, like one of his possessions. That was her charm for him.'

'And for you?'

'She was like her falcons. She had to be free. I adored her. She was – laughter and creativity and fun.' He smiled. 'We used to come here and put on capes and boots and play Robin Hood in Sherwood Forest. Uncle Harry was always pressed into service to play Friar Tuck.'

The fire began to crackle.

'Just your everyday normal childhood,' Catherine joked. 'I wish I had really known her.'

He was in a reverie. 'My mother never concerned herself with practical things, and she despised unpleasantness. Others dealt with the less magical side of my childhood. Every morning, I'd leave the nursery and be turned over to the care of this nanny or that, or Mrs Crenshaw, the housekeeper. Sometimes I still remember the white-capped maids, and how they scurried in fear from the butler whenever he appeared.' Alfred shrugged. 'My mother wasn't part of my day-to-day life, really. Day to day was too ordinary for her. She loved everything that was beautiful *passionately*, whether it was good or not for her. Falcons, games, music, paintings, men.' He paused and then his voice became rueful. 'Women. Anything that was rare, ravishing, or elegant.'

The dogs trotted to his side and stretched out in front of the fire.

'She committed suicide when she was forty years old.' His voice was flat. 'She was having an unhappy love affair.'

Cathering didn't know what to say. She'd heard rumors of the legendary baroness and her overly warm friendship with Sybil, the woman with the fedora she had seen on the train. She could now understand why Alfred had chosen the complaisant Camille, but she decided to say nothing. He obviously wanted a listener.

'It's possible to love one's parents in spite of their imperfections.'

'I know.' She thought first of her mother, who had never been there for her, and then of her father, whom she still hated.

They sat quietly together.

'My father left when I was very young. My mother –

well . . . But I still love them both.' The words just came out, surprising her. But they were true, she realized. She still held on to the good memories of her father, the bicycling, the bedtime stories, and the baseball games. She really didn't hate him. It was anger, more than hatred. And disappointment.

'Parents are only human beings,' said Alfred. 'Just being a parent doesn't grant you sainthood or give you expertise. You can't blame them for not being what they're not.' He turned away and faced the fire. 'As it ends up, I've turned out rather ordinary. Hard working, old-fashioned in my values, some would say boring. I must be a throwback.' He turned back to Catherine. Tears were streaming down her face. 'Have I upset you?'

She hardly heard him. All she could think about was her father, the sound of his voice as he soothed her in a thunderstorm, the dozens and dozens of letters that her mother had sent back unopened over the years, and the picture that was still in the bottom of one of her dresser drawers. Alfred's honesty was unlocking a disturbing revelation within her. She realized that she had never been able to love someone without judging him. If she stopped judging her father, she would be free to love him again. And she would also stop trying to replace him. It suddenly became clear that she had spent her life either ignoring or looking for him.

'I'm sorry,' she sniffed.

'Here, have my handkerchief. You can start a collection.'

She smiled and cried at the same time. 'You must think all I do is cry and eat.'

'I do seem to bring out your indulgent side.'

She blew her nose. 'No. Really. You make me – ' She searched for the right words. 'See things.' Was it coincidence that the few times she was with Alfred were the times she'd been able to think most clearly about her life? Or was he very special? 'I think Lady Camille is very lucky.'

'Yes, she is. I have no faults at all.' His dimples framed his smile. 'And just what do you think are ideal characteristics in a man?'

She thought for a minute. 'Well – dependability. Respect. Solidity. Someone you can look up to.'

'Terrific. That sounds like the perfect father.'

She blinked, startled. Did he think he was her psychiatrist?

'And what characteristics do you find appealing in a woman?' she asked testily. Probably proficiency in needlepoint, she thought.

'Certainly not fencing without foils.'

They stared at one another. Cathering felt a cacophony of strange emotions. She wanted to be angry with Alfred, but she wasn't. She didn't know whether she wanted to hit him or embrace him. Maybe she should just sock the aristocratic cleft in his chin.

'Are you still wet?' He touched her jacket.

'No.'

They were still studying each other. Neither said anything until the fire had diminished to one glowing ember and the dogs were asleep.

Alfred leaned towards the last flicker of light and held out his wrist to check his watch. 'Seven-thirty-three. Dinner was served three minutes ago in the dining room.' His voice sounded disturbed. 'Oddly enough, I don't care. I feel I can talk to you,' he said. 'I hope you don't mind.'

'I hope you do run for the House of Commons, Alfred.'

'You're the only one who does, I'm afraid.'

'You understand things. That's very special. I would

imagine that gives you parliamentary qualifications.'

Together they stood up and walked out the door, and Catherine felt an empty space inside her, as if she'd left something behind.

Catherine and Alfred were met at the side porch entrance by the baron's butler, a Teutonic relic who had perfected the art of the blank expression and who now arched a disapproving eyebrow. Nobody was ever late for dinner at the baron's table.

'Have they gone in yet?' Alfred asked.

'Yes, sir. A full five minutes ago.' He nodded to Catherine. 'Your bath is drawn, Miss. If you hurry you can make the main course.'

'And if we don't, we can *be* the main course.' Alfred pulled off his muddy boots and left them by the antique butter churn filled with walking sticks and canes, where sixteen assorted pairs of Wellingtons and hiking shoes were already lined up along the wall.

Catherine kicked off her muddy Nikes and pushed them into the row.

They hurried up the stone steps and paused at the top. 'I'll see you in a few minutes, then,' Alfred said, as Catherine rounded the corner to the guest wing hall.

The ladies' maid was in Catherine's room, waiting to help her out of her clothes. Every detail had been taken care of. Her ankle-length black velvet skirt and white satin blouse with pearl buttons were laid out on the bed, along with her underwear. On the dresser were the tickets for tomorrow's flight from London to Chicago, and her suitcase had been opened and was lined with tissue paper.

'Miss, I didn't know what you planned to wear in the morning, so I haven't packed your things yet. But your bath is ready in the dressing room, and I've lit the fire in there for you, so it'll be nice and cozy.'

Catherine suddenly felt exhausted, whether from jet lag, overtiredness, or the emotionally draining conversation with Alfred, she didn't know. But the thought of facing an evening of polite conversation at a formal dinner was more than she could face. She needed to be alone with her thoughts and let the last whirlwind of days sink in. She didn't want to disappoint the baron, but she felt so tired. Their business had been done. Billy was set. She had such an early flight tomorrow, which meant getting up at dawn, that it would be better to skip dinner, she rationalized.

'Would you please sent word down that I won't be joining them for dinner. Please give my apologies, but I seem to have caught a chill.'

'I'm so sorry, miss. But you really should eat something. I'll have a tray made up for you and bring it right up. Then we'll pack you up and you can have a good night's sleep.'

'Thank you. That would be wonderful.'

The maid disappeared. Catherine dropped her still-damp jogging clothes onto the paisley carpet and made her way to the adjoining dressing room. The air was warm and humid and smelled of lavender from the scented bubble bath. Towels were set out along one wall on racks heated by a hot water system, and even her toothbrush had been set out for her and prepared with her toothpaste.

Catherine eased herself into the free-standing antique cast-iron tub and reached for a sponge and a bar of soap. She leaned back into the warm bubbles, stretched out, and pointed her toes. She wanted to erase everything from her mind. It was easy to do in this atmosphere. The only light shone from the fireplace, and she concentrated on the mantlepiece decorated with delicate Chinese ginger jars, antique perfume atomizers, and malachite bowls of bath salts.

She pulled up her hair and closed her eyes, putting the thick natural sponge behind her neck as a cushion. Even though she tried not to think, Alfred, Graham, and her father all came rushing into her head in a montage of images.

Graham. He'd be in Lake Forest now. Would he be sitting with Eve, reliving their memories?

Her father. Where was he? Wasn't Van Nuys, California, the postmark of his last, unopened letter? She had a sudden urge to call him for Christmas, but how would he react? She'd better not. Nothing could be accomplished by a transatlantic call from the ghost of Christmas past.

Alfred. What about Alfred? He had certainly confused her feelings about Graham, yet whenever she was around him he made life so uncomplicated. Was that just English charm, Catherine wondered?

She had everything, didn't she? Graham Donaldson had been her idol from her business school days. He had left his wife for her and they had a life plan together. She was senior vice-president of a billion-dollar company where she controlled her own white Formica empire. So why was she sitting alone in a bathtub a few days before New Year's, in an English manor belonging to a German baron, feeling confused?

She heard a knock on the bedroom door and assumed it was the maid bringing her dinner tray. Maybe she would feel better after she had something to eat.

'Did you send my message to the baron?' Catherine asked.

'What message was that?' Alfred Grunewald, outfitted in a tuxedo, stood framed in the doorway of her dressing room.

He looked startled to see her not dressed and ready and took a quick step backward as she half-sat up in the tub, bringing her knees to her chest.

'I – was just coming by to bring you down to dinner,' he explained.

Catherine knew she should tell him she wasn't coming. She should ask him to leave. She should tell him she was embarrassed. He ought to apologize for intruding and leave.

Instead, neither of them spoke. And when he came closer and picked up an oversized towel and held it open, Catherine rose out of the tub. Her body glistened in the flickering light. There was no shyness, no rationality in her compulsion to move toward him. She stepped out of the tub, her arms by her sides, and, as if choreographed, took one slow, measured step, then another, until he dropped his hands to his sides, letting the towel slide to the black-and-white marble floor, and enfolded her in his arms. For a minute, she rested her head on his shoulder as water ran down her body, soaking his dinner jacket. She lifted her face to his, and he traced a stray drop of water down her shoulder and then to her breast with his finger. As his hands ran down her back, they kissed, and soon all Catherine felt were his lips on her mouth, throat, eyelids, and cheeks. Nothing else seemed to matter as she curled her fingers in his hair and pulled his head down to hers. Her tongue traced his mouth and Alfred moved his hand to cup her face as they kissed again and again. She wanted him in a way she had never experienced, as if he alone could fill the emptiness within her. Every inch of her body yearned for his touch; every part of her psyche told her this was right. She rested her hands on his chest and caressed the damp, pleated shirt that fitted tightly across his chest. Alfred's hands moved down the length of her body as if he too sought something. She leaned into him, bursting a thousand tiny soap bubbles, and rubbed her nipples against the fabric of his dinner jacket. She parted her legs slightly, pressed Alfred to her, and felt him harden at her touch. He gently guided his hand between her thighs and his fingers quickly found her moist center. Catherine wanted to tear his clothes off, push him onto the floor, and melt into him. She wanted them to lose themselves in each other; she wanted them to be one person. It was instinct, it was lust, it was something she couldn't understand.

But suddenly she remembered where she was, who he was, and she pulled away. She picked up the towel and covered herself in one motion. 'Lady Camille will be waiting for you,' she whispered.

He looked down at his water-stained tuxedo and drew a deep breath.

'You're right.'

He backed toward the door, tripping over a cast-iron doorstop.

She heard him close the bedroom door on his way out. She had no idea how many minutes she had stood there motionless before she heard another knock, wrapped herself in a towel, and opened the door expectantly. The maid entered, carrying a tray on which rested three silver *cloches* to keep her dinner warm.

# 11

With all the windows boarded over, Drucilla couldn't tell if it was day or night. She had no way of counting the days or the hours. She didn't even have any idea how long she'd been on the boat. Her hair had now grown to chin length, so she guessed two months had passed.

After what seemed like an eternity, she had been let out of the closet. Her seasickness then waned and so her life improved slightly. At least she now had a bed to lie on, and a blanket. They still let her out for her daily shower, and she was given an occasional paperback book to read.

She knew she'd lost weight. Her ribs and collarbones protruded beneath her thin T-shirt. At first, she could hardly bring herself to eat anything, but now she found herself looking forward to the canned meats, vegetables, and rice. The meager routine of eating was a way of putting some order into her life.

She saw her two captors frequently, but only with stockings over their faces. The woman droned on and on about the Badera Roja and social injustice. She lectured her with fiery tirades about capitalist pigs, colonization, and cultural imperialism. Drucilla didn't care what she was talking about. She always nodded in agreement, no matter what the woman said. She had made up names for the man and the woman: Butch and Bitch.

Bitch was worse than Butch. She made her stand for hours reciting propaganda from the Bandera Roja until the words made no sense. Dru could now repeat them from habit. Sometimes Bitch would come in late at night, shine a light in her face, and taunt her for hours about her father, the capitalist pig who had chosen his company over her.

Escape was impossible. The door of her cabin was locked from the outside. She had tried screaming for the first few days, but no one came except Bitch and Butch. Crying did no good, either. It only made her feel worse. Nobody came to comfort her, so what was the point of tears? She was beyond depression. Her only hope was that Arnaud and her father would rescue her.

Lying on her bunk, her fantasies were her only diversion. She relived her wedding over and over and began to see herself in the role of the kidnapped heroine, the maligned countess, waiting to be rescued, like a princess in a tower.

Today had begun like all the others. The box of cereal, the canned milk, the morning shower. Except that Bitch had given her a newspaper to read – the *New York Post*, although she forced Drucilla to say thank you three times before she put the paper in her hands.

Drucilla checked the date. February fifteenth. If this was today, it had been three months since the kidnapping! Then she flipped to her horoscope. She was a Gemini. Maybe this would be the day she would be rescued! But her forecast was for good luck in a business deal.

She flipped back to the front page and saw a story about the Pope. She read on. On the top of page three was a picture of Arnaud. Poor Arnaud, he must be so worried. Another picture at the bottom of the page was taken from their wedding. But wait, that wasn't her dress. She wasn't the bride! Drucilla looked quickly back up to the headline: 'Ex-Husband of Kidnapped Victim Marries Shipping Heiress.' She looked at the picture again.

Arnaud was with a *new* bride, Olimpia Papadapolos. Mouthing the words out loud, she read, 'Nineteen-year-old heiress married on Isle Saint Louis.' Arnaud was quoted as saying that he was convinced Drucilla was dead, and the marriage had been annulled. She read the story twice in a state of shock. Then she crumpled up the paper in a fury. 'No! No!' she shouted. How could he have done this? She wasn't dead. Had everyone given up? Would she be a prisoner forever? After she stopped crying, she timidly unfurled the paper. Arnaud's new wife looked like an idiot, wearing the family tiara. They deserved each other. Maybe her captors were right. He was a stupid capitalist and he looked ugly besides. She remembered that he hadn't even fought for her – she'd had to defend *him* from the kidnappers. Drucilla yanked off her engagement and wedding rings and threw them under the bunk.

Bitch was always telling her that her family had deserted her, that they were capitalist imperialists. And here was Arnaud's bride wearing a crown. A shipping heiress, daughter of one of the world's richest men. Bitch always told Dru her family cared for nothing but money, that only the simple life of working people made any sense, that luxuries were evil, that selfish people deserved to die. Maybe she was right. Dru didn't know what she believed anymore. 'Oh, Daddy, please come,' she whispered.

Suddenly Bitch came in wearing the stocking stretched over her face. Drucilla was almost glad to see her. They finally had something in common. They could laugh about Arnaud and his silly new wife together. 'See? Look at the pig. He only wanted money. See? You're nothing. You've done nothing with your life, you've never helped anyone. Why would anyone love you except for your money?' She pointed a fat finger at her. 'Maybe if you gave your money to help poor people someone would care about you. But you only spend it on your makeup and clothes. No wonder he married another woman.' Her features were like melted candlewax beneath the stocking mask.

Drucilla sat on the bunk, nodding.

The door flung open and Butch pushed his way in. There was barely room for them all in the little room. They hauled Drucilla up from the bed, bound her wrists, blindfolded her, taped her mouth, and pushed her with a swift heave into the closet.

The closet! It was the one thing she dreaded most. She would die in there, she knew it. They were going to kill her. She heaved her body against the door and sobbed through the tape until she was too weak to move.

All at once, the closet door opened and someone pushed up against her. She couldn't see, but she sensed it was a large person, a man. Was he going to taunt her with more propaganda or kill her? She kicked out with her legs and realized that the closet door was still open, but she could not get away.

He ripped the tape off her mouth, put his hand across her face, and dragged her to her feet. She didn't dare bite him, thinking he might have a gun.

But then he started to stroke her hair, as if to comfort her. She felt his body close to her. He had a strange, sweet smell, like a woman's perfume – musky and sweet at the same time. Was it violets?

His comforting caresses felt almost good. She at once resisted and yet welcomed them. It was the first time she'd felt any human touch that wasn't brutalizing since her wedding night. And then his touch went beyond comfort, becoming insistent, until he ripped open her shirt, pushed his hairy chest to hers, yanked down her jeans, slammed her into a corner, then down onto the floor. He sat on her legs and forced them open, pressing his thumbs down on her pelvis.

She didn't resist. She tried to stop breathing. If she pretended she was dead, maybe he would finish faster. He was shoving himself into her, once, twice, she lost count. Gasping for breath in the humid closet, she wished she *was* dying. But within seconds it was over, and just as suddenly he was gone, leaving her alone with the lingering smells of musky sex and violets.

She swooned, hitting her head against the back of the closet, and slouched flat to the floor.

By the time she came to, the boat was moving again, carrying her once more into oblivion, she was certain. But far off on shore, the man who had just left the closet stood on the deck of Miami's Jockey Club and watched the Hatteras as it pulled out of the slip and blended in with the Swans, C and C's, and Cigarette boats and Bertrams, as if off for a leisurely Sunday cruise.

# 12

There was a dead, eerie silence on the boat. Drucilla had grown so used to the buzz of the generators and the whirr of the fan that without them she felt as if the boat had dropped off the edge of the earth. For the past two weeks – as she counted it – they had been constantly moving through seas so rough that she was tossed around in her bunk and felt sick to her stomach. She had seen little of Butch and Bitch, although Bitch had actually brought her some fresh fruit.

When she woke up this morning, her cabin was dark and there was no sound or movement on the boat except for the rocking of the waves. The narrow cabin was like a steambath. Her T-shirt was soaked through, her short hair was wet with sweat, and her thighs stuck together. Although no air had managed to get into the cabin, flies somehow landed periodically on her arms and legs. She brushed them off and lay still on the damp bunk. She didn't care. Ever since the rape, she'd stopped caring about anything. She didn't even care if she were pregnant, since she felt as good as dead anyway.

The air was stifling as she lay in a daze in the dark. Why wasn't the electricity working? What were Butch and Bitch up to now?

Off in the distance, she heard a motor. It came closer, until she could tell it was next to her boat. And then, there was the sound of footsteps. Someone was coming. Was it Butch? Bitch? The rapist? She sat up. Maybe she was being rescued. Should she call for help? No, if it was

Butch and Bitch they'd probably punish her.

She cowered on the floor, curled up in a ball, trying to make herself as small as possible. Maybe no one would be able to find her. If only she had some strength, Dru thought in a state of panic. She would then be able to fight them off.

A shattering blast hit the door, and she winced, expecting the next blow to touch her.

With a splintering crash, the cabin door burst off the hinges, and what looked like a sea monster in the blinding light stood there facing her. Dru squinted in the sudden brightness but soon focused on the barrels of two shotguns, which were pointed straight at her. They were going to murder her! Frantically, she screamed and covered her eyes.

And then she heard a familiar voice. 'Put those guns down, you're frightening her! Drucilla, it's me. It's okay. Everything's okay now. We're here.' Michael Picol was suddenly beside her, his arm around her shoulders.

She grabbed his wrist in a vise-grip as he and the frogmen half carried her to a small Coast Guard cutter that was tied to the lee. She stumbled aboard; her knees felt weak, her eyes were half-blinded by the first sunlight she'd seen in three months. Overhead, two white helicopters hovered.

'Go! Let's get out of here,' shouted the frogman. 'They said we have five minutes before this thing blows!' The cutter took off toward shore, where Graham Donaldson stood watching with binoculars.

Was that really Drucilla, Graham wondered. She was so white and frail, so unlike his big, healthy girl. God knew what tortures they'd inflicted on her to make her look like a skeleton. But at least she was alive, Graham quickly reminded himself. He strained for a better look.

Thank God for Picol, whose persistent negotiations had finally ended his family's worst nightmare. Picol had worked out a plan to return one of the Place in the Sun islands to the Venezuelans, along with its mineral rights and a package of job concessions for the rebels. Graham had to argue with Rex to achieve that, but while Rex was President of the United States, he was also Drucilla's godfather. The Venezuelan government had, in turn, put pressure on the Bandera Roja for Drucilla's release.

Graham felt his body tensing. God, why didn't they hurry? The kidnappers had been explicit on the last tape they'd sent to Michael Picol. The conditions stated that only four men could board a boat anchored five miles off A Place in the Sun, and the boat would he detonated minutes after Drucilla's release.

He had wanted to be part of the rescue team himself, but Picol had said it was too dangerous. The FBI had convinced him that Drucilla had a better chance if her father didn't participate.

Now he stood anxiously on the dock, ringed by Intercon security guards.

The Hatteras was still in the wake of the cutter when the big powerboat exploded into a huge ball of flame. A cloud of white smoke peppered with debris shot up sixty feet into the air. Fire-colored sparks splintered through the sky, then dropped like comets to the cool, blue ocean. 'Thank God she's clear,' Graham said, as he fell to his knees, shielding his eyes from the heat of the flash.

'One of them must still be in the area with a detonator,' shouted an FBI man into a radio as he twisted toward the shore.

On the cutter, Michael Picol grabbed the rail and steadied Drucilla, throwing his jacket over her shoulders as she clung to him, eyes tightly closed in the glare of the sun and the blazing fire.

The frogman who had swum under the Hatteras before they boarded frowned. 'How the hell did they get the timing so close? They must still be in the area.'

Michael Picot shot him an impatient look. 'It's your job to know that. Thank God we're all off.'

When they reached the dock, Picol pried Dru's hand from around his wrist, one finger at a time. Graham rushed over and lifted her off the boat and into his arms. Her legs could barely support her, and she collapsed into his arms sobbing hysterically, 'Oh, Daddy, Daddy!'

Picol, strangely pale despite his tan, watched silently.

# 13

Bambi sat in a damp canvas chair with *Green Mansions* stenciled on the back. She was cramming for her exams with Reutie, her tutor, and simultaneously studying the simple lines for her role as Rima in her new film. The grades were important to her since she'd gotten early acceptance at the University of Kentucky's veterinary medicine program, as long as her final grades were acceptable. She didn't want to blow her chances. Out of the corner of her eye, she could see the catering crew setting up a buffet lunch on the long, metal tables under the thickly leaved trees. That meant it was one o'clock, and they still hadn't gotten the first shot in the can, though she didn't particularly care. When she modeled for Valeski, she'd been able to get caught up in the fantasy of the camera, to lose herself into the Bambi persona. She'd known Valeski for so long that it was almost like playing one of Hughie's make-believe games. She hadn't liked making television commercials nearly as well as modeling for Valeski because repeating every move and work ten or fifteen times was boring. But since commercials only took a day or two to shoot, she had tolerated it. For the Bambi sportswear line and her fragrance *Fawn*, they shot ten commercials in two weeks, and she didn't have to work again for months. She wasn't so sure that filling up her free time with making films was such a good idea. *Hollywood* – the word always stuck in her throat. Movies took months to shoot. She looked up through the thick canopy of leaves, searching without success for sun. Being on location was like being in exile, Bambi thought. She dropped her eyes again onto the grammar study sheet Reutie had prepared for her.

She and Hughie had been ferried by helicopter from Honolulu to the rain forest of Waialeale on the island of Kaui to shoot the jungle sequences for the remake of *Green Mansions*. Hughie had said that this was the perfect choice for her second movie. Rima, the role that was still identified with the young Audrey Hepburn, would catapult Bambi into film stardom. After Bambi's success in the made-for-TV miniseries, *National Velvet*, which, according to Nielsen, got the biggest prime-time ratings of the season, it was important for her first feature film to be exacly the right vehicle. Bambi herself had chosen the part of Rima the Bird Girl, who lived among the lush trees and orchids like a wild, untamed wood nymph.

Bambi glanced up at Hughie, who was in a whispered but heated debate with the stylist and director near the wardrobe tent. What could be taking so long, she wondered. She wasn't even dressed in her costume yet – she was wearing her jeans and makeup smock. She flipped through the pages of her math textbook. There was so much material to cover, and it was so hard to study with all these distractions. Every half hour it seemed to rain. The technicians were always underfoot and people were always poking brushes at her face or skewering wigs to her head.

The atmosphere, exotic as it was, was depressing. The hundred-foot-high canopy of green leaves blocked out most of the sunlight, even though wide-angle areas for the master shots had been cleared. A misty bank of fog hung in the air, and the ferns, mosses and hanging maile vines created a primeval atmosphere referred to by the Hawaiian natives as The Abode of the Gods. They provided the perfect backdrop for the director's deep-in-the-jungle look, but seemed confining to a girl accustomed to open midwestern spaces. A lacy waterfall tumbled down a mossy hillside, and lights, generators, and camera were set up on the river bank to capture Bambi as Rima swinging overhead on the vines.

But there was a problem.

'Listen to me, Hughie,' the director said, as Bambi turned back to her math book to concentrate on her integers. 'This is just not going to work. You know I love Bambi, but I have a picture to make.'

Hughie waved a week-old copy of *USA Today*. 'Without Bambi, you have no picture. Read this poll. She's the most admired teenager in America.'

The director shook his head sadly. This was only his third feature film, and he couldn't take a chance. 'Hughie, I have so far shot this entire movie in two angles – close-up and extreme close-up because I cannot shoot Bambi below the shoulders because she is twenty pounds overweight.' He enunciated every word as if Hughie might miss his point.

'She looks beautiful.'

'To you. To me. But *not* to the camera. I shouldn't need to tell *you* that the camera adds twenty pounds to her figure.'

'The starving orphan was never Bambi's look.'

The director tapped his script.

'Besides, you can let out those costumes in five minutes,' Hughie continued.

The director was not moved. 'Rima is supposed to be lighter than air, a sparrow, ephemeral. We signed Bambi for those qualities. What the hell's the matter with her? She looks more like a water buffalo on a pizza binge than a wood nymph.' He shouted, 'Look at the goddamn proofs, will you? Look!' He flung a handful of glossies, wrinkled by the sticky humidity, into Hughie's face.

Hughie bore down on him. 'Your idea of beauty is passé. Nobody looks like Twiggy anymore.' He crumpled the proof sheets. 'She's the epitome of modern American women. Strong, muscular, well-defined, broad-shouldered . . .'

'Well this part calls for reedlike, doe-eyed, sylphlike. Read the script.'

'Be quiet,' hissed Hughie, 'she'll hear you.' He turned on the wardrobe stylist. 'It's your costumes! They'd make Audrey Hepburn look like an overblown Studebaker.'

The director took his arm and they walked a few steps together. He tried to be sympathetic because of Bambi. She had such a vulnerable quality in her eyes, no one ever could stand to hurt her. 'You saw the dailies. Her face is just hidden under all that excess baggage. Chipmunk cheeks, like a kid who's been on a six-month pig-out.' He sighed. 'This is just not working. It's costing a fortune and the producers are on my back. If she can't drop those twenty pounds in a week or two, I'm going to have to let her go.'

Bambi was looking in their direction now, and she caught the frown on Hughie's face. It looked like he was having a hard time with the director. She closed her book again and said to her tutor, 'Can we go over this later?'

She had a feeling she knew what this was about. She'd seen the dailies. She knew she looked more like a body builder than a wood sylph. All those late-night cram sessions with potato chips and cokes had added pounds. And with all the exercising, riding and outdoor country life, she was growing into her seventeen-year-old, broad-shouldered inherited frame. And she wasn't going to starve herself for this movie or anything else until she fit somebody else's anorexic image of beauty. She was almost six feet tall and she needed her energy.

Maybe this film had not been such a great deal, she said to herself. Being an actress had sounded glamorous, but all she did was sit around bored, getting orders to do this or do that. She was sick of it.

She walked over to Hughie's side. 'What's up, guys?'

Hughie put his arm around her. 'Bambi, we're going to take a break for a few days.'

'For my finals?'

'No. We'll go up to La Costa for the crash diet program. Barry would like you to be a few pounds lighter.'

She shook her head emphatically. 'Forget it.'

'You'll lose that twenty pounds in a week. It won't be hard.'

She faced Barry. 'Does this movie show me in Bambi clothes? Does this movies sell the Bambi line? We don't sell leaf tunics. There's nothing in this film for me.' She turned to Hughie, who was suddenly silent as he smoothed a wrinkle in his linen shirt. 'I think we should go,' she announced. 'When's the helicopter due back?'

'We can work this out, Bambi,' Barry said. She was surprising him again, and he hated surprises.

'No, I don't want to work it out.'

'They've shot most of your close-ups already. You can't walk out without ruining the film,' Hughie pleaded.

'Yes I can. Radio the helicopter.'

Hughie trotted alongside Bambi as she headed back to the wardrobe tent, and Barry scrambled to catch them.

'Bambi, honey,' said the director. 'Fifteen pounds?'

'No.' She kept walking.

'What is Barry going to do?' Hughie said, just loud enough for her to hear. 'You're letting him down.'

She tossed her head as she picked up her books. 'He

can get a body double for all I care.' She stopped and said slowly, 'I'm tired of being the ice princess, or Rima the Bird Girl. If I want to eat normal meals, it's not going to kill me. Can't I just be Elizabeth Ann Stuart for a change?'

The director watched Bambi and Hughie until they moved on and disappeared into the tent. Then he motioned to his assistant. 'Get me that girl from the mermaid movie.'

# 14

'Come on, darling. Why don't you try to get up and eat a little bit?'

Eve pushed aside a clutch of Beatrix Potter animals in their pinafores and gingham and cleared a place for herself on Dru's bed. She could understand why Drucilla hadn't been able to return to the penthouse, even though Lolly was still there, but Drucilla just wasn't pulling out of her depression fast enough. She should be able to leave the kidnapping and Arnaud behind her and get on with her life. Instead, she was becoming more and more withdrawn, retreating into her childhood ways. She seemed comfortable only in her bedroom, with its half-canopy organdie beds, floppy-eared, faded stuffed animals, and memories of the time when she was a little girl.

Dru lay curled up in a flannel nightgown, clutching a pastel-checked stuffed mouse to her chest, staring at nothing in particular. It broke Eve's heart to look at her like this, her face was so gaunt and pale. She wouldn't watch TV, read, or even answer the phone, except to speak in monosyllables to her father or Michael Picol.

Eve clasped her daughter's hand. It felt clammy and cold, as if she had no circulation. 'Are you sure you wouldn't like some lunch? It's twelve-thirty. Maybe a tray with a little salad or soup?'

'No, thank you.' Dru's voice was barely audible. She'd been throwing up again this morning, Eve knew. She couldn't seem to keep food down. Dr Corbett seemed to think she'd been brain-washed into rejecting anything from her family, but Eve was getting worried. Maybe he should get a few more tests run. She might have picked up some unusual parasite that wasn't easily detected.

'I know what, Dru.' Eve forced her voice to be cheerful and soothing. 'You know what a kick you get out of Aunt Pollyanne, how she makes us all laugh. We can go with her on an all-girls' retreat to the Greenhouse. We can be pampered and rest, and the best part is, we'll eat whatever we want. Milkshakes every day! You'll be the envy of everyone there!'

Dru rearranged three of the rabbits on the pillows.

'Would you like that, dear? What do you think? Let's make an effort.' Eve took the untouched breakfast tray off the bed and put in on the white desk Dru had used before boarding school. Eve knew that Dru had been through a terrible crisis, and she wished she could be more adept at handling the situation. But there were certainly no role models that she cared to emulate in these circumstances. Eve made a mental list of all the kidnappings she could recall. In the Getty kidnapping, they had cut off a child's ear. At least Drucilla had only lost her hair. That would grow back. She recalled the Hearst kidnapping. Hadn't it taken their daughter years to readjust and settle down into a normal, happy life? Maybe Eve was expecting too much too soon.

She mustered all her determination. 'I'll tell you what. We'll call Aunt Pollyanne right now and set it up.'

Dru turned her head. 'Do we have to?'

Eve picked up the phone and dialed Pollyanne's private line, which rang on the third floor of the White House and was only answered by the immediate family. The phone rang five or six times, and finally Pollyanne picked it up.

'Pollyanne, how lucky to find you in.' Eve's voice was light.

'I'm sitting here with your goddaughter, and we were thinking how much fun it would be if we had a nice girls' retreat at the Greenhouse.'

'How is Dru doing? Any better?' Pollyanne sounded preoccupied.

'I think she'd do even better after a couple of days of total pampering. I was thinking about the end of the month. It is about time for our annual pilgrimage.'

The First Lady hesitated. 'I'm looking at my calendar, and I'm so busy right now with the Van Cliburn International Competition. We have different pianists playing every night right through next month. I'm head of the committee.'

'Not even for a weekend? I think it would really cheer up Dru.'

'Darling, the final dinner is at the White House. Rex is presenting the awards.'

Eve had an idea. 'That might be even better. We'd love to get her out a little bit. As a matter of fact, Alex Levin won that competition when he was first out of Juilliard. Perhaps you could squeeze in the three of us?'

'Oh. Is Drucilla seeing Alex Levin? She deserves something nice after that French no-count.' A note of interest sounded in her voice.

'N-no, he's – ' Eve decided not to explain. She wasn't sure that Pollyanne was ready to hear that she was seeing a man fourteen years her junior. She could fill in Pollyanne later. Right now, Drucilla was more important.

Pollyanne's reply was straightforward. 'That's not going to work, lovie. Graham is coming. And he's bringing that Catherine girl. Pat over at protocol made that decision, not me, darling. The seating would just be impossible. You understand . . .' Her voice trailed off.

Eve felt as if her best friend had just thrown ice water on her, but she forced herself to show nothing. 'Of course. After all, the divorce *is* final. Perhaps we'll go to the Greenhouse *next* month, dear.'

'Actually, I've got a whole new regime. A colonic every three months. It cleans out *everything*. Drucilla should try it. She'd feel like a new person. It takes all the toxins out of your system. Afterward you fast for three days. And then eat only grapes for five days.' She started to drone on in her boarding school tones.

Eve could hardly believe that Pollyanne could relegate their friendship to a back burner and try to solve Drucilla's condition with a colonic. She barely listened to the laundry list of new diet and purification techniques. Pollyanne was obviously caught up in the advice of her sycophants, her hairdressers, nutritionists, personal trainers, interior decorators, and dress designers. The color of her hair, her weight, artificially emptying her colon to reduce the size of her stomach to pancake-flat proportions, and antiaging skin preparations were turning her brain to mush. Pollyanne babbled on about making sure the colonic was given in conjunction with wheat grass and friendly bacteria and assured Eve that it was well worth any discomfort.

'Listen, Eve. I'm having a ladies' garden lunch thing here in June. Why don't you come to that? You won't need an escort.' Until that last phrase Eve hadn't realized why Pollyanne had been so *busy* since the divorce. In Pollyanne's world – Eve's former world – Eve was no longer in the same position of power she had held as the wife of the country's leading oil executive and counsel to four Presidents. And since her goddaughter had somehow lost her titled husband and been kidnapped by unsavory terrorists, she was apparently also out of favor. But Graham and the girl were somehow acceptable. She didn't really hear how Pollyanne got off the phone, but after she clicked off, Eve continued to talk into the empty receiver. 'Thank you, Pollyanne. As soon as we're ready we'd love a quiet qeekend with you both at Camp David and I'll tell Drucilla that you send her a big kiss. Love to you both.' And she hung up the receiver herself.

As she turned on the television and plumped Dru's pillows, Eve collected her thoughts. Polyanne had been her best friend for so long that her defection stung. She tried to make excuses for her friend. She was probably in a room full of people demanding her attention and hadn't really thought about what she'd said. And their friendship *had* always been based on the exteriors of life, not the deep issues. Eve had learned long ago never to rely on Pollyanne to solve any problem more serious than skin care.

She handed Drucilla the remote control. 'I know what would be fun,' she announced. 'Remember how you used to love our Sunday brunches at home? Let's have one this weekend. Nothing fancy. A few friends. People you know.'

Drucilla tensed. 'I don't want to see anyone from the wedding.'

That was going to be a problem since half the city had been invited to the wedding. Well, Eve decided, she'd just have to invite some of the friends from her music class at Northwestern. Alex's friends were interesting young people. Drucilla would accept Michael Picol and Bambi and Hughie.

'You won't have to get dressed up,' Eve forced a laugh as best she could. 'But you will have to get out of your flannel nightie.'

# 15

Eve hugged her knees to her chest and sat, enraptured, as Alexander Levin soared into the third movement of 'Study of a Winter's Eve.' The juxtaposition of themes was so personal and lyrical, it spoke to her like a secret language between the two of them. The leitmotif that ran through the piece was clearly the first unfolding of their feelings for each other. She looked around the room, surprised that the others could not decipher the meaning behind every note. Hughie, Bambi, and Dru were seated with Michael Picol to her left. The dozen or so students from Alex's master class, Dr Corbett, and Paula Deutch, president of the Women's Board of the Chicago Symphony Orchestra, were on her right, listening intently. Eve focused on the intimate, personal shadings of the music that meant so much to her.

Alex was presenting her a treasured gift. This wasn't jewels that anyone with money could buy, but a homage to her, which meant more than anything that had ever come in a velvet-lined box.

She turned to see if Drucilla was relaxing. This afternoon Dru had received the most ludicrous letter from Arnaud, whom she still referred to as her husband. Eve had been worried that it would upset Dru, but instead her daughter seemed amused for the first time. The note was full of bravado and pomposity, elaborating about Arnaud's failure at becoming Orpheus to her Euridyce. He should have gone to the shades of hell for her, the letter confessed – but he was sure that Orpheus never had to deal with the American press. He was of the vine and lyre. Drucilla was too American to understand his Gallic ways, and she was certainly better off without him.

Dru had taken the letter and dropped it unceremoniously into the wastebasket, an action that Dr Corbett had optimistically viewed as a cautious reentry to reality.

Around Michael Picol, Eve noticed, Dru seemed to feel calm and protected in a way that even she could not provide. Dru saw him as her heroic rescuer, the man who had freed her from the horror of the kidnappers. She leaned against him, her fingers clutched around the sleeve of his sweater, looking so very fragile. At least she was out of bed, dressed, and in the living room enjoying other people for the first time since she'd come home, Eve thought. With her short, tousled hair and pale, unmade-up face, she in no way resembled the carefree bride of the year of only a few months ago. But at least she had ventured from her room and there was a look of genuine enjoyment on her face. Eve and Dr Corbett exchanged glances. Maybe everything would turn out all right after all.

As Alex's graceful hands flurried across the keys in what almost seemed like a gesture of passion, Eve's mind flickered back to that evening at the Deerpath Inn. It had been a romantic fantasy, Eve thought, almost blushing at how they had pretended to be strangers without the ubiquitous bodyguards, without responsibilities, or accountabilities. They had met in the dining room of the charming country inn, and during their light supper and wine they had asked each other about their childhoods, dreams, and desires, as if there had been no kidnapping, divorce, or past. Eve had lived out her secret fantasy that night as he led her up the stairs and into a room where she had never been as Eve Donaldson, so she did not have to *be* Eve Donaldson. She would never have had the courage to go to his rented gatehouse in Highland Park, and being with another man in her own house had seemed somehow sacrilegious. She had always been a wife, never a lover. But now *she* made love to a man. In the past she had been passively receptive, while Graham hurried through the motions of lovemaking the way he conducted business deals, but now Eve found herself surprisingly sensual, taking the lead in a subtle seduction of which the cool, aloof Eve became a passionate aggressor. She had imagined she was Grace Kelly seducing Cary Grant, playing out all the elegant little eroticisms she had only conjured up in secret daydreams.

On the outside, she was still the proper Eve, wearing her trademark tweeds and cashmere. But as she removed her clothes, a new Eve emerged from a crysalis. Alex had unhooked her silk stockings from a lacy garter belt borrowed on impulse from Drucilla's drawers, something borrowed she said to herself as she unrolled the stockings one at a time, handing each to Alex as if it were a gift.

With her back to him, she took a tiny flagon of *Fracas* perfume from her evening bag. Turning to face him, she traced the fragrance down her throat and across both breasts.

Reaching back, she pulled the hairpins, one at a time, from her chignon and laid them on the pine dresser.

And then Eve unfolded like one of her late-blooming hothouse orchids, her arms and legs like soft petals opening at last to reveal a delicate, velvety center.

Shyly at first, and then intensely, she had ridden the swelling, warm waves as the act of lovemaking never seemed to end, one position simply leading to another until she soared and flew, holding onto Alex for balance as they surged together and found themselves in an unorchestrated, quiet place neither one of them had ever found before. She remembered finally lying there, his head on her stomach, her hair cascading over the edge of the bed, staring at the beamed ceiling, released from role-playing.

She no longer had to be Mrs Graham Donaldson of the engraved calling cards. She was simply a woman.

A few days later, she had driven downtown to Marshall Field's and bought dozens of pairs of high-cut French silk bikini panties. Her hips and thighs were still taut from all her years of riding and show jumping, and her body now took on a new appeal for her in which she luxuriated. She bought real silk stockings, a Fernando Sanchez negligée slit high on both sides, and retired her Fabergé egg to the safe, since it did not suit her new freedom. Eve would never again be encumbered by things from the past.

She ran her hand up and down her cashmere-sweatered shoulders as the music floated across the room. She had a decision to make. Alex had told her last night that he had been appointed conductor of the Boston Symphony Orchestra. He would be moving to Boston, and he had asked her to come with him as his wife.

What would marriage be like to a man so much younger? True, he was brilliant and loving, and had his own position in the world. He needed her, not for her social standing or her estate, but for the compassion and inspiration she brought to him. It suited Eve to see herself as the stirring inspiration of a musical genius. If not a childlike Constanza to a brilliantly creative but impractical Mozart, she romantically envisioned herself in terms of the great Romantic composer, conductor, and pianist Franz Liszt. Yes, it was only after Princess Carolyne von Sayn-Wittgenstein had entered his life that he wrote the first twelve symphonic poems, the *Faust and Dante* symphonies, the piano sonata, and more. But then she remembered, too, the Princess was never able to obtain a divorce to marry Liszt. Eve was free to marry Alex.

How would people perceive her romance, once they knew? She'd had some hint today, when Paula Deutch had seen Alex lift up her hair to kiss the nape of her neck. Paula, who had gone to school with Eve and Pollyanne, had visibly drawn back, blinking in horror as if she were witnessing an act of incest. Lake Forest could somehow accept Graham's relationship with a woman thirty years younger, but she was obviously relegated to the dowager woodpile, to spend her life escorted by the likes of Cary Leggett.

Drucilla, at least, had seemed to have accepted the situation. She made no value judgments on anyone since her return, and she had even smiled at her mother when Alex took her hand. Perhaps she'd have a delayed reaction in the future, but Dru seemed to be turning away from Eve's old world as much as Eve was. Perhaps Eve's recovering from her life-shattering divorce would encourage the same in her daughter.

As she looked at Dru, Eve reminded herself that she wasn't a child with pink ribbons and pinafores. The best thing she could do for her was to let her live her own life and in time, perhaps with the right man, even Dru's wounds would heal. If she had brought her up well, she would manage.

Even Bambi seemed happy for Eve. She certainly wasn't model-thin anymore, but Eve thought she looked more beautiful. Studying seemed to agree with her. Looking at Bambi now, propped up on her elbows as she lay casually sprawled on the Savonnerie rug, Eve was reminded of Franklin Stuart's natural grace. There had really been nothing delicate about him, yet he had projected the same vulnerability that had made his daughter a superstar. But Bambi would never suffer as her father had, out of her element, in a world passing her by. Bambi set her own standards, and she rose quickly to the top.

Bambi was not a helpless high school girl. She was confident in all she attempted and not afraid to turn down a million-dollar-film contract. Eve only worried that she had never had a normal social life. Growing up with Hughie, even under Eve's supervision, was admittedly unorthodox. For a long time, Eve had wished she could have done more for Bambi, who could have so easily been her own daughter, and whom she had loved as one for so long. But what-ifs and the past were of no use now. Bambi and Hughie did not need her anymore.

Alex did.

Eve focused on Alex's soft, curly hair, falling on to his forehead as he bent over the piano, and wondered what it would be like to live in Boston. She knew that Tanglewood in the Berkshires, the summer home of the symphony with its lush greenery and engaging musicians and aficionados, would be much to her liking. A house in Martha's Vineyard, a place to practice, and garden, was their dream. Boston offered the world of music, fresh starts, and new dreams. The roomful of guests burst into bravos and applause as Alex finished his sonata, and he then looked not into the face of the music critic from the *Chicago Tribune* for approval, but into Eve's own eyes.

# 16

The sun in Portugal was somehow softer, Eve thought. It didn't have that scorching, dry Palm Springs feel or the humidity of Palm Beach in season. On the Algarve, the sun seemed filtered through the almond blossoms that scented the ocean breeze. Eve slipped off the stern ladder of the *Ebony Eve*, the ninety-two foot black-hulled vintage sailboat that had once belonged to Barbara Hutton, and dove head-first into a wave. She had purchased the boat on an impulse when she discovered that Alex loved sailing almost as much as he loved music. The boat was completely automated, with roller-furling sails and an anchor that could be dropped at the push of a button. Only Captain Manuelo was needed to sail it, so Eve and Alex could have their privacy. They would be equally at home cruising the Mediterranean or sailing off Cape Cod this summer.

Eve plunged into wave after wave, swimming toward the shore with strong, sure strokes.

The beach was contoured by mammoth rock formations that jutted twenty feet out of the sand. Standing in shallow water, Eve leaned over, cupped her hands, and scooped up as much water as she could. Then she ran up the beach. Her feet sank into the topaz-colored sand as she looked down at her legs, which, for the first time she could remember, were actually tan.

'If I can't get you into the ocean, I'll bring the ocean to you.' She opened her hands and shook them out playfully, splattering salt water over Alex's shoulders and back, as well as the papers on which he was writing.

'You've just drowned the adagio.' He smiled up at her. 'Luckily, it's all up here.' He pointed to his head. 'Waterproof.'

Eve dropped to her knees beside his orange-striped beach chair. 'How can anyone possibly compose on a beach miles from a piano?'

'I don't need a piano. After all, Beethoven wrote half of his life's work when he was stone-deaf. It's like math – I make sense of it in my head. Listen.' He started to hum a refrain. 'It's to be played with a chamber group. You can hear it, can't you?'

'I love being in love with a genius,' Eve said, smiling.

'Well then, do me a favor, don't drip all over the work of a genius. Besides, you're very distracting in that white bathing suit.'

'Wasn't that the point of this vacation?' Eve and Alex had looked forward to this week together away from everything. The villa in Albufeira had been his surprise. It belonged to Helmut Hermberg, a cellist with the Viennese Symphony Orchestra and his wife Monika, who were taking much delight in introducing Alex and Eve to the charms of this seaside artist colony. They climbed up and down the steep cliff, where whitewashed, terracotta-roofed villas hung over the sea, perilously clinging to the hillside. Mornings were filled with the beach and the pool, everyone wrapped in terrycloth robes. Afternoons were for lazy naps and cruising to the nearby fishing villages, where they sat outside and ate fresh sardines grilled over hot coals. At night, they drank local wines and talked and laughed for hours. The Hermberg villa was always filled with the sound of music, and the two men often practiced together, each building on the other's interpretation, sometimes joined by Eve on the second piano while Monika played the flute.

Alex stroked her ankle, and she leaned toward his chest. He pulled a grape from the woven basket and put it into her mouth with a kiss.

When Eve opened her eyes, she saw Monika on the balcony of the villa, waving a white towel. 'I think I'm being signalled,' she whispered. 'Our picnic must be ready.' She stood up and waved back to Monika. 'Continue being brilliant,' she told Alex as she headed toward the weathered wood steps. Without turning around, she could tell that his eyes were following her all the way up the ten flights of stairs. His obsession with her was almost as great as that with his music.

Alex had been pursued by women on virtually every continent. The musical groupies, as he referred to the never-ending stream of available, easy-to-bed celebrity worshippers, were annoyingly persistent. Eve Donaldson was a rare entity. She was a paradox, he felt, combining a veneer of cool aristocracy with almost naive passion. Alex felt proudly responsible for releasing Eve's suppressed sensuality; together, they had discovered it. And because she understood his music was his first passion, she was willing to let him put it first in his life.

Eve Donaldson didn't play games like the women he'd known before. She knew her priorities, had learned from her experiences, and had been jaded by none of them. She looked at everything and every situation as if she were seeing it for the first time.

He couldn't believe his luck. Graham must be a half-baked fool to let a woman like this go. But if Alex was the recipient of Graham Donaldson's stupidity, he wasn't going to complain.

In the house, Monika was waiting with three urgent

messages, all of them from Bud Felsenthal, Eve's broker, a man she spoke with twice a year at most, and who should have no reason at all to track her down in the Algarve.

Monika shrugged. 'Maybe he has a big, new deal for you.' The words sounded almost quaint in her thick accent.

'But he *never* calls me.' Eve stared at the phone number. 'It must be six in the morning in Chicago.'

She frowned. Graham had always taken care of the financial side of things. Well, now that she was divorced, she supposed she'd be hearing a lot from the broker, the insurance man, the real estate agent. Alex, brilliant and sensitive as he was, was even more inexperienced than she in these areas. Although in the last ten months, she had found that she was much more capable in such situations than she'd ever imagined. She'd set the sale price for the house herself, negotiated the purchase of the *Ebony Eve*, and was closely involved with the complicated separation of her and Graham's finances. Severing the ties that had been so firmly in place since she was eighteen years old had brought out a new side of her that even she hadn't suspected existed. Eve found herself not only accepting her new responsibilities but enjoying them.

She placed the transatlantic call, and Bud Felsenthal came on the line. 'Eve, so sorry to disturb you on your vacation, but this needs your immediate attention.'

'I don't know how helpful I can be. If you have any questions, Graham . . .'

'It concerns your Intercon stock. I got a call from First Corporate Finance. A premium has been offered for your holdings.'

Holdings? Graham had put stock in her name over the years, but her real holdings were the shares from the first issue left to her by her parents. 'My holdings are not for sale.'

'You realize you personally own twenty-five percent of Intercon's outstanding shares. Then there's Drucilla's and the Elizabeth Ann Stuart trust, which you vote. That's a total of forty-six per cent. There's been some unusual activity in the stock. It went up six points last week. Someone's willing to pay a big price for all those shares.'

'Who is it?'

'We don't know. They're buying through a blind – a firm who shields the identity of the investor.'

'I know what a blind is.' Why did financial people always assume everyone else was ignorant? She'd spent enough time with Graham to be familiar with the basic terminology. 'But I don't want to sell. This is my family's company.'

'I realize that, but we're talking megabucks.'

Megabucks. She already had three or four million in her own name. And Bambi's stock was the child's only legacy; Eve had never touched it, and she had no idea, really, what it was worth now. 'What does Graham say?' Felsenthal was his broker, too.

'That's the thing, Eve. Your holdings are separate from Graham's. I think there is a bigger issue at stake here than just the stock. Somebody's making a move, and I'm under obligation to advise you that this could be a chance for serious profit for you, Drucilla, and Bambi. Michael Picol tells me the trusts are very complicated.'

'Should I discuss this with Graham?'

'I'm sure he'd be very interested.'

'Well, how much stock do they want?'

'All of it. They obviously want to assume a position in the company. They're offering seven dollars over the book value.'

Eve knew the book value was now ninety and something. That was almost a ten percent premium. They were talking almost fifty million dollars, Eve calculated. The commission on that would certainly have been an incentive to roust Bud out of his bed in the predawn hours. She looked down at the beach, where Alex was just getting up and collecting his things to come back to the house.

'Listen, Bud. We're just about to go for a picnic sail, and I don't want to keep Alex waiting.'

'Eve, this is important.'

'I'll be home in a few days, Bud. We'll talk about it then. Best to Peggy.' She hung up.

As she went up to her room to shower, she decided she'd call Graham after lunch . . . or dinner. There was no hurry. The money meant nothing. She had enough to live very well. She and Alex were happy. Their life was not based on money, but on music and love. She'd let Graham handle the wheels of fortune, since he was so good at turning them.

She smoothed some aloe cream onto her suntanned face and throat, combed and rebraided her hair, and hurried out of the house, stopping only to pick up the picnic basket. She and Alex would be alone today. Monika and Helmut were planning to visit an artist in Lagos.

Eve handed the picnic basket to Pedro, the houseboy, who ferried it out in the skiff. She and Alex would swim to the boat.

Once they were on the polished teak deck, Eve rubbed Alex's deeply tanned shoulders with a towel as he signalled Captain Manuelo to cast off. He would take the wheel himself after lunch. He and Eve relaxed on black canvas-cushioned deck chairs at a small drop-leaf table, and she laid out the wine, cheese, bread and strawberries as the five billowy black sails unfurled, puffing out one at a time in the Mediterranean sky. As the bowthruster positioned the *Ebony Eve* into the wind, the boat effortlessly pivoted a hundred-and-eighty degrees in fiften seconds and they close-hauled under full sail at twelve knots.

The sleek, black-hulled boat with its ebony sails sliced through the water to the strains of Liszt's piano 'Sonatto del Petracho.'

Eve dipped a ripe strawberry into her wine glass, then licked the wine from the berry.

Alex looked across the table at her. 'I can't wait,' he said, and hurriedly taking her wrist, led her below deck to the cabin. Below deck, the sunlight glinted warmly off the Honduras mahogany paneling. The boat could sleep twenty-three, but they were only interested in one bed at the moment.

A few months before, Eve had been convinced that her life as a woman was over. But now, at forty-nine, she felt like a *femme fatale*, rather than une femme d'une certaine age, as the French politely called middle-aged women. After the hysteroctomy, Graham had never touched her. She had donated his guilt-gift, the obscene sapphire heart, to the jewel collection at the Field Museum and taken the tax deduction. She wished she could have written off the last two years as easily. She had come so close to self-defeat, but she had ultimately made it. Like the phoenix rising out of the ashes, she was a new woman, burning with desire instead of languishing in middle-aged insecurities. She again knew fire and passion and romance. How much more satisfying it was to be made love to on a sleek sailboat off the coast of Portugal than to be an untouchable icon in the cover of *Town & Country*. How much better it was to have Alex's graceful fingers graze her breast than a million dollars' worth of jewels shimmering at her throat.

A powdery white film of dried sea salt made their bodies slightly rough and sandpapery to the touch. They passed through the grand salon, into the black-carpeted master stateroom, and through a brass-fitted, louvered mahogany door. The master bath had a whirlpool tub, but Alex and Eve stepped into the teak-lined shower, where they took turns rinsing the sand off each other's bodies. It was not the warm water she felt on her bare body as he slipped off her suit, but his touch. As Alex traced the lines of her body, she stood straight and tall, confident about her lean, elegant figure. Her breasts and thighs were still firm, her stomach only slightly rounded. What imperfections there were he seemed to love, including the six-inch keloid scar that dissected her belly. Alex knelt and kissed the scar gently, tracing its length with his tongue. She followed his face with her hands, knowing he loved to watch her touch herself.

He turned her around and caressed her buttocks as his fingers explored parts of her body that had never been touched. Once they had dried themselves, Alex rubbed her with almond oil until they slipped against each other in a rhythm.

'Show me your body,' he whispered.

And she did. Eve Donaldson, who had always made love in a nightgown in the dark, relished every moment she stood naked before Alex. Their images were reflected in the vanity table's mirror, and Eve watched Alex clear away a collection of shells before lifting her onto its polished surface. He spread her legs open in front of him, and she watched his fingers caress her skin until she shivered at every gentle touch.

'Do you like this?' he breathed as he moved into her.

'Or this?' He moved more quickly, his hand stroking small circles on her breast.

Eve loved hearing his voice when they made love. Graham had always echoed a series of groans in the darkness, but when Alex spoke to her she felt connected. Love flowed between them, and their sex life was an extension of their closeness.

'Touch me. Yes,' she bit her lip. 'Touch me there.'

Eve threw back her head, her spine pressed against the glass, and she watched their bodies come together, molding into one continuous form. She wound her legs tighter around Alex's waist and pulled him to her. Running her fingers through his hair, she was reminded of how much younger he was. There was not a trace of gray there, his body was slim and smooth, and he had enough energy to make love over and over again, pleasing Eve as frequently as he pleased himself. She was excited by the mere sight of him, by his desire to thrust them both into unparalleled ecstasy. She wanted him as she had never wanted any man in her life.

'What to you want? Tell me?'

She felt a muscle in his arm tighten behind her neck, and she answered. 'Fuck me, Alex. Fuck me again.'

Arms around his chest, cheek on his shoulder, eyes turned toward the open porthole and the sky, she thought, if my friends could see me now.

# 17

'So what the hell was going on here? Were all you guys sitting around with your thumbs up your asses?' In all the years at Intercon no one had ever heard a venomous tone in Graham Donaldson's voice. Irv Turner fidgeted uncomfortably in the chair directly opposite Graham's desk. A silent Catherine anxiously watched a vein twitching in his neck.

'Bill Ackerman must be asleep at the switch,' Graham fumed. 'I thought those bankers of his were supposed to watch the stock. Instead, I get a call from my ex-wife!'

No cne was willing to say it, but ever since the kidnapping the company had lain virtually dormant. During the reign of the triumvirate, there had been more infighting than decisions. The lines of responsibility had been hopelessly confused. Bill Ackerman might very well have tried to contact Graham, or even Michael Picol, but communication had not been terribly efficient.

Turner shrugged. 'What would we have done if we had known? I couldn't order a fucking paper clip without getting a three-way consensus. We're lucky twenty-five companies weren't down our throats.' He mumbled under his breath, 'You know what a camel is? It's a horse put together by a committee.' He shot a look at Catherine, who was seated cross-legged on the window sill. Michael Picol was a few feet away, his features obscured in the darkened corner.

Graham raised a hand. 'All right, all right. We're not

getting anywhere. The question is, what are we gonna do about it? Picol?'

His voice was measured, 'Legally, we can't respond to what hasn't happened. They're doing all their buying in street name, and they don't have their five percent yet, so they don't have to file . . . but still . . .'

Graham cut him off. 'I'm putting Ackerman on the speakerphone,' Graham said, leaning forward in his swivel chair. 'I've got Picol, Turner, Sam Adams, and Catherine McBride here in my office.'

Ackerman's voice came over the speakers, barely masking hysteria. 'The cloudburst has started. They've already got four point nine percent and the fat's in the fire.'

'Who is it?'

'Trans-Oceanic.'

Turner looked confused. Catherine sat straight up.

'How big are they?'

'Big enough,' Ackerman answered. 'Very interesting company. They're South American. No visible assets except for casinos in the Caribbean. Credit line up to six billion dollars, which means their holdings are hidden. This is not amateur hour!' Ackerman's voice rose. 'With that kind of money, for all I know they own my firm! What does Picol say about these guys?'

'I know them. They're a holding house for South American money. Very glitzy. Intercon's not their style. If they were after an oil company, they'd go for Occidental or Global.'

'Talk to you later.' Graham cut off the speakerphone. 'So. We have ten days. Who's got what to say?'

Turner made an attempt at levity. 'Why don't I get a golf game with their chairman?'

Nobody laughed.

The temperature of the room seemed to drop by ten

degrees as everyone realized they were in for a seige.

Sam Adams adjusted his glasses. 'How secure is the Donaldson trust?' He leaned over Graham's shoulder.

'I'm in control of that. We've still got forty-six percent, don't we, Michael?'

Picol nodded. 'Yeah, but some of that's in trusts you don't vote.'

'Eve and Dru will vote with me,' Graham said confidently.

'Well then,' Catherine jumped in. 'How about taking the offensive?' She purposefully did not look at Turner. He had continually vetoed any suggestion that came from her. She had sat quietly on the windowsill for the past hour, except for a curt, occasional question, but she couldn't hold back when all Turner could come up with were jokes. Graham needed her now.

But he just shook his head. 'You're talking a Pacman strategy. Problem is, they're probably a bigger fish.'

'We could issue some junk bonds to raise capital,' Turner suggested, hiking up his pants.

Sam Adams threw up his hands. 'The risk is too high here. Their capital is limitless, isn't it? Who's making their decisions?'

Nobody seemed to know.

Graham continued, 'I don't believe in acquisitions financed by debt. We'd be putting all our money into paying off the interest. We'd have no equity left. Six billion dollars. Shit.' He carefully emptied the tobacco from his pipe.

Picol straightened up and moved away from the wall into a patch of light filtering through the blinds. 'Look, this is probably nothing more than greenmail. As far as I know, this move is totally out of character for Trans-Oceanic. They don't even own a refinery. What would they want with us? Cash is their specialty. They can jack up the price of the stock and force us to put all our capital toward buying them out at a profit. I would base our defense on that strategy.' He moved back into the shadows as if his performance was over.

Graham nodded. 'Okay, let's reconvene at noon and meanwhile I want a complete rundown on Trans-Oceanic and all their people. Catherine, hold on a minute.'

When the room was empty, Graham, motioned for her to close the door. He rubbed his forehead.

'Graham, I'll stand behind you a hundred percent, but I think it's time to let on about the oil find. It's too dangerous to have secrets when we're under the magnifying glass.' She tapped her silver belt buckle. 'Besides, if this thing gets serious, we could use it for a crown jewel defense.'

'No.' Graham pushed his chair a good three feet away from her. 'A Place in the Sun stays as is. Understood? Those oil deposits are only preliminary reports.' He emphasized the word, accentuating all five syllables.

'What about Eve? What if she decides to sell?'

He brushed the air. 'Eve's never made a decision on her own except picking out the drapery fabric. She doesn't even know what her holdings are. In all the years since we've been married, she's always relied on me.'

Catherine winced. 'But you're not married anymore.'

'Eve is totally incapable of deciding things without me. In fact, there's a family problem I want your help with. Eve called in a panic this morning.' Graham was visibly troubled. His voice was grim. 'Drucilla is pregnant.'

Catherine didn't say anything. Poor Graham, she thought.

'She was raped on the boat . . . by the kidnappers.' He looked at her.

Catherine calculated the months since the kidnapping. At best, she'd have to be three months pregnant.

'Can she still have an abortion? What do the doctors say?' Damn Drucilla. she thought. She pitied the girl, but she also resented Dru's insistent dependency, which kept distracting Graham from equally grave business matters. It was almost as if she were trying to undermine Graham. She was a grown woman, like Catherine. Why did she demand all her father's emotions?

'Well, that's the whole thing. For some weird reason, she wants to keep it. It's insane.'

The whole thing was insane, Catherine thought. She sat down on the edge of his desk. 'She's confused. She's probably still suffering the shock of the kidnapping.'

'She won't listen to her mother. But I was thinking, she might listen to somebody closer to her age. Like you.'

Catherine almost groaned aloud. She wondered how Graham could be so blind. Didn't he realize that his daughter blamed *her* for the divorce? And clearly Drucilla was off-balance. They should just put her under medical supervision. Pregnant! That was the last thing Graham needed with this takeover battle beginning.

'I've scheduled lunch tomorrow with Dr Corbett and Drucilla. I'd like you to be there, Catherine.' He suddenly looked vulnerable.

'Graham, she wouldn't want me there. And I'm going to be very busy here. So are you. Honey, she's a grown woman. She needs professional help.' Would this ever end? Would an ex-wife and daughter always rule this man? The company needed him now. *She* needed him now.

'Graham, I just can't go.'

'Well, I can't let my daughter have some rapist's child. God knows what kind of creature it would be.'

Catherine thought carefully before she spoke. 'It would be your grandchild.' She paused for a moment. 'Maybe it should be her own decision.' The best thing she could do for Graham was to help his daughter get back on her own two feet. 'Whatever it is, it would be half her child, too.'

Graham stared at her. 'She can't keep it. It's ridiculous.'

Catherine felt herself sag inside. Every time it seemed as if there would be a chance for the two of them, something out of her control seemed to pull them apart. 'I'll see you at noon.'

She patted his shoulder and closed the door quietly behind her.

# 18

As Eve breezed through the sixth floor of Marshall Field's in the elegant Water Tower Place shopping complex, she knew she not only looked different, she felt different. It was good to be making purchases for a new life, not just for a different charity party. Let's see, she'd bought a complete set of hand-thrown pottery, some pewter cutlery, and even pewter salt and pepper shakers – all for the house in Martha's Vineyard that she and Alex didn't even own yet.

'Oh, don't bother putting them in a box,' she smiled at the enthusiastic salesgirl as she clipped on the new Paloma Picasso topaz-and-sterling octagon earrings. 'I'll wear them.' The earrings went beautifully with the ivory-and-topaz necklace Alex had had made for her in Greece. She'd retired the Fabergé egg to the safety deposit box last month and had decided to put it up for sale at Sotheby's. Real women with real lives didn't wear a dead czarina's jewels, Eve had decided. They were for murky museums, not her vibrant new world. Eve had even considered giving the Fabergé egg to Pollyanne, since during the last election Pollyanne had seemed to be campaigning for czarina as opposed to First Lady. Her old school friend appeared to have lost her perspective and was consumed by her press and public appearances. The significance of the gift would undoubtedly be lost on her. And besides, the egg would fetch a good price at Sotheby's and with all of her and Alex's plans, Eve was going to have to sell off some of the Benton and Donaldson paintings and jewels to finance a new life for Mr and Mrs Alex Levin. It turned out that much of the Donaldson's extravagant lifestyle – the planes, cars, travel, entertainment – had been company money. There wasn't nearly as much as she had anticipated, and she and Alex had dreams for a scholarship program, a new orchestra, a cozy house . . . well, it all cost so much to be done right.

She glanced quickly in the mirror as she adjusted the earrings. It had been only two weeks since she'd had her eyes done but you could hardly tell. The stitches were out, there was no swelling, and the microscopic scars were hidden completely in the natural movement of her expressions. With the help of a dab of foundation, all you could say about Eve was that she looked fresher and her skin smoother. She hadn't mentioned the eye lift to anyone, not Alex, or Dru, and especially not to Pollyanne, who would grab onto any beauty secret and spread it around like a press release. She had spent two hours last week extolling the virtues of bee jelly on toast for breakfast.

Eve had the eye lift for herself. Having cried so many tears, she felt the surgery was like removing the sadness from around her eyes. In her white Krizia sweater and knit skirt, with her hair down and her skin still aglow from the Portuguese sun, she looked nothing like the older woman who had been 'deserted by her husband for a younger woman.' Instead, she looked the way Grace Kelly would have if she'd married Cary Grant and lived the life of Eve's fantasies. In fact, she could almost sympathize with Graham for finding a younger woman attractive. After all, hadn't Alex brought something vibrant and special into her own life?

She picked up her silver-gray shopping bag from the counter-top. The plates and her whole wardrobe for Martha's Vineyard could be sent, but she wanted to give

Drucilla the half-dozen French men's shirts that she had adopted as her pregnancy uniform. Actually, for the first time since the kidnapping, Dru looked alive. At first, Eve had been appalled by the thought of her daughter delivering a child conceived in rape. But as the new life grew within Drucilla, her daughter's own life seemed to return. And, after all, who was Eve to condemn anyone's choices? Her own life, which had been a so-called fairy tale, had been, she now realized, a façade in which she had played a Lake Forest geisha to a corporate megalomaniac. Perhaps it was better not to make judgements.

Eve had only met Grace Kelly once, at a Red Cross ball in Monte Carlo, but she now wondered if the rumors about Her Serene Highness and her young daughter on the day of that fatal drive down the Corniche were true. Eve had heard from her friends who summered in the South of France that there had been a heated argument in which the princess, who epitomized 1950's values, had tried to impose her views on her New Wave teenage daughter. Nothing constructive ever came out of nagging, haranguing, and attempts to force the issue. It was the relationship that counted. She had learned that from Alex. And Eve wasn't about to sacrifice her relationship with her daughter, or her future grandchild. If it was to be, she would accept it as a gift, not a curse.

Eve stopped at the stationery department on her way out of Field's. She hated department stores, but the classic marble atmosphere of Water Tower Place was more like an elegant candy store, and shopping there resembled moving through a colorful bazaar overflowing with exotic temptations where you could always say, 'Charge it.'

She looked at a wonderful crocodile notebook that would be perfect for Alex, who was always rushing around looking for scraps of paper. As she stared at the samples of engraved invitations, Eve wondered whether it would be appropriate to send out birth announcements when her grandchild was born. Her old sense of decorum was hard to shake. Well, there was plenty of time to decide. She closed the heavy sample book. She'd have to be sending out her own change-of-address cards soon, but somehow she wasn't quite prepared to deal with that publicly yet. She'd get to that later. It was almost time to meet Hughie.

She breezed across the street. It was one of those rare Chicago days when the weather was perfect, the skies clear and sunny, with a clean wind off the lake. Cricket's was only a block away, so there was no need to move the car.

Eve shuddered and averted her eyes as she passed the massive Gothic church in which Drucilla and Arnaud had been married. There was no way she could avoid it, since it stood smack in the middle of Michigan Avenue on a corner she had to turn. If things had gone according to their well-laid Lake Forest plans, Drucilla would be married and expecting an heir to the de Cotrille title, not the child of an unknown assailant. Eve resolutely turned her head and focused on a flock of red and blue umbrellas in the windows of Crate and Barrel.

'Hello, Mrs Donaldson.' The doorman at the Tremont Hotel opened a pair of doors and ushered Eve into the small private lobby. She walked through the darkened bar to the main dining room, where the maître d' kissed her on both cheeks before escorting her to her usual booth, which was variously occupied by Ann Landers, Christie Hefner, the former mayor, the head of the Art Institute, or served as headquarters for whoever was currently reigning in Chicago's power lunch set.

Eve settled into the banquettes and laughed as she looked up to see the three-foot-long toy Intercon oil truck, perfectly sized to scale, dangling from small chains directly above the table. Aside from the red-and-white check tablecloths, the decor of the restaurant was focused on the ceiling, which was covered with enough miniature trucks, tankers, airplanes, boats, and logos representing all the major corporations and companies in Chicago, to fill FAO Schwartz. These were big boys' toys representing the highest level of success. The stuffed Harris Bank lion, the Gould missile, a tiny *Chicago Tribune* truck, the US Steel hardhat, and the red-and-yellow cement mixer from Material Services symbolized the patronage of some of the most important officers in the biggest businesses in town.

'Well,' Eve looked up. 'Here I am, still under the Intercon wing.'

Hughie adjusted the table between them. 'Would you rather have sat under a sausage?' He pointed to a giant salami bearing the Beatrice logo.

'Well, maybe this is an appropriate table after all.' Eve pointed to the signature of sisters Abigail ('Dear Abby') Van Buren and Ann Landers, which were scrawled on the wall behind them, just to the right of a framed signature of opera tenor Pavarotti. 'Advice to the lovelorn,' Eve said. 'This is a perfect place for me to sit.' She smiled.

'Who needs Dear Abby and Ann Landers when you've got Hughie?' he said. 'Haven't I always steered you in the right direction?'

'Well, you *did* send me to Dr Kirby.'

'And your eyes make you look ten years younger. There's not even a trace of a bruise.'

'Maybe all that vitamin C and zinc Pollyanne made me take helped,' said Eve.

'That woman,' Hughie leaned over, 'has gone totally over the edge. Did you see she missed two official receptions in a row? I heard from one of my stylists that she wouldn't go because her hair didn't look right.'

'I'm sure that's not true, but maybe she does need a little attention from Rex.' She put down the menu.

Eve ordered a half portion of grilled swordfish. 'I think we ought to pool all of our advice and give it to Graham.' She sighed. 'Poor Graham. His little friend had him running in circles. In fact, he has *big* circles under his eyes and his color isn't the same. I'd hate to have him keel over like Henry Hudson. I wish I could help him. He blames himself for everything, especially Drucilla.' She sipped her Evian and lime.

Hughie took a big gulp of his Kir Royale. Poor Graham! He banged the glass down on the table so hard, the champagne spilled over onto his hand, catapulting Antoine, the always-alert maître d', over to the table to mop it up. Although it had been rumored that Antoine had just put down a six-figure deposit for the two vintage brownstones down the block, he always treated his customers as if he had been born to serve them.

'Sorry?' Hughie hissed. 'How can you possibly feel compassion for someone who broke up your home, humiliated you in front of the world, and cost you most of your friends?'

'They weren't really my friends,' Eve whispered. 'Alex saw right through them.'

'Graham deserves everything he gets,' Hughie snorted. 'Even the Catherine McBitch. *How* can you defend him? Most women would have had him hung.' He buttered his roll with vengeance. 'Sweetheart, maybe I should send Graham to Dr Kirby. But then, he doesn't do lobotomies, just baby eye lifts.'

Eve folded her hands and rested them on top of the table. 'Hughie, I would like you to remember, I am still a

Donaldson. We're still a family. And you and Bambi are still very much a part of that family.' Her rigid back inched even farther from the banquette. She'd tried so hard for so long to bring Hughie into the Donaldson fold, but somehow he always resisted. But then, he was Franklin Stuart's son. He'd inherited his father's pride.

Hughie leaned forward, so intense that the waiter carrying a plate of crudités backed off before setting it down. 'The Donaldson name has nothing to do with this. It was my father and your father – my father's stock and your father's stock.' He gave a bitter snort. 'How dare you give yourself so little credit?' Hughie couldn't believe that Eve still didn't separate myth from fact. 'Your father left you with his life's inheritance, Eve, and he'd be doing a tarantella in his grave if he ever knew you were risking it for a victim of male menopause. Graham has gone crazy. Everything he's doing is totally irrational, Eve, why can't you realize that?' Hughie shredded his roll, leaving crumbs all over the table.

'Shh!' Eve warned. 'Kup's at the next table. Do you want to read about this in his column tomorrow?'

'It's true, Eve. He stinks. The guy's deranged. Walks out on one of the most beautiful women in the world, a woman, incidentally, who brought him a dowry of a company.'

'A little company, which he built into one of the biggest in the world.'

The waiter discreetly inched up to the table, placed Hughie's appetizer of escargots and Eve's salad before them, making himself as invisible as possible.

'At least you'll make a fortune on the stock,' Hughie mumbled.

'Sell? I wouldn't think of selling. We're not going to let foreigners take over father's and Graham's company.'

'It was *my* father – and grandfather – too, and Bambi's. Graham did us out of what should have been ours, just like he'll do you out of what should be yours if you don't stand up for yourself. A million-dollar divorce settlement is peanuts, Eve, compared to what you'd get out of that stock.'

Her mouth tightened. Why did Hughie have to rummage through the drawers of the past in a public place? And especially since she'd succeeded so well in putting everything in its place, out of sight, out of mind, and focusing on the future with Alex. She and Alex had plans. There was the new orchestra endowment, which would allow Bach to be played on the original instruments of the period of the composition. There was the school for gifted students that they wanted to set up at Tanglewood. There were so many positive things happening that she couldn't understand why he had to dredge up the past. She tapped a fingernail against the edge of her salad plate. Well, perhaps Hughie wasn't totally to be blamed. She'd never really told him the whole story, preferring to let Franklin remain a glorious image of fatherhood to his children. She'd never seen the point in letting Hughie and Bambi know how their father had sunk into debt or that she had bailed him out secretly time and time again by buying his worthless Benton and Stuart stock at twice its book value. Nor did she tell them of how Franklin had mistaken her generosity for renewed love. She would never, ever tell Hughie about that night when Graham was in Saudi Arabia and Elizabeth was pregnant with Bambi, when she had held Franklin Stuart in her arms as the aristocratic, sensitive soul sobbed out his failures and weaknesses. And out of sympathy, not passion, she had allowed him to make half-hysterical love to her. It had been a terrible mistake, she had realized immediately. Franklin's despair had only increased; his obsession with Eve became maniacal and suicidal. She had finally had to put a stern halt to his insistent letters and phone calls.

After Bambi's birth, when the Stuarts had gone to Austria, Eve had sent a final telegram that spelled out the fact that Mr and Mrs Graham Donaldson would not be joining Franklin and Elizabeth. They would be happily spending the summer together in their newly acquired ranch in Wayzata. Between the lines, her meaning was too clear for the fragile Franklin Stuart. Of course, she would never have sent such a telegram had she realized that Franklin's recent outside investments, his last hope for the future, had been such an abrupt disaster. He had lost virtually all of his capital and was deeply in debt, all in a matter of days. She had not taken his frantic transatlantic phone calls, not realizing that Franklin's passion was a misguided cry for help, for a return to the safety of the charmed days of sunset rides and afternoon sails. In his alcohol-wasted mind, she later realized, Franklin had rationalized that if he recaptured Eve, he could recapture those days of irresponsibility and innocence. Even Bambi, the world's most charming baby, could not save him; in fact, he saw her as a barrier, one more burden to shoulder, one more responsibility to weigh down his imagination.

When Franklin had ranted on about taking his own life, Eve had dismissed it as another ploy for her attention. But when word of the 'accident' reached them, she knew, in a sickening realization, exactly what had happened.

Out of remorse and guilt, she had rushed to Europe to make the arrangements and take care of the children. At her imploring, Graham, Hughie's guardian, had worked for months to sell the Stuart mansion, which had been Hughie's inheritance in the absence of any cash, and cover Franklin's debts so the children could have a fresh start. Eve knew that Hughie had never forgiven Graham for the sale of the house. But it had never dawned on Hughie that Graham had had no choice. And Eve had taken all the stock she had bought from Franklin Stuart and put it in trust for Bambi, adding it to the shares her father had left her. Hughie did not have to know about everything, but perhaps he should know about this.

'I have a trust in Bambi's name,' Eve announced quietly.

'Trust?'

'I did what I could. I did everything to protect both of you. And Graham allowed me to do so.'

'*Allowed*? But Eve, that was *your* stock.'

'It was stock that I purchased from your father. Franklin had fallen in debt and I had secretly purchased some stock from him. I added it to the shares he left your sister in his will. She got the stock, you got the house. The details aren't important. After all, you have been left the house . . .'

'Which Graham sold.'

'Because he had to,' she continued. Her stomach was in knots, but her voice remained calm. How could Hughie doubt what she and Graham had done for him out of sheer love? 'It was quite – undervalued – at the time.'

Hughie frowned incredulously. 'Well, where-the-hell-is-Bambi's stock?' The sentence tumbled out like one long word.

'Her proxies are voted with mine, just like Dru's. You see, Graham did treat Bambi like our own daughter. I really don't know,' she continued coolly. 'It was Benton and Stuart stock. I'm sure it was all handled properly. The Northern Trust handled everything for me. We've always viewed this as a family affair. Everything is handled and voted as a block.' She shrugged. 'I couldn't even tell you how much stock *I* have. I just get the interest statements. Bambi's interest is automatically reinvested by the Northern people.'

'Are you telling me that Bambi is a major Intercon shareholder?'

Eve was getting exasperated. 'Darling, I don't *know* about these things. I haven't seen her stock certificates in fifteen years. I planned to look into it when she turned eighteen since there was no point in doing so before the trust matured.'

'Well, I'd like to know. Why wasn't I told?'

'Darling, you were a little boy who had just lost his mommy and daddy.'

'Lost? Bullshit. He shot her and turned around and killed himself.'

Eve couldn't move. She stared at the checkered tablecloth, struggling to keep her composure.

'I found letters in the attic. Those poems to you. My father saved every scrap of paper you ever wrote to him. Graham Donaldson destroyed my father just like he robbed my father's part of the company.' He jabbed his fork in Eve's direction. 'You and Bambi and I are in the same boat, Eve. And if you have the trust for Bambi, which you do, and you have plans for the future, which you do, then, yes, let's vote as a block. Vote that son-of-a-bitch out.'

He skewered three escargots on his fork and kept jabbing the rubbery creatures into the scalloped plate. 'Graham always had a mistress, Eve. Before Catherine McBitch, it was Intercon. And your divorce settlement was snail shit,' he snorted. Looking up, he saw her stricken face and his voice softened. 'What are you doing after lunch?' He reached out and took her hand. He hated to hurt her, he really did. But Bambi's rights were at stake.

'I . . . I . . . I'm meeting Alex later at Orchestra Hall,' she stammered.

'Via a detour to the Northern Trust.'

# 19

'Oh, Michael, I'm so excited! You're here!' Her bare, milk-white breasts bouncing, Winnie Lifton hiked up her high-cut bikini bottom and bounded across the wrap-around sixty-foot terrace to the glass sliding doors. Picol stepped out onto the balcony of his penthouse on the top floor of Miami's Jockey Club. Even without her customary three-inch heels, Winnie propelled herself on tiptoe as she threw her arms around his shoulders.

'Don't get all that suntan slop on my suit,' he said. He was dressed for a meeting, perfectly tailored in his custom-made Italian suit.

She tugged at his tie, teasing. 'It's so *hot* here, why don't you take off some of these clothes.'

He pushed her away with a half-grin. 'Turn around and let me get a good look at you.'

She spun around *en pointe*, careening dangerously against the flimsy railing that defined the view of the harbor and cool, blue bay forty floors below. On the Jockey tennis courts, multitudes of girls not unlike Winnie Lifton vied for sixty-five-year-old men distinguished by their racquets, varicose veins, and gold chains.

'Did you miss me? I watered all the plants.' She pointed to the hibiscus that rimmed the terrace as if they had bloomed in honor of his arrival. 'I've gone marketing at Publix. Got all your favorite fruits and drinks and health food stuff . . .' She rattled breathlessly, counting off the shopping list on her fingers. 'I've been working the juicer for *hours*. There's fresh pineapple and papaya juice in the 'fridge.'

'Good girl. Get me a glass.'

She bounced across the sharp carpet like an honors graduate from a go-go geisha school and returned with a silver tumbler garnished with a strawberry.

'Your ass is sagging.' He took a big gulp of pineapple juice.

'What!' She twisted backward in panic. 'Where? That's ridiculous!'

'Well, it's drooping.'

'It couldn't be. I work out every day.' A frantic expression crossed her round little face. 'It is not, and you're mean. And I squeezed the fruit and everything.'

He reached out to grab her behind. 'I'll squeeze this.'

She hit his hand away. 'If you don't like the merchandise, don't touch it.'

'You can get it fixed. Don't worry. Forget it.'

'No!' She pouted. 'I'm a movie star.'

'That's why you've gotta be perfect. I'm doing you a favor.'

She was still petulant. 'You fly all the way from Chicago to Miami to tell me I'm not pretty enough!'

'A big ass is cute. Some men like big asses.'

She checked out her left thigh. 'Are *you* some men?' Winnie reverted back to a more whimsical attitude. She coerced more out of him with teasing and her ability to make him laugh than arguing. He could get very mean and ugly when he got angry enough. Her ability to keep things light, make him forget business and laugh at her or with her was the basis of their relationship. And sex, of course. She coyly lifted up one hip and slid an arm across the opposite shoulder.

Picol pulled off his tie. 'Stop looking at yourself. It

makes me nervous.' He unbuttoned the top of his shirt, reached out, caught her by her twenty-inch waist, and wrapped it with the Hermès tie, emblazoned with gold and blue bugles.

'You were just teasing, right?' She threw back her hair and slowly sank down to her knees on the bright yellow sunbathing mat that was laid out on the brick terrace. She untied the tie and handed it back to him.

'Just keep this thing away from my neck,' he grimaced.

She gave him a wounded look. 'Don't remind me! Poor Romulo! It's just too awful.' She had had to sublet the apartment after the nasty incident with Perez, since she could never take another bath there again. She'd managed to stay out of LA by shooting on location, and in two days she was scheduled to begin an episode of *Miami Underground*. No one had ever linked her with Perez, thank God, but Winnie still felt her career had stagnated. She'd gone against her agent's advice and not renewed her contract on *Southwest*. She had decided that she belonged on the big screen, not on videotape reruns. But after Perez's death, the Winnie Lifton Film Retrospective had never materialized. Maybe Michael could help her. He knew everybody. Then again, maybe he was right about her figure. She was due in a few weeks to read for a movie in which she would be cast as an aerobics instructor/ undercover detective. Sort of a female Rambo. Ninety percent of her character's scenes were to be shot in revealing leotards. She'd have to shape up fast. Michael was very perceptive, and he usually was right. Even the Perez thing hadn't been a total disaster. She had ended up with a flawless collection of unset emeralds as magnificent as Merle Oberon's once had been.

Michael stood over her, looking into her eyes. She could tell by his expression that his hard edge was softening. He really did care for her. She knew it.

'I know a doctor. He does that fat vacuuming,' Picol suggested.

'Where they suck the fat out?'

'They can do it any place. Suction lipectomy. You ought to get it done.'

Winnie was horrified. 'I'm a big star! I can't be seen going into a plastic surgeon's office.'

'Call Theresa at the office. She'll give you the name of this guy who comes to the house. He's a friend of mine. Real discreet.'

He tossed her the Hermès tie. 'Here. Tie this around your eyes.'

'Oh, are we going to play Blind Man's Bluff?'

'I don't like you staring at me.' He jerked down her bikini bottom and she giggled. Michael was so unpredictable, she thought.

Picol pushed her against the mat with his full weight. There was no need to take off his jacket. Who was she, anyway. She was nothing. She was a whore, no different from any other woman. If you let them get a hook into your soul, Michael thought, they'd leave you. Ruin you. They pretended to fall in love, to care, but they didn't. Women were all like his mother. When it came right down to it she hadn't really loved her child. She'd walked away, and Michael had never trusted any woman. They'd turn on you in a second.

Women like Winnie, however, were easier. They could be bought. But lately he suspected she might be trying to weasel her way under his skin, even love him. He had decided not to let her get too close; to punish her even, by using her for a quick fuck. It was easier blindfolded, where he was anonymous, impersonal.

He unbuckled his belt, opened his pants, and guided

Winnie's mouth onto his erection. The more he pulled at her or tugged at her breasts, the harder Winnie sucked him. He wanted to fuck her, and so he pulled out, shoved her down onto the mat again and, holding her hands above her head, he thrust into her. Michael ignored her whimpering cries, and concentrated solely on pleasing himself.

When he was done, he got up without looking back toward the terrace, walked inside, picked up the phone, and dialed his secretary.

'Theresa. It's me. I just came in from the airport. Any word from Herrera?'

'Mr Herrera will be arriving at the Palm Bay Club at five o'clock. And Catherine McBride has been trying to reach you. She's left four messages. Oh, and I sent flowers to Henry Hudson. The secretary is going back to the office today.'

'Hey, thanks. You take pretty good care of me.' An important part of Theresa's job was to smooth over his own idiosyncratic and social faux pas. After a long recovery, Hudson was returning to work even though it was only a ceremonial gesture. 'Transfer me to McBride.'

'Michael, thank God. Where are you?' Catherine wondered how any one man could disappear so completely so frequently.

'Getting ready for an important meeting.'

'You've got to get back here right away. Something's happened.'

'Hold on. We can handle this over the phone. I'm right here.'

Her voice was edged with fatigue and exasperation. 'Well, I wish you'd bounce back in here because Graham's just gone right over the edge. He's planning to run a full-page open letter to the board of directors of Trans-



G. I. H. P. - 23

Oceanic in Wednesday's *Wall Street Journal* and *New York Times*.'

'Oh, shit.'

'Yeah. The letter states that under no circumstances will we be taken over, and while he's at it he takes a few shots at Trans-Oceanic. And he says that the Intercon family is committed to research and development and the defense and betterment of America, all that stuff. He makes it sound like an institution on the level of the Founding Fathers is going to fall into the hands of a bunch of wetbacks without green cards. This verges on libel. You've got to get back here and stop this. I think I almost had him ready to listen to reason about using A Place in the Sun as the crown jewel. But then this Drucilla thing came up. He's put it on the line between my loyalty to him and my loyalty to the company.'

Winnie teetered out of the dressing room like a tigh-trope walker, balancing seven shoeboxes, which she put down carefully on the living room floor.

Picol turned his head.

Winnie pulled each pair of shoes from the tissue paper and lined them up in a row on the couch. Two of the Susan Bennis/Warren Edwards shoes cost five hundred dollars a pair, but she loved the ones that spelled out 'Pop' in pink hand-tooled leather. The Maud Frizons and Mario Valentinos were over three hundred dollars. She hadn't bothered to ask the price of the Gucci hunter-style boots. Winnie darted to Picol's side, turned him around to face the couch, pointed to the shoes, waved the bill in front of his oblivious face with a kiss, and tucked it into his pants pocket, absolving herself of fiscal responsibility. After the Perez incident, Picol had given her carte blanche at three different Madison Avenue stores. He'd felt so terrible that he couldn't comfort her in person.

He shrugged Winnie off as she put her arms around his waist.

'Listen to this.' Catherine dropped her voice. 'Drucilla is pregnant. It's really blown Graham away. This thing is a nightmare. All he does is talk to psychiatrists and obstetricians. You've got to get back here and put some pressure on.'

He took off his jacket for the first time since he had landed in Miami. The room was suddenly very warm. 'What do you mean she's pregnant?' He waved off the Winnie Lifton circus.

'She was raped. During the kidnapping. And Graham's hysterical because she's insisting on keeping the baby. And she doesn't even know what the father looked like because she told Eve she'd been blindfolded when it happened. And Eve, Mrs Coat-of-Arms and guardian of the DAR who can reel off every ancestor on the family tree, is actually siding with Drucilla. God knows what the baby will be, and Graham's a basket case over it. He isn't exactly ecstatic over his first grandchild being a mystery guest.'

The heat was getting oppressive in the apartment. God, didn't Winnie ever turn on the air conditioning? Beads of sweat broke out on Picol's face. 'Hold on.' He put down the phone and walked over to the thermostat. It was set at sixty-eight. He turned it down to forty-five. The damn thing was probably broken.

When he got back on the phone, Catherine was going on about the legal ramifications of a dissident shareholder.

'I'm not so sure we can count on Eve, either,' she was saying. 'She has a new life now. Maybe she'll want to cash out. Graham can't believe it, but I do. That woman is bitter, and . . .'

'So is she going to have the baby or not?'

'Haven't you been listening? You're as bad as Graham. I'm talking about the *takeover*.'

'When is the baby due?'

'God,' she sighed. 'In a few months. What are you worried about, that she'll make you the godfather? Maybe you'd better stay where you are, on second thought. Eve's got her net out for potential husbands to give the baby a name.' She laughed. 'Even Hughie Stuart's name came up. What a joke! Then they tried to name it a de Cotrille, but Arnaud went on record on the *Today Show* when he got the annulment during the kidnap interview, that the marriage was never consummated.'

'I'm coming back tonight. I'll be in the office at eight o'clock tomorrow morning. I'll talk to you then.' Picol dropped the phone.

Winnie playfully tickled the back of his neck.

'Lay off me,' he spat. 'Don't touch me.'

Winnie backed off timidly. Had she bought too many shoes?

'Shut up, you whore!' he shouted.

Picol had lashed into her before but never with such unbridled contempt.

'But – but Michael, I love you. I've always loved you.' Tears were welling up in her eyes.

'You've loved half of Caracas and most of Beverly Hills. Do me a favor and get lost.' The combination of violence in his eyes and disgust in his voice sent her running to the bathroom, where she locked herself in.

Picol stood for ten minutes on the balcony watching the boats moored at the club dock. Winnie was the last thing on his mind. All his attention was focused on one ship, which looked so small below.

Then he gathered up his things and left for the meeting with Herrera. For the first time in Michael Picol's life he was distracted by something other than business or sex.

In the bathroom, Winnie Lifton examined her red, puffy eyes in the mirror. What had she done to set him off like that? She was only twenty-four, but her face seemed to sag in front of her. Maybe she should call Theresa and have her make an appointment for fat vacuuming. It sounded so simple. Like running the Hoover over the living room rug.

# 20

It was like a funeral, Catherine thought. She remembered how many times she had sat with this group around this table and been excited and invigorated. But now it was as if the lifeblood had been drained from the corporate giant and the board was convened to ceremoniously lower a casket of stock certificates into the ground.

The corporate secretary took a perfunctory attendance. All ten board members were accounted for in the roll call except Eve Benton Donaldson, whose absence surprised no one, since she had not attended a board meeting for fifteen years. Eve had always preferred to make her appearance at the annual stockholders' meetings, sitting elegantly silent in the first row, lending off-stage support with her presence.

Catherine herself held only minor stock compared to most of these men, to whom Intercon had been a life's work. Most of them bore the pallbearerlike expressions of men who by five o'clock could become gray flannel nomads, cut loose to deal with psychological impotence that no severance pay could counteract. In contrast, Irv Turner seemed as relaxed as if he were about to sink an eagle on the eighteenth green at Old Elm Country Club. Of course, no matter how the vote went, he could bail out on the wings of his golden parachute. His contract with Intercon was ironclad and assured him of his full presidential salary through his sixty-fifth birthday, after which he would receive a substantial pension. Even without his customary six-figure bonus, Catherine knew that Turner's stock alone could support a small Third World nation, especially at Trans-Oceanic's offer of six times book value.

If Graham were worried, he hid it very well at this moment, even from Catherine. She searched his face for some sign of what he might be feeling, but saw only the façade of the corporate helmsman and family patriarch. For days, they had tallied up how the votes would fall. Secluded in a hotel suite at the Marriott, the defensive team had sifted through every conceivable option, and Graham had come to the conclusion that if everyone held true to his word, he could retain control. After all, he and Eve personally controlled forty-six percent of the stock. There seemed to be no cause for worry, but Catherine was not so sure. Eve had still not sent in her proxy. There were too many unanswered questions. Catherine hated going into any deal open-ended, but she supposed Graham knew what he was doing. If she no longer saw him as the infallible, godlike figure of two years ago, Catherine still supported Graham's decisions. Although she objectively felt that some of his decisions were wrong, her love and loyalty to Graham forced her to back him up. It had been naive to view him as a perfect man, she now realized. His shortcomings were due as much to her own fantasies as to real human inadequacies.

Where *was* Ray Acconti, she asked herself. His usual seat at Turner's right hand, was empty. Since his demise as Graham's fair-haired boy, Acconti had turned into a parrot, perpetually perched on Turner's shoulder.

The door swung brusquely open and Acconti appeared, breaking the somber gloom. He marched in with a splay-footed self-assurance so completely foreign to him that it didn't seem to fit his body, let alone the tone of the room. The fact that, like Catherine, he now held a board position, was not enough to explain his new posture, she thought. Their appointments had been created out of the chaos of the kidnapping, and neither one of them held any real power. If the kidnapping had never happened, neither one of them would be sitting in this room at this moment. She knew they both carried weight only as swing votes. Could someone have bought his vote, Catherine wondered? Probably not. His shares, like hers, were too insignificant. And as reptilian as he was, he prided himself on his devotion to the environment rather than the pursuit of business.

Acconti sat on the edge of his seat as if he were only touching down momentarily, ready to take flight at any instant, and Catherine noticed him nod imperceptibly to Michael Picol, who was eating dry-roasted nuts from a Steuben dish etched with some no-longer-significant commemorative date.

The issue at hand was simple. They were going to vote on whether or not to agree to the terms of the Trans-Oceanic stock offer. Carla passed around a typed agenda for the meeting, but before she had made it halfway around the table, Ray Acconti rose to his feet. 'Gentlemen,' he said, ignoring Catherine's presence, 'I have an announcement of note. I must abstain from this vote, and I hereby tender my resignation.' He handed Graham a sealed envelope. 'Just this morning, I received and accepted an offer to replace Henry Hudson as Secretary of the Interior. Contingent on the appropriate confirmations, of course.'

Turner turned to examine Acconti as if he had just announced he were pregnant. He ran his eyes hurriedly down the itinerary almost as if to see where 'R Acconti defects' was listed.

Graham said nothing, and for a moment heavy with

dreadful expectation and annoyance there was a quiet raising of glasses and polite round of congratulations.

Catherine and Graham exchanged glances. She knew for a fact that President Savage had not let Graham in on his appointment. Such a breach of business etiquette was tantamount to raiding. How long had this been in the works, she wondered. Cabinet appointments didn't just happen out of the blue before breakfast. Who was the instigator, then? Graham was going to be furious when he found out. Although it was always good to have a friend in the secretaryship, Ray Acconti was no Henry Hudson.

Catherine looked suspiciously at Michael Picol. He was connected at every level with the Department of the Interior. How could *he* not have known? He sat there crossing his legs so calmly, he was even yawning.

Of course he was calm, Catherine realized. He *knew*. How and why Picol knew she did not understand. But she was suddenly positive that not only did Picol have advance notice of Acconti's departure, but he probably had something to do with the appointment itself. Graham had certainly spent years positioning Picol in a situation where he could do just such a thing. A horrendous train of thought clicked through Catherine's brain. If Picol was capable of this betrayal, what else was he up to? And she had given him the oil find papers! She shuddered and hoped she was wrong.

'Of course, it would be a conflict of interest if I were to stay on in this meeting,' Acconti pontificated. 'I should not be privy to any confidential dealings of Intercon at this point.' He glared at Catherine. 'This appointment is a culmination of my life's work, and I intend to dedicate myself to *preserving* the environment.'

There goes the new Alaska site, thought Catherine.

Graham stood up to shake Acconti's hand. 'I'm sure

we'll enjoy working together on this new basis as we have in the past,' he said, although Catherine knew from the unusually soft pitch of his voice that he was incensed. Graham's link with the Department of the Interior was effectively severed, and he knew it. Acconti's self-righteous immobility would focus on saving the tree with great emotion, but never the forest.

Acconti left the room.

The canvass of votes continued. The chairman of the board of Hoagland Steel Company, the former chairman of the board of Statewide Insurance, and Professor Polanski from the University of Chicago all voted not to sell, which was expected since they were longtime cronies of Graham Donaldson. Admirable, thought Catherine, but combined the three held about enough stock to fill a paper-clip box.

Of course, R. J. Williams, chairman and founder of the country's largest pharmaceutical company, voted his substantial block of stock with Graham. 'This is an American company,' Williams interjected, interrupting the vote. 'And I mean it to stay American. I don't think we need to infest this country with bolivars. There's nothin' the matter with good old dollars. Might I add *petrodollars*,' the pontificating old man continued, and would not have stopped had the private door from Graham's office not opened. Eve Donaldson, accompanied by a small, balding man whom no one recognized, walked into the room.

My God, thought Catherine. That *couldn't* be Alex Levin.

Two chairs materialized, and Eve introduced Terrence Hutchison, Jr., a senior vice-president at the Northern Trust. 'Mr Hutchinson is here representing Miss Elizabeth Stuart.'

Catherine took in Eve's black Adolfo suit and felt her

studiously avoiding her eyes. As before, Eve's perfect grooming made Catherine self-conscious. She hadn't had a manicure in weeks and the gray sweater-dress she'd been wearing for the last two days, since they'd been closeted in the hotel, was wrinkled. All her time, around the clock for the past two weeks, had been spent racing from room to room within the suite, sequestered like a jury with the takeover combat team, making frantic phone calls and wiring Hong Kong and Zurich at all hours of the night.

Graham stood up and said, 'Pardon me, sir, but this is a private meeting. Surely you know this.'

Hutchinson pulled a barrage of papers from his attaché case. 'The Elizabeth Stuart trust represents the largest single holding of Intercon stock. Her father, Franklin Stuart, had bequeathed some shares to his daughter and the rest were purchased by Eve Donaldson sixteen years ago in the name of Elizabeth Stuart. Mrs Donaldson was trustee until two days ago, when the Northern Trust became trustees for Elizabeth Anne Stuart.'

'Who the hell is Elizabeth Anne Stuart?' Michael Picol spoke for the first time. The arch of his eyebrows revealed real surprise, as opposed to his nonchalant response to Ray Acconti's sudden announcement.

Catherine turned to him and answered, in a drop-dead voice, 'Bambi.'

'Let us see those papers.' He stood up and walked over to Hutchison.

Eve took Graham aside for a private conference. 'You never returned my calls for two days,' Catherine overheard her say before her voice dropped to a whisper. The woman was amazing, Catherine had to admit. She had to be almost fifty, but, except for the matronly suit, she barely looked forty. She was tan and radiant. Her hair was shiny and loose. And she was slim. Catherine felt a twinge of the old rivalry, but pushed it back.

Michael Picol joined Eve and Graham. After a ten-minute conference, they returned to the table, and Graham addressed the restless group. 'We'll continue with the vote now, with Mr Hutchison representing Miss Stuart.'

'The trust of Elizabeth Stuart votes to sell its shares to Trans-Oceanic Corporation.'

The room went stone-still. 'Miss Stuart's trust consists of seven percent of the total shares of Intercon stock,' Hutchison explained.

Why hadn't anyone mentioned this trust before, Catherine wondered angrily. Was it a secret? How could Bambi, of all people, a teenager, end up with stock that much? Was Bambi Eve's daughter or what? She had no more time to wonder, though, because Eve was casting her vote.

'I vote all my shares to sell to Trans-Oceanic.' She couldn't look at Graham, as a communal shudder radiated through the room. How she hated to do this to Graham, and so publicly, but she and Alex had finally decided the music school and their new life together came first. She had to cut all ties to the past, particularly to this company, which had been her rival since childhood. She felt no emotional attachment to the company which had taken away first her father, then her husband.

'My daughter Drucilla, however, votes against this sale,' Eve continued.

A glazed look went over Graham's eyes. The company was slipping away. He looked at Picol, who sighed heavily.

'This is probably the wrong time for such personal

announcements,' he said. 'We wanted to save this for an appropriate time.'

Catherine stared. Was he going to the Cabinet, too?

'Drucilla and I were married yesterday.' His voice was even, as Eve dropped her pen onto the speckled tabletop. 'I'm sorry, Eve, Graham. Drucilla wanted to tell you herself, Eve, but you were in Massachusetts, and she didn't have the heart to disturb her father.'

Eve and Graham each instinctively reached for the other's hand, causing Catherine to wince. Was it comfort or habit or – love? If the announcement hadn't taken place at this inopportune moment, they would both have been delighted that their grandchild would have the legitimacy of a father and a name.

'Drucilla has given me power of attorney. And she votes to sell.' He held up his hand. 'Believe me, Graham, after much serious personal soul-searching, I have concluded that this offer is extremely generous and comes at a time when the international economy works in our favor.'

He looked around the room. 'As I understand it, Graham would receive very favorable terms, and would even be included in the new slate of directors. Trans-Oceanic has, I feel, some progressive ideas for this company which could make it much more profitable for us all.'

Catherine couldn't believe what she was hearing. Picol was obviously on the opposition team.

'They'll be filing their 13D tomorrow, and their Hart, Scott, Rodino with the Justice Department shortly. During the thirty-day waiting period before they can get approval, they've suggested we meet for some constructive talk.'

He turned to Graham. 'By the way, due to the special

circumstances which you and Arnie Welles so brilliantly put together in the Caribbean,' he paused for impact, 'all our interests are protected.'

Damn him! He was using the information she'd entrusted him with to blackmail Graham. She herself had unwittingly armed Michael Picol to tie Graham's hands. She felt like getting sick, like a murderer, an idiot. And every bit as much a traitor as Acconti, Eve, and Picol.

Picol didn't mention that Trans-Oceanic had already gone to Eve and offered her a secret deal for an option on her stock at a special price, which she had accepted.

'Of course, Graham,' he continued, 'when it's this obvious that a deal is in the company's best interest, we know you're going to recognize the facts and not lobby for some nonexistent self-interest.'

If there had been as much as a letter opener on the table, Catherine would have hammered it into Michael Picol's heart, if he had one, which she doubted. But it was all she could do to keep the tears from running down her cheeks as she watched the public humiliation Graham was experiencing.

The rest of the meeting was a blurred daze to her, and she remembered only that when she cast her own vote, it was for Graham Donaldson.

There was no chance in the confusion after the meeting to even speak with him. She raced down the hall in her high heels to her white Formica corridor, shoving mail carts and any thing or person who came into her path out of her way. She was thinking faster than she could articulate. If anyone had asked her what she was going to do now, Catherine probably wouldn't have been able to answer, wouldn't have consciously *known* the answer.

All she cared about now was saving Graham from the terrible position she'd unknowingly helped put him in.

There was nothing she could do about Picol at this point. He was obviously planning to put himself at the helm, and she'd let him get away with it.

Well, she was going to fight back.

She picked up the phone and dialed the private number of Baron Eric Grunewald.

# 21

For some women, the definition of loyalty was simple: you married a man and you stayed faithful to him. For others, like Catherine McBride, loyalty was more complicated. What made you loyal? Standing by a man when you knew he was in the wrong and saying nothing? Or trying to alter a disastrous chain of events to save him, in spite of himself? To go along with Graham, Catherine grimly thought, was tantamount to rearranging the deck chairs on the *Titanic* after it had hit the iceberg. No, this was not for her. She was going for the lifeboats.

The lifeboat took the form of one man in a rubber bathing cap and black rubber goggles who was now breaststroking his way through the living room of his apartment on the forty-fifth floor of the Trump Tower.

'Perhaps if we sweeten his departure,' Baron Grunewald suggested as he flipped over in the water and switched to the backstroke, 'your chairman would be more agreeable.' The underwater lights of the pool gave the clean white room an undulating, blue-gray cast that matched the New York winter dusk.

'No, if it were a matter of money, he would have cashed out like everyone else,' Catherine said, leaning forward in the black leather Barcelona chair at the edge of the white tile pool. She was used to unusual settings for business meetings by now. In fact, she was utterly convinced that no really important transaction ever took place in an office. The setting was irrelevant. What was important was the deal, not whether it was negotiated on a car phone or at poolside.

It was fortunate that the baron had been in New York, only two hours away from Chicago. There was no time to lose, since Trans-Oceanic had already announced the takeover to the press, but no legal document had yet been signed. What appeared on the surface to be an oversight born of overconfidence seemed, to Catherine, a lucky legal loophole – through which the baron could squeeze, if he was interested and could move quickly enough. There were other companies she could go to, but none with a CEO as autonomous as Eric Grunewald, who could make a decision without getting bogged down by a yammering board. Heads of most mega-companies were usually figureheads, but the baron's company was privately held, and he made his own decisions.

From the moment she had stepped off the private elevator of Trump Tower and through the double bronze doors that opened into the living room of the enormous apartment the baron and his son shared when they were in New York, they had discussed nothing but the strategies necessary to persuade the baron to emerge as a white knight in the Intercon takeover. The fact that he was submerged in chlorinated water, swimming his daily hundred laps in his own Olympic-length pool, was not the least bit distracting to him. The baron, Catherine knew, did not have to sit behind a deck to concentrate on business. She had seen him make billion-dollar decisions while playing with his miniature toys. His ideas seemed to come to him as he put everything into perspective, played out in miniature, as it were, before he played it out in real life.

The goggles and white cap moved closer to her end of the pool again.

'Graham is an idealist,' Catherine called out. 'That's why he hid the oil find. A Place in the Sun is his immortality. A man like him will never sell out on his ideals.'

'It is never good to trade your ethics for your ideals.' The baron disappeared briefly beneath the surface for a racing turn against the side of the pool. He reemerged and switched to the sidestroke. 'He has to tell. Now. Billy is looking at the figures now with Dieter in the office downstairs. But the figures are the least of it, my dear.'

'Yes. I'm aware Graham could go to jail for withholding information from the stockholders.'

'That, yes. But he is in real danger. I think there are – unhealthy forces involved.' She had to wait for him to elaborate until he swam closer again. 'That kidnapping is only one example. Things can get very – untidy – when one deals with Raoul Herrera.' He reached for a toy submarine at the side of the pool.

She clasped her hands together. 'Well, Michael Picol and Herrera seem to get along pretty well.'

'*Very* well.' His tone was pointed. 'I think you should know, they had several meetings in Miami and Caracas preceding the kidnapping and several more preceding the buyout, and so the plot thickens.' As he pulled off his swimming goggles and handed them to her she could see that his eyes flickered just as they did at chess before he would pounce on his opponent and announce checkmate.

'Are you sure?' It was a rhetorical question, a chilling reminder of her own unwitting part in Graham's manipulation. She knew that the baron was right, but it was confirmation of her own suspicions that she had handed Michael Picol the nails for the coffin he had built for Graham.

'There are certain bankers in Frankfurt that Trans-

Oceanic have utilized who are financed by the Grunewalds. The checks to Michael Picol's Swiss bank account are, shall we say, significant.'

Catherine focused on a half dozen place settings of broken crockery that jutted out of an enormous muddy-gray Julian Schnabel painting across the room from the high-tech pool.

'Don't worry, my dear. We shall protect your chairman, Graham Donaldson. I have an old score to settle with Herrera myself.'

'Why do you think Herrera would want Intercon? They must have other ways of getting into oil.'

'Intercon has the pipelines and refineries in place that would take a dozen years through South American channels. Instant credibility, top-line banking connections, and Venezuela has a potential oil field in the south that would eclipse Maracaibo, maybe even challenge Saudi price control for a while with all their own ready-to-go refineries and world wide distribution system. With this new oil source, my dear, for *starters*, all they have to do is float some offshore equipment in the Caribbean, and it's a turnkey operation. And the way the deal's structured, down there, it's *domestic* petroleum.' The baron climbed up the bronze pool ladder, his unexpectedly toned body wearing a skimpy European swimsuit. 'The same reason why Intercon might make sense for my acquisition program. Would you hand me my robe, my dear?'

'Will there be a place for Graham?'

'Why should there be? The man is an imbecile. He left himself vulnerable. You, who play chess so well, should realize that you never leave yourself unprotected.'

'Still, the stockholders are mainly his family. I'm sure they'd rather sell to a company that will keep Graham on the board.'

'Trans-Oceanifc will file suit.'

'Don't the numbers make good sense for Darco? What does Billy think?'

'Even on the surface it looks difficult. Rough.'

Catherine wondered what the baron meant, but before she could ask, a plump blond man carrying an attaché case with the Grunewald crest materialized from behind the elevator doors.

'Dieter, you have the figures?'

'Yes, Baron. Right here. The building office has been calling, sir. Apparently the pool is leaking into the apartment below you.'

The baron sighed. 'This is why I hate modern construction.'

'The owner is a most hysterical Palm Beach woman. She has called her attorney, your attorney, Donald Trump and *Sixty Minutes*.' There was a look of piqued annoyance on his face. 'Evidently, her living room has become a waterfall. She says her floor and carpets are ruined and a priceless rare albino Macaw has drowned.'

The baron jerked the sash of his robe. 'Her *parrot* drowned!' he snorted. 'How much water is there? Maybe we can float junk bonds. Right, Catherine?' He laughed and marched toward his private quarters.

'Call Bernie Goldblum,' he yelled over his shoulder.

'Is he your counsel?' Dieter frowned. 'Didn't he represent that American socialite when the tanker rammed her seawall and crashed into her pool?'

'No. Bernie Goldblum is the pool man. He's with Aqua-Pool. See you in an hour, my dear. We will continue this discussion at dinner tonight. Alfred and Camille are in town for our newspaper chain and the Metropolitan Museum opening.' He hurried a towel over his sparse hair as he stopped walking. 'He's trying to buy the *Daily Telegraph*.'

'Are they married now?' Catherine followed him to the doorway.

'A Christmas wedding is planned. But you will enjoy this evening. They have a rock-and-roll band. Camille's brother is in it.' He disappeared through a darkened doorway flanked by more New York art than was commonly seen at the Whitney Museum's Biennial. His voice boomed back at them. 'And get that woman downstairs a new bird! A mallard or something else that swims.'

One hour barely gave Catherine enough time to race back to the Carlyle Hotel on Seventy-sixth Street, hurl herself into the shower, and dress for the gala. Thoughtfully, the Carlyle kept a blow-dryer under the sink, along with shampoo. She had learned to keep a bag ready and packed at all times at the office, with a few mix-and-match basics, her black velvet Vicky Tiel dress, and black satin-and-sequin evening pumps. The dress was simple, but somehow it always seemed appropriate. She decided to leave off the velvet bolero jacket.

She stood in front of the mirror. Right now she looked just about right for a cocktail party in Chicago. But this dinner was at the Metropolitan Museum, and the women would be decked out in all their jewels and furs. As she had hurried through the lobby, she had seen two women led behind the front desk by a distinguished-looking man in a black suit and an armed security guard to the hotel vault room, obviously raiding their safety deposit boxes. Catherine had heard the ladies excitedly referring to the Metropolitan opening. Vaults meant serious jewelry. She had no jewelry save for the ever-present Grunewald crest, which now, however, hung on a *real* gold chain.

The black dress was a pretty simple number, curved,

strapless, molding her bosom, tightly nipped-in waist, perky short skirt – very short. All the ladies would be wearing voluminous ball gowns, she thought and frowned. She laughed to herself thinking that she might send for sequins from room service. The Carlyle was the most accommodating hotel in the world. Once, when Graham had been having a kidney stone attack there, the concierge had hand-delivered a special prescription pain killer and a choice of two doctors as if it were three o'clock in the afternoon and not three A.M. on a Sunday morning.

She stood before the mirror and the reflected image startled her for an instant. She *had* changed since that first Dallas ball. Confidence, as well as her smooth skin and clear blue eyes stared back at her. Catherine noticed the reflection of the complimentary flowers sent from the hotel manager. She walked over on impulse, pulled out a spray of tuberoses, pushed her hair to one side, and twisted the flowers and her hair into a French braid. Her earrings seemed too tailored. If every other woman would have dazzling jewels, she sensed that it was better to take them off entirely.

Her trench coat was reversible, lined with dark brown, sheared mink. She never wore a fur coat to the office because it would have seemed too extravagant, but a fur-*lined* coat was an accepted necessity in Chicago. She shook the coat inside out, smoothed the soft fur, turned up the collar, and was off.

'Don't you step on my blue suede shoes,' wailed Lady Violet Crosswich as she hiked up her thigh-high electric-blue satin mini-skirt three inches higher, revealing the tops of her unmatched silk stockings and hot-pink garters. Her pale, bare shoulders shimmied to the beat, precariously straining the bustline of the dress, which threatened to at any minute reveal in full the endowments of the youngest daughter of Great Britain's third-highest-ranking duke, although according to the *Tatler*, England's glossy chronicle of the aristocracy, these breasts had already been bared, to the tune of a seventy-five-pound fine, in the back of a speeding car on the M-1 Motorway. Behind her, in black-suited formation, her rhythm-and-blues backup band, the *Heirs Apparent*, rocked in synch down the grand staircase of the Metropolitan Museum, expressionless behind Ray-Ban sun glasses.

'That's Charlie, Camille's brother on saxophone,' Alfred Grunewald shouted into Catherine's ear, attempting to compensate for the decibel level. Alfred, Lady Camille, Billy Wright, and Catherine stood at the edge of the grand staircase, taking in the spectacle.

The baron, escorting Mrs Priscilla Bosworth, New York's most blue-blooded collage artist, was lost in a crush beneath a row of Van Dyck ancestral portraits. Mrs Bosworth's silver chignon was stacked so high it added at least an inch to her already imperial height, and her gown of a thousand crowded, colored sequins and bows covered every inch of her almost anorexic frame. The baron's tuxedo jacket was velvet and Cathering noticed the Grunewald crust emblazoned on both of his gold-and-sapphire cuff links.

'The whole Queenie Bopper crowd has turned out for this.' Alfred pointed out several minor members of the Royal Family. 'Camille's family was quite reluctant to ship their heirloom Chippendale to New York for this exhibit, so they sent their collection of Georgian silver, race cups, and ash trays, inscribed with the names of Crosswich's winning horses.'

Camille elegantly rotated her wrist in her brother's

direction, the enormous taffeta structured sleeve of her Bruce Oldfield dress deflecting a dancer spinning off-axis in her direction. She looked like a Princess Diana clone – very tall, pale and capable of giving a sidelong glance and a blush. 'Charlie hasn't missed a note – I don't think,' she said.

'Who would know the difference?' Alfred shrugged, smiling indulgently.

'Oh, look, there's Linley.' Camille pointed out the son of Princess Margaret and Lord Snowdon. 'Let's go see him, shall we? I want to ask him how his carpentry's coming along.'

'You run ahead.'

'Don't leave this spot, then, Alfred. You know how lost I get when I can't find you.' She disappeared into the gyrating crowd.

Catherine and Billy drifted to the edge of the dance floor, where they exchanged sympathetic glances. They were both swept along with the baron's after-dinner entourage, regardless of the fact that joining the Queenie Bopper crowd was the last thing either of them felt like doing. Catherine felt like a widow, dancing before the body was cold. But what else could she do? The baron was her one chance to salvage Graham and his company. However the baron wanted to do business was up to him, and he usually insisted on extending the business day into dinner and beyond.

At least she and Billy had had a chance to bring each other up to date. Billy had folded quite comfortably into the baron's network and had regained all his former enthusiasm for his career. Running Darco definitely agreed with him.

'I was pretty damn shocked,' Billy commented. 'I never thought Graham would sell out. He seemed to be a man who liked to be king of his own realm.' Catherine noticed that Billy was still wearing the same scruffy cowboy boots he'd worn in the halls at Intercon. 'There's more to it, isn't there, than what's on the street?'

No wonder Billy was such a good wildcatter. His instincts were so clean and clear-cut. But she would never betray Graham by telling Billy the whole truth. If she could do nothing else, at least she could preserve the façade. She couldn't lie to Billy. But she couldn't tell him everything, either. It was time to make a tactful exit.

She gestured to Billy that she'd be back and maneuvered her way into a cavernous room at the far side of the museum. Her footsteps echoed on the hard floor as she wandered through the awesome reconstruction of the Temple of Dendur. She had to clear her head for a few minutes. The artifacts of the three-thousand-year-old temple put her problems in perspective. She sat down and plucked at the flowers in her hair, pulling them out and unpinning the French braid, shaking it loose.

'Taking up the worship of Osiris, are you?' She hadn't even heard Alfred coming up behind her. He sat beside her on the marble bench.

'I'm considering it. Isn't he the god of the dead?'

'Death. But also resurrection.'

'I'm waiting to get to the resurrection part.'

'Trust me. There is life after Intercon.'

She smiled. As usual Alfred managed to focus in on what she was thinking. She got that strange feeling again, as if she'd known him before, known him always. 'How are you always so perceptive?'

'It's my job. I'm in the newspaper business. How are you always so pretty?' His eyes slid down her face and throat. His hand reached out and she sat very still. Was he going to kiss her? Hadn't they worked this out in

England? He was still engaged and she was still in love with Graham. Wasn't she?

He touched neither her face nor throat, but the ornament hanging around her neck. He picked it up, his hand lingering on her chest. 'The Grunewald crest?' He looked startled.

'I've had it since I was in school. It's my only jewelry, and it means a lot to me.'

'I'm glad you're not one of those jaded types who doesn't admit anything means anything to them. What else means a lot to you? Your family?'

'I haven't got any family.'

'I thought you said your father was still alive.'

Catherine hated discussing her father. To her, he was dead. He dropped the ornament gently back onto her chest, and when he removed his hand, she missed its warmth.

'Maybe you should take a lesson from Osiris after all,' he said. 'Resurrect your father.'

'What?'

'Find out who you really are. Then you'll know what you really want.'

'What I want is what I can do for myself.'

'You are your résumé, then?'

Why couldn't he just leave her alone? If anything, she wanted comfort now, not interrogation by an investigative newspaperman. She sighed. 'I'm suddenly very tired. Please give my regrets to Camille and the baron. I'm going to have to miss the Palladium.'

She stood up.

'I envy you. But Camille promised her brother we'd meet him there. If you change your mind, we'll be in the Michael Todd Room. It's a little quieter up there.'

As she turned to leave, Catherine felt the same inexplicable pull to Alfred she had felt in Chicago and then England. It seemed that no matter what was said or not said, they both understood without words that they should not get closer because there was no telling what even the slightest touch might set off. Catherine still felt the confusion in her memory of the kiss in the bath at the country house. It was an absurd feeling that had no place in real life. She forced herself to walk away and not look back.

Back at the hotel an hour later, Catherine flipped on the stereo and sat in her cocktail dress thinking. There were suddenly so many questions, and no answers at all. She thought about what Alfred said. Her father! She didn't need her father. She had Graham.

Her father. Graham. Graham. Her father. Catherine knew that if a psychoanalyst got hold of her, he would probably say that her attachment to Graham was based on an unconscious desire to finally have a father.

Ridiculous. Her feelings for Graham had been based on his intelligence, rapid-fire decision-making, and his ability to win under pressure. What had happened to those traits? It seemed she had assimilated them somehow, as if their relationship had drained off his strength from him to her. She remembered a quote from Gloria Steinem: 'We have become the men we want to marry.' She had always wondered what that meant. Now she knew in spades.

Two calls to Graham rang endlessly. Guiltily, she remembered that she hadn't even told him that she had left. She even tried her own apartment, in case he had gone there. He must have gone to Eve's. They were probably pondering Dru's marriage together. She wondered what it must be like to have a snake for a son-in-law. She yawned lazily and kicked off her shoes.

The doorbell to her suite jolted her, and she padded barefoot into the tiny, taupe-and-peach, fabric-shirred entrance hall. Peering out the three-inch space allowed by the security chain, she saw Alfred Grunewald, his coat slung over his arm.

Catherine opened the door, and they stood facing each other for several minutes.

A room service cart clattered by, and several expensively attired couples crossed from the elevators to their rooms.

Finally, she was the first to speak. 'Lady Camille is waiting for you,' she said, trying to sound pointed, but coming out, instead, regretful and almost sorrowful.

'Yes,' he murmured. 'I'm being very unfair to Camille. But I thought you might have changed your mind and wanted to come with us after all.'

'No. I haven't changed my mind. I'm really very tired and could use the rest.' They both stared at each other, and finally Catherine stepped aside. 'Would you like to have a drink before you join the others?'

'Thanks, but they're waiting downstairs in the car,' Alfred said.

'Of course,' she said, thinking to herself that she should have realized he wouldn't have come here by himself. 'Well, I do hope you have a good time – it's been nice seeing you again, Alfred.'

'It's always much more than *nice* to see you, Catherine.' He turned to go, and she closed the door. That was her relationship with Alfred, Catherine decided. A series of doors opening and then closing. Suddenly, she felt she'd never been in such an empty room.

Three hours later, she was sleeping when she heard the faraway ring of a doorbell, which gave way to a knock, and then someone calling her name through the door.

It must be almost dawn, she thought as she threw on her robe. 'Who's there? What is it?'

'It's Alfred. Please . . . May I come in?'

Alfred! Now Catherine knew what it meant when the romance novels said *her heart leaped* – because hers did. She fumbled with the chain and yanked the door open, not even thinking about her hair or lack of makeup. It didn't matter.

They held each other, and she lay her head against his chest. *Home*, something deep inside her said. *This is home*.

Then remembering, she pulled back. 'Your fiancée . . .' she whispered.

'I've broken my engagement. I told Camille. It's all right.'

'She must be so upset.'

'Actually, she wasn't. She suspected, you see.'

'What?'

'That I'm in love with you. After all, she's known me since I was a child.' He kissed her hair. 'But then again, so have you.'

They smiled at each other and he held her close. They kissed and Catherine felt the most complete contentment she had ever known. Nothing existed for her in that moment.

Alfred kissed her fingertips gently, as if each one were a treasure. He stroked the nape of her neck softly as she curled in his arms at the edge of the bed. And when they made love it was not frenzy or passion, but a promise neither voiced but each knew. He stroked her breasts afterward and said, simply, 'We're together,' and she understood. He felt so right inside her. Whispering and laughing softly, they fell back on the bed. And Catherine, who rarely cried, found herself sobbing in Alfred's arms; her tears were of happiness, and as he wiped away their salty tracks on her face, she knew she could never again sleep with Graham Donaldson. Or anyone else.

There was only Alfred. Kind, loving, exquisite Alfred. His eloquent touch, his compassion, his limitless love was all she wanted. 'I love you,' she breathed over and over into his throat as her lips traveled across it. 'I love you.' Of this, she was certain.

# 22

Chicken sandwiches and champagne. No matter what *The Wall Street Journal* had reported, that was how the deal had really gone down, not at a sleek, terrazzo table in a paneled conference room, not at the elite, old-guard Chicago Club, but in an ordinary hotel suite in the O'Hare Hyatt Regency. The living room had been littered with wadded-up papers, empty Coke cans and Perrier bottles, half-eaten food and wrappers, and all the flotsam that surfaces after ten people spend forty-eight hours closeted together in close quarters.

Once the baron had offered one hundred and twenty-five dollars a share, the verbal agreement with Trans-Oceanic no longer mattered to the serious shareholders. While Trans-Oceanic frantically filed suits in federal and state courts and lodged complaints with the SEC, offers and counteroffers for control of Intercom were lobbed back and forth. The phones rang every few seconds, and the corporate campsite crawled with advisers. Meals were delivered by room service. Graham barely slept, afraid that if he permitted himself to be less than alert, he might not be able to handle an immediate decision required by a late-night call. Superstitions and irrational rationales suddenly overtook men who normally behaved only by the book. The atmosphere had some of the spirit of school games in which people chose up sides and pledged fealty. Promises and allegiances were made and altered a dozen times each hour. An open line had been cleared to the banks in Zurich with a seven-hour time-zone difference, and Hong Kong, thirteen hours ahead.

Two of the glass-enclosed elevators in the Hyatt Atrium were commandeered by various groups of stony-faced investment bankers, strategic planners, and corporate lawyers. At one point, at two in the morning, a team from Salomon Brothers was being whisked up, while a group from Bear, Stearns and Company was heading down, each team eyeballing each other from their respective illuminated elevators in the semidarkness of the Atrium.

After one particularly promising three-in-the-morning conference call, Graham thought he might be able to bring in a third party and propose a partial white-knight maneuver to keep control. The thought of Trans-Oceanic splintering his life's work into shreds infuriated him, but he was stymied when the aggressors raised their bid.

Finally, the baron's counterproposal offered Graham a deal with which he could reckon. He would remain on as chairman with Billy Wright moving in as president. Beyond that, Graham would be given complete credit for the oil find, secret immunity from any repercussions that might result from the fact that he had withheld the news of the discovery and a three-million dollar golden parachute. Most importantly, he would be appointed head of the Graham Donaldson Research Center, and a generous grant from the Grunewald Foundation was written into the merger to fund it. Catherine's carefully constructed plans for a money-generating resort were quickly eviscerated, leaving only a shell of a clublike resort for eighty members in search of calm seclusion. That was all that was left of all the grand plans for A Place in the Sun.

Four days after the baron's second offer, the merger was ready to be consummated, pending SEC approval and a favorable stockholder vote.

No one actually saw the baron. During the entire course of negotiations he remained sequestered on his private Boeing 747-300. Only when an agreement had been verbally reached did he extend an invitation to Graham Donaldson and Catherine to join him on board. The rest of the merger team celebrated in the suite with French champagne, German beer, and chicken sandwiches.

The party was subdued. The adrenalin level that had carried the group along for days crashed, and exhaustion had set in, in spite of the tempered jubilation that they had managed to keep Intercon intact. Most of the team managed to hang onto their jobs, which was enough cause for relief.

Both Catherine and Graham knew that the merger was the lesser of two evils. They didn't go into the whats and whys or dissect the demise of Intercon or who was to blame, as if it were a failed love affair. What was the point? There was no going back.

Catherine felt as if she were operating in a fog, with no point of reference to lead her on to any patch of clear visibility. Graham never did thank her for bringing the baron to the rescue. She figured he had probably appraised the situation in his neatly compartmentalized mind and come to the conclusion that the takeover would be something the baron, being the consummate businessman and strategist, would ultimately have seized upon himself. It would never occur to him that Catherine would have been dealing in trade-offs and debt collecting on her own to bring the normally cutthroat Baron Grunewald to the table in a conciliatory mood. Still, he must have known from the turn of the conversations that she was the catalyst. Perhaps Graham was waiting for the right moment, when he was less distracted, to show some sort of appreciation. But Catherine chastised herself. She had known up front that there was a chance that he might even resent her for taking such an initiative. A lesser man than Graham might even have resented her efforts out of pure chauvinism. And she had never expected Graham to bow down in gratitude. Catherine had set out simply to save him from disgrace, and Intercon from being parceled up into little pieces. Professionally, it was a simple matter: she had no choice. As for her own feelings, she didn't know what she felt, or if she felt anything at all, except hatred for Michael Picol and disdain for the betrayal of Graham's family.

Her feelings for Graham were the most confused. She knew she didn't love him the way she loved Alfred. They hadn't slept together for months, and their business relationship was no longer one of mentor and student. The man she had loved, she realized, didn't exist. Their whole affair was based on the fact that she had idolized him. Idolatry was not love. When she could no longer idolize him, she could no longer love him.

Alfred had been in her thoughts despite the unromantic atmosphere of merger and acquisition. It was Alfred's voice on the telephone and not Graham's that she heard before she fell asleep since she'd come back from New York.

Catherine saw the events of the past few weeks as a giant sorting-out process. Even if Graham was incapable of responding to what she'd done for him and his company, it didn't matter. If he saw her actions as a threat to his omnipotence, she saw them as a gift that freed, if not him, herself. She had paid back in kind everything he had done for her. They were even. Maybe even equal. Indeed, now that they were just two people, that wasn't enough.

These thoughts raced through Catherine's mind as she sat in the expectant atmosphere of the Intercon auditorium, waiting for the press conference that would sanctify the merger announcement. She glanced at the glossy press kit in her lap, with the new logo depicting the Grunewald falcon haughtily perched atop the Intercon globe. She nodded at George Lazarus from the *Chicago Tribune* in the audience. The business press had turned out in force. *The Wall Street Journal, Crain's, Forbes*, and *Fortune* had all sent reporters. Even *M* was there. Why, Catherine couldn't imagine, except to report on what a baron wears to a takeover. In that case, they would have to be left wondering, for the baron wasn't coming. Hardly ever making an unnecessary move, it would have been redundant for him to come. For him, the deal was completed; while his swat team moved into place, he moved on to another city with another deal to be done. He always allowed the press to photograph him at play on Marbella or Saint Moritz, but never while he did his real work.

Still, the press wouldn't be disappointed. They had come for a briefing on the merger, but would leave with the news of the biggest oil find of the decade. On the stage were Billy Wright and Arnie Welles. Welles had been named the director of research and development at Darco-Intercon, the new merger company. The fact that Billy, a former Intercon employee, was moving in as president only reinforced the consensus that Graham Donaldson had pulled off a coup and had been part of selecting the new team. As Graham walked up to the stage, congratulations and handshakes accompanied him every step of the way, his peers and associates acknowledging his brilliant handling of a difficult situation. The Old Boy Network applauded one of its own on a graceful exit.

No one talked to or even acknowledged Catherine. She sat quietly in the first row in what was formerly Eve's place, and watched Graham have his moment. He might have come into the room as a man who had been forced to play out a losing hand, but she knew he would emerge as a hero. That had been part of her deal with the baron. The oil find that so excited the room was deemed a Graham discovery and Graham deal, as if he had pulled it out of the hat in the middle of stymied negotiations. There would be no kudos for her; her role would never even be acknowledged. The press was already calling this a 'brilliant strategic fit.' For once, the credit didn't seem to matter. She was at peace with herself and happy to save Graham's dignity.

The room quieted as the lights dimmed, and Graham stepped up to the podium, a few more wrinkles around the eyes, perhaps a little grayer at the temples, but still the vibrant man she had first met that day in the New York office.

Catherine glanced around the room to see how the press would respond to him. His strong public voice was authoritatively filling up the room when suddenly a vise-grip closed around her upper arm, and Michael Picol loomed over her like an apparition.

'Let's go.' He yanked her to her feet and propelled her up the aisle, out of the auditorium, and into the elevator bay.

Was this Picol's idea of strong-arm tactics? Catherine planted her feet on the glazed tiles and wrenched her arm free. He was cutting off her circulation, and she shook her tingling fingers in disgust. 'If there hadn't been fifteen photographers sitting there,' she said through clenched teeth, 'I would have called security.' She glared at him. His usual calm façade was missing, and he looked more like a vicious, street-fighting, switchblade-carrying kid.

'What the hell are you doing here?' she demanded.

'Why don't you crawl back to Trans-Oceanic where you belong? And take your Swiss bank account with you.'

He shoved her roughly against the elevator doors, and the stainless steel ash tray ground into her back. For a minute she thought about hitting him, but the terrifying look in his eyes made her afraid of how he would react. Her eyes searched the familiar face she had never really seen before. He had the look of a crazed dope dealer who had lost his connection.

He breathed into her face. '*Call off the kraut.*' He emphasized each word. The sticky-sweet floral odor of his cologne nauseated Catherine. She wondered how she had ever even thought he was attractive. The whites of his eyes looked sallow, but the pupils flashed with fury. 'You made this deal. You can kill this deal,' he said coldly, his voice coming out as if he were a ventriloquist, without his lips even moving. 'And if I were you, I'd kill it dead. Do you get my drift?'

Someone was finally giving her the credit – or was it the blame? 'I don't have to answer to you.' She was at once terrified and mesmerized.

'Herrera will tie this deal up in court for years,' he shot back.

'You're the one who left the legal loophole. You were too busy running off and getting married.' She watched him carefully as she spoke. 'I guess I should thank you.'

He deliberately took her chin between his forefinger and thumb, clenching her face into his fist. 'If I were you, I'd buy a prison visiting wardrobe, because I'll send lover-boy to Club Fed. And you can go too, for withholding information from the stockholders.' He grinned. 'I've still got that document from Arnie Welles. Signed and dated.'

Club Fed. That was Danbury, the white-collar prison. Catherine recalled that a Watergate trickster had been sent there. Could he possibly do that? She'd covered all the tracks so far. The elevator doors opened behind her and two men got out, as she jerked her face away from Picol's hand.

'Stop threatening me, Picol. You can't touch the baron.'

'Don't count on it. There's a few people in Washington who still remember World War II. They'd just love to pull the plug on that old Nazi.'

She started to turn away.

'Look,' Picol barked. 'You're not getting a thing out of this deal. Not even a head-nod. Trans-Oceanic is a very generous company. You could write your own ticket with them. You'd never have to work again.' So he was threatening her, intimidating her to offer her a deal, Catherine thought. He would never have done that if he were in control.

She was disgusted. The creep was actually trying to bribe her. 'Is that Herrera's way of doing business? Is that how they got to you?' She could see it now. Herrera, Picol, and those South American vultures sitting around planning a takeover based on everyone's weaknesses. She wondered just how far they would go. 'Money. Is that the answer to you, Picol?'

'It's the golden rule. He who has the gold rules. You better cut yourself in before Daddy-O cuts you out.' He turned and strutted toward the garage entrance like a gang member going to a rumble. 'I'll call you,' he shot over his shoulder.

What kind of people had she been working with? How could she have worked with somebody every day and so misjudged him. God, she'd even let that creature kiss her! Picol, Acconti, what was this system that made people turn on each other for profit? Was even Graham any better? She'd heard the stories about Franklin Stuart, and others, too. What was this, the Crusades, where slaughter was justified in the name of the Holy Cause? This was not the world she wanted to be a part of.

Catherine walked slowly over to the auditorium door and reached for the handle. Her hand hung in the air. Suddenly she couldn't think of a single reason why she should enter the room. She turned around, took out her special key, and went up the elevator to Graham's office.

When he came up, two hours later, she was sitting there in the dark.

'Where'd you go?' Graham asked, loosening his tie and throwing it onto his desk. 'I saw you one minute, and the next minute you were gone.' He walked by and ruffled her hair. 'Well, we did it, kiddo. I couldn't have done it without you.'

She stared at him.

He went to the bar, pulled open the cabinet to reveal an array of glasses, and poured himself a Perrier. 'Want anything?'

She was still silent.

'What do you say we go to Gene and Georgetti's and get a steak?'

'I don't eat meat anymore.'

'Right.' He sat down on the couch beside her. 'I know you must be exhausted.' He heaved a heavy sigh. 'Well, it didn't come out so bad for us. I'm a lame duck, but I still have things to do. And more time. I've got the island,' he put his arm around her. 'And you. We'll have more time to go down there and be together.' He got up and turned on a light. 'Funny, when things got really rough, what kept coming into my mind was this picture of the island. Water. Sand, Palms. The fish. And you in your baseball cap and bikini. I guess the dream's going to come true.'

'Whose dream?' Her voice was coming out of a tunnel somewhere.

'I'll be glad to get out of this rat race. And it's no place for a lady.'

She felt her stomach churn.

'I don't want my future wife to have to live on a treadmill. I'm going to take care of you.'

Future wife! They'd never really discussed marriage. Two months ago she would have been ecstatic to hear those words. But somehow they just tumbled out and drifted into space. What could she say to him? How could she tell him about Alfred when she didn't know herself what she was going to do with Alfred?

Somehow, she found the words.

'Graham. I have to say this. Maybe it's not the time, but there is no good time. And I respect you too much not to tell you. Now.'

He stared at her, puzzled.

'You know how much I care for you. Truly, I do. But marriage . . .'

He took her hand. 'I know it's not right to spring this on you, sweetheart, but I thought . . . since the separation I'd *assumed* . . .'

She bit her lip. 'I'm sorry, Graham.'

'Sorry?'

'I can't marry you. It wouldn't be fair.'

'Fair to whom?'

'Either of us.'

He sighed. 'You're exhausted, Catherine. We all are. You have every right to be shell-shocked.'

Her brows furrowed together. 'No. I know what I'm

saying. I can't marry you. I need to think things over. For a while. On my own.'

He put his arm around her. Her independence was confusing to him, and he tried not to show the hurt he felt. 'Maybe so. Maybe you should take some time off, think things over. Then we can take this up again. And while you're thinking, I can have Cartier's make something up . . .'

'No!' Her voice was firm. 'I – I mean. Not now.' She looked up, pleading with her eyes. 'I need to be on my own now. Please.'

Graham took her face in his hands and looked closely into her eyes and he saw it there, the warm weariness that had taken over where once he had seen only sparkle and passion. A rest. That was what she needed. Then they'd talk again. Meanwhile, he could always spend a few weeks in the company apartment to humor her.

'I was thinking,' Catherine mumbled as she leaned her head against his chest, more in fatigue than from emotion. 'I'd like some time off. A few days away.'

'Where? the island?'

'No, Los Angeles.'

'Los Angeles? What are you going to do there?'

She smiled for the first time that day.

'I think I'll go ghostbusting.'

# 23

Catherine ran her finger down the names in the Los Angeles phone book, stopping short in the middle of the first column. There it was! Ed McBride. No pseudonym, no camouflage, no mystery. Could it be so easy as this to get in touch with him?

She blinked helplessly at the page. What would she say? How do you articulate your feelings – what do you say to a long-lost father? Are you the Ed McBride who used to have a daughter named Catherine? Are you the one who left your wife and child in Pittsburgh for the Avis Rent-a-Car lady? What do you have to say for yourself?

Maybe she should just take the address down and write a letter. It probably wasn't even the same Ed McBride.

But what if is *was*? Hadn't she come to Los Angeles to confront her past, to come to terms with her father at long last? She finally decided to check it out a little before she made a fool of herself. It was Saturday afternoon – somebody would probably be home. Besides, the address was only a few minutes from the Beverly Hills Hotel. She could drive over and back before Aggie returned. Before she could change her mind, Catherine forced herself to copy down the address and walk out the bungalow door.

Minutes later, she found herself sitting in the car in front of a white stucco house. Catherine noticed the window boxes filled with pink geraniums and felt a sting of sadness and loss as she remembered the window boxes at their little house in Pittsburgh.

The screen door banged open and a fourteen-year-old

girl, who looked so much like Catherine at that age that she had to look twice, came running out of the house and raced into the back yard. 'Dad,' she yelled. 'Mom wants you.'

So this was the sister who'd replaced her, the dimpled baby from the hated Christmas card. Catherine's shoulders started to tremble, but she was unable to cry, her tears had been used up years ago. What must it be like she wondered, to grow up like this girl, safe and secure, knowing both your parents slept in the next room? To come home knowing your father wanted to talk about grades or boys, or just to cuddle in his lap and be held? To not spend half your life with an empty space in your chest where your ability to love and to feel things used to be? Catherine envied the girl, her almost-mirror image.

She brushed through her hair with her fingers and took several deep, measured breaths. It was okay, she reassured herself. It was okay to feel things, even if they made you unhappy. For so long, her rationality had blunted her. Her instincts for self-survival would have made this reunion totally impossible until now. Now she had some jagged edges. She could face her father, because she knew he *was* part of her life. She had not severed him so neatly as she had thought, after all. He always would be there, even if he turned his back on her.

Her father walked into the back yard. It *was* her father. She was instinctively sure of it. She examined his features, his walk, his voice, as if he were a biological specimen on a glass slide. But her feelings were more the result of intuition than any combination of physical characteristics. Yes, this was the same Ed McBride as in the picture she had kept buried at the bottom of her dresser drawer all these years. She had taken it along to Los Angeles to remind herself, and pulling the frayed photograph from her purse, she could see that the man in the yard looked less like the man in the picture than the little girl resembled Catherine. Still, she knew it was he. And she knew it was time.

She walked up the three steps, rang the buzzer, and he answered the door. He seemed startled at first, then a slow look of recognition came over his face. He knew exactly who she was.

They made false moves toward one another like football players taking each other out and then there was an awkward silence. Who should do what first? Do you embrace, are you glad to see one another, do you hurl insults, accusations? He shyly took the initiative and opened the screen door for her, then reached out for an awkward hug. How long had she wished for this simple touch, Catherine wondered. And yet it brought no rush of emotions, just a sense of the end of a journey. Her father introduced her to his wife Veronica and Catherine shook hands politely, as if meeting a suburban family who had invited her for lunch. The girl in the yard was Kim, and there was another teenage daughter. Her sisters. The fact that they were almost grown further emphasized the distance between Catherine and her father.

Veronica discreetly motioned her daughters out of the room, and Catherine was alone with her father. There were no tears, no apologies, no declarations of regret. But the question hung in the air between them. Why? It was as though two old lovers had met for the first time in twenty years after one had left the other waiting at the altar. The love, the hatred, all the emotions were dissipated, but the question remained as if an answer would assuage the ego of the deserted girl or salve an old, keloid wound. *Why*? She had finally said the word she had wanted to ask her mother, Effie, anyone who could tell her. Why, she asked him.

The answers were anticipated: no bombshells were dropped. Because he had been in debt. Because he had been in love with Veronica. But mainly it had been because Elaine McBride was so weak, so needy, so unstable, the victim of moods that whiplashed from gay, flirtatious coquetry one moment to deep, black depressions the next. They had medication for that now, didn't they, but then it had seemed so hopeless.

He had tried to keep up, he explained, his eyes pleading *don't hate me*. He had sent letters, called, sent money. Elaine McBride had evidently sent them all back, unopened. Catherine listened as her father tried to explain that he had wanted her to come and live with his new family. But Elaine had insisted that her child was the only thing that kept her going. She wouldn't let him take her away. And then it was too late. Things had slipped away from him. Catherine nodded quietly as if the situation had been a series of misunderstandings, rather than the greatest single tragedy in her life.

She stared at this balding, paunchy, ordinary-looking man who had been the source of so many dreams and frustrations and thought about all the letters her mother must have intercepted, all the messages she had never gotten. Why had her father not called her after her mother's breakdown? She had expected him to know intuitively that she needed him. And yet she had never picked up the phone and called her father herself. Certainly a girl who got straight A's in school could be resourceful enough to locate her own father. It had been so easy, in the end, leafing through the Los Angeles directory. Thinking about it now, Catherine realized that she had been afraid all these years of a second rejection.

But rejection had made her what she was, Catherine concluded as she sipped iced tea, her back ramrod straight, on the flocked velvet couch. She rubbed the fuzzy gold fabric. There were crumbs on the cushions. If she had been brought up in the secure cocoon of a middle-class family, would she have been as motivated as she was to succeed on her own? When you had an allowance coming in and keys to the family car, how pressed would you be to spend all your after-school hours working at McBride Vanity Cleaners, learning the basic rules of business and management firsthand? Would you still be so desperate for approval and attention that you compulsively perfected your papers and reports to win yourself a Grunewald Scholarship?

Maybe she could never completely forgive her father, but she could finally acknowledge that he was just an imperfect man, like Graham, and now that they had met again, she could never really hate him either. In fact, she realized that he didn't deserve all the blame. Her mother had deserted her, too, emotionally. Her strength, she realized, came not from either of her parents, but in spite of them, almost in direct reaction to their inabilities to cope.

*I can't tie myself to the past anymore*, she thought. *My mother is buried. My father is what he is, a familiar stranger from another time. But I don't need to spend my life looking for their replacements, either*. Whether or not she ever saw him again, Catherine knew now that she did have a father, and for now that was enough.

Catherine and her father hugged each other and promised to keep in touch. Veronica invited her for Christmas. Then, just as she was walking out the door, Catherine felt Ed McBride's hand on her arm. 'I'm proud of you,' he said. 'We all are.'

'Thanks, Daddy,' she whispered. That was the only name she had ever called him. The word spilled out so naturally.

And it was over. And all so anticlimactic.

The glass sliding door slid open and Aggie Palmer stepped sideways into the lanai of Bungalow Number Two, negotiating clearance for her broad-brimmed black hat. The sun glinted off of the three-million dollars' worth of emeralds that constituted her 'funeral jewelry.' A fifty-two carat cabochon stone formed the body of a golden-legged spider that was pinned to the brim of her black hat. An obscenely large multifaceted emerald brooch that had once belonged to the mother of the Shah of Iran weighted down the lapel of her simple black Givenchy suit, and the thirty-two carat solitaire on her left hand was almost as big as her fist. A gold mesh cuff studded with smaller stones completed the ensemble. Catherine wondered if Aggie were wearing emeralds on her toes beneath her French pumps.

'Too bad that bitch in the coffin couldn't get a load of these rocks,' Aggie snorted as she pulled off her hat and flipped it onto the wicker table. 'At least I looked better than she did. You should have seen the woman! Serves her right! She looked like she was held together with a staple gun! I think she was lifted to death!'

Miss Aggie plopped into an overstuffed wicker ottoman with an elfin grin. 'I always swore I'd dance on that *actress's* grave, and now I've done it. If I don't live five minutes more, I've lived enough.' She propped her feet up, rubbing a swollen bunion.

Jarred out of her reverie, Catherine started to laugh. Agnes Palmer had literally come all this way to bury her late husband's mistress. She had turned out in her widow's weeds and decked herself out like a queen at a coronation just to get the last word with a dead person.

Aggie smirked. 'She used to have this huge entourage. Six personal maids, an agent, a manager, a cheetah on a leash, don't you know. Well, you should have seen her entourage today. Six pallbearers and me. Everybody else was there because they wanted to get their picture in the paper when they write about the death of a legend.'

The old woman focused on a potted plant. 'Up until the day he died, that woman never left my husband alone. Don't you know, I had to sit there while she turned the Colonel's funeral into a circus. Did I tell you she brought the cheetah to his funeral?' Aggie pitched her purse onto the table, where it bounced and landed beside her hat. 'I never hated anyone in my life, but I'm glad that woman is dead. I spent forty years telling the press that she was a *dear family friend*.' She paused. 'Well, maybe Colonel Jack would have liked her better now. Dead lovers are faithful lovers.' She slapped her hands together with finality. 'Done! Now she's in the ground.'

Aggie had a way of putting everything in perspective. My God, if *she* could dance on her husband's mistress's grave after the indignity of having shared him for years during their marriage, Catherine could certainly find a brighter point of view on the reunion with her father.

'How were your ghosts, dear? Tell me all about it.' Aggie patted Catherine's hand and shot her a no-nonsense look.

'He was just regular. I guess I expected something more.'

'More than what? That's what men are – regular. They laugh, they cry, they get up in the morning, they put on their pants. That's all there is. It's not like in the movies.'

Aggie had an answer for everything.

'What did he say when he saw you? Was he in shock?'

'I – I think he was kind of glad to see me, like he'd been waiting for me to show up.'

'Well, he probably was. Figured you'd turn up some day. What did *you* say?'

'I wasn't sure *what* to say.' She twisted a strand of hair. 'I wanted to hate him and love him both at once. But when I saw him, I couldn't really do either. He wasn't the father I loved when I was a little girl, but he wasn't the monster I'd turned him into in my mind either. He was just a guy who didn't know what to do any more than I did.'

Miss Aggie leveled a perceptive glance at her. 'Wouldn't you know that Emily Post doesn't have a single chapter on how to act when you meet your father after he's run off and left you.' She stood up with authority. 'Ghostbusting always makes me hungry,' she announced. 'What do you say we go to that Bistro Garden place, and then let's hit Rodeo Drive. I could use a new hat. And let's think of somethin' special for you.'

Catherine didn't answer. She wasn't in the mood for shopping.

'C'mon, dear. We're both a couple of survivors. Now let's go do somethin' fun.' Aggie tugged her sleeve and they were off.

Three hours and two arugula salads later, Catherine felt, if not distinctly better, completely distracted as she and Aggie Palmer attacked Rodeo Drive like Santa Ana at the Alamo. They left a wake of empty hangers, exhausted salesgirls, and blizzards of sales receipts as they foraged down one side of the street and up the other armed with checkbooks and credit cards, dumping their packages into the white stretch limousine that trailed them from one boutique to the next.

The distinctive scent of Giorgio's perfume engulfed them a full ten yards from the store's entrance as they checked out the window displays under awnings of yellow-and-white canvas. Catherine bought herself a T-shirt that spelled out *Giorgio's* in brass rivets, a Beverly Hills bargain at one hundred dollars. On Rodeo Drive, Catherine could see, you didn't buy merchandise. You bought escape. Catherine had never really enjoyed shopping, but she now understood its function in many women's lives. There was something therapeutic about the trying on of a dress, the rustle of tissue paper, the feel of the fabric, the glitter of the accessories, something that transported you away to an anesthetized limbo for a few precious hours, where your most difficult decision might be whether to take your purchases or send them. Like a visit to a psychiatrist, a new outfit gave you hope for a new you, an opportunity to see yourself differently, even if only for a few minutes, in a fitting-room mirror. The cost of the T-shirt was the price of admission.

At the Chanel boutique, Catherine lined up several groups of costume chains and a rainbow of jewels with faux stones, but was abruptly chastized by Miss Aggie for buying anything that wasn't real. She doubted she would ever own real jewels, and resolved to come back when she was on her own again.

Gucci, Cartier, Valentino, Fred the Jeweler, Nina Ricci, Gianni Versace, Fendi, Courreges – the unlikely pair mowed down the doors and raided the boutiques of the Pantheon of the chic. At Hermès, Aggie Palmer bought herself several pairs of riding gloves and ordered a new set of bits and bridles for her hackneys. On the east side of the street they took in Elizabeth Arden, Férre, Krizia, St Laurent, and Georgette Klinger, with its filigreed, silver Art Nouveau doors. Catherine tried on a clean-striped business suit from Versace, but settled on a sequined Mickey Mouse sweater from Theodore. She felt ready for a little lightheartedness in her life, even if it took the form of a sweater.

Back on Wilshire Boulevard they tallied up their conquests of purchase and walked west past Saks, Gumps, and I. Magnin's.

'I got an idea,' Aggie announced as if she'd just struck oil. 'Let's go to Neiman-Marcus.'

Moving up the escalator, Aggie finally popped the question in her own inimitable style. 'So now that you've found your father, made your deal and saved the company, who are you gonna marry?'

'Marry?' Catherine gulped. 'I don't even know what I'm going to do Saturday night!'

'Well, what about Graham? He's dying to marry you, isn't he?'

'Oh, Miss Aggie,' Catherine sighed.

'What about that nice Billy Wright?'

'We're just friends.'

'What are you looking for? A fever of a hundred and three?' They stepped off the escalator. 'That baron looks pretty impressive. How about him? You could be the baroness.'

Catherine giggled at the thought of marrying the Teutonic baron. Fortunately, she hadn't told Miss Aggie about Alfred, or the old lady would be ordering the christening cups. 'Why do I have to get married at all?'

'Nonsense. Of course you will. You don't want to be my age and all alone with your awards and plaques and six-figure salary.' Aggie stopped suddenly in her tracks and dropped her voice to a stage whisper. 'Look! I'd know that walk anywhere.' She squinted in the direction of a tiny blond tottering by in lizard boots with stratospherically high heels. 'That's Winnie Lifton.'

Catherine looked up. That couldn't be Winnie Lifton. The woman's mouth was grotesquely twisted, as if she'd had a stroke. 'That woman could never be in front of a camera. Look at her face. One whole side of her mouth looks paralyzed.'

'Oh no, dear, it's her. I never miss an episode of *Southwest*,' Aggie persisted. 'The poor child does look awful. I was reading about her in the *Enquirer*. They say she had some sort of face lift that went haywire. Cut the nerves.' She peered more closely as the blond pulled her face down into her upturned leather collar and covered her mouth with her hand.

Catherine and Aggie now found themselves standing in front of the third-floor bridal department. Aggie nodded approvingly as she appraised a luxurious ivory wedding gown with a seven foot train and an illusion veil. 'Now *that's* the kind of thing a girl like you should have,' she proclaimed.

'The perfect outfit to wear to a merger.'

'Now don't tell me this dress doesn't tickle your fancy.'

'I think *you* should have it, Miss Aggie,' Catherine teased. '*You're* the romantic.'

Miss Aggie hooked a thin arm through hers and literally dragged her into the bridal salon. The woman was amazingly strong for an octogenarian.

'For what?' Catherine protested.

'For fun.' Agnes Palmer had spoken, and Catherine knew she had no choice.

Miss Aggie ensconced herself on a couch in the mammoth fitting room, and Catherine stood limply before the mirror, in her underwear, while a small fleet of enthusiastic saleswomen, all of whom seemed to know Aggie

Palmer, carried in six wedding gowns and ten headpieces and veils.

'I can't believe I'm doing this,' Catherine groused. 'They're going to throw me out of here. I don't even have a fiancé.' Her words were muffled as a twenty-five pound dress encrusted in seed pearls dropped over her head.

Aggie Palmer swiftly appraised the situation and put down her flowered teacup. 'Oh, no, no, that dress is too southern belle.' Aggie almost whistled. 'That's not you at all, dear.'

Catherine found herself laughing. Buying a wedding dress was fun. She had to admit she had fantasized about a beautiful bridal gown hundreds of times. Almost every time she had walked past a department store wedding window display. What woman didn't?

The salesgirls were not laughing. The manager had notified them that Mrs Agnes Palmer of Palmer Point, Texas was in the LA store the moment she had activated her charge with a purchase of dusting powder on the first floor, and they were warned and ready to keep the store open 'til midnight if Mrs Palmer so desired.

'Really, Miss Aggie,' whispered Catherine. 'We can't lead these poor ladies on like this. They're working so hard to find something I like.'

'You *should* have something you like.' She patted the settee. 'Come sit by me. I'm getting tired now.'

Catherine gathered up the opalescent folds of the organdie skirt, whisked the veil around her arm, and sat down gingerly, careful not to wrinkle the material.

'Listen, my dear. Humor an old woman. Today I buried my husband's mistress – a thorn in my side for forty years. Let me do something for the future. If I can bury her, I can marry you. Oh, you can just leave it in your closet if you will, and wear it 'round the house! Who knows when a husband will turn up and you've got to be ready.'

Catherine grabbed her temples with both hands and groaned. 'Oh, Miss Aggie.' Wasn't it enough that she'd faced up to the first half of her life today? Did she have to go shopping for a husband, too?

'No, let me finish. I'll pick out the dress. You can pick out the man.' She took the unused funeral handkerchief out of her purse and dabbed dramatically at her eyes, proving she was a much better actress than her husband's ex-mistress. 'I'm not going to live forever. Maybe I won't be able to dance at your wedding. But whenever it is, I'll know you'll be thinkin' of me, and you'll know I'll be there if I picked out the dress.' She sniffed and waved the black lace handkerchief. 'And your taste is *sooo* plain.' The tears vanished. 'I like the one with the bustle.' She winked at her young friend.

# 24

'Darling, are you going to feel funny about seeing the house again?' Eve looked up the long driveway that she had spent her entire life traveling, waiting for the moment when they would pass the clutch of weeping willows and the house would come into view. She wondered how she would feel when she walked into her house, which since the closing three months ago was no longer hers. Even though Eve was staring through the windshield of the Jaguar, she felt Alex watching her. Their months together had only increased his uncanny ability to read her thoughts.

It was the first time since she'd sold the house to Bambi that Eve had set foot back on the property. Eve and Alex had been living in Massachusetts since their quiet marriage on Nantucket two months ago. How different it had been from her first wedding with the entire social register and all of Lake Forest east of Sheridan Road in attendance. The only witnesses on Nantucket had been Bambi and Alex's mother. Michael Picol hadn't allowed Drucilla to travel while she was pregnant, and Eve hadn't even bothered to invite Pollyanne. The First Lady's snubs after Graham had left still smarted. Now that she was Mrs Alex Levin, of course, a wife again, married to a conductor of a major orchestra whose artistic reputation was growing into the world-class stature enjoyed by only a small circle including Leonard Bernstein or Sir George Solti, she received incessant invitations to the White House from Pollyanne. The size of the wedding and who had attended was irrelevant. What mattered to Eve was Alex's hand on the small of her back in the night, their taking turns cooking breakfast in the morning while they listened to opera on his compact disc player, and the way he brushed her hair before she went to bed – the way they loved each other.

The plans for establishing Alex's new school and his conducting schedule had taken up all their time since the wedding. If Alex hadn't been conducting Mozart's *Sonata in A Minor* at tonight's benefit performance for the school, they probably wouldn't have gotten back to Chicago at all before Dru's baby was born in two months. Eve loved to hear Alex conduct Mozart. He applied such an unaffectedness to the music somehow, and elicited both passion and trust from his musicians that she wondered about the legendary artistic temperament. He attributed everything good and positive to Eve, who shared equally in every decision that was made. She was even composing a little and was chairman of his new school.

She checked the time on the sporty leather Piaget that she wore. It was five o'clock and the concert at Ravinia wouldn't begin until after seven. There was plenty of time to visit with Hughie and catch up on how Bambi was doing at college.

As they pulled up in front of the house, it seemed just the same from the outside, except that all the draperies were gone. An army of trucks and huge-haul bins parked under the deep arches at the side and rear entrances was a new touch, too.

She leaned over and stroked the nape of Alex's neck. Then she tenderly slid her hand under the fabric of his shirt. 'Your shirt is a little big, maestro. Who dresses you?' They were both wearing Armani tuxedoes, his black, hers white, like the negative and positive of a photograph.

'A very classy broad,' he smiled at her, and stopped the car.

In front of the stone stairway, Hughie, wearing a flowing caftan, rounded the corner from the garden, followed by a chattering entourage that, Eve had heard, was continuously recruited from the ranks of certain boutiques, hair salons, and photography studios. Eve noticed the handsome son of a local horse breeder tagging along, as well as six or seven young men of almost seraphic good looks.

'Well,' Alex announced. 'I don't know if I ought to leave you with all these good-looking young boys.'

'I don't think I'm their type,' Eve closed the car door and leaned through the open window.

'You're everybody's type. All men fall under your spell.'

It always amazed Eve how Alex could be so worldly, yet naïve at the same time, as if his talent had insulated him from the realities of the world.

'Eve! The empress of the music world! How are you?' Hughie came rustling up, his caftan flapping, trailed by his happy following. 'Bravo! It's the maestro and his wife!'

Eve waved over her shoulder to Alex as she was swept up with the group, which was en route to an inspection of the living room.

As she watched Alex drive off, a workman pushing an unwieldy wheelbarrow rumbled across the stone courtyard. Eve frowned when she saw that it held the heavy silk flamestitch wallpaper that she had chosen for the living room, wadded up in clumps of blue and beige in the bin. An involuntary shudder quivered across her shoulders. How many months of her life had she devoted to choosing that wallpaper, to making sure every nuance of the custom colors and design had been perfect?

'Just a moment,' she called to the workman. She reached down and picked up a torn fragment and held it up, examining it like a little corner of her life. It was only wallpaper. She dropped it back into the rubble and walked into the house.

In spite of herself, Eve almost gasped when she poked through the gutted house where she had been born, bred, and married, and where she had raised her own child. The grand stairway had vanished, as had most of the second floor. Now a forty-foot ceiling dominated the space, and walls had been replaced by random columns, placed here and there for structural support. A glass brick catwalk rimmed the entire perimeter of the huge room, with architectonic arches leading to what remained of the second floor. Everything was open in this new unfamiliar place. It would be a house with no secrets.

'Hughie,' she touched his arm. 'This looks like a French railroad station.'

Hughie made a sweeping gesture. 'André Putman. She's a whiz. It's the first job she's ever done in Chicago. Of course, it was wonderful when you had the house, Eve, but *now* it's *moderne*. It's going to be completely black and white. Black and white marble, furniture, floors . . .'

Eve was about to ask what had happened to the eighteenth-century paneling when she thought she recognized Bambi sulking across the room. But as the familiar figure moved, or rather stalked closer, she realized something was off-kilter. It was Bambi's tall, lean build, Bambi's signature cropped hair, Bambi's doe-like eyes and thick, dark lashes that cast shadows on high, chiseled cheekbones. It was Bambi's body wearing a white cotton shirt and *Bambi* jeans with riding boots. Still, something was amiss. Eve froze when she suddenly realized that it was not Bambi, but a young *man* standing in front of her, a close friend of Hughie's, she gathered, by the way he created an aura of intimacy as he moved to Hughie's side.

'Sasha, meet the most beautiful woman in the world.' Hughie turned to Eve. The young man lifted his Bambi eyes to greet her. 'Sasha's just defected from the Kirov Ballet. He's staying here while he gets acclimated. You should see the pictures Valeski did of him for *Vogue*. You'll faint.'

Eve held out her hand and looked uneasily at Hughie. He must certainly not be unaware that this person was an androgynous clone of his sister. How bizarre, she thought, suppressing a shudder. A psychiatrist would have a field day with this. 'How – how is Bambi?' she asked, casting about to initiate a normal conversation, as if the asking would reassure her that this creature before her was not Elizabeth Anne Stuart.

'Dedicated to the pursuit of veterinary medicine. She's signed up for summer school. We're all going down to visit her on campus. Morale.'

Eve could envision this bevy of puerile pulchritude descending on an unsuspecting, sleepy southern campus, where the hottest thing that happened was probably sex between boys and girls.

'I left the cottage intact for her. She wouldn't let me touch a thing.' Hughie groaned as he nodded at a fabric sample. 'But I'm redoing the new horse farm from scratch. We're building the house out of an old stable. You know, lots of sandblasted beams and old hurricane lamps. If I don't lose my mind first.' He waved his hands in the direction of the plasterers, who were experimenting with finishes.

Eve wondered what Drucilla and Bambi thought of this transformation of their childhood home. Bambi probably wouldn't care, since she spent most of her time at school now and had even discounted the city of Chicago as her home. 'Have the girls been out lately?' she asked.

'Dru's waiting till it's done! But Lolly Bishop adores it! Loves change, you know,' Hughie called out as he climbed a small ladder to nowhere. 'When I saw Lolly she was going balling in Vienna. Princess W is giving a serious birthday ball. Lolly was on the phone here, hustling an extra seat for her ballgown. She wanted them to credit it with extra mileage points.' Sasha steadied Hughie's hand as he tottered backward down the ladder.

'She thinks the Concorde is a station wagon,' chimed in Oliver, who cut Eve's hair when she was in town.

Sasha leaned over and whispered into Hughie's ear.

'Thank God for Sasha,' Hughie extolled. 'What a mind! He just reminded me, Eve, you have a message here from the White House.'

Oliver perked up. 'It was all over the newspapers. Pollyanne didn't make it to the dinner for the King of Spain last night. Evidently, your girlfriend spent the whole evening in her room.'

'Where on earth is the phone? Is there a phone in this house? It used to be *here*!' Hughie threw his arms up in the air. He had put on about fifty pounds since the family fortune had increased so dramatically with the sale of Bambi's stock. Although the money was legally Bambi's, she had set Hughie up with an allowance, which, from the hangers-on and the amount of spending, Eve judged to be enormous.

Sasha led Eve to the greenhouse, which was equally as

changed as the main house. Hughie was turning it into a Nautilus and dance studio, although the thought of Hughie lifting more than a shrimp fork was inconceivable. Clearly, the studio was for Sasha, who moved through the grounds like a panther and into the greenhouse leading Eve past the statue of Diana as if she'd never been there before.

Eve knew she'd been remiss in not calling Pollyanne. The First Lady's aides had left several messages, and that fact in itself had irritated Eve, who still thought their relationship had been worthy of dialing direct and talking in person. But if the White House had taken the trouble to track her down here, Eve thought, it must be important.

She dialed the private number in the family quarters. Private or not, she had to go through three frosty aides before Rex himself came on the phone. This was unusual, she thought. No one ever picked up this line except Pollyanne.

'Eve, when can you come up? I think it would do Pollyanne a lot of good to see you.'

'Alex's schedule since the wedding has been so full,' she apologized. 'I miss you both, but . . .'

Rex lowered his voice. 'Pollyanne hasn't been well.'

Eve wondered if one of Pollyanne's self-prescribed age retardants hadn't finally done her in.

Rex went on to describe a horror story in which Pollyanne seemed to have undergone a progressive psychological disintegration. In other words, according to Rex, she'd gone stark, raving mad, and it was as embarrassing as hell. The symptoms had first shown themselves at the last state dinner, when she had achieved the zenith of calorie counting by surreptitiously spitting an entire five-course dinner into her napkin in front of the President of France. It wasn't even bulimia, according to the staff physicians. She didn't even swallow the food or let it work its way down her gullet. Rex sounded as if he were in total anguish as he described how Pollyanne had spent the past month spitting out everything from crudités to a box of chocolate Turtles into tissues, handkerchiefs, and napkins.

'She's got it down to an art,' he moaned. 'It sort of looks like she's dabbing her lipstick. So we've managed to keep it out of the press, but it's getting worse. She stays in her room getting her legs waxed and facials and God knows whatever, and then we can't get her to come out. Except last night. Last night was the worst, Eve.'

'I heard she missed the state dinner,' Eve said. 'Maybe she's just exhausted. She has a lot to live up to.'

'That's the whole point. She thinks she can't be perfect till she looks like one of her magazine covers. And those are all touched up anyway!' The poor man sounded distraught.

'Rex, that's terrible. She's such a strong girl.'

'Well, last night she flipped. She went down to the Rose Garden and cut all the heads off the Savage roses. We were frantic looking for her – the Secret Service, me, Mother. And there she was in her nightgown hacking away with a fire ax.'

'My God.'

'We had to call in Bloomers to replant the entire garden before it got light, so nobody would find out. Placido Domingo is entertaining the King of Spain in the East Room, and the First Lady is out decapitating roses in the garden.' Rex's voice broke. 'She won't talk to the doctors. Why don't you come? We'll send a plane.' It was more than a request.

Eve was horrified. Poor Pollyanne. One of her 'minidepreshes' had gotten out of hand. It had all gone to her head – the politics, the press, the fishbowl life. This is what had come of devoting herself to Rex and his ambitions. Eve considered herself lucky to be off that merry-go-round, safe with Alex in a world of love and music. Funny, how the separation which Pollyanne and the others had pitied her for had led to the most fulfilling time of her life. Poor Pollyanne.

But then again, it wasn't Eve's fault. She had to think of herself first. Alex and Drucilla needed her. The new school needed her. Pollyanne needed professional help. 'Rex, dear, I'm going to do something better than come myself. I'm going to ask Dr Corbett to come immediately. He's brilliant. He's the one who saved Drucilla. Pollyanne knows him. So she'd be comfortable with him.'

'You're her friend.'

'Well, you're her husband, Rex. She needs *you*. Why didn't you stay upstairs with her instead of going to that state dinner? The Vice-President could have stepped in.' Eve couldn't believe she was telling off the President of the United States! But it was as if she were telling off Graham, too, for all the years when she was a corporate widow. That life was behind her. She had escaped. But she had not forgotten.

'But the publicity,' Rex protested sharply. 'It would be horrendous if this got out.'

'Rex, you're in your second term. You have a mandate behind you.' An idea occurred to Eve. 'Why not turn this into something positive? Look what Betty Ford did for breast cancer and alcohol abuse. When Pollyanne pulls through this, she'll be a heroine.'

'I'll be looking for you.'

'Dr Corbett will be there tomorrow. And I'll do what I can.'

After she'd hung up, Eve knew she wouldn't be going at all.

In the corner of the greenhouse – the former greenhouse – she spotted a trio of clay pots holding a few abandoned sprays of cymbidium. She plucked one of the blooms, tucked it into her lapel, smoothed her ruffled satin shirt, and left to join her husband.

# 25

'Michael, it's cold on my tummy. Besides, you're no doctor,' Drucilla giggled as her husband moved the stethoscope over her pregnant abdomen.

'Quiet. I've been practicing medicine for years without a license. I know what I'm doing.'

'Can you hear both heartbeats?' Drucilla had known she was carrying twins for the past three months. Michael had taken an uncharacteristic paternal pride at the news, but Dru wondered how he would feel when he learned the twins were girls. But Dru hadn't told Michael the sex of the babies. She hated to spoil his excitement, and he naturally assumed that they would be boys, to carry on his family name.

Because this was a pregnancy conceived in rape, her obstetrician had insisted on an amniocentesis test to determine if there was any evidence of congenital defects or disease. Dru had convinced herself that the babies were really her husband's by blocking the rape from her mind. She and Michael had agreed to keep the babies no matter what they looked like – black, Oriental, whatever. They would raise them as their own. Even her mother had understood. Plenty of people adopted foreign children, didn't they? And these babies *were* one-half Donaldson.

Michael's reaction had been extraordinary. He acted as if these were his own children and he'd been waiting for them for most of his life. He'd insisted on joining her for Lamaze classes, and he'd devised his own special nutritional program for her on his computer. He'd even taken a maternity tour of Prentice Woman's Hospital to check out the facilities and make sure they were up to his standards. Dru was amazed. Michael was turning out to be father of the year, and the twins weren't even due for six more weeks.

Everything had worked out better than she had imagined. Michael was so protective of her, she finally felt safe. He'd hired round-the-clock bodyguards for them both, and purchased the apartments on both sides of his in the Lake Point Towers, so they could have privacy as well as more space for a nursery. Of course, there was not much room for romance. Her husband never touched her, except to stroke or pat her belly. Maybe he was being overprotective of her. Sometimes, Drucilla thought, she envied her mother and Alex with their easy hand-holding and touching. But, on the other hand, she was relieved. She could not completely erase the memory of the musky-sweet violet scent and the weight of an unknown person pinning her down, and she still couldn't close the bathroom door behind her or walk into a closet by herself.

Only Michael seemed to understand and put up with her fears. People had been so wrong about him. Underneath his hard shell was a core of caring and love. He was so sensitive to her needs. He would only let people he knew and trusted into the house, for instance. He did not want to hire a strange nurse for the babies. Instead, he had sent Singh, the houseman, to nanny school in London. She wondered what kind of bonus he'd given Singh to get him to push a pram.

She giggled again as Michael pushed the stethoscope across her abdomen. It tickled.

'Okay, I've got the heartbeats now,' he announced excitedly. It was wonderful how anything to do with the babies made him beam with genuine delight.

'How many do you hear?'

'Five or six. I must not be doing this right.' He sat up and took a jar of vitamin E oil from the night table drawer. 'Here, rub this on your stomach.'

'Can't you do it? You do it so much better. The babies – they can tell.' She tugged at his elbow petulantly. She wanted him to stay. To get into bed with her, so she could put her head on his chest and feel safe. She didn't want him to go out.

'No. I gotta go.'

'At eleven-thirty at night?'

'Business. You and the kids stay at home and rest up.'

'But I'm bored with staying home.' She hated the jangling of the phone, his abrupt exits and apologetic absences.

'Watch a movie on the VCR.' He pointed to the long shelf of black boxes. 'There's got to be something you haven't seen here.' He carefully tucked a pillow under her legs. 'It's better to sleep with your legs raised. Otherwise there's a tendency for the blood return to be impaired. I read it in Lamaze.'

'I don't know why we've got this team of doctors lined up. You could probably deliver these babies yourself.'

'I intend to.'

'I thought you hated the sight of blood.'

'I'll let the other guys handle the knives. That's their department. I'm just going to bring them into the world.'

Dru looked alarmed. 'Oh my stars.'

'Don't look like that. I'm prepared. Half these nights I'm over at Prentice observing.'

'Observing what?'

'Delivery techniques. Dr Rosenberg lets me scrub in.'

'What do those women think?'

'Most of them are so out of it, they think I'm their husband.'

Dru was sure he was teasing. He had such a sense of humor. Nobody saw that side of him but her.

She held out her cheek to be kissed, but he bent down and nuzzled her belly instead. 'See you later.'

'But I'm afraid to stay here alone,' she whispered.

'Okay. I won't take the bodyguards. I'm leaving them all with you.'

It was too bad, Dru thought, that many of his meetings took place at night. But since that British company had taken over Intercon, Michael was on his own, and she knew how hard it was to set up business for yourself on a normal person's schedule. He was starting an international legal consulting firm and it seemed as if practically all his clients were on different time zones.

Dru wasn't sleepy at all. Her eyes wandered up to the ceiling. She purposely avoided looking behind her. She hated that Madonna picture, with the Angel Gabriel and the Immaculate Conception and all. It only highlighted the fact that her babies were the result of a rape.

She wrapped herself in one of her extra-large men's shirts and padded into the kitchen for a glass of skim milk. Michael made sure she drank some every day. She passed by the Lucite console with its three TV screens, went back to the bedroom, and pulled out a tape at random.

*Wuthering Heights*. Perfect. Michael reminded her of Heathcliff. She fast-forwarded through the tape, stopping only at the Heathcliff parts.

What else was there to watch? She'd seen all these tapes a dozen times. Dru wandered back to the console, where she remembered seeing a rack of unmarked tapes and pulled one out. Maybe there'd be something new in there. Or at least a business tape so boring it would put her to sleep.

She slid the tape in and lay back on the bed. The first shot was of a crotch. Good Lord. A porno tape from Michael's bachelor collection. A cheapo, clearly. No music, no credits, just a disgusting close-up of a woman's crotch. A man's hand was fondling her. 'Oh, yuk,' she said. She tried to reach the remote control to turn it off, but her distended belly made it hard to sit up.

As the camera pulled away, she recognized one of the Scarron bridesmaid's dresses from her own wedding. Suddenly riveted to the set, Drucilla was unable to look away as she focused on the scene and recognized Lolly Bishop yanking off the Scarron dress. Then the tape went blank for a minute, before it picked up a picture of Lolly diving into a bathtub to perform oral sex on – good Lord, it was Michael! It was her, all right, and *him*! The bridesmaid's bouquet was floating in the water beside her. My God, her best friend was giving her husband a blow job in the bathtub!

Dru rushed, nauseated, into his bathroom. It still smelled of that pungent sweetness of musky flowers that was suddenly all too familiar. *Violets*. It was the smell of the closet! The man in the closet . . . the sensations of the rape whirled around her. With every ounce of strength she had, Drucilla pushed against the sink, as if to push the memory out of her mind. She didn't want to remember! She never wanted to remember!

A sharp, deep pain doubled her over and she felt her knees on the bathroom floor. This couldn't be labor. There were still five weeks to go!

She groped her way to the front door, where the bodyguards were stationed, holding the walls to keep her bearings as a burst of warm fluid trickled down her legs.

She had to open the door, get help, before she lost consciousness. The pain jolted through her again. She'd never make it, she realized.

She crawled on her hands and knees back to the bedroom, leaving a smeared trail of blood. It felt as if a gash had opened up somewhere deep inside. The panic button was just on the bedside table. She pounded on it with her fist and collapsed at the foot of the bed, pulling the sheets off as she fell backward.

Michael Picol got off the elevator at the penthouse floor. What could Winnie's latest problem be? She had said it was urgent. He hoped she wasn't going to put the move on him tonight. God, one side of her face looked like a melted candle. He'd run out of excuses to keep from touching her. He was better off with A, B, and C, he smirked to himself. The three stewardesses nobody knew, whom he could count on to be gone the next day, when they had to fly somewhere else.

He had to be careful where he went these days, and whom he saw. Herrera and his men would love nothing better than to get their hands on him. Trans-Oceanic had gone out on a limb in anticipation of money from the oil oasis that would have been created by the Intercon acquisition. Although eighty percent of the Venezuelan population would have still been impoverished, the thought of the twenty percent that would have benefited from an enormous influx of petrodollars had prodded Herrera into bringing in the South American Mafia to build casinos and control the terminale, a lucrative if illegal lottery. Organized crime had committed millions of dollars and build several major casinos on Herrera's prediction. Now he was left holding the bag, with egg on his face, and Picol hadn't been able to convince him that his sudden marriage to Dru was not a sell-out. He had married Dru for his own reasons. He'd been in enough deals with Herrera to know that this was a guy with a long memory, whose machismo balanced a hair-trigger revenge mechanism. If he was let down in a deal, there was hell to pay.

He would meet Herrera, Picol had decided, but on his own terms. After the twins were born, he'd be ready to move on a new deal. There were already some things in the works. He'd cut Herrera in. They would smooth things over.

The problem was he never knew how angry Herrera really was. Over the phone, he sounded cool and aloof. But he had a Mafia mentality, though Picol was sure it was nothing he couldn't handle. He'd been cornered before.

He wondered how far out on a limb Herrera had gone over all this. He couldn't have lost money. When the Grunewalds took over, Trans-Oceanic's Intercon holding had gone up. But Herrera had lost honor, and this made him a very dangerous man. Picol took in a big breath of air as he turned to the penthouse-floor corridor and sauntered into the Ambassador Suite.

Winnie's rooms were dimly lit. She had draped scarves over all the lampshades. She turned her good side to him. 'So, how's the happy groom?'

He put his feet up on the table as she handed him a drink. 'Did you hear – it's twins. I'm gonna get two for one.' He smiled – the first genuine smile Winnie had ever seen on his face. 'They're going to be big boys.'

'Come off it. How do you even know whose they are? How can you get so excited over this? She should have had an abortion. You made me have one. Or have you forgotten?'

'Don't look at me with that face.' It looked like someone had twisted a wire inside her lip.

'If we'd had our baby, you would have known you were the father. But now – who would want me?' She started to cry little rabbitlike sobs. 'You'd rather have some kidnapper's kid with some rich socialite than mine.'

He looked at her, his face in the shadows. 'Twins. They're mine.'

'What?'

'I am the father.'

'Right.'

'You don't have to believe me. You'll see when they are born. They'll look like me.' He smiled. Every time he thought of his babies, he felt good. They *would* be his! For the first time he could remember, he loved something without reservation. Even before they were born, they were taking over his emotions, making him feel as if at last he could have the chance to redeem those days when his father locked him in a closet and forced him to shut down his feelings in self-defense. 'My kids are going to be great.'

'But she was kidnapped.'

'Yeah. It was what Herrera and I called a diversionary tactic. I set up the whole thing.'

'You're disgusting.' She jumped up from her chair.

'Nobody got hurt.'

Winnie paced across the room in a rage. '*Me*! I got hurt!' She was shrieking and pointing at her face. 'No one but you would want me now, and you're married. You went and got *married*!'

Picol brought his feet down with a crash that shook the coffee table. 'I don't know why I even came here in the first place. I don't need some freak-faced bimbo trying to give me guilt.'

Winnie started to fly at him, but she caught herself and choked off her angry comeback. She had to remember what she'd gotten him there for. Herrera had been right. Picol would never do one thing for her, just insult her. Herrera had given her the villa in Brazil and a blank check in her name for Dr Pitangy, the world's top plastic surgeon, to resurrect the damage done by Michael's matchbook-school doctor. The operation had seemed so simple . . . just vacuum off the fat under her cheekbones. But the incompetent creep had sucked out a nerve ending, paralyzing one whole side of her face.

She had had some doubts tonight. After all, she had once loved Michael Picol. But he had taken that love and squashed it like yesterday's newspaper to be thrown out with the trash.

She had to do what she planned. There was no future for her as an actress in front of the camera. And what man would want her now? Herrera was the only one who answered her calls. He was helping her. Now she was helping him. Whatever settling up he and Picol had to do, it was none of her business. Her instructions were just to get him into the suite without his bodyguards and keep him there so Herrera could have his undivided attention. If Michael would think that was a betrayal, so what? He'd already betrayed her so many times, it didn't matter.

You're an actress, she reminded herself, resetting the facial features she could still control. 'Michael,' she said seductively, 'couldn't we make love one last time?'

His expression was blank.

'I brought a friend. She's very beautiful. She's down the hall. Let me go get her. Maybe the three of us could get something going. You'll wait, won't you?'

He was interested, she could tell. 'Who's your friend?'

'My replacement on *Southwest*.'

'The kid who married that rock star?'

'Right. Faust. He's on tour – and she's dying to meet you. Just let me go get her. We could have dinner together and then who knows? I haven't entirely forgotten what Michael Picol likes.'

Picol sat down on the couch and leaned back with a yawn, stretching his chest.

'Two minutes, baby,' Winnie said. 'All my California goodies are in the bedroom. Why don't you go in there? You might be pleasantly surprised to find out who all joins you.' She slipped out the door, closed it behind her, and ran as fast as she could to the elevator, which was being held for her by two men wearing windbreakers and open shirts.

Michael Picol had just sauntered into the bedroom to poke through the tackle box where she kept her makeup and drugs, when he heard the door open. Nah, he wasn't interested. He turned around expecting to see Winnie and the eighteen-year-old bride of the infamous rock star. Instead, he came face to face with three huge men. In a split second he assessed his options. The bedroom was at his back. His gun was there in his jacket. He could shoot one, block another, maybe, if he moved fast enough before they got him. He backed up slowly, but the three men matched each of his steps, forcing him deeper into the corner.

'Señor Piccolini,' said one. 'You're very impolite. You have not returned our calls.' He picked up the phone and slashed the cord with a razor-sharp knife.

Damn Winnie. He hadn't thought she had the brains to figure out a trap, much less lead him into one.

'Where's Herrera? I want to talk to him,' Picol bluffed. All of his street instincts told him that these men were on a payroll, and whatever they were being paid for was not in his best interest. Maybe if he offered them more than Herrera . . .

'But Señor Herrera has no reason to talk to *you*,' replied the tallest man, and as he moved toward Michael Picol he pulled a length of piano wire from his pocket and snapped it taut between his hands.

# 26

'Danny, I really wish I could go with you – but Hughie and the boys are coming down this weekend.'

'Again? The "magnificent seven" were just here last week, Elizabeth.' He obviously didn't approve.

She could never expect Danny to understand Hughie, 'I'm his only family. He misses me, that's all. He likes to come down and visit.'

'Seems to me he has plenty of company.' Danny rolled his eyes. 'He always bring along the entire audience from "Let's Make a Deal."'

'Try to be more understanding. They're fun.' Bambi ate the crust off the last piece of pizza. She wanted her brother to be happy. Hughie was actually much busier and more involved now that he had the new house to fuss over, and if that included a crazy collection of friends, what difference did it make? She knew that her leaving for college had devastated him. Sasha was the evidence. She grimaced when she thought of Sasha, her twin brother, as Hughie liked to joke. What was that creep doing pandering up to her brother? Hughie's sex life was his own business, but this went beyond sex. It was weird. She knew Sasha was just an effort to fill the empty place she'd left in Hughie's life, but every time she saw him with his Bambi face she felt like heave-hoing him out the door with a horse kick in his pretty little behind.

Hughie and the boys found some reason to show up almost every weekend. They were adorable, but she was serious about her studies now and couldn't really spare

the time to look after them. She certainly didn't want to offend her brother, but she'd have to cut his visits back to once a month if she wanted to have any personal life of her own.

She'd worked so hard to get into college and to shed her Bambi image. It had finally worked. Nobody even knew her as 'Bambi,' super-model. In this small college town, she was just Elizabeth Ann Stuart, another pretty freshman. Hughie's weekly appearance with his peacock entourage of stylists and makeup artists did not exactly help her blend into the woodwork. She'd had enough of notoriety.

The Bambi line was still going strong. She never modeled for it anymore, and they reran her old pictures in the ads. She still got scripts to read and calls about movies, but she and Hughie now paid her agent to turn everything down. Hughie had been right. Modeling had been a way out. But now she had another escape route. With the money from the stock sale, she didn't have to do what she didn't want to. She'd never really enjoyed bein in the limelight, and acting was worse. She loved Valesk of course, but she could still see him whenever she we home. The life she really cared about was here, at scho

Bambi was enjoying life as Elizabeth Ann Stuart. could eat whatever she wanted, and if she gained a pounds, nobody cared. She could have a roommate own age, someone to talk to about boyfriends an nighters. She could ride her horses all afternoon in of spending her only free time getting her make hair perfect for the next shot. Hughie thought this life was hideously boring, which was why he cam to 'rescue' her every weekend. But Bambi lo mixers, the classes, the sororities, the dates wit boys, not the *Gentlemen's Quarterly* hopefuls

on shoots. It meant she was accepted, she was normal, not an accident of nature with a beautiful, photogenic face, an ice princess without parents. And most of all she loved learning to be a 'horse doctor' and still have time to compete in all the equestrian contests that would qualify her for the Olympic trials.

She hadn't told any of the kids at school about her horse farm outside of Louisville – not even Danny, or any of the guys she went out with. It would just make them wonder and set off a lot of talk. Everybody thought the horse farm she visited was Hughie's, and that was fine. Now when somebody asked her out, she knew it was because they liked Elizabeth Ann Stuart, not a millionaire model with thirty-five magazine covers and ten thousand acres.

Bambi brushed her hair out of her eyes. She'd let it grow long again. Looking around the off-campus restaurant, she could see fifteen girls with variations on her old Bambi haircut – short, uneven and boyish, and spiked at the nape of the neck. Now that everyone was wearing it, it held no interest for her. She still gravitated instinctively to a look of her own, usually throwing on a patterned skirt, ankle socks under sandals, a long vest over a man's T-shirt, pinned with a clutch of old medals, tucking her hair under a tweed cap. Without makeup and with her hair now shoulder-length, Bambi bore little resemblance o the androgynous creature she'd made so famous. ltogether, she looked far more appealing with no effort han the Bambi-haircut girls who spent hours in front of eir mirrors. Like many women born beautiful, she rely studied her looks. She didn't have to. She could ke them for granted. Her intelligence was another atter. That, she never took for granted. She knew that en with her new fortune she'd need to keep her wits

about her to build up a world-class horse farm. Money was a factor when a yearling could cost a million dollars, but everybody in the field had money, old money, huge money, and no amount of money could breed a champion. You had to know your bloodlines and your training. Horses were a business that she intended to do better than anybody. Everything she'd done so far had simply been a means to this end.

Any man she got involved with would have to understand her way of life. She knew it would take a very special person, and she hadn't met him yet. That would come later. In the meantime, she liked traveling in a pack. It protected you from intimacy, gave you an excuse not to be alone with someone you didn't like, and shielded you from casual campus sex.

Her roommate waved from the next booth. As Bambi got up, one of the girls at her table noticed her jeans.

'Do I detect Bambi jeans?' she said. 'I never thought I'd see Elizabeth Ann Stuart wearing a designer label.'

'Whatever happened to that Bambi person, anyhow?' asked Danny. 'She was pretty hot for a while there.' He and Elizabeth grinned at each other as she pulled her cap further down over her eyes. Danny had figured it out a long time ago, but he had also figured out she didn't want anyone else to know when she pulled the Bambi poster off his wall and stuffed it into the waste-basket.

'Just dropped from sight,' said the girl.

'Right,' shrugged Elizabeth Ann Stuart. 'Like Andy Warhol said, everyone's famous for fifteen minutes.'

# 27

Ray Acconti's retouched face stared back at Graham from the cover of *Time* magazine. 'Plan for a Small Planet,' he muttered to himself in disbelief, astounded at the gullibility of the American public. Here they were, turning him into a Baby Boomer folk hero for his unheard-of challenge of the Secretary of Defense. Acconti had come out in condemnation of the Star Wars program on the grounds that deploying nuclear weapons in space polluted our entire planetary system. What the hell did he think he was going to do – declare Mars a national park? The man's only experience above the ground was flying in the company plane. And here was Acconti being lauded as the Mr Clean of the ionosphere! Where was the press when it came to people who knew what they were talking about, like Dr Io? Why would they put a yes-man on the cover instead of a great humanitarian and scientist who was devising ways to feed the world? Maybe the Graham Donaldson Research Center wasn't as extensive as he had once hoped, but the nature of Dr Io's work was monumentally important.

Well, what was the use of getting all worked up? The whole point of this island was to escape the pressures of the mainland world and concentrate on the work that had to be done. He and Dru had come down for a month, while he caught up on Dr Io's progress.

He looked up to see Singh walk by carrying a tiny hand-carved outrigger that he had been meticulously whittling from a coconut shell most of the morning. The immobile face of the threatening-looking Sikh dissolved into a gap-toothed smile as he knelt at the water's edge and presented his gift to the two little girls who were perched in their mother's lap, their identical starched sun-bonnets shielding them from the cloudless Caribbean sun. The little boat bobbed out to sea toward Antigua, and Dru held their tiny hands and helped them wave it on its journey.

Graham tossed aside the *Time* magazine and picked up a pair of sterling silver buckets engraved with his granddaughters' names: Hope and Michele. Dru had named one of the twins after Michael Picol even though he had disappeared on the day of their birth. Since that day, no one had seen or heard from the son-of-a-bitch. If he ever did show his face around his girls again, Graham would personally bash it in. It was bad enough that Picol had sold out the company; the fact that he had betrayed Drucilla was unforgivable.

But then, who wasn't in the business of betrayal these days? Hadn't everyone knifed him in the back, even the women in his life? He kicked at a hermit crab that was slowly inching its way across the sand. At least it had a shell to protect itself, even if it was stolen from another animal.

Graham had thought he knew Eve so well. He would have taken her back, even after she had gone off with someone he could better see matched with Dru. He had been astonished that Levin had actually married Eve. Didn't he realize that she was a grandmother, a woman who'd been raised to stay out of the limelight and tend to her family? Now here she was cavorting around with a bunch of intellectuals and aesthetes, wearing her hair swinging around her shoulders, making a display of herself for the world to see in half the magazines in America.

He thought about Eve and conjured up a picture of the woman he used to know. A woman whose husband and children came first. A woman who had her values in place. His ideal woman. Why then had he jeopardized his happiness and her devotion? Right now, he couldn't imagine why. He should have been able to handle it like other men in his position and have a wife and a mistress. But Eve had given him ultimatums. As had Catherine. Why did women have to do that? They forced you to act prematurely. If Eve had been smart, she would have closed her eyes to what didn't concern her. His love for her was different from his love for Catherine. Nothing could have ever changed the feelings he had for Eve. She should never have forced his hand.

He had always known where he stood with Eve. What was it with the 'modern woman' who puts herself before everyone else? How did two people ever get in the same room if one of them wouldn't follow the other? No wonder Catherine was such a bad dancer – she always had to lead. She had appeared to be his woman, his love, his future wife. Yes, she gave the appearance. She was good at making people believe what she wanted. Catherine was a person with mixed-up priorities, a woman without the soul of a woman, who didn't know how to take care of a man, and didn't care. A self-centered brat when the chips were down. She should probably never have children.

Graham picked up the *Time* magazine, rolled it up, and swatted a sand fly. It must be getting close to five. They came out about then.

'Dru, you'd better think about getting those babies back to the bungalow so they won't get bitten up.'

'In a few minutes, Dad. Look how *happy* they are.' Her voice lilted up and took on the animation it did only when she was around her daughters. The rest of the time,

Graham thought disconcertedly, she seemed unapproachable, shrouded in her own world. He was glad the twins had been girls – Dru seemed to have such a repulsion toward men. Since the night the babies had been born, she literally shrank from the touch of any man except himself and Singh, who Graham was sure was a eunuch, with all his nanny-school affectations. She'd even propped Dr Corbett in favor of a woman psychiatrist.

Dru seemed to have adopted the celibate looks of a nun. She wore no makeup these days, paid no attention to her clothes, wearing her plainness like a penance. Dru now lived in a baby world, eating the twins' food from their spoons, napping when they napped, bathing with them, talking baby talk, and letting herself be cared for by Singh like one of them.

As far as Graham knew, her last adult act had occurred in the hospital, when she pulled a picture of Picol from her purse and very deliberately lit a match and burned it, twirling it in her fingers, letting the ashes drop into the ash tray by the bed, as if she were exorcising him from her life. After that, she had never mentioned his name again, as she sat by the incubators anxiously waiting until her premature babies were strong enough to go home. And now home was wherever her father was.

Graham wondered what had happened between Dru and Picol. It seemed odd that he should vanish after demonstrating such love for these babies even before they were born. Much as he depised Picol, he almost wished he would return for Dru's sake. Since the kidnapping, only Picol had been able to penetrate her forlornness. Graham had hired detectives, but they had all come back empty-handed, which did not totally surprise him considering the vindictiveness of those with whom Picol had been operating.

Well, thought Graham, shaking some sand off his fishing hat. If you lie down with dogs, you get up with fleas.

Strange though, he hadn't felt as betrayed by Michael Picol as by the women in his life who professed to love him.

Dru carried over one of the little girls wrapped in a terrycloth towel lettered 'A Place in the Sun,' who beamed at him with a toothless chortle. Little Hope, or was it Michele? He couldn't really tell them apart yet.

He gently held the baby and looked into her trusting eyes. Her eyes were beautiful, dark brown, almost black, in contrast to her fair hair and complexion.

His granddaughters. Unspoiled, uncharted. He would make sure that they lived protected and loved, so they would never know betrayal.

Singh handed him the second baby, and he bounced them both in the crooks of his arms. These babies would grow up into real women who would know how to be supportive of a man and his dreams, who would not lose themselves in some greedy, self-centered climb for their own position.

Not that he wanted them to be clinging vines. They'd be modern girls. But they'd know the meaning of loyalty.

He waved a tiny sterling silver shovel at them and four tiny hands reached for it as it glinted in the light of the sun hanging low in the Caribbean sky.

He'd do everything for these little girls. They'd have their Place in the Sun.

Every girl should have her place in the sun.

# 28

Catherine McBride Grunewald set down the Dictaphone and put her feet up on the chintz ottoman. She stared at the pattern, with its pastel floral bands on ribbons of lemon, white, and fuchsia, and tried to refocus her concentration. She still had to go through a stack of fifty résumés and two hundred letters of recommendation. She couldn't just skim through them. She knew all too well that each one of these pieces of paper represented somebody's dreams, potential, and hopes. But no matter how hard she tried, any concrete thought of her work drifted off and lapsed into luxurious daydreams. She let a manila envelope slip to the plush burgundy carpet.

Before today, the countrified coziness of the cabin had been a quiet sanctuary where she could clear her mind after a long day. But now, the marbelized wallpapers, stippled finishes, and the muted forest colors of thistle, pine cone, autumn, and dark wood only seemed to unravel fantasies that no longer were impossible. Sitting in the large room on the main deck, which the Mayfair firm of Colefax and Fowler, London's most British decorating house, had given an embracing aura of age and stability, Catherine stared out the window at the continuous sunrise over the Atlantic, but imagined instead a tousle-haired child on a pony.

Catherine had barely gotten used to being a bride – four months was still a bride, wasn't it – and taking over the directorship of the Grunewald Foundation. She had taken a big leap from the corporate world into the not-for-profit sector, but that was exactly what she had wanted and needed. She was ready for that kind of change in her life. And now she had to get used to the idea of being a mother!

She unfastened the sterling silver belt with its familiar Grunewald crest. The belts and the signs over the overstuffed couches that discreetly instructed 'Do not occupy during taxi, takeoff, and landing' in German, French and English, reminded Catherine that she was in transit on the Grunewald Boeing 747-300, on her way home after three weeks of lecturing and interviewing on college campuses and not in a baronial drawing room.

Until yesterday, Catherine hadn't even suspected she was going to have a baby. She had gone to the campus doctor in Cambridge, thinking her lack of energy and queasy stomach were due to the flu, or perhaps jet lag.

When she was sure, she had felt such an instantaneous maternal surge that she wanted a few hours alone with this person growing inside her before she told Alfred, even though they had been planning this since the first time they made love as man and wife on their wedding night on this very plane. She leaned her head back on the overstuffed cushion and remembered.

In Los Angeles, Catherine hadn't been able to decide what she wanted to do, but shc had decided what she *wouldn't* do. She wouldn't stay at Intercon. She wouldn't stay in Chicago. She wouldn't even stay with Graham. It was over, for a variety of reasons. And meeting her father had freed her from the needs that had held them together.

She hadn't consciously decided to marry Alfred that night in New York, but she hadn't been able to get him out of her thoughts. When he'd arrived in Los Angeles and walked into her bungalow, she knew what she wanted. She knew what *she* felt.

Suddenly Alfred held her to him, her cheek to his throat, and her hand slipped under his shirt, tenderly touching his chest when they kissed.

'I'm scared to death,' he whispered.

'So am I.' There was no logical reason to keep them apart.

The room service waiter had to knock seven or eight times before they even heard him, and they stepped apart only long enough to make way for a cart heaped with what looked like every Viennese pastry in California and a magnum of Cristal Roederer champagne.

'It's the best I could do at this hour,' Alfred grinned, tossing his white silk scarf over the arm of a chair.

'I don't know which to try first,' Catherine laughed at this display of spun-sugar excess.

'Well, let's try a little bit of everything.'

But that night the pastry cart had gone untouched.

Alfred's proposal had been unorthodox, but then, being both a Grunewald and a newspaperman was unorthodox to begin with. He had arranged to have a special edition of his London paper hand-delivered to her apartment the morning she got back from Los Angeles. It had been a witty self-parody of one of his own racy London tabloids. The sensationalist headline read: 'Pastry Thief to Marry Chauffeur.' Underneath was a huge picture of Catherine, captioned, 'His driving drives me wild.' The accompanying story related how their childhood romance had been rekindled when the American lady in question had mistaken Alfred Grunewald for a hired driver, and it had been instant love in the rear-view mirror. Whether they would be married in London or Chicago was a subject of rampant speculation. At the end of the article was a coupon with fine print instructing the reader to check one of the two boxes marked 'yes' or 'no,' clip along the dotted line, and give it to the messenger who would be arriving in one hour.

Catherine found herself hesitating only as long as it took to find a pen in her purse. She checked off 'yes,' and scribbled in the margin, 'Please sign me up for a lifetime subscription.'

There was no ambivalence and no indecisiveness. She knew it was right for her and Alfred. At last she knew there was a word for this crazy confusion, this sense of touching the soul that she had felt every time they were together: Love.

When the doorbell rang, she had rushed to the door, sure it was the messenger.

It had been Graham.

Their conversation had gone like a Noel Coward song:

'How are you?'

'I think I'm engaged.'

'To me?'

'Not quite.'

A scene like this would have been more original set to music:

*The man who took over the company you spent your life with is taking over the girl you hoped to wife with.*

To Graham, the scene was more Greek tragedy than musical comedy. His fury had been mildly suppressed when Catherine had convinced him that she was marrying the son, not the father.

He was still enraged. And there was no way she could explain her feelings, which in fact made no real sense. All the things she should have said about being grateful to him, still caring about him, would have only hurt him more. There was no place for rationality. What man wanted to hear the woman in his life tell him that he was loved dearly – like a friend or a brother – but that she planned to run off to marry someone she scarcely knew a continent away because the chemistry was right?

She had not heard from him since, but she felt no guilt. Hadn't she given as much as she'd gotten from the relationship? She would always care for him, but she wouldn't marry somebody because he expected her to. It was over. In love, she knew she had to lead with her feelings.

The wedding had been an elopement with all the frills. The only witnesses to the ceremony in Chicago's City Hall, an example of architectural mediocrity at its best, were B.J., who hoped to catch the bouquet, Effie, whom Alfred had insisted on flying in, Aggie Palmer, who had arrived with fourteen pieces of luggage and a Lear jet filled with bluebells for the bridal party, and of course, the baron himself. Uncle Harry would have fit right in, but he'd been hospitalized for the past month.

The bridal party had made a colorful entrance. Aggie Palmer, carrying a parasol, Effie in a wheelchair, the baron, trailed by his bodyguard and valet, who insisted on giving the bride away, and Catherine, negotiating her way through the urban construction barriers and pneumatic drills in her hoop-skirted bustle gown, the train in one hand and Aggie's bouquet of Texas prairie bluebells from Palmer Point in the other. The groom, ever the intrepid photojournalist, ran ahead taking pictures with an Instamatic while B.J. ran interference.

Somehow, this Fellini-esque ceremony had more meaning to Catherine and Alfred than any stained-glass extravaganza in Westminster Abbey. Everyone who mattered was there.

The baron had offered to send a plane for her father, but Catherine knew that her relationship with him and

Veronica wasn't ready for that yet. Perhaps in the future they could share family rituals. But the phone call Alfred and Catherine had made from a phone booth after the ceremony had made both Catherine and Ed McBride feel they were still sharing something.

At the wedding breakfast on the Grunewald 747, which was festooned with thousands of pink and white balloons tied to the wings in bunches like pastel cumulus clouds, the baron toasted his new daughter-in-law and announced that he was turning over the reins of the Grunewald Foundation to her, to run as she chose. This was her real wedding gift, in spite of the fact that he presented her with a dollhouse-size castle and moat, an actual, to-scale miniature of the real thing, which awaited the newlyweds on fifty-two thousand acres bordering the banks of the River Dee. Aggie Palmer's gift had been 'his and hers' right-hand-drive Toyota jeeps customized from the Neiman-Marcus catalog and delivered to Alfred's London office for use as town cars. They had honeymooned at the Scottish castle.

Catherine turned away from the plane window, went to the desk, and looked at the calendar, counting backward. It wasn't hard to figure out exactly when the baby had been conceived – the first weekend in Scotland, after an early-morning ride through the moors on two Appaloosas named Aubergine and Smokey. She pulled her knees up onto the overstuffed chair, remembering how they'd made love, lying naked in the heather, their clothes strewn across the purple dappled grass, with such impetuousness and intensity that she'd been glad fifty thousand acres separated them from the closest observers. 'If the baby is a girl, I'll call her Heather Elaine,' Catherine said aloud.

'Pardon me, ma'am?' the steward asked. He was carrying Midnight the cat. 'Midnight was loose in the cockpit.'

He deposited the purring ball of fur into her lap.

She heard the flaps descending on the big plane, and the steward reminded her politely that they were landing. She slipped her tweed jacket on over her leather pants and silk T-shirt and took the elevator down to the second deck, where she joined the pilot and copilot in the cockpit.

'May I?' she slipped on a headset and strapped herself into the seat behind them.

'Of course, Mrs Grunewald.'

The pilot set the channel and she waited for Alfred to come on the radio from the jeep near their private hangar at Heathrow. She smiled fondly. He was still her chauffeur. No matter how busy he was, he always managed to meet her, usually accompanied by the ever-disobedient dogs, Günther and Lotte.

'We're waiting for you,' she heard him say. She squinted into the rising sun.

'So are *we*.'

'Who's "we"? Did you bring guests, or has the future baroness become accustomed to the royal "we"?'

'No. This is just the plain old American "we." And *we'll* tell you about it when *we* see you.'

She was willing the plane to land sooner, so that she could fly on her own speed into his arms.